Nobody's Perfect

For information on how to order, or for quantity for place orders,
please write to Addison-Wesley Longman, Inc. 180 18 Yellow Spring
[...] (aloha) or visit us on the web at [...] abookst.com.

Special sales of [...] by individual organizations, corporate, educational institutions[...]
[...] discount on the purchase of 10 or more copies of a single
title for special markets or premiums.

Nobody's Perfect

a novel

BY

Patricia Haley-Brown

ANOINTED VISION
www.anointedvision.com

This novel is a work of fiction. Any resemblance to real people,
living or dead, actual events, establishments, organizations,
locales, is intended to give the fiction a sense of reality and
authencity. Other names, characters, places, and incidents are
either products of the author's imagination or are used
fictitiously, as are those fictionalized events and incidents that
involve real person and did not occur or are set in the future.

 Published by ANOINTED VISION
P.O. Box 80735   Valley Forge, PA 19484
www.anointedvision.com   (610) 337-2251
Email: pop@anointedvision.com

Library of Congress Catalog Card Number: 98-92837

Haley-Brown, Patricia.
      Nobody's perfect : a novel / by Patricia Haley-Brown. --
1st ed.
      p. cm.
      I. Title.
PS3558.A35N63 1998   813'.54
                                      QBI98-387

ISBN: 0-9663174-1-6

First Printing: May, 1998
Second Printing: August, 1998
10 9 8 7 6 5 4 3 2

Nobody's Perfect was printed by Bawden Printing
Website is maintained by Net-Ez WebMaster

THIS BOOK IS DEDICATED TO MY FATHERS

To my heavenly Father, the only perfect man I know. I thank you for the gifts and talents that you have given me, and for your anointing on this project. My Lord, this, my first book, my first fruit, I offer as a sacrifice to you.

To one of my earthly fathers, Robert (Bob) Thomas, Jr. I thank you for the faithful love and support throughout the years. You have been a true blessing to me. Some would label you as 'step-father', but I say where there is unconditional love, there is no 'step'. I love you, and happy 70th birthday (July 8, 1998).

ACKNOWLEDGMENTS

How do I begin to thank the multitude of people who have unselfishly helped me see this project come to a successful completion?

I'll start with my family. To my mother, Fannie Haley, thank you for carrying those first three unedited sample chapters around and showing them to people. I can always count on you to take anything I do, and make it seem super-ordinary. I love you, Ma. I also thank you for taking care of my dad, Fred Haley, during his bout with Alzheimer's. May you be abundantly blessed for your sacrifice.

To my brother, Frederick Lane Haley and wife Tanya, thank you for believing that I will sell a million copies, even before the book was anywhere near print. Your grandiose thinking keeps me encouraged as well as laughing.

For my deceased brother, Erick Lewis Haley, completing my book comes with a bittersweetness. I am thrilled to be at this point, but sad that he is not here to share it with me. Fortunately, the seed of unconditional love he sowed into my life will always be present.

To my cousin, Kimberla Lawson Roby, I am proud of how you've taken the literary arena by storm. Keep on writing, girl. I am blessed to have such a close-knit family. In recognition of my aunts, I have found some place in the story to use your names. It is my small way of saying thanks for always being there.

Jeffrey W. Glass, saying thanks is so inadequate when it comes to all that you have done to help me complete this project. You got involved at a critical time, and utilized your strong project management skills to the fullest. In the final stretch, when it would have been too much of an imposition to ask others for help, you unselfishly volunteered above and beyond any expectation. You truly, truly helped me to make it happen. Thank you, thank you, thank you, my dear, dear friend.

Mr. Stephenson Clarke (Phila.), you have been involved in this book process from the early stages, in one way or another. Words cannot capture how much I appreciate all that you've done.

Ricardy Banks, (webmaster@net-ez.com) I am well pleased with the work you have done with the Anointed Vision website. In a computer literate age, internet access is critical for a new business like mine. Thank you for the creative presentation of my book and company.

Andre & Pam Seals, Joan V. & Frances Walker, Jeffrey Glass, Kimberla Roby, Michelle Keene, Carolyn Howell, Roscoe Burks, Doreen Amster, Tiana Allen, Ernesa Lloyd, Shannon Norman, Audrey Williams, Stephen Faleti, Rayford Reed, Leslie Walker, Heather Gerhardt, Julie Newman, Alicia Dillihay, and Angie Viloria, thank you all for reading the draft and providing necessary feedback.

Those of you who had to read it multiple times, Rena Burks, Tammy Lenzy, Emma Foots, Dorothy Robinson, Laurel Robinson, Renee Lenzy, thank you, my dear friends, for the professionalism you exhibited in editing. Rena, of course you read the first page and many subsequent pages over and over and over, but who's counting. I love you sis. Tammy and Dorothy, I appreciate the spiritual eye you kept on the manuscript's content. Love you both.

Keith & Shari Grace (Grace Design - Rockford, IL), what can I say? You were among the first to read the early draft. Even with all the typos and corrections, your compliments where a source of tremendous encouragement, back when I was uncertain about where this project would go. Thank you for sending kind words at a pivotal time. Also, I am well pleased with the cover design. Great job.

Don and Mary Bartel, thank you for believing in me back when I didn't know where Stanford University was. If more high school counselors cared like you, then the future of the education system and students would be much brighter.

Diedre Campbell, Patricia Hill, Regeanna Wallace, and Don Brown (my Sanford, Florida connection), thanks for the emotional support. Pastor Gus & Carolyn Howell, Pastor John & Roxanne White, and Dorothea Kendrick, your anointed prayers have carried me through.

Bawden Printing, thank you for aggressively pursuing the business with Anointed Vision. You have exemplified the concept of true customer service. IRN Payment Systems and Book Expo America, thank you for taking the extra time to usher a newcomer into the publishing arena. Your help is not taken lightly.

Ms. Audrey D. Williams, (jsoninv@aol.com), girl, we're doing it. A thousand thanks for your efforts with the publicity and promotional tour. Your energy has been a breath of fresh air. Thank you Sheila Murray for your creative suggestions.

Wanda Gates, I am so very grateful to you for jumping in and helping me keep the Anointed Vision office operating efficiently. I didn't forget you, Michelle K. Mitchell. I appreciate your promotional efforts. I wish you success in the entrepreneurial arena.

Doreen, Emma & John, Sr., Joan, and Rena you not only helped me with the editing, but you also helped to coordinate the four pre-publication receptions. Thank you for carrying the weight of planning those events for me in your respective cities.

For your immediate interest in participating in the promotional activities surrounding the book, I say thank you to my alma maters, Stanford Univ. and Univ. of Chicago. Special thanks to Student Life, Diversity Affairs, and AAMBAA. To my other affiliations, Delta Sigma Theta Sorority, Inc, Dominion Christian Center (Rockford, IL), Christ Tabernacle (Rockford, IL), New Covenant Church (Trooper, PA), and W.E.N. (Phila.), thank you for providing another means of getting Nobody's Perfect into the marketplace. Also, I thank Rockford Register Star, Barnes & Noble (Rockford, IL), Hair Gallery (Norristown, PA), Mona Lisa's Pa'lour Salon (Pontiac, MI), Mae's Salon (Rockford, IL), Dr. Thomas R. Moss' office, and the numberous independent stores and media sources.

Thanks to all of you, and some that I'm sure to have inadvertently omitted, we have achieved a major milestone. I could not have done it as smoothly without the individual and collective input of you all. I am truly blessed to have such a powerful support group.

May the Lord richly bless each of you for all of the love, support, and work that you have sown into my life.

PRELUDE

Rachel couldn't help but wonder if she was, possibly, losing her edge? Was this her fate? Would she ever find Mr. Right, or would she settle with a Mr. Interim.

It seemed like just yesterday when she was twenty-two-years-old, the youngest, and most promising woman on her job. She had the world at her fingertips. Men were falling at her feet, fine ones at that. In her twenties, when she had the clear advantage, it seemed like there was plenty of time to get married and have kids. Now that she was thirty, her professional edge was far greater than her romantic one. Most of her co-workers were already married with kids. She was behind the eight ball. Ideally, Rachel wanted the same success she'd experienced in her career to spill over into her romantic relationships.

It appeared that she was looking for love in all the wrong places, because her pretty-boys, or so-called Mr. Rights, were all wrong. Over the years she'd met plenty of guys, dated some and befriended others. The dating scene had been bumpy. Through it all, no solid relationship resulted from her efforts. There were times when Rachel wanted to call it quits and embrace being single.

At least one motivation she had left for getting marriage was to have a child. In the past, there had been plenty of opportunities to have a child with any number of men, but she wanted more. She had no intentions of having a child out of wedlock and intentionally joining the ranks of unwed, typically struggling single mothers. She wanted a baby, with a husband 'first'. Anything less was unacceptable to her, and certainly to her God-fearing grandmother, Big Mama.

Her maternal clock was no longer chiming faintly in the recesses of her mind. It was now pounding heavily in the forefront, like a grandfather clock. Time was running out for getting hitched and having kids. Unless something happened soon, Rachel envisioned herself being forty with a couple of pre-schoolers at home. Mr. Right had to show up in a hurry.

When Rachel was twenty-one, she created a short checklist of characteristics she preferred in a man. Consequently, her prayers, were much shorter. The only real consideration, at the time, was that Mr. Right be handsome. In ten years of dating, her checklist had grown from a meager three to a whopping twelve. She was going from one extreme to the other, from the potential suitor not having a job at all, to being financially stable, from merely being single, to not having any pre-existing kids. Finding a compatible mate hadn't been easy, but, for Rachel, it would prove to be more a spiritual journey than merely a destination.

<u>1</u>

With her internal clock, the summer sunlight piercing through the blinds, and the energetic cat, Boots, Rachel was sure not to sleep past 6:00 most mornings, including the weekend.

"How am I going to get everything done today?" Saturday was filled with errands, bills, housework, sorority meetings, and if lucky, occasionally a movie. Today was more intense. She had to focus on getting herself together for a blind date. Against better judgment, Rachel let her co-worker, Sharon, talk her into going to a cookout. It was an opportunity for Rachel to meet Sharon's brother, Kenny.

Rachel held her hands up and spread her fingers out in front of her, like a fan. "I'm glad Tanya is able to squeeze me in. I couldn't, dare, meet this man without getting my hair and nails hooked-up." She was glad to get the 7:30 time-slot. It was early for a Saturday morning. Being the first appointment was the only way to ensure that she wouldn't be sitting up in the beauty shop all day. Any other time, she could tolerate it. But not today.

She had procrastinated long enough. Rachel sat up, placed both feet on the floor, and created a to-do-list in her head. "Hmm," she exclaimed. "Women always have to put in the extra effort. We're expected to look stunning on each date. All men have to do is show up. I bet this Kenny guy isn't going out of his way to impress me." On second thought, she said, "Then again, I don't want a man who spends more time primping in front of the mirror than I do." She stretched. "Been there enough times. In one way or another, I always end up having to pay for it." She stood up and stretched, again. "Boy, it's tough being a man, but tougher being a woman."

Although it seemed like so much preparation for such a brief moment, she didn't consider it to be optional. Even if Kenny turned out to be nobody-special, she still owed it to herself to look fabulous.

She walked to the bedroom door and pulled her robe off the hook. Today was going to be hectic. She decided to take a few minutes for herself and headed downstairs to get a cup of tea. She couldn't help but think, enthusiastically, about the cookout.

She was at a slow period in her dating. In her ten years, or so, of dating, Rachel had never experienced a drought, a voluntary rest, but never a real drought. Summer was in the air. Rachel felt it was time for a whirlwind romance. She loved the Chicago summers, and loved, even more, having an exciting companion with whom she could enjoy the fun-filled days and nights.

The rare occasions when she got with Gary did not qualify him as a significant other. The poor fellow was one of her many has-beens. Even on his way out, he was still trying to hang on. As far as Rachel was concerned, she was definitely available to meet someone new.

After the recent flow of nobody-specials, she was ready for some spice in her life. Maybe Kenny was precisely what she was looking for. Although she wasn't eager to admit it, she was excited about meeting him.

She leaned her back on the refrigerator, and took another sip of the lukewarm tea. "It seems odd that a perfectly good man is still available." She was referring to Ken. "All women talk about is the shortage. Why hasn't someone snatched him up if he's all that?" She walked to the stove and poured some more hot water into her mug. "This better be worth it," she said in between sips of her tea and bites from the bagel.

2

When she got to Sharon's place, she could tell from the number of parked cars that a lot of people had already arrived. "I hope some other people from work come, just in case this Kenny doesn't have it going on."

She was especially hoping Kenny was already there. "I don't believe that I let Sharon talk me into this. How do I get myself into these messes? Boy, I want to get this over with."

The plan was to meet him right away, get the introductions over, and get past her nervousness. The other motivation for meeting him early was to take full advantage of her glow. It was the result of an extra effort she put into fixing up when meeting a new beau. The longer she waited, the more likely her oily nose would start shining, lipstick would wear off, or even worse, hair would blow out of place. Rachel didn't consider herself a vain person needing to glance into a compact mirror every five minutes. However, she was self-conscious enough to want to make a good impression.

"Why am I so nervous? I don't even know this guy. It's not like I have anything to lose."

She pulled the lipstick tube from her small purse and painted her lips. "Let me see." She tilted her head up, gazed into the rear view mirror, and smacked her lips together. She turned slightly to the side, but kept her eyes focused into the mirror. Not a hair out of place. The anxiety was mounting. She put the keys in her tiny purse. "Well, here it goes," she said, and opened the car door.

She noticed Sharon's car parked in the driveway. The knot in her stomach tightened as she got closer to the house. "I sure hope there are some people here that I know," she mumbled.

As she approached the house, her feelings about the party were mixed. Get-togethers were always uncomfortable when she went alone, and then didn't really know anyone, except the hostess. She spent the time acting entertained when, really, she was bored to tears.

"Oh, well, I'm here now. I guess I'll see what's going on," Rachel uttered as she approached the house.

She walked towards the backyard, in the direction of the music and loud talking. The smell of barbecue got stronger as she got closer. There were about twenty-five people already there. As Rachel glanced through the crowd, she didn't recognize any faces. Everyone seemed to be in pairs and small cliques.

"Great," she muttered, "it's going to be like that."

She walked towards the beverages, giving the impression that she was confident, and felt comfortable being there. Whatever she did, it couldn't be obvious that she was nervous.

"Rachel!"

As she turned around, she saw Sharon calling her from the back steps. Rachel was relieved to see a familiar face.

"Hey girl. I'm glad you made it," Sharon said.

"I told you I was coming."

"I know, but you never know. You know how things always seem to come up at the last minute. Anyway, I'm glad you're here." Sharon leaned forward and gave Rachel a hug. "Guess what?" Sharon said with undeniable enthusiasm.

"What?" Rachel retorted with a tone of reluctance.

"Ken's here." Sharon had a big smile on her face. Rachel struggled to show no reaction, when in actuality the knot she had managed to loosen in her stomach was starting to tighten all over again.

"Let me introduce you. Finally, you'll get to meet. He's excited about meeting you." Sharon grabbed Rachel softly by the arm and pulled her towards a group of three guys and one young lady.

By Rachel's standards, one guy was too short. With heels on, she would easily tower over him. On top of that, he was on the chunky side with a bulging belly, the dreaded receding hair-line, a tacky pair of run-over sandals, and a pair of polyester shorts.

This plump fellow was probably a nice guy. Sad for him, he reminded her too much of Brian, a fellow she secretly dated on the rebound from a serious relationship gone sour. In her opinion, he was the typical 'worshipper', nerdy and physically unappealing. He was extraordinarily nice, treated Rachel like a queen, did everything for her, and made himself available at her beck-and-call.

Sad for him, niceness hadn't proven to be enough to make Rachel completely happy. She wanted a guy who was physically and romantically appealing, although, he seemed harder and harder to find. It was as if every man she met had one or two redeeming qualities. Never all of them operating at the same time. She could never understand why it had to be 'either or'. Combining bits and pieces of all the guys she knew, into one package, seemed to be the only way she was going to get Mr. Right.

The second guy was tall, at about six-one or six-two, and quite handsome. He was dark-skinned, and from what she could see, he didn't have a receding hairline, or the infamous bald spot that men get in the center-back-part of their head. It was obvious his body was in exquisite shape, to the point of being sculptured. He fit all of the pretty-boy requirements. She discounted him as being Kenny. He was too fine. Also, he didn't look anything like Sharon. He was much darker, handsomely darker.

Without staring, Rachel noticed a ring on his wedding finger. "Oh, well." She wasn't interested in a married guy, even though, many were interested in her. She had gone through it with a married man, Luc, and never again wanted to be a third-wheel in the marriage scene. It took forever for her just to be able to function without him, let alone fully recover. As a matter of fact, she wasn't even one hundred percent recovered as it was, and the breakup had been almost two years ago. The thought of being with a married man made her nauseous. 'Been there, done that, ain't going back', was her new philosophy.

It was refreshing for her to see a handsome man wear a wedding ring, in public. She knew enough guys that deceivingly didn't. Luc waited until she was hooked, emotionally, before he revealed the important detail that he was married, hoping she was in too deep to let it matter. The married men were always claiming to be in the process of leaving their wives. Rachel wholeheartedly believed men never left. Her line was, "They might get put out, but they don't leave."

The petite lady standing next to him must be his wife, Rachel speculated. They seemed comfortable together. "Wouldn't you know it. The fine guy is taken," she uttered. He was probably a playboy anyway, she rationalized to ease the disappointment.

To Rachel, the lady did look quite a bit younger than her handsome husband. However it didn't surprise her. She hypothesized that men typically ran around in their younger years, and then settled down in their late thirties and forties with a younger woman. They got the whole fairy tale, wife and kids, at any age.

It was always lopsided. When she was younger, the men her age wanted older, more established women to take care of them. Now that she was older, the men her age were looking for younger women to breed for them. Rachel wondered if she'd ever get a turn to date someone closer to her age.

The third guy wasn't bad looking. His hair was a little bit longer than she liked. Not enough to be a show-stopper. Since he was facing her, Rachel could see his smooth skin glistening in the sunlight, and his hazel-colored eyes radiating. She liked his features. If it turned out to be him, she could anticipate some pretty kids. He also seemed to have all of his hair and teeth, which she never took for granted in men over thirty. His ring finger was bare. Maybe he was available. She couldn't tell for sure, not solely by the absence of a ring.

The one nagging factor that bothered Rachel was his youthful demeanor. Either they were too homely, too short, too young, or just plain married. How would she feel with a twenty-some-year-old man when she was already thirty! What would he know about life? She was not interested in watching a man-child grow up. They seemed hard to come by, but she was still holding out for a settled, mature man. She didn't have any kids of her own, but Rachel had done plenty of mothering, compliments of the men in her past. Leah, her college-friend, had a much younger husband. That was fine for Leah, but it wasn't something Rachel could deal with for herself.

"Excuse me, I want to introduce you all to my friend, Rachel," Sharon interrupted.

Here was the big moment. However it turned out, Rachel was glad to get it over with.

"Rachel, this is my sister, Dana."

She was shocked to know that Dana was Sharon's sister. "Her sister," Rachel replayed in her mind. Boy had she guessed wrong. Rachel couldn't decide whether to be formal and shake hands after each introduction or to be casual, and acknowledge each with a simple 'hi'. Feeling slightly nervous about meeting Kenny, she opted without completely thinking it through, to be casual in her response. She didn't want to come across as being snobby by shaking hands at an informal yard party. First impressions were long-lasting, and even if Kenny turned out to be something less than wonderful, she still wanted to present herself stunningly.

"Hi," Rachel responded as she made eye contact with Dana.

"Hi, Rachel. Nice to meet you."

Working her way around the circle, Sharon then introduced the young guy, who Rachel suspected to be Kenny.

"This is Terry, Dana's husband."

Wow, what a surprise, Rachel thought. Dana's husband! No wonder he looks young, he is, she concluded. She knew Dana was the baby in the family, being somewhere in her early twenties. Rachel figured Terry was around the same age.

Well, at least she had gotten one thing right, married men, like Terry, didn't always wear a wedding ring. The ring definitely threw off her assessment of who was who.

"Hi," Terry and Rachel spoke simultaneously. The picture was becoming rapidly clearer. Short and chunky, who reminded her of Doughboy, must be the man. At least they were meeting early. Her new plan was to eat, socialize for a few minutes, and then make the great escape. One thing was for sure, she wasn't going to be eating with Doughboy. By the looks of his stomach, he had already eaten enough.

No matter what, she decided there was no point in giving up her phone number to this Kenny guy, even if he was Sharon's brother. Rachel was hoping this was not going to affect her working relationship with Sharon. That was the danger of being introduced to someone by a mutual friend. Another reminder of the very reason why she disliked blind dates.

"This is my cousin Ty." As he reached out to shake her hand, she hesitated. The shock of him not being Kenny was staggering.

"Hello, Rachel," Ty said in a soft spoken voice and a slight grin. "Nice to meet you." Although his hand was a little moist, it was of no consequence. Her focus had switched to the tall, dark, handsome, and exquisitely-built man standing before her.

Rachel was usually good at sizing up people. Much to her heart's content, she had batted zero in figuring out who was who this time. Her worst fears had been put to rest. She composed herself quickly for the big introduction. She didn't even think about how she looked. She wanted to come across natural and together. All of the preparation she had gone through early in the morning was for this one moment.

Before Sharon could introduce Kenny, he spoke out in a deep, authoritative tone. "Hello, Rachel. I'm Ken." He softly took her hand and looked directly into her eyes.

A man with some confidence was refreshing to Rachel. She wondered if it equated to him having positive self-esteem. It had been difficult enough for her to find working, healthy men over thirty who were neither married, nor shacking-up. It was absurd for her to go even further by wanting a man with reliable transportation, decent credit, a few goals, no significant baggage, and not living with his parents. Those were the preliminary requirements a man needed before she could even begin to seriously evaluate him on the twelve-point checklist. Rachel had definitely gone off the deep-end if she also wanted him to have some self-esteem. The expectation had become a joke to her.

"It is a pleasure to meet you. My sister has told me a lot about you," said the handsome man standing before Rachel. His smile was electrifying. The contrast of his perfect white teeth against his mahogany skin was flattering to her. He immediately received his first two check points for being tall and gorgeous. She was in awe, although she did manage to contain herself.

Without thinking intensely, Rachel responded, "I hope good things."

"All good."

"Sharon," someone yelled from across the yard. She turned around to see who it was. It was another guest arriving. "Excuse me, please." As Sharon prepared to walk away, she looked at Ken with a grin and said, "I'm sure you will make Rachel feel welcome." Rachel felt a little bashful, being the center of attention for a brief moment. She was already feeling a little squeamish. Ken hadn't taken his eyes off of her since the introduction.

"So, Rachel, how do you know my sister?" Dana asked.

"We work together."

Rachel felt some dampness in her hand. As luck would have it, her cup was leaking. She didn't know for sure, but suspected that the cup had been squeezed too tightly in her excitement. She had to get napkins before it made a real mess. She was about to excuse herself when Ken chimed in and said, "Here, let me help you." She had both hands cupped together holding the dripping drink. He put his hands under hers, and before she could say that's okay, he was ushering her towards the garbage can. After she rid herself of the cup, she realized that they were now standing alone, away from the crowd. This was ideal. She couldn't have consciously planned this random happening any better.

"So, are you from around here?" Ken asked.

"Kind of. I live in Wheaton right now."

"Ooh." He was impressed, knowing that Wheaton was a very nice, upscale area. But then Sharon had told him weeks ago that Rachel was classy, so it really wasn't too big of a surprise. Ken liked what he saw in Rachel. Unknowingly, she had made the first cut with him. Since Sharon hadn't given him much information, he continued with the questions. "Why did you say, kind of?"

"Because, I've only lived here about five years. I lived in Atlanta before coming here, and Detroit is my home."

"Oh, the Motor City? What area?"

"Uhm, right around Outer Drive." Rachel didn't want to get into too much detail, because she wasn't sure how familiar Ken was with Detroit.

"By Eight Mile?" He was smooth in his approach, discretely checking her out.

She was still nervous as evidenced in her arms being crossed and fingers tapping on her forearm.

"Yeah!" His knowledge of her hometown allowed her to feel like they had made a connection, no matter how insignificant. The nervousness began to subside. For the first time in the conversation, she dropped her arms and relaxed.

"Okay. I know where that is. I was up there a few summers ago for one of the festivals. What's that place called downtown?" Ken was snapping his fingers trying to remember the bit of detail.

"Hart Plaza?"

"Hart Plaza? Nah, that doesn't sound like it."

"Belle Isle?"

"Yeah, that's it, Belle Isle," he nodded in confirmation. So you're a Motor City girl?"

"I love Detroit, if that's what you mean."

"All righty then. Is that where your parents live?"

"Actually, my parents died in a car accident when I was five."

"Oh," Ken responded for lack of anything else to say. "I, I didn't know." He felt uneasy and at a loss for words.

She sensed his discomfort and tried to ease it. "That's all right. You didn't know."

"Sharon didn't tell me."

"She may have forgotten herself. I only mentioned it to her once, and if I remember right, it was a long time ago. Don't worry about it. I'm not offended. My folks died a long time ago. I'm long over the emotional part of it. My grandparents were the ones who raised me, and they, or I should say, my grandmother still lives in Detroit. My grandfather died a few years back."

Even though Rachel told him she wasn't offended by the comment, he still felt awkward. He managed to innocently direct the conversation towards himself.

"I know how it is to lose a parent. My mother died of cancer three years ago, but it's like it was just yesterday." His voice faded off near the end of the comment. "I still miss her."

"That must have been hard for you to lose your mom. The good thing, if you can call it good, is that I vaguely remember my parents. I only have faint memories of them in my mind. For all practical purposes, my grandmother is my mom."

"At least you have your grandmother. That's good. Family is important."

"Sure is." Unknowingly, Ken had earned his third check point on her list for being family-oriented.

"What brought you here from At-lanta?"

"My job."

"Sounds like you've lived all over the place. Moving around doesn't bother you?"

"Not really. As long as there is a phone and a plane nearby, I can live practically anywhere." Those close to Rachel playfully referred to her as the 'operator', because she was rarely ever without a phone glued to her ear.

"So, do you like it here?"

"Love it. I've met some good people, including your sister."

"Yeah, she's an all right little sis," Ken affectionately stated. "Do you get downtown much?"

"Yeah, I do. I love going down to Grant Park and North Beach in the summer, like everybody else," she said with a slight grin.

"It doesn't take much to have a lot of fun in Chicago," Ken affirmed.

"No, I guess it doesn't." Although she never cared much for small talk, somehow it seemed perfectly fine with Ken.

"What?" they both blurted out at the same time.

"Oh," they said simultaneously, again.

Rachel started to laugh. Ken bent slightly over and touched her arm while laughing.

"Want to try for three?" she asked in the midst of chuckling. The laughter was good for her. It seemed to completely eliminate whatever tension she had left.

"I'm sorry," he stated. "You go ahead. What were you saying now?"

"Not really anything. I was saying how much I like Chicago." Actually, in those brief moments, Rachel had forgotten exactly what she was intending to say. She decided to play it by ear. "I was wondering what kind of things you do in the city for fun."

"Well, I'm into bike riding and swimming. Every now and then I play some ball, but, of course, every brother plays some ball," he said jokingly.

"Yep, or at least everyone thinks they can play. Are you any good?" Before Ken could answer, Rachel chimed back in. "Now that I think about it, that's a stupid question to ask a brother. 'Of course' you can play. I haven't met a brother, yet, who honestly admitted he couldn't play ball. "Rachel was feeling much more comfortable, and her body language confirmed she was relaxed and enjoying the conversation.

"Oh man, how can I answer, now." As Ken boyishly spoke, he flipped his head back briefly and gazed up at the sky. "Believe it or not, I'm actually pretty good." Ken had to laugh. He knew that, by and large, she was right about the brothers. "Let's get off of me. What is it you like to do? With you being the together sister that you obviously are, I know you're good at everything. Out of your unlimited talents," he teased, "what is your biggest claim to fame?"

"Actually, I'm into golf."

"Golf, huh! A female golfer. I didn't know sisters got off into golfing. Are you any good?"

She was into the conversation. It was another rare opportunity to educate a potentially unenlightened man about women. Since this was a brief meeting, she wouldn't be able to give him the entire lesson.

"I'm decent, but I'm always looking to improve my game." Rachel was being extremely modest. She was, actually, a sensational golfer.

"Do you play for money?"

"Sometimes. My best friend and I do several tournaments a year. He taught me how to play about ten years ago. I've been playing ever since."

"Interesting. It sounds like you're a serious golfer. You're a first for me!"

"It's fun. Do you golf?" she asked while briefly placing both of her hands on his lower arm.

"No more than putt-putt. I've never played a full game. It's not my thing."

"Don't knock it, you might like it. Maybe sometime when you're free, we can go play a few holes."

"Maybe. I can't promise to go golfing with you, but I like your other idea."

"What was that?" Rachel was barely smiling on the outside, but she was overjoyed on the inside. The way he was wearing the

silk summer shirt was putting a hurtin' on her eyes. She always did
have a weakness for good-looking men. Ken was no exception.

"Your suggestion about going down to the lake front and
checking out some of the festivals."

"That sounds nice." She wanted to strike the fine balance
between letting him know she was interested in going out, while not
appearing easy or anxious.

Ken was charming Rachel with his captivating voice,
seductive gestures, and interesting responses. She knew it was
intentional. He was smooth, though. She didn't feel offended at
all. She felt like a giggly school girl in the company of this
handsome, suave brother.

When he looked away for a moment, she whispered, "He is
too sharp. Goodness. I should give him an extra credit point." He
was safe, so long as he respected her, and didn't gaze up and down
her body like she was a piece of savory meat. She hated when guys
would be talking to her, while combing her body with their eyes. It
disgusted her. Thank goodness Ken was a classier act.

"So, what else do you like doing, Ms. Rachel?"

"I like going to movies and plays."

"Oh, so do I. As a matter of fact, my church just had a little
play. When they have another one, maybe I can let you know."

She didn't mind the continuous charm. It was all harmless and
tasteful, not to mention flattering. Ken was a church-kind-of-guy,
and definitely warranted a fourth check on her list.

She was quite relaxed. The conversation had gotten good, now
that they were past the basics. She hadn't been paying much
attention to her surroundings. The party was in full swing. People
were spread out across the yard. She had no idea what time it was,
and thought it rude to glance at her watch. She didn't want to give
Ken the impression that the conversation was uninteresting. It was
anything but.

Ken spotted someone from across the yard. "Excuse me,
Rachel. I'll be right back."

She looked at her watch and realized they'd been talking for
almost two hours. To her surprise, it was almost 5:00. Before
coming to the party, she had dropped her cat off at the vet to get the
annual routine done. In order to get Boots before the vet closed at

6:00, Rachel calculated that she needed to be leaving by no later than 5:25.

When she looked in the direction where Ken had gone, she noticed him talking to a lady who had just arrived. It looked like there was a little girl standing next to the lady. Sharon also joined the threesome. "I wonder if that's one of their sisters?" Rachel softly questioned. She only remembered Sharon mentioning one sister, but wasn't sure. Sharon turned around and glanced at Rachel. Sharon was too far away to be heard. Rachel thought maybe Sharon wanted her to come over and be introduced. She started to go on over, but decided to wait until Sharon or Ken gave her the clear signal to come and meet their sister.

Rachel didn't know how long Ken was going to be. She would have to be leaving shortly. It didn't make sense to strike up another conversation with anybody else. It would be pointless with her planning to leave any minute. Besides, she wanted to close out with Ken. She rushed over to the table and grabbed a bag of chips. In the midst of all the excitement, she hadn't eaten anything, and the food smelled great.

She saw Ken pick up the little girl and twirl her over his head. It looked to Rachel like he was going to be tied up for a while. At first, she thought it was rude of him to interrupt their conversation, and then, on top of that, to be gone so long. After she thought about it some more, she realized he was not her keeper for the party. Rachel also reasoned that she, not Ken, was being rude by trying to dominate his time on their first meeting.

Nevertheless, she had to go and get Boots. No way was she letting her cat stay in that place all weekend. She glanced at her watch, saw 5:20, and decided it was time to go. It was too bad Ken was tied up. He never got a chance to ask for her phone number. She wasn't the type to go and slide it into his hand, unsolicited. His little interruption couldn't have come at a worse time.

As she approached the circle, Ken's back was to her, and he didn't know she was coming. She overheard him say something like, "What do you want me to do?" The lady, Rachel figured to be their sister, didn't seem overly happy. Once Rachel was near the circle, she sensed the seriousness in the conversation. She didn't want to interrupt, but also did not want to leave without saying goodbye to Ken and thanking Sharon for the invite.

"Rachel," Sharon said in a strained tone.

Rachel didn't know what was going on, but felt awkward interrupting. "I want to thank you for inviting me. I had a nice time." She looked Ken directly in the eyes to let him know she enjoyed his company.

"You're not leaving are you?" Sharon inquired.

"Yes, I have an errand to run by 6:00."

"Do you have to leave?" Ken asked disappointingly.

"Yes, I do. As a matter of fact, I'm already late." For some strange reason, Rachel could feel the woman's eyes on her the entire time they were talking.

"Then I'll talk to you later," Ken said.

Rachel noticed that the attractive lady didn't resemble the other sisters, but neither did Ken. The lady was slightly taller than Rachel, fair-skinned, sandy-colored hair, and shapely. She was the kind of woman men were physically attracted to. Rachel was glad the woman was family and not the competition. The most noticeable thing about her were the tight, tight shorts. Her hips were more curvy and her behind much larger than Sharon or Dana's. The shorts appeared to be two sizes too small. Something about this Sanders' sister didn't mesh with the other two for Rachel. For some reason, the mystery sister appeared more flamboyant and assertive than Sharon and Dana. The lady reached her hand over Ken, towards Rachel and said very sternly, "I'm Sandra, and you are?"

Rachel responded by reaching her hand out to shake Sandra's. "Hi, I'm Rachel. Nice to meet you."

"Nice to meet you, too. This is my daughter, Ariel."

"Hi, Ariel."

"Hi."

Something had disrupted the pleasant mood Ken was in earlier. However, Rachel had neither the time to figure it out, nor the desire to get into what seemed to be some family mess.

"See ya," she muttered disappointedly and started towards her car. She was hoping Ken would excuse himself from the little huddle and, at least, offer to escort her to the car. She was interested in getting to know him better, and also eager to get a better read on his interest level. The closer she got to the car, the less likely it seemed that she was going to be able to give him her phone number. Evidently he was engrossed in the conversation with Sandra and Sharon. He wasn't going anywhere, anytime soon. The goodbye didn't go as hoped. All in all, Rachel chalked the cookout up to an afternoon well spent.

3

The crowd of people had vanished and only the immediate family was left to finish cleaning up the remains of the cookout. Sharon's husband, Nick, was cleaning out the grill. Terry and Ken were putting some of the lawn furniture into the storage shed. Sharon was gathering up the plates and utensils. Dana was playing with Ariel. Sandra was making herself useful, here and there.

"Since you're going to be here until Monday, why don't you let Ariel spend the night with me and Terry? We'll take her to Dad's tomorrow, and you can pick her up from there," said Dana. She bent down to Ariel's eye level and asked, "Do you want to come home with me and Uncle Terry."

"Yes, yes," the happy little girl responded, as she leaped up and down.

"That's fine with me. Kenny or I will pick her up tomorrow," Sandra stated.

Sharon handed Sandra a dish wrapped in cellophane to take into the house. Sharon lead the way up the four steps, into the kitchen, with Sandra right on her heels. It was the opportunity Sandra had been waiting for most of the evening, to catch Sharon alone.

"Sharon, who was that lady, what's her name, uh, Rachel?"

"She's a friend of mine."

"Of yours!" Sandra seemed surprised. "I thought she was Kenny's friend?"

"I introduced her to him, and Dana, and Terry, and a bunch of other people."

"So, she's not Kenny's girlfriend?"

Even though Sharon knew exactly what relation Rachel was to Ken, she didn't want to give any details to Sandra. She didn't want to open a can of worms, knowing Sandra still had feelings for Ken.

"Not that I know of, Sandra. But girl, you can't ask me. You have to ask him about his women. You know I can't keep up with his business and mine, too." Sharon wanted to get the point across, without coming down too hard on Sandra, so she opted to go with the humorous approach.

"I know, but since you and I are cool, I thought I'd ask."

"That's fine, but the only thing is, I don't know anything." Sharon headed back outside to get the last few remaining dishes. "I guess you have to check with Kenny."

Sandra was dissatisfied with the answer, but she did respect that Sharon didn't want to get involved. She took no offense. As a matter of fact, she decided to take Sharon's advice. Sandra walked towards the back section of the lawn, where Ken was trying to wedge a plastic chair into the already crowded shed. "Kenny?"

"What, Sandra?" he sighed.

"What's with the attitude?"

Ken continued trying to wedge the chair into the shed, and her interruption seemed to cause him additional irritation. "You should be asking yourself that?"

"What does that mean?" Sandra snidely asked.

Ken stopped what he was doing, and looked directly into her face. "You show up over here, without telling anybody that you're coming. Then you expect me to drop everything and be available for you, although you claim it's for Ariel. Please!" He turned his back to her and continued working with the chair.

"You should be glad that I brought your daughter to see you. It's not like you make it a habit to come see her."

"See, there you go. What's up with you? You need to get a life, and get out of mine. I am so sick of this crap with you."

"Sick! Sick! Sandra leaned back and shook her index finger at Ken in total frustration. "You have some nerve, you so-called-father-figure. You don't even send the money, regularly, like you should."

"So what? What does that have to do with you showing up here? You could have called a couple of days ago, and let me know that you were coming. I could have made plans to spend time with Ariel. But you couldn't do that," Ken paused as he stepped closer to Sandra, "could you!"

"Forget all that. Let's deal with what is. Are you saying that you're not going to spend time with your daughter this weekend, because I didn't call ahead of time? The point is, she's here now."

"No, the point is, you need to stop with the games. I'm really tired of this act of yours."

Up to now, the arguing had been kept to a semi-low level. No one else had been able to overhear their tense conversation. Ken slammed the storage shed door closed, looked at Sandra, and walked away leaving her standing there with her hands on her hips and jaws tight.

Ken walked over to where Ariel and Dana were playing. He came up behind his daughter and scooped her up into the air.

"Ahhhhh," Ariel playfully screamed. "Daddy, you scared me."

"I did, huh. Well, Daddy didn't mean to. Give me a hug."

As Ken squeezed the little girl, Sandra brushed by him and went to sit on one of the few chairs still left out. Although he could look directly at her, he chose to avoid eye contact, and focus his attention on Ariel.

"Daddy, uhm, I, uhm, Mommy said I can go home with Auntie Dana and Uncle Terry."

"She did."

"Yes."

"Are you going to be a good girl?"

"Yes."

"Good. Daddy will come by and see you tomorrow, before you go to bed, okay."

"Okay, Daddy."

"I love you sweetheart."

"I love you, Daddy." Ariel gave him a kiss on the cheek.

Ken stood up and took the car keys from his pocket. "Where's Sharon?"

"I think she's inside, man," Nick responded.

Ken ran up the steps and opened the back door. He called out, "Sis?"

"Yeah," Sharon peaked from a squatting position in front of the opened refrigerator, crammed with leftover potato salad, baked beans, and barbecued chicken and ribs.

"Oh, there you are." Ken walked over to Sharon and kneeled down beside her. He didn't want anyone else, especially Sandra, to overhear his conversation. "Look, about your girl, Rachel, I really liked talking to her. She seems like good-people."

"Ah, see I knew you'd like her."

"Well, with Sandra showing up and trippin', as usual, I didn't get a chance to get her phone number. I guess it's all right to call her at home. Do you know if she's living with anybody?"

"No!" Sharon firmly stated. "She is not living with anybody."

"You know for sure?"

"Yes, Kenny. She's kind of religious, at least her grandmother is. Now that I think about it, the only man she mentions regularly is her brother, Neal. I never hear anything about a boyfriend. Why do you think I'm trying to hook the two of you up?"

"What does religion have to do with her living with someone? I go to church and I don't see anything wrong with two people living together, if the hook-up is right."

"If you say so. I just thought you church-folks didn't see things the same way the rest of us did about shacking-up. You know it doesn't bother me one way or another, but I'm not into the church like you."

"Yeah, well, whatever. Listen, I need you to do me a favor."

"What?"

"Let me have her number."

"What about Sandra?"

"What about her?"

"You and Sandra need to quit. Your raggedy relationship with her is going to keep messing you up until you take care of it, once and for all. You have the nerve to be asking me if Rachel is living with somebody. I should be asking you that question."

"Don't even go there. You know I don't have anything going on with Sandra. She's the one who keeps all of this nonsense going. Anyway, what about the number?" Ken whipped his charming smile on. It had been quite successful in helping him get his way with women. Even Ken's sister found his charm persuasive.

"You're lucky Rachel doesn't have a private number. I guess I'll go ahead and give it to you. If it was unlisted, you'd just be out of luck. Next time, you better handle your business better."

Sharon took her loosely balled up fist and playfully pushed it into his shoulder. Flowing with the moment, he exaggeratedly leaned back, as though her punch had made a real impact.

"Okay, okay, sis. Don't be so hard on a brother." He playfully put his arm around her in appreciation.

"Brother, nothing!" She comically rolled her eyes and right before turning back to the business in the refrigerator, she gave Ken a smile of affirmation, letting him know that all was cool.

After Ken got the number, he headed back outside and gave his final good-byes to everybody, except Sandra. It was obvious to everyone there that they were not on speaking terms, yet again. The cookout was over, but the unsettled bitterness between Sandra and Ken definitely was not.

4

Rachel was too excited to relax. Her head was still spinning from the wonderful afternoon she had spent with Ken. The party turned out to be fun after all. She was glad that Sharon talked her into going. Instead of going to bed right away, she decided to watch some late night TV.

Boots jumped up onto the sofa, close enough to Rachel to avoid falling off. She rubbed the top of her cat's head and Boots responded by purring in a soft, almost whispering sound. In a semi-animated voice, she said, "I had a great time." Although she wasn't always in the habit of sharing her inner thoughts with the cat, Boots would have to do tonight. It was too late to call up her cousin, Roz, or her closest and longest standing friend, Neal. She was extremely close to them both, to the point that most people assumed Roz and Neal were her sister and brother. She was wondering if Ken was also reflecting on the afternoon at this very moment.

"If only I could have given him my phone number."

Ding Dong.

"Who could that be?" She wasn't expecting any company. "Nah, it couldn't be Kenny. I didn't give him my address." She tucked her shirt in and patted her hair down before opening the door. "Who is it?" she curiously asked.

"Me, Rachel, Gary."

"Gary!" She took a deep breathe and rested her forehead on the door. "Gary!" She closed her eyes and shook her head. Finally, she slowly opened the door. She stood in the doorway staring at him. He was standing there beaming with excitement.

"Hi, Rachel. Can I come in?"

"I guess so," she curtly blurted out while trying to camouflage her irritation.

He grabbed the screen door and came in.

She was stand-offish with him. "Gary, did we talk about you coming over here tonight?"

"Ah, nah, nah, but I was in the area. Thought I'd stop by and see you. Is it okay if I stay a little while? I'm sorry for not calling first." He reached towards her in an attempt to be affectionate.

His clinging was a big turn-off to her. Rachel wondered if he had any inkling of how annoyed she was with him boldly showing up, unannounced. She brushed by him and headed for the sun room. He had no choice but to follow.

Rachel sat on a chair. Since the sofa could hold two people, she didn't want to give him the wrong idea. She flipped the station to the movie channel, and picked up the popcorn to munch on. She was content, after successfully dodging his desperate romantic attempt.

He grabbed a handful of popcorn from the bowl, sat down on the sofa, and began to chomp on it. His chewing annoyed her. At this point, everything he did irritated her. She was simply tired of him.

She could feel his disgusting eyes combing her body. The last thing on her mind was intimacy with him. They had only been intimate twice in their six months of dating. The short romantic interlude had really been over before it ever got started. As a result of the unsatisfactory experience, she secretly nicknamed Gary 'the minute-man'. His sexual shortcomings added to the incompatibility, but she never had the heart to shatter him by revealing the truth. Sex was not happening tonight, or any other night according to Rachel.

Her goal was to watch some TV until she could tactfully figure out how to get rid of him. He bent over and untied his shoes. He was getting comfortable. It was clear that he wasn't making any effort to leave on his own.

A couple of hours elapsed. Rachel was ready to turn in for the evening. Gary was already snoring on the sofa. She looked over at him and shook her head. She had grown unbearably tired of him. She was too easy-going to feel comfortable telling the man to get out. She was hoping he would wake up, leave on his own, and spare her the inconvenience of having to kick him out. Although she wasn't romantically attracted to him, she didn't want to be mean to him. She decided to set the exit plan in action by letting out a big yawn.

"Oh boy," she yelled in his direction. "I guess I'm really tired," Rachel said while stretching out her arms.

"Want to go to bed?" Gary sat on the edge of the sofa, anxiously awaiting her response.

She wanted to go to bed, but not with him. Why was he making it so difficult for her to dump him. She tried to be humane about it, but he didn't leave her much choice."

"Gary, I'm really tired, and I want to go to bed, alone," she emphasized.

"Can I sleep down here, then?"

She wondered what would it take to get him out. "I think it would be best if you went home."

He was disappointed by her response. With no other options, he finally got up, pulled some keys from his pocket, and headed for the door. She walked behind him and sighed with relief.

He put his hand on the door knob, and right before opening it, turned to her and said, "Are you sure you don't want me to stay?"

"I'm sure," she responded in a soft, non-threatening voice.

"I'm glad I got a chance to see you. I'll call you tomorrow."

Rachel nodded slowly. She didn't actually want to encourage him to call. Gary leaned over to kiss her on the lips, and she casually turned to the side, while fingering her hair behind her ear.

"Talk to you later."

As Gary walked out, she closed the door behind him. With her hand on the knob, she took a moment and leaned back against the door in relief. It was times like this which made dating a not so pleasant experience. She flipped off the lights, and headed up the stairs to her bedroom.

She knelt down, with her hands clasped on top of the thick, rose-printed comforter that draped across the queen-sized brass bed. From childhood, Big Mama had instilled in her how important it was to pray. Although Rachel wasn't adhering to all of her Godly teachings, she faithfully said her prayers every night, before going to sleep. Actually, it had become her source of hope in the search for Mr. Right. Even in her lukewarm religious state, she recognized that it was going to be nearly impossible to find Mr. Perfect by herself. Only God was going to be able to find her man, with all of the twelve characteristics that she was looking for.

"God, please bless me with a husband. I still want to have a family. Please let me find the right man."

Kenny briefly crossed her mind, but Rachel didn't dare pray specifically for some man that she had met only hours before. It seemed too much like hypocrisy. She could hear Big Mama's words ringing in her head, "Chile, just take the request to God. He don't need yo'r ideas on how to fix it."

With Big Mama's influence and direction, Rachel kept on track with her prayer. "After you bless me with a husband, please bless us with some kids, too. Thank you Lord." She prayed for some other things, before winding down. "Take care of Big Mama. Amen."

It seemed like the more Rachel perfected the twelve-point checklist, the longer her bedtime prayer became. She couldn't understand what the big deal was. She was only asking for the basics: a good-looking, down-to-earth, mature man who had his own money. And most of all, she wanted a strong man who knew how to treat his woman and make her feel special, without feeling threatened or inadequate. Maybe Kenny was the man who could make her fairy tale a reality.

Rachel got off of her knees and slid into bed, between the cool sheets. Without realizing it, she dozed off. In her dream, she could faintly hear the phone. When Boots jumped up on the third ring, she knew that it must be the phone and chaotically reached for it. Even when she was delirious, she answered the phone in an alert tone. Consciously or not, she always wanted to give the impression that she had it together.

"Hello." There was a pause on the other end. "Hello," she said again, this time with an irritated tone. She was in no mood for prank calls this late at night, or even worse, an undesired call from Gary.

"Hi."

She knew the suave voice was coming from none other than Ken. She had an uncanny ability to recognize voices over the phone, even after meeting someone once, particularly this someone.

"I apologize for calling so late. I hope I didn't wake you."

"Oh no, you didn't wake me." Even though he had, she wasn't about to let him know it.

"I got your number from Sharon. I hope you don't mind?"

"Not at all. As a matter of fact, I'm glad you did."

"Well, I wanted to call and let you know that I enjoyed meeting you today. I also wanted to apologize for getting tied up before you left. I didn't get a chance to properly say goodbye."

Her heart was racing. She wanted to say all of the right things without it appearing to be an effort. She decided to let him do most of the talking.

"I was wondering, if you're not too busy tomorrow, maybe you'll take me up on my offer to go down to the waterfront."

"I don't have any real plans tomorrow," she said instantly, without much thought. "Yes, I would love to go."

"Great."

"Around what time?" she asked.

"Well, I normally go to church in the morning, and I'm usually out by 1:00 or 1:30. I could pick you up around 2:30. Is that okay?" There was a brief pause on the phone. "If you want, you're welcome to come to church with me."

Rachel did go to church, but not as often as her grandmother liked. Going to church with Ken seemed too much like a date, and she didn't think it would be appropriate. Although she wasn't acting as religious as she was raised, Rachel definitely didn't want to discourage anyone else from being gung-ho about church, especially Ken. She found it difficult enough to find a man with the basics, let alone one who was also religious. If he goes to church, he could only be but so bad, Rachel thought. For a brief moment, she contemplated how he might react to her not wanting to go to church with him? She didn't want him to label her as a heathen this early in the game. Regardless, it was a chance she had to take.

"I won't be able to go to church with you tomorrow morning. Maybe we can go together another time." The word 'maybe' took her off the hook. It meant, she really hadn't committed to anything.

"Two-thirty, though, is fine for me," she responded.

"Okay. Well, I'll pick you up tomorrow. Oh yeah, give me your address."

Rachel wondering if, maybe, she had finally hit the jackpot and found the right man, a good church-going guy. "324 Ferdie Lane."

5

Rachel spent most of the morning preparing for her date with Ken. Yet, she found herself rushing to be ready on time. It was already 1:30, and she hadn't completely decided on what to wear. She stood in front of the full-length mirror and held the long, floral-printed, crepe dress up to her lingerie-covered body. She spent several minutes flipping back and forth between the comfortable dress and the classy-looking linen skirt. She wanted to impress Ken, without over doing it. With her conservative, self-conscious nature, she was only willing to go but so far in dressing seductively. Because of the reserved way she dressed, most men didn't initially know that she had such a knock-down shape.

Rachel was considered petite. Her golden brown complexion, coupled with her radiating personality, captured the attention of many men. She had no problem meeting men. She ran into trouble when it came to finding and keeping a good one.

Being this was the first date, she decided to be comfortable, and go with the dress.

The cat was curling up next to her leg as she was getting dressed. "Poor Boots. What? You feeling lonely? It's a good thing I don't wear a lot of make-up, because I sure wouldn't have time to put it on today," she stated while glancing in the mirror. Last month, she had her hair cut and wrapped for the hot Chicago summer. It was classy, and most importantly, easy.

Rachel was straightening up, when she heard a car pull up. She looked at her watch; it was exactly 2:30. Right on time, she acknowledged. "Good, he isn't one of those late-kind-of brothers."

She had opened the door earlier to get a breeze, and to let Boots sit in its favorite spot by the door. The cat loved listening to the sounds made outside. That's as close as Rachel would let Boots get to the outside, in fear of the cat getting lost, or even worse, get hit by a passing car. Poor Boots was nurtured like her child.

As Ken came up the walkway, she could see that he was tastefully dressed with a cream-colored short-sleeve shirt, slightly darker shade of pants with extra-thin brown stripes, and expensive looking Italian shoes. His comely face was accented by a pair of small, wire-framed, circular, trendy-looking sunglasses. As Ken got closer, he looked up and saw her standing inside, several feet from the door. He greeted her with a warm smile. Rachel was taken. She unconsciously responded with a smile.

"Hi."

"Hello."

"Can I come in?"

"Please," Rachel offered as she pushed open the screen door.

"We picked a nice day to be out on the waterfront."

"Yeah, it should be nice. Can I get you anything, water, juice?"

"No, I'm okay. With all of the food at the waterfront, we can get something down there, if you're hungry."

Boots surfaced and sat down near her feet. The scrunched look on Ken's face indicated that he wasn't exactly fond of cats.

"Oh, don't pay any attention to Boots. My cat is harmless, right Boots." Her words didn't seem to bring any relief to his stressed look. "You're not afraid of cats are you?"

"No, I just don't like them."

"Oh, I'm sorry to hear that." Great, she thought. Finally, something was wrong. She actually felt better now that everything wasn't perfect; it was seeming more realistic.

"Well, I'm ready." She grabbed her purse, and they headed for the door.

Ken opened the passenger side car door for her.

"Hmmm," she quietly moaned. She found it refreshing to be with a man who had some manners. She resigned herself to the fact that men, nowadays, didn't even think about opening the door for a lady. Even worse, several times she had to provide the car and, on top of that, do the driving. Rachel never did care much for a man riding shotgun on the passenger side. In some cases, it was either that or give up gas money, which she chose not to do. Neither choice was ideal, but driving the man around seemed a bit more palatable than coughing up money. She strongly believed that every man, calling himself so, should, at least, have some kind of old jalopy to get around in. To her, there was nothing worse than a date walking. It was clear Mr. Right was going to have money and a car.

On the ride downtown, she was casual in her approach, but no doubt, she was checking out Ken. He put on some John Coltrane music and turned it down low. So far, he was doing okay. She suspected he might be putting this kind of music on to impress her. She visually scanned the mini-music collection in the car and noticed many of her favorite jazz-type artists like Charlie Parker, Billie, Ella, and Miles. Perhaps he wasn't pretending at all. She was relieved to see that Ken wasn't into the hip-hop, bee-bop type of thumpin' and bumpin' music heard screaming out of the cars of youngsters. She was feeling pretty good about spending this time with Ken, who unknowingly, had earned four check points in two days.

"It was nice meeting your family yesterday."

"I'm glad that you came. I'm glad I finally got a chance to meet you."

There he went again, laying on the charm with ease.

"Your sisters seem very nice. Of course, I know Sharon from work, but it was nice to meet Dana and Sandra."

"Sandra's not my sister." She assumed Sandra was his sister since they were all talking so intimately at the barbecue. "She's my ex."

"Oh, I'm sorry." Rachel felt embarrassed and a bit surprised. No wonder, the meeting with Sandra felt a little strange. Rachel hadn't been able to put her finger on it before, but she knew something was out of sorts. It never crossed her mind that Sandra was Ken's ex. Sharon never mentioned that he'd been married.

"No, I'm the one that's sorry."

"Sorry she came, or sorry that I didn't know?"

"Both. I apologize for not introducing you to her yesterday. I was surprised to see her there. She caught me off guard."

"Ken, you really don't owe me an apology. We just met. There is no need for you to involve me in your personal affairs."

"Trust me, I have no secrets when it comes to my relationship with Sandra. What can I say? We don't get along. I love my daughter and all, but it's difficult for me to deal with Sandra. I guess, in a way, I didn't want her to meet you."

"Why?" Rachel asked out of curiosity.

"Because Sandra has not cut the string yet. She uses my daughter to keep hanging on. She also tries to befriend whatever woman happens to be in my life. Now, how pathetic is that? I admit, at the risk of being rude to you, I didn't want to get into anything deep with her yesterday."

Rachel had no idea the little girl was his daughter. She was surprised, disappointed, and didn't know exactly what to say in response. So, she decided it was best to lighten up the subject. "Your daughter is very pretty."

"Yeah, she's my girl."

"How old is she?"

"She's five."

"Do you see her often?"

"Not really. She lives in Ohio."

"Oh, so she's only in town for the weekend?"

"I guess."

What did he mean 'I guess', Rachel pondered. Didn't he know?

"See, that's how Sandra is. She called this morning to see if I would pick Ariel up from my dad's, and keep her this evening. I told her no, because I already had plans. Sandra just shows up and expects me to change everything around to accommodate her schedule."

"If you want to get together another time, I'll definitely understand," Rachel sincerely offered. She assumed that Ken, like most good daddies, would want to spend whatever time possible with his child, particularly since Ariel lived out of town.

"No, I'm not playing into Sandra's games. Besides, once I make a commitment, I stick by it. I do want to see my daughter, but I have to put my foot down with Sandra, otherwise nothing will change."

Rachel was impressed and pleased to be in the company of a dependable man. Off hand, she couldn't remember if dependability was a characteristic on the checklist or not. If it was, that would be number five. Either way, it was at least worth a brownie point, those extra check points given to those who needed help making the twelve-point checklist. She was taking all of his conversation in by listening and not saying a word.

"I'm sorry to dump all of this on you," he apologized.

She didn't exactly know how to react to this Sandra thing. Perhaps Ken was on the rebound. If he was, Rachel was definitely not going to get involved. She was all too familiar with how those relationships were destined to fail.

"So, how long were you married?"

"Married! We weren't married. We did live together, though, for about three years before my daughter was born, and about a year after that."

"You guys were together for quite a while, and never married, huh."

"Nah. She wanted to get married, but it never seemed like the right time. We didn't plan on having the baby. Things weren't going so well for us then. After the baby came, we tried to stick it out, but we both got tired. Or, I should say that I got tired and decided to leave."

"How did she end up in Ohio, if you don't mind me asking."

"I don't mind. Sandra requested a job transfer to Ohio. She has some family there and wanted to start over in a new place. Sometimes I think she was hoping I'd follow her there."

"Did you consider it?"

"Not really. Our problems would have followed us to Ohio."

"What about your daughter? Do you miss not being a daily part of her life?"

"Yeah, and that's something I did have to accept. I can't let Sandra's decision to move away stop me from getting on with my life."

Something about this conversation left Rachel a little bothered. She prayed that he wasn't the hands-off kind of father who kept the child's picture in his wallet for display. The kind who showed up at the graduation as the proud dad with a card and maybe fifty bucks. The one who hadn't done any nurturing, role-modeling, bedtime storytelling, or providing of consistent financial support. In fear of getting too deep into her feelings about absentee-fathers, she stayed on the surface with the dialogue. Besides, they were at the water-front, and this was her opportunity to have a good time. She kept reminding herself that this was only the first date with the man, and there was no need to size him up this early for anything serious. Today, she was just going to relax and have a good time.

Rachel loved going to the Taste, as the locals called it. It was one of her favorite activities in the city. The Taste of Chicago was a big waterfront festival held annually in Grant Park, right between Michigan Ave. and Lake Shore Dr. There were literally hundreds of restaurants selling samples of food. There was plenty of good food and music. The ethnic festivals she used to go to in Detroit's Hart Plaza and Atlanta's Underground were mini-versions of the Taste. The only thing Rachel hated about the Taste was the fact that it always seemed to be held on the hottest week of the year, around the 4th of July, and this year was no exception.

"Since you're a regular, is there anything in particular you want to do?" Ken graciously asked.

"Not right now, but at some point I want to get a barbecued turkey leg and some Eli's cheesecake. We can walk around for a while, if you want."

She knew that the food could be kind of expensive and had already decided, beforehand, to contribute to the purchases. She determined a long time ago that on a first date, she would pay her own way. That way, the man wouldn't expect anything in return, like sexual favors. In her early relationships, guys were often eager to get personal on the first meeting, following, what Rachel termed, a $2 date. In order to nip the sexual expectations in the bud, she typically went Dutch on the initial dates.

There was a drawback to her approach. Often times, guys were offended and felt threatened by her need to be independent and wouldn't follow-up with a second date. On the flip side, some guys would like it, oh too well, and wanted her to contribute regularly. It had been difficult for Rachel, a self-sufficient woman, to find the balance between allowing the man to pay, as is traditional, and not putting herself in a compromising position by letting him put out a few bucks.

"By the way, I meant to tell you that you look nice today," Ken said without establishing eye contact, "and yesterday, too, for that matter."

Her cheeks were blushing. "Thank you very much," she calmly and politely replied on the outside. Internally, she was screaming, "Yes, yes, he noticed. All the hard work I put into the preparation paid off. Yes." The compliment put a little extra pep in her step. This date was going well, so far.

Overall, she hated the dating process. There were so many do's and don'ts. Typically, it took her eight solid months to really get to know whether a guy was compatible. The men she dated, in recent years, hadn't made it to the eighth-month mark. She figured her tolerance level for rejects was decreasing as her age was increasing. Older and wiser was what she liked to believe. Her new philosophy was, "Why invest time if there's no future in it?"

What she hated most was starting over each time. Once she got to know a man, even with all of his flaws, there was a tendency to stick it out. It was too much work to get to know a new person. She speculated that it was why many people stayed in bad relationships. She always said, "A bird in the hand, even if its lame, beats two in the bush." Rachel wanted to meet Mr. Right, skip the superficial infatuation period, get hitched, have some babies, and move on with life. It was unrealistic, but it didn't hurt to dream.

Ken parked several blocks away.

Walking towards the center of the festivities, she didn't feel confined to any schedule. She merely wanted to have a nice relaxed afternoon. As an afterthought, Rachel said, "I would like to check out the jazz groups."

"That's fine. Where are they?"

"They're usually by the water fountain," she pointed.

"Let's go." Ken extended a hand to her, and once her hand was securely nestled in his, he took off in the direction of the water fountain. She felt secure and special as he maneuvered his way confidently through the crowd.

There were literally thousands of people at the Taste. Nevertheless, she always managed to run into someone she knew. She learned the hard way that it was indeed a small world after all. Four years ago, she had agreed to go to the Taste with Luc. Even though she was kind of seeing Rick, the playboy, at the time, it seemed like a safe idea. With so many people at the Taste, she figured the chance of running into anyone she knew was slim to none, particularly Rick. Lo and behold, she ran smack dab into Rick's friend. She remembered how uncomfortable they both were, and she vowed not to be caught in such a position again. She never did really know if Rick found out, but the guilt alone ate her up.

It felt good to be out with a man. Her love life had been non-existent of late. She had decided to take a breathing period from the dating scene. She went downtown alone from time to time, but it wasn't the same as being out on the waterfront with a handsome guy.

"Are you sure you don't want anything? Something to drink maybe?"

Ken seemed accommodating to her, and she liked it. It had been a long time since she had attention from a man, or at least from one that she wanted to be with.

Admittedly, both Gary and Brian were attentive, but they didn't have the magic touch. She spent more time dodging them than having fun. They were all right until she could do better, and by the looks of Ken, she had.

"Okay. Yeah. I'll take something. I don't drink beer, but anything else is fine." Rachel assumed that he didn't drink alcohol either since he was a church man.

After what seemed like forever, they finally got to the jazz display. "There's a spot over there. Do you want to sit on the grass?" he pointed to an area where many people were already planted.

She focused in on a vacant shady spot, right under a tree.

"Over there, in the shade will be fine."

There were people everywhere. Moving through the seated crowd, with her hand affectionately locked in his, Rachel felt captivated by the sensual touch. Something about him was captivating to her. At least for the moment, he was someone special. She was too, too familiar, though, with how wonderful guys always were in the beginning. She didn't know why women did that? They would meet a man, then immediately size him up for the altar. All kinds of thoughts were flooding her mind. Could he make the eighth-month cutoff? Only time would tell, but for right now, holding hands was a good sign.

She sat with the long crepe dress completely covering her legs, chin resting on her knees, and hands clasped together. He laid on his side and rested his head on his hand. The group playing looked like locals, but the music was top notch. "This music is decent," he acknowledged.

"Yes, it is," she agreed. The music had a romantic overtone. Surrounded by people, yet, it was as if they were alone, listening to the passionate music. They were hitting it off.

She was still curious about his relationship with Sandra. Rachel was sure that Sandra's view of the relationship was totally different than his. It always amazed her how two people in the same relationship, especially when not married, tended to see the status so differently. She considered herself to be like many other woman who usually labeled a relationship as serious, once intimacy got underway. On the other hand, guys would usually down-play a serious relationship, and leave a door open to pursue other women, by saying that they were just friends.

When Rachel thought about it, she was actually relieved not to have known who Sandra was at the cookout. It would have made things prematurely awkward. She admitted to herself that it was good to be in the driver's seat. It was always better to be the woman of choice meeting the wanna-be or has-been girlfriend. Rachel remembered how much it hurt when she ran into two-timing Rick and his new woman at the movie theater. It didn't feel good, unexpectedly being put out to pasture for a new filly. If the truth was as Ken described, with Sandra still wanting him, then she couldn't help but feel a little sorry for Sandra. In Rachel's estimation, Sandra was just another sister driving blindfolded through the rocky roads of love, and her man was navigating.

All in all, Rachel had a strong interest in Ken, but Sandra was a wild card. The problem Rachel had with wild cards was that she never knew how or when they were going to show up. Battling with the ex was not something she was interested in doing right now, no matter how appealing he was.

She didn't know if this was a good time or not to dive back into the conversation with him. Maybe she really didn't want to know anymore, right now, but her curiosity won out. "So, do you have any more kids besides your daughter?"

"No, just Ariel. Do you?"

"No," she quickly answered.

"Oh, a career woman, huh?"

"No, just a single one. Call me traditional, but I always wanted to have a husband, backyard, and some money before starting a family. Ten years ago that seemed like a simple request. I didn't think it would take so long to make it happen."

"So you want to get married."

"Perhaps, at some point. That is, if the opportunity presents itself."

There was a time when her answer would have been a definitive yes. But time had worn the response down to a perhaps. If Ken was anything like the other single men she dated, the mere mention of marriage would send him into a tailspin.

"As attractive and personable as you are, I would expect you to have plenty of men asking to marry you?"

Rachel heard that line in varying forms, but it always seemed to be used by guys as a lead into asking about her current dating status. She didn't know why he couldn't cut the crap, and just come right out and ask?

"And they say women play games!" she said to herself.

In response to Ken, Rachel didn't want him to think she had been involved with some countless number of men. But, she also wanted him to know that, yes, she had quite a few admirers and was not hard up for a date. It was good to let him know early that he wasn't the only show in town. "Sure, I get many offers, but none have been right for me."

"So, you've never been married?

"No, I haven't." She inquisitively asked, "Have you?"

"Nope, I haven't met Mrs. Right, yet."

"You know, when we first met, I thought you were married."

"Married! What made you think that?"

"The wedding band you had on yesterday," she said glancing at his ring finger, which was not sporting the band today.

He looked at his ringless finger and said, "Oh, okay. I guess you would think that I was married with the ring. Well, I'm not married. I wear the ring sometimes. It belonged to my mother's father. After Mom died, I took it as a keepsake. Unfortunately, it only fits my ring finger. So, every now and then I'll wear it.

When she looked up, their eyes met for a moment. She was wondering how he felt about the date, and now she knew. She could see by the twinkle in his eyes, he was attracted to her as well. The good thing was he liked her back. The bad news was, it was going to be important to keep the heat turned down and not allow things to progress too rapidly. She didn't feel like getting into another crash and burn relationship, the kind with a fast take-off and generally ended in a big explosion. She had lost enough weight in recent years resulting from the depressive, broken-relationship-recovery periods. She had more than her share of nights when she cried herself to sleep. If anything was to come of this, she knew it was going to take time.

"So, are you seeing anyone?"

There, he had finally asked it. She couldn't understand why men were so anxious to find out her availability status, but so often neglected to share theirs. She wasn't really seeing anyone. As far as she was concerned, the relationship with her most recent suitor had been over months ago. That was around the time she stopped calling Gary, and making any effort at all to see him. It was rare for them to see each other, and on the few occasions when they did, it was at his initiative. Rachel really hated breaking off relationships. She was hoping Gary would fade off into the sunset with some dignity, but he was definitely lingering. With her luck, she wouldn't be at all surprised if they ran into him at the Taste. Although she wanted to get rid of Gary, she was hoping for his sake, more so than her own, that he didn't see her with Ken. It would be cruel and hurtful, as she knew from her own personal experiences.

Since Gary was well on the way out, she responded confidently, "No, I'm not." Besides, why should she feel guilty. She knew plenty of guys, like Rick, who prided themselves on smooth transitions. They felt good having someone new on the scene before the other woman was completely out of the picture. Smooth transitions were only a problem for the person who didn't know that they were on the way out. It didn't cost a man anything to have two women during the transition period. The worst that could happen was that he had to be sexually active with both women on any given day. Rachel didn't know for sure, but figured Rick hadn't considered the double work to be such a bad thing. Matter of fact, it was probably more like a bonus than a punishment.

"That's surprising for someone like you!"

"I think everyone needs a break in their life, whether it's from work, a relationship, family, or whatever. I'm learning how to enjoy being by myself. Don't get me wrong, I enjoy companionship, but there's a time and place for everything."

They were deep into the conversation, and hadn't noticed most of the people leaving the grassy area. Glancing at her watch, she noticed it was already a little past 7:00. The jazz group was packing up. She had totally forgotten about eating. It was low priority compared to her chat with this handsome beau. Ken had no idea how captivated she was with his voice and sensuous demeanor. He definitely had it going on in her eyes.

"I guess we should find another spot."

"Let's sit here a little while longer. I like the conversation." As Ken reached out to touch her arm, she felt jittery.

"Well, since you're not seeing anyone, I guess it's okay to see you again."

She decided not to respond and therefore let the silence lead him into more dialogue.

"If you're interested, I have tickets to an art exhibit, tomorrow. I wasn't going to go, but if you go, I'll go."

Wow, a man with some class, she noted. She wasn't a big art buff, but if it meant another date with Ken, then why not? It seemed harmless enough.

Unconsciously, she glanced at her watch one more time. This time he noticed.

"Is it getting late for you? What time is it by the way?"

"It's 7:40, and yes, it is getting late." She did have to be at work early tomorrow, especially since it was the middle of the billing cycle.

"Rachel," Ken softly said while lightly picking up her hand and looking into her eyes. "I am enjoying our conversation, but I know that we both have things to do. I'll let you go, for now."

Rachel tried not to show any signs of excitement, although Ken's charm was making it difficult.

"On the way out, why don't we grab that food you wanted," he suggested.

"That sounds good."

Ken got up first, and then extended a hand to help her up. She felt refreshed to be with a gentleman. She was eating up the long deserved attention.

"Do you want the turkey leg?"

She decided not to get her favorite barbecued turkey leg. The sauce was too messy to eat on a first date. She didn't want to be smiling in Ken's face, with meat, unknowingly, stuck between her teeth.

"All I want is some Eli's cheesecake and maybe a piece of fried chicken from Gladys' Kitchenette. Wait, is it Gladys?"

"If you are talking about soul food, it is?"

"Right, it is Gladys. I always get the name mixed up with Sylvia's in New York and Delilah's in Philadelphia."

"Yeah, I know about Delilah's. I have some family in Philly."

Exiting the Taste, Gary briefly crossed Rachel's mind. She was almost home free, having escaped the claws of a chance happening. For all of their sakes, she was glad they didn't run into Gary, and probably a few other folks.

On the way home, they listened to the jazz music in the car. Every now and then, one or both would interject something. They pulled up to her townhouse. Ken turned the park lights off, but left the motor running.

"Hang on, let me get your door."

"That's okay."

"No, let me get it. I'll feel better if you let me walk you to the door."

Rachel had been minimally exposed to this kind of good treatment in the past, but had no doubt that she could sure get use to it in a hurry.

As she turned the key in the door, she stopped and turned towards him. "Would you like to come in?"

"No, I'll let you get settled in, and I'm going to see my daughter. I promised to stop by before she goes to bed, and it is getting to be about that time. But, remember, the art show is tomorrow. If it's okay, I will pick you up at 6:30. That should give us plenty of time."

"That's fine."

Now that the first date was over, they'd broken the ice. She was wondering what he was going to do next. She had mixed feelings about a kiss. It was only the first date, after all. On the one hand, he looked seductive, and seemed aggressive. On the other, his kissing her was bound to tarnish her image of him being the perfect gentleman. By her standards, he was in a tough spot and didn't even know it. Doing nothing, he came across as a wimp. By taking charge and acting out his emotions, he would come across as too assertive.

He took her hand and softly kissed the back of it. "I will talk to you later. Thank you for spending the afternoon with me. It was nice, and I really enjoyed it."

"Me too." Cool, Rachel affirmed with her heartbeat racing from the anticipation. He had managed to show affection, without compromising her opinion of him. He was too good. She figured it was going to be fun getting to know him.

6

It was the middle of the hospital's billing cycle. Rachel's day was hectic, but going smoothly. Ken, no doubt, was the source of much of her contentment. She found herself constantly reflecting back to the romantic time they had at the Taste. Daydreaming about Ken was unavoidable: holding hands and casually walking along the lake, lying on a blanket in the park and reading poetry together. Her mind wandered from one scene to another. She constantly reminded herself that she needed to keep the fantasizing in perspective. Ken was nice. So were many others before him.

She had often been deceived by fine guys. They came in great packages, but the contents didn't usually turn out to be as appealing as their outer looks. Rachel knew from first-hand experience, all that glittered was definitely not gold. She had dealt with enough gold-plated, perpetrating brothers; the kind whose shiny and polished physique attracted her to them, but the shine quickly rubbed off as soon as she got involved long enough to know what they were really all about. She was looking for the real thing now, no more gold-plated stuff.

Ken seemed to be batting a thousand, so far. Handsome, with a car, a job, able to hold a conversation, sexy, and polite just for starters. She took nothing, including the basics, for granted with men anymore. She'd been burned too many times.

When the phone rang, Rachel saw Sharon's name spelled out on the digital display and smiled. She was expecting Sharon to call, sooner or later, for the update.

They worked in different areas of the hospital. Sharon was an administrative assistant and Rachel was an accounting supervisor. They didn't normally talk during the work day, except for lunch time. This was different today. They both had a reason to talk.

"Hello, Sharon."

"How did you know ...," Sharon said before pausing. "Oh, that's right. You have a display phone. You're man-age-ment," Sharon teased.

"Don't even start."

"So girl, how are you today?" perky Sharon inquired.

"Fine."

"I'm calling to see what happened to you at lunch time."

"Oh girl, you know how crazy it is when we're going through billing. I worked through lunch so that I won't have to stay late tonight," Rachel explained.

"That's unusual for you to be rushing out. Why? You must have plans or something?"

"Yes."

"Uh huh. With Kenny?"

Rachel reluctantly answered, "Yes."

"Uhm."

"Uhm what?" asked Rachel, as if she really didn't know.

"I guess there's no need to ask how things went."

"I'm sure the curiosity is killing you."

"You know it is," Sharon excitedly said. "So, go on. Tell me."

"What can I say? It was a nice afternoon at the Taste."

"And," Sharon paused, waiting for Rachel to volunteer more scoop, "go on."

"There's really nothing else to tell." Although Rachel was excited about Ken, she was reluctant to give too much information to Sharon. In case something did materialize between them, she preferred to keep it private. She vowed that whatever Sharon found out on a personal level would come from Ken. Besides, Sharon was his sister, and Rachel knew blood was always thicker than water. Rachel figured if she never started the process of confiding in Sharon, then there would never be any need to break it off later.

"We had a good time. I'll see him again tonight for another date."

"I knew it. I knew you two would hit it off."

"And how did you know that? Are you psychic, or something now?"

"No, it's just that you're both looking for somebody nice. Well, I'm happy for you."

"Thanks. Also, thanks for inviting me to the cookout. I had a great time."

"Well, my break is almost over. I'll probably see you at lunch tomorrow. But then again, maybe not. With you dating and all, you'll probably work through lunch so you can get a jump on an early evening." Sharon was in a playful mood. Rachel didn't mind the kidding at all. As a matter of fact, there was some truth in Sharon's comment.

Rachel was curious about Sandra. Perhaps, Sharon could give her some quick insight into that relationship. She wanted some information, but didn't want to seem nosey or overly concerned. Sharon was obviously interested in her brother's love life. Why else would she go to the trouble of introducing him to somebody in the first place. Rachel figured it wouldn't hurt to see what Sharon knew and, more importantly, what she was willing to tell. Before she hung up, Rachel asked, "So, why didn't you tell me about Sandra?"

"Sandra? Huh, there is nothing to tell. She's Kenny's ex-girlfriend."

"She is a bit more than just that." Rachel was alluding to Sandra being the mother of his daughter. "And, she sure didn't act like an ex to me."

"Yeah well, to Kenny she is an ex. They get along for the sake of Ariel, but as far as I know, that's it." It was clear that Sharon didn't want to say more than what was necessary. "What did Kenny tell you about her?"

"Basically the same thing." Rachel could have let the discussion drop, but her curiosity had not yet been satisfied. She decided to probe a little bit further. "The question is, do you think she is going to be a problem if we're dating?"

"Definitely not!" Sharon stated in a firm tone.

"How can you be so sure?"

"Because I know Kenny. He wouldn't go for that. He'll handle his business, especially where Sandra is concerned. Just go out tonight and enjoy your date. Don't worry about Sandra. Get out and have some fun."

"Okay. I guess we'll talk later then. Oh yeah, I'm not sure about lunch tomorrow. It's not because of dating either. It's the billing cycle."

"Yeah, okay."

They both said bye and hung up. Rachel immediately got back to work, because today, by hook or by crook, she was leaving at 4:30. That would give her plenty of time to get home, freshen up, and be ready for Ken by 6:30.

Sharon's reassurance wasn't enough to put her mind at ease, but then again, it wasn't Sharon who needed to make her feel comfortable about Sandra. She figured that Sandra was indeed a non-issue at this point. She had just met Ken, so it wasn't like she wanted or needed to make any demands on the handling of his personal affairs.

Her primary concern stemmed around getting involved with an unavailable man. 'Been there, done that' was her motto regarding unavailable men. It was a road she cared not to travel again. The mere thought of getting caught up with an already-hooked-up man was painful. It had been six years ago, and she still had a vivid memory of the encounter with Paul's girlfriend.

Like most of her men, Paul was no exception. He too was a gold-plated, pretty boy. They hit it off well in the beginning. Everything was wonderful, until Ann showed up. Apparently, Paul had either forgotten to tell Rachel that he was still involved with someone, or forgot to tell Ann that he was seeing someone new. Either way, it wasn't such a good spot for Rachel to be in.

Paul played on a basketball league with a group of friends. At his request, Rachel attended one of his games a couple of months or so after they'd started dating. She felt honored to finally meet his friends. Meeting the family and friends was a significant sign to her that the relationship was progressing. It also meant she was in the prime-time spot. Based on her experience, she knew men tended to be secretive, and only exposed the family to their women on a need-to-know-only-if-serious basis. The men in her past were good about reserving the main-woman spotlight for the chosen one. By getting personally invited to his basketball game, Rachel assumed that she was in the main-lady seat. She was in his spotlight, and enjoying every bit of it.

Recounting the scene, she remembered that it had been a beautiful, hot sunny day. To survive the heat, she had worn a spaghetti-strapped sun dress that tied around the neck. In order to partake of various summer activities, she had recently opted for the hassle-free braids. Rachel sat in the team's section of the bleachers. She sat with Barb, the girlfriend of Paul's friend, Jeffrey. Rachel and Barb were talking, as well as catching glimpses of the game, here and there. At half-time, Paul and Jeffrey came over to talk with the girls briefly. Paul was sweaty, so he didn't hug Rachel, but he did give her a big kiss.

After half-time, Rachel was enjoying the conversation with Barb, when all of a sudden, she thought she heard a woman yelling behind her. She turned around to see if her mind was playing tricks on her. Sure enough, there was a woman standing one level up on the step behind her. The woman seemed to be focused on Rachel. Until that moment, she hadn't really paid any attention to the woman's babbling in the midst of the crowd.

"Yeah, you," the upset woman shouted.

Rachel didn't recognize the woman, and so figured she wasn't talking to her and turned back around. The robust woman then leaned over several people and tapped Rachel on the shoulder. Rachel was starting to get curious. She turned slowly to the woman. "Yes? Are you talking to me?"

"Yeah, I'm talking to you, tramp." The woman's hand was placed solidly on her hip.

"Excuse me?" Rachel exclaimed in complete shock.

"Excuse you my butt!"

"Miss, do I know you?" Rachel's tone was serious. She was not appreciating this person talking to her like this, particularly in front of a crowd.

"You ought to know me. You sure seem to know my man real well. So, it seems to me that you ought to know me since I'm his woman."

"His woman!" Rachel was taken aback. When she originally met Paul, he claimed his former relationship had long been over.

"You're the sleaze he's been taking out and spending what little money we do have. What is it? You can't get your own man?"

She didn't know what to say. If it was true, and this was Paul's woman, then he had some serious explaining to do. "Look, Miss, I had no idea." The woman was in a fury. Rachel mainly wanted to get her calmed down. It was embarrassing being approached in public by someone with such allegations. There was also the concern of the angry woman becoming violent.

"No idea. No idea. Ya know, honey, you ought to find out who you're sleeping with, tramp, before you get yourself caught up into something you can't handle."

If it were true, Rachel could empathize with the woman's position, but the name-calling was going to have to stop if she wanted to continue with any type of productive conversation. "Ma'am, you are obviously upset. Let's go outside and talk calmly. I'm sure there's some misunderstanding!" Rachel exclaimed.

"Misunderstanding my butt. The only misunderstanding going on here, is you. You better know that I've put up with too much in this relationship to let somebody come along and benefit from the work I've put into my man. It ain't happenin' today, slut."

That was it. For all of their sake, Rachel tried to be civil and approach the mess with some sense. But this woman didn't want to hear any of that. Rachel became angry, and decided she had been called her last name by this woman.

"Look, I'm through with the matter. If you are Paul's, whatever, then you need to deal with him and not every woman out here you think he's seeing. Do yourself a favor, girlfriend, get to the source of your problem." With that, Rachel turned back around in her seat in hopes that the woman would go away.

The woman didn't take too kindly to Rachel's smug tone. She reached over Barb and several other people to get to Rachel. It wasn't clear if the woman was trying to snatch Rachel up or what, but she managed to grab the spaghetti-strap and ripped it right off the dress. Within moments, her breasts were completely exposed. She was too shocked to respond. Barb, immediately pulled the drooped down portion of the dress up to cover Rachel. While they were getting her clothes together, the woman, snatched at her head and pulled a braid completely out, from the root of her hair. When her head jerked back, the woman punched Rachel in the face.

Paul caught wind of what was happening, and Rachel saw him running up the stairs towards them. Half-way up the stairs, he angrily yelled, "Ann. Ann. What are you doing?" He did get her attention momentarily. It was just long enough for Rachel to start exiting out the other side of the bleacher. She wasn't going to stay around and find out who or what Ann was to Paul. Humiliated, all Rachel wanted to do was get out of there. When she looked back across the bleacher at Paul and Ann, she saw them yelling directly into each other's face.

Later, she found out that Paul and Ann either were or used to live together, with their kids. He had lied about not having any kids. His excuse was lame. Paul claimed being a single man gave him the freedom to see whoever, whenever, and for whatever he wanted. He told Rachel, until there was a ring on his finger, he was foot-loose and fancy-free.

"Please," was all Rachel could say at the time.

Even today, some six years later, she found herself amused when thinking about the wanna-be-a-player, Paul. She chuckled.

Paul may not have had the decency to marry Ann, but as far as Rachel's interests were concerned, he was definitely committed.

Paul told her he had taken care of the situation with Ann, and so the incident shouldn't stop them from seeing each other. Yet, Ann had made it very clear that they were still intimately involved. Rachel speculated they were still sleeping in the same bed. With Ann, as Rachel figured to be the case, sex equated to a relationship. Whereas with Paul, sex was merely a nice alternative to a cold shower. It in no way implied commitment. Rachel didn't know if she was angrier at Ann for approaching her and not the man in this case, at Paul for being the typical dog, or at herself for not reading the warning signs beforehand, and stupidly getting involved.

In the end, Rachel was insulted he had even asked her out. What kind of a person did he take her for? How was she supposed to feel about going out to an expensive dinner, only to realize he had three sucklings at home who needed this and that? Once she got the truth, it was no wonder he always preferred to spend time at her place instead of his own. That's why she could only get a hold of him by cellular phone and beeper.

That explained why he had that episode with the money access machine. The second time they went out, Rachel was bent on going to a new live jazz supper club on the south side of town. When she thought back, Paul had tried to talk her out of it. When he couldn't, he agreed to go.

He stopped to get some money from the electronic teller and fumbled at the machine for fifteen minutes. Rachel had already learned that wasn't a good sign. Anyone with money in the account didn't take more than sixty seconds to get it out. As predicted, he came back to the car talking about the machine was broken. She pointed out that someone else was using the machine, and it seemed to be working, now. He continued on with the farce by saying his card was scratched. She was disgusted, and hind sight was saying the incident should have terminated the date. Instead, she offered to pay the tab. Since she was already dressed and set on going to the new supper club, money was not a reason to turn back.

After that incident, Paul always came with money. Where he was getting the money became clear. The brother was nice looking and all, but he didn't appear to have a fat, Rockefeller wallet. Besides all the other reasons why she didn't want to see him again, she definitely couldn't stomach the thought of, knowingly, taking food out the mouths of his kids. She was disgusted the jerk didn't see it as robbing his children. As far as she was concerned, it didn't matter what Paul thought, he was history.

Rachel vowed to stay away from committed men, and that included anyone who was shacking, married, engaged, dating, separated, with kids, or even paying someone's bills. She learned the hard way, men didn't always come clean with the status on their other relationships. For some reason, the men she got involved with didn't equate commitment with dating, separation, shacking, and being in an unfulfilling marriage. In spite of their connections to a woman, some of them actually considered themselves to be available. In Paul's case, however, Ann made it clear that, with or without a ring, they were a couple and all other women better recognize it, even if he didn't. To avoid any more pitfalls, Rachel was determined to learn how to read the signs. She couldn't trust men with such critical information. She wasn't in the mood for finding out the hard way, again.

Rachel sat back in her office chair and smirked. "Paul, huh. What a joke. With three babies at home, a woman snoring in his face every night, a joint apartment lease, and knee-deep in bills, that fool was talking about being fancy-free." She shook her head in amazement, and said, "Uhn-uhn-uhn." All she could do was laugh and chalk it up to experience.

As nice as he was, Ken was no exception to her avoidance rule. His daughter, Ariel, was beautiful, but having a child from a previous relationship prevented Ken from getting a perfect score of twelve on the checklist. On top of that, Sandra had shown the first sign of commitment. Rachel was learning to read the signs in an effort to survive in the dating game.

7

As Rachel pulled up to her house, her watch displayed 5:15. Perfect, plenty of time to change before Ken arrived.

Once inside the house, her usual ritual began: head to the bedroom, kick off the pumps, drop the briefcase into the corner, playback the answering machine messages, and change into some sweats or shorts, depending on the season. She'd conclude the routine by going downstairs, feeding Boots, and preparing her dinner. Tonight, it wasn't shorts or sweats.

As she walked into the bedroom, Rachel could see the message light blinking. The excitement started to build up, in hopes that Ken had left a message. She hadn't given him the work number. For now, the only phone contact to be initiated by him would be via the home line.

She pressed the play button on the machine. "You have five messages" the computerized voice sounded.

As the messages started to play, the first one was Neal. "Where are you, and why didn't I hear from you this weekend? I want to find out what happened at the picnic with that guy. Call me back. Later."

The second message was a hang-up followed by a call from Gary. "Hello, Rachel. Just calling. Nothing important. Hey, if you're free one night this week, perhaps we can go to a movie. Call me when you get a chance. This is Gary. Bye."

The fourth call was another hang-up. Rachel associated the hang-ups with Gary. She hadn't seen or talked to him since Friday. She knew he was calling, probably so many times he felt guilty about leaving any more messages.

The fifth message was another call from Neal. "Hey Rach, I forgot to tell you, I'll be in Boston for three days. I only found out

Friday. I'll probably leave tomorrow night and be back by the end of the week. If you get in tonight, call me. Otherwise, I'll call you when I get to Boston. See ya."

"Boston." It was just like Neal to always let her know where he was going. She wondered what he was doing in Boston, knowing he didn't have any clients there. Neal was a successful technology salesman, and did a great deal of traveling for his job. No matter where he was or who he was with, Rachel was always able to reach him.

She'd known him all her life, and they had been friends for well over twenty years. Rachel felt more like they were family. They'd gone to grade school and college together. They knew most of the same people. They both loved traveling, when their schedules permitted. She was very comfortable with Neal. Traveling together was always enjoyable and stress-free. She didn't have to worry about dressing up and being on her p's and q's at all times. Neal was the only male she didn't mind seeing her first thing in the morning, before she was perfectly groomed. No other man, including her former fiancé, got the honor of seeing her quite so comfortable.

In all the years they'd known each other, they had never been sexually involved. It had never been an issue. There was one instance in college when they contemplated intimacy, but it was too awkward for them both. They jointly agreed to steer clear of any sexual encounters. Both feared the sexual experience would jeopardize their solid friendship. After they both came to the realization, the issue never came up again. Neal was definitely her best friend, and she was his.

She glanced at the clock. She didn't have time to call Neal before the date. She planned to catch up with him tomorrow. She was eager, however, to talk with him and share the details of her weekend with Ken. Since they were so close, they shared many personal thoughts with each other. He was her insight into the male species, and often had to shed light on why men did and didn't do certain things. In this case, she wanted the objective male view on the Sandra-piece-of-the-puzzle.

Sandra was a red flag Rachel wasn't too anxious to overlook. Overlooking flags in past relationships had been her downfall. She was finally starting to not only learn from her mistakes, but to actually apply what she had learned.

She didn't know what was appropriate to wear to an art show. She finally decided to wear a tailored suit and go for the conservative look. To keep the feminine look in perspective, she opted for the fuchsia colored suit hanging in her closet with the matching colored pumps. To add a little flare to the outfit, she decided to wear a white silk body suit underneath with a purple scarf wrapped around her neck. It was classy, yet sexy. Exactly the look she wanted.

What seemed like a lot of spare time was rapidly diminishing. She took a quick shower and touched up her hair and make-up. She put her clothes on in a rush. It was already 6:15, and 'dependable' Ken would be there any minute. She grabbed the pumps and tried to put them on while holding the door frame, careful in her haste not to put a run in the pantyhose. It was the only skin-toned pair she had left; there would be nothing worse than to get a run at this moment. It would definitely destroy the sexy look she managed to hook-up with the outfit.

Rachel was almost down the stairs when she remembered cologne. She'd forgotten to put some on. She rushed back, grabbed the Trésor lotion and rubbed it on her wrists, neck, and a spot behind each ear. She haphazardly sprayed the same spots with the cologne. Just as she set the bottle down, she heard the doorbell ring.

Before she went to open the door, Rachel took a glance at herself in the full-length mirror located in the hallway. She turned sideways, backwards, and lastly faced front. She was pleased with her appearance for the evening.

"Show time." She had never been to an art show and, therefore, didn't know what to expect. However, Rachel had already reconciled in her mind that no matter what, it was going to be another fun-filled evening with Ken.

When she opened the door, Ken's face lit up. His eyes brightened and a grin formed out of one side of his mouth. He nodded his head slowly, acknowledging how nice she looked. "Looking good, Rachel, real good."

His reaction was all the confirmation Rachel needed to know she was looking exquisite. The tailored suit fit her body perfectly. It wasn't tight, but fitted.

"Why thank you."

Ken didn't realize how shapely she was. Rachel intentionally camouflaged her body the day before with the loose fitting summer dress. This time, he was seeing Rachel in her natural form. His eyes discretely encompassed her entire body within a matter of moments.

No words were spoken directly about romance, but the sensuality was heavy in the air.

"I don't know if you've eaten, but if you haven't we can pick up something quick on the way."

"That would be fine." Rachel replied. "Normally I cook, but there wasn't enough time tonight."

"Are you a pretty good cook?"

"As good as I am at golfing," she said with a smile.

They both chuckled, as a reflection of the conversation they had about golf at the cookout.

"Well, maybe one day you can have me over for dinner."

"That will be my pleasure, Mr. Sanders."

"We better get on our way then."

"I'm ready," said Rachel as she grabbed her purse. Three days in a row, was starting to feel like a whirlwind. As she closed the door on the way out, she knew the evening was well on its way to being wonderful.

<u>8</u>

"Everything has to be perfect." After all, this was the first opportunity Rachel had to impress Ken with her hospitality. She was rated by her friends as an excellent cook, and attributed it to growing up with her grandmother. Rachel could hook-up some good down-home cooking with fried chicken, red beans and rice, mixed turnip and collard greens, cabbage, potato salad, and candied yams. As much as she loved the taste of soul food, she didn't like to eat heavy meals on a regular basis. She limited it mostly to holidays and special family occasions.

Tonight, she decided to cook an Italian dish Neal taught her. The menu included chicken scaloppini, wild rice with mushrooms and shaved almonds, steamed broccoli, and a salad with an array of lettuce greens. For dessert, there was chocolate fondue with an assortment of fruit and bite-size pieces of cake. She envisioned eating the fondue in the sun room with soft music playing in the background. Except for dessert, everything was about done.

The meal was only a small factor in the overall success of the evening. Rachel and Ken had spent a great deal of time together in the past two months. Reflecting, she said, "This dating thing has been good, but there is still a lot that I don't know about him." She casually wiped off the kitchen counter. "Man, he has been a perfect gentleman, but I know something is bound to come up." She put the towel down and walked towards the sun room. "He is wonderful," she fondly admitted. "Oh well, we will see. I guess I should have learned by now that only time will reveal the kind of man Ken really is. Boy, I hate this dating thing. Patience is not my virtue. For my sake, I hope what I am seeing in Ken is really what I'm getting." Based on her past track record, the probability of it really being as perfect as it seemed was slim to none. As a final thought on the matter, she said, "Well, I'll just have to ride this wave of happiness with him for as long as it lasts. Why not! It's not like there is anybody else ringing my phone or knocking my door down. At least there's no one I'm interested in. Ken is it." She leaned over and fidgeted with the stereo.

Rachel turned the Time & Circumstance song on low. She left the patio doors open to catch the breeze. Normally the August Chicago nights were hot, but, tonight, it was pleasingly mild. The gentle breeze could be felt throughout the sun room. She decided to chill some wine in case Ken was interested in a mid-summer night toast. With the church thing and all, she suspected there was a good chance he didn't drink, not even socially. She knew he didn't drink beer or hard liquor. Just in case, the wine would be there.

The only thing left to do was to freshen-up her hair and make-up. The home-cooked meal had all the makings of a quaint, romantic restaurant. As a matter of fact, she figured if all went as hoped, it would be even better than any old public, impersonal setting.

She expected Ken to arrive around 8:00. She glanced at her watch, and it displayed a quarter to eight. She took a final glance around the place and nodded in satisfaction. Nothing had been left to chance.

"He's going to be here any minute. Is everything ready?" She scoped the room. The music was soft and soothing. The food was ready. The wine was chilling. The vanilla candles were creating a sweet, exotic smell throughout the house. Even Boots had been neatly tucked away in the basement, particularly since Ken didn't have a great appreciation for cats.

When Rachel heard the car pull up, she dimmed the lighting in the dining room.

"I'll wait for him to ring the doorbell before I go to the door." Since the front door was not visible from the dining room, she could be afforded the opportunity of making a grand entrance.

Ding Dong, the doorbell sounded.

Rachel smiled to herself and strutted to the door, fully visible to Ken as she approached.

"Hello gorgeous." Once inside, he leaned over and gave her a kiss on the forehead.

She hadn't determined if it was his voice or his charm that drove her crazy. Whichever it was, she was excited. "Can I interest you in something to drink?"

"No, not right now."

"Well, dinner is ready. So, shall we eat?"

"Sure. Lead the way," as he extended his hand to her.

She eagerly took his hand and headed towards the dining room. So far, so good. The table had already been set for two with fine china and a breathtaking bouquet spread across the center. Only modest light filled the room. The light from the chandelier reflected off of the crystal curio, creating a sensuous setting. She stopped at his designated seat.

"Ken, would you please sit here?" Rachel asked while pulling the chair slightly from the table.

"If you don't mind, I'd rather wait for you to be seated," he said.

She was pleasantly surprised. A gentleman to heart. He started it in the beginning of their dating and was managing to keep it up, seemingly with ease.

Unexpectedly, he hugged Rachel and gave her a kiss on the side of her neck. Before letting go, he whispered ever so delicately into her ear, "Rachel since you've dedicated so much time and effort into preparing this dinner, why don't you let me take it from here. Why don't you sit down and let me serve you." There was a brief moment of silence which seemed to add to the mystique. "It would be my pleasure to serve you."

Rachel was beside herself. There was no way she could decline such an offer. This was a nice break. With most guys, she had to buy the food, cook it, clean up afterwards, and entertain in the process. She had to do everything, but burp them. Yes, this was a nice change. "I would like that very much."

Ken pulled out the chair for her to sit down.

The food was served, and they began to eat. The conversation during dinner flowed, and Rachel felt wonderful. It was going exactly as she planned. The mood was right on target. "Ken would you like some wine?" she asked in a reluctant tone.

"Sure," he quickly responded.

His rapid response generated a bewildered look on her face.

"Why do you look so surprised?" he inquired.

She hesitated before answering. After collecting her thoughts, she spoke. "Well, since you're into the church, I thought you might not drink. When we were at the Taste, you didn't drink any beer. So, I just assumed you didn't drink at all."

"I do drink on occasion. My drinking doesn't have anything to do with religion. I'm just not a big beer drinker. As far as church goes, I believe it's okay to drink, so long as I don't get drunk."

"I see." Interesting, she logged. She was finding out that going to church didn't preclude him from having a liberal view on social issues. With the new found knowledge, she poured him a glass of wine. "How about a toast?"

"Absolutely," he said. "Please, let me do it."

She nodded and said, "By all means. Please do."

They lifted the glasses and touched them together. "To another month of happiness." Ken toasted.

"… and another, and another, and another," she chimed in.

Unexpectedly, there was a knock on the door. She wondered who could be dropping in at such an inopportune time, since she wasn't expecting anyone. "Excuse me please."

When Ken arrived earlier in the evening, the screen door had been left open in order to partake of the breeze. As Rachel looked at the figure standing in the doorway, she became very nervous.

"Gary!" she softly said. "What are you doing here?" Internally, Rachel was outraged that Gary had shown up without calling ahead.

"I happened to be in the area."

"Yeah, right," she wanted to say. All she cared about was getting him out of there before Ken saw him.

"I wanted to make sure you were doing fine. I left a lot of messages for you, but I didn't get any call backs," said Gary, trying to convince her that he was there out of concern for her welfare.

Rachel knew the first indication of a man's lack of interest was his unwillingness to either initiate or return a phone call the morning after. She couldn't understand why the unspoken signal didn't work the other way around.

She wanted to tell him, "Get a clue. Obviously, I didn't want to talk to you. That's why there were no call backs." But, she couldn't bring herself to say it. Even at this point, she didn't have the heart to crush the poor guy.

"Rachel, you look real nice, as always." His eyes glided down her body like a slice of butter on a hot roll.

That tacky little line wasn't getting him anywhere, and the roving eyes didn't help his cause with her, either.

"Can I come in?"

She wanted to say, "No, and go away," but didn't have either the heart or courage, whichever it was. Taking the diplomatic way out, she responded, "Well, this is not a good time."

"Why? You have company?"

Not that it was any of his business, but she felt obligated to respond in a decent fashion. "Yes, I do."

"Oh, I'm sorry." It was easy to see his ego was deflated.

"It's okay, but you should have called."

"I did, many times. You didn't answer." Rachel wanted him to leave. She was afraid Ken was going to walk out of the dining room into eye's view of Gary. He was clearly hurt, but what could she do. What was the big deal with hanging on? Gary was like Sandra, an ex who had been fired, but hadn't accepted the pink slip.

She didn't know what else to do with this man. Admittedly, she shouldn't have let the relationship drag on for so long, but Gary caught her at a low period. He wasn't intimately satisfying, but she did consider him to be good company. He wasn't quite as bad as the old worshipper Brian, but he definitely wasn't a Ken. Regardless, she couldn't have him showing up whenever he wanted, and, potentially, messing up her good thing with Ken. Something had to be done, quick.

"Gary, I'm sorry, but things aren't working out between us. We need space, to move on." There, she had said it.

"But I still like you Rachel. We have a lot of fun together. I don't think we should make any hasty decisions. Let's not throw this away," Gary implored. Clearly, he was at her mercy.

Hello-oo, Rachel thought. Was he deaf? Why was he making it so difficult for her to end this farce? He looked so pathetic to her. At this point, she desperately wanted him to leave. She was ashamed for anyone, especially Ken, to know she had spent any time with this man. His pesty behavior was a direct reflection of her brief moment of desperation and desire for companionship.

It was apparent he wasn't going to accept 'no' for an answer tonight. All Rachel could think about was getting him out of there, at least for now. She noticed Gary was no longer looking at her. His eyes were focused on something over her shoulder.

"Rachel, is everything okay?" Ken asked.

"Oh no," she faintly mumbled. Her worst fear was happening. Ken was at the door. Her heart was pounding. "I'm fine," she stammered.

"Is this someone that I should meet?" Gary inquired.

No he didn't, was her reaction. What nerve! She couldn't believe how clueless this man was. Didn't Gary understand what was going on? She was having a romantic dinner with her man. Did Gary really think he was her significant other deserving of an introduction? Rachel wanted him to acknowledge that she had spent the past ten minutes trying to break off the relationship with dignity? She was wondering what it would take.

She didn't want to do it, but the awkward circumstance didn't leave many outs. She pushed the screen door open and let Gary come closer. "Gary, this is Ken. Ken, Gary," she said with her eyes rolling, and a subtle tone of frustration.

Ken walked over to the door as Gary stepped inside. Ken extended his hand. "How you doing, man?" Ken greeted.

"All right. Nice to meet you, brother," Gary retorted.

"Likewise."

Rachel didn't know what else to say, so chose to be silent. She noticed Gary giving Ken the eye, which wasn't surprising. Ken came across as a man's man. His demeanor was very commanding. Poor Gary was intimidated. It also didn't help ease his plight to see Ken standing directly behind Rachel with his hands on her shoulders. It was obvious, they were a couple. As ridiculous as Gary was being, she couldn't help but feel sorry for him. She had been there enough times herself to know how it felt, to know how much it hurt. As irritating as he could be, Rachel felt that not even diehard Gary was deserving of his feelings being crushed. It wasn't really his fault she had no significant attraction to him.

"Rachel, just thought I'd stop by. I'll call you later to discuss that business."

What business, Rachel wondered. She figured he was only trying to save face in front of Ken, and make it seem like there was important business between them. She decided that the least she could do was to let him have that one. After all, she wasn't out to crush his manhood. She actually felt good about helping him to walk away with some dignity.

After Gary left, Rachel knew the air needed to be cleared with Ken. But, she did not know what to say. He didn't ask anything else about Gary, so she didn't volunteer.

Ken caressed both of her hands and glanced into her eyes. "By the way lady, the dinner was uhm uhm uhm."

"I'm glad you liked it," she graciously accepted.

"Liked it! I stuffed myself. You know, a woman who can cook has a lot going for herself." He learned over and gave her a peck on the cheek.

Rachel was blushing and bubbling over with contentment. Since they were both finished eating, she suggested they have dessert in the enclosed sun room. The sun had gone down, but the temperature was perfect as evidenced by the breeze coming through the French doors leading out to the deck. The ceiling fan was whisking air gently throughout the room. Rachel dimmed the lights. The candles were also giving off a nice glow. Finally, before sitting down, she put on several mellow songs to add the final necessary touch.

This was her favorite room in the house. It was multi-functional, intimate with the right man, perfect for a small party group, but mostly a place of meditation and solitude. The setting was romantic. She sat on the wicker sofa with her legs folded sideways. Although there were other seats in the room, he sat down next to her.

She didn't know how to take his move. Rachel had gone to great pains to create a romantic environment, but now the reality of it was sinking in, it frightened her. They had been together over a month and had not engaged in any real intimacy. Both had flirted with each other over time. Yet, she wasn't ready for anything serious. Too often she had gotten intimately involved too early in the relationship and regretted it afterwards. She really liked him, but engaging in intimacy now, would only end up clouding her judgment and, ultimately, her feelings. She wanted everything perfect. She hadn't held back on sex in the past, but this was different. Rachel had already decided that in case Ken was Mr. Right, she was going to save herself for something special and more permanent between them. This was possibly the makings of her fairy tale.

Deep down, she had used Ken's religious practices as a safety net. Between his religion and gentleman-like ways, she didn't view him as a sexual temptation. Therefore, she flirted with comfort, but this move of his, to sit next to her, was unexpected. She had misjudged his beliefs on drinking. Perhaps she had done the same regarding intimacy. She couldn't overlook the fact that he did have a daughter out of wedlock, making the thought of him getting too touchy-feely very possible. She was still hoping he was not going to make a move.

"This room is very relaxing," Ken acknowledged.

"Yes it is. I love this room. Sometimes, I just come out here and meditate, or read, or whatever."

"Rachel?"

She could tell he was serious about whatever he was getting ready to say. She was hoping he wouldn't destroy her wonderful image of him being unlike the other men, and wanting sex after a nice, quiet meal. Here goes, she suspected, the typical male in him is about to rear his ugly head.

Ken started to set the mood. "This music, actually the whole room is romantic. I was thinking we could …,"

Before he could finish, she cut in. "Ken, I think I know what you're about to say, and I, well, I'm not ready to make love with you."

"Rachel, I didn't ask you to. I was only going to ask you if you wanted to lay your head on my shoulder while we listen to the music?"

Embarrassed, all she could say was, "Oh."

Without another word being said, he extended his arm across the back of the sofa. She slid closer to him and laid her head on his shoulder.

Time seemed to stand still. Their time together was innocent, yet sensuous. Whatever fear she had of being with him quickly vanished. The music and his heartbeat hypnotized her. Without realizing it, almost three hours had passed since they first sat down in the sun room. The only thing that alerted them to the time was the stereo clicking off. The three hours of music she pre-set early in the evening had played completely through.

"Rachel?"

Quite comfortable, "Hmmm?" is all Rachel could muster up. About halfway through the music, she had stretched out, laid her head on his lap, and fallen asleep.

"I need to be going." He stretched his arm up and in the process caught a glimpse of the time.

"So soon?" Rachel dragged.

"I know, but it's well after midnight, and I have to get ready for church in the morning."

"Oh yeah. It is Sunday," Rachel realized as she started to sit up.

"Yes, it's Sunday. I'd better get up, otherwise I'll continue to sit here and get comfortable."

In order to be supportive of his need to get up and out, she hopped up. Holding hands, they both walked slowly towards the door. They stood face-to-face, hand in hand.

"Rachel, I had a wonderful evening. You are such a classy lady." He leaned forward and kissed her on one cheek and then the other. "I'll call you tomorrow," Ken said as he reached to open the screen door. He turned back towards her and said, "Thank you."

"You're welcome, anytime."

"I bet that's what you tell all the guys," he teased.

Good one, she noted. She assumed he was talking about the run-in with Gary. Thank goodness that was the only off-handed comment he made about the unfortunate mishap, and even that was with humor.

"Ha ha," was all she could say to acknowledge what he was really implying.

"Good night."

"Good night," Rachel responded as Ken let the screen door close behind him. She watched him get into the car and pull away.

She went to turn off the lights in the sun room as well as blow out the remaining candles. She noticed the fondue had been untouched.

"I guess we didn't need that." She smiled as she carried the dishes to the kitchen.

Before going up to bed, she let Boots out of the basement. Rachel was sleepy, but content.

The message waiting indicator was blinking. Apparently some calls had come in during dinner, but she had turned off the ringer. That was normal procedure, especially in the midst of a new relationship. She didn't want to be disturbed. More importantly, she didn't want to deal with stragglers -- men like Gary who had a hard time accepting that it was over. Smooth transitions were preferred. Out with the old and in with the new. It tended to be awkward trying to talk to stragglers when she was entertaining company. She was too tired to deal with the messages tonight. Whoever it was would have to wait until the morning. She did turn the phone ringer back on, in case of an emergency. She knelt down to say an abbreviated prayer. Since she was tired, and more importantly, things were going so well with Ken, she didn't feel an urgency to have a long drawn out prayer tonight.

Before falling asleep, Rachel reviewed her Mr. Right checklist. Of the twelve, Ken had five so far: family-oriented, church-going, tall, handsome, and dependable. Not bad for this point in the relationship. Even though he had lost a critical check point for already having a child, Rachel still saw him as a viable candidate. He was still glittering, like real gold. Filled with joyful thoughts, she brushed Boots furry back and drifted to sleep.

<u>9</u>

The ringing phone startled Rachel from her sleep. Before completely opening her eyes, she was wondering who could be calling so early. Slowly she sat up, got her bearings, and reached for the receiver. Exhaustion had really set in during the night. It was already morning, and Rachel felt like she'd only gone to bed an hour or so earlier.

"Hello," was the best she could do in her groggy condition.

"Yeah. Hi Rachel."

"Gary?" she inquired, unsure whether it was actually him.

"Yeah, it's me." The tone of his voice definitely did not exhibit the excitement he normally showed when talking to her.

It was only 6:30 in the morning. This was the only day she had to sleep past 6:00.

"Boy, this is an early morning wake-up call." It was her tactful way of letting Gary know he'd called too early, especially after her late night with Ken.

"Can you talk now? I mean, do you have company?"

Then it hit Rachel why Gary was calling so early. He wanted to know if Ken had stayed overnight.

"No, I do not have company." Her tone was sharp and seasoned with a bit of irritation. "And other than being sleepy, yes, I can talk now."

Gary obviously had something on his mind that wouldn't wait. "Rachel, I've been thinking about our relationship and I've come to some decisions."

Reluctantly, she answered "Okay."

"Rachel, this is tough for me, but I've decided we're going in different directions. We've had some good times, but somehow things changed." His voice sounded overly dramatic.

She wanted him to get to the point so she could, at least, go back to sleep for another hour. She decided to speed him along in making his point. "What are you saying Gary?"

"Well, Rachel, I'm saying that I need to break off the relationship," he reluctantly said. "I'm sorry."

So it was going to be like that, she acknowledged. Hadn't she already broken up with him in at least three different ways over the last five weeks, with the most recent being last night. Yep, Gary was determined to break off the relationship even after she had already broken-up with him. Rachel labeled it as a 'manly' thing, whereby he needed to be the one to call it quits. To her, it didn't matter how it happened, so long as it was done quickly and painlessly, before she was fully awake.

"So, that's your decision?" She was going through the motion of showing concern.

"Yes. Again, I'm sorry."

"Well, I have to respect your decision." She was thrilled, but obviously couldn't let on with Gary. For some reason, he needed to carry on the horseplay. Far be it for her to burst his bubble. It didn't cost her anything to play along. Rachel was sure Gary wanted her to say something else to keep the conversation going, but she thought it too risky. Too much response on her part might give him the impression she was still interested.

"Well, Gary, I wish you the best."

He was silent for a moment, knowing that once they ended the call, it was probably the last time they would talk.

"I wish you well, too."

She knew he was trying to hold on, but Rachel was eager to move towards closure on this conversation.

"Take care Gary. Bye."

Hesitantly he responded, "Bye".

Rachel hung up the receiver and rolled over. "Done. Finally."

She was glad to be able to get some more sleep. This was going to be the busiest week of the month. The more refreshed she started the week off, the better her chance of getting through it stress-free.

10

Thursday was always a crazy day, at least every other week. Rachel had to get out of the office no later than 5:00 in order to get to the board meeting. She sat on the board of a local non-profit organization and took the job seriously. Before running out of the office, she ran to make some copies. The phone was ringing, but she didn't get to it in time. Thinking it might be Ken, she quickly dialed into her voice mail to find out if he'd called. It turned out to be a message from Neal. Running the chance of being late, she decided not to call him back until after the meeting.

As soon as Rachel got home, she went through the normal routine. There was an urgent message from Neal. He had called twice. She assumed it must be something serious for him to leave an urgent message. Without doing anything else, she immediately picked up the phone and dialed his number from the memory space #1.

"I got your urgent message. Is everything okay?" she asked excitedly.

"Hello to you, too," Neal humored. "Everything is okay."

"Well, you're the one who had me all worried, so don't get on me for being overly excited or worried or whatever," she said.

"With your busy social life, it's hard to catch up with you these days, or should I say evenings. I can't ever catch you. Ken's getting top billing these days. Just forgot about your friends." Neal was obviously having a great deal of fun teasing Rachel about her dating. As close as the two of them were, he could easily joke without her being offended.

"Don't even try it. I keep in touch, the same as I always do. Anyway, what's up?"

"Remember the chairman's ball coming up this Saturday?"

"Yes," Rachel responded.

"Well, Nicole can't go."

"Why not?"

"She broke out with chicken pox. Can you believe that. Of all times."

"That's too bad. I know you were really looking forward to going. What are you going to do?"

"Well, what are you doing Saturday, buddy?"

"Ken and I are getting together, I suppose?"

"Oh well."

"But," Rachel jumped in. "I know how important this is to you. I can go with you to the ball."

"Wait, what about Ken? I don't want to mess up your plans," Neal sincerely stated.

"It's all right. We were probably going to the movies or something simple like that. He'll understand. Besides, this is important to you."

"Are you sure?" Neal implored.

"Yes, I'm sure. What are you going to wear?"

"My tux."

"Which one."

"The black one without the tails."

"Oh, it's black-tie formal!" Rachel emphasized. "I don't really have anything to wear. Hey, this would be a great opportunity for me to buy the black dress I saw at Lord & Taylor last month."

"Well, if you're going to buy it, stop by tomorrow and pick up my credit card."

"No, I didn't mean for you to buy it."

"Look. I'm glad you're going on such short notice. The least I can do is buy your dress and, knowing you, the shoes and bag."

"I'm not letting you buy it."

"Rachel. Stop being so stubborn. Let me do this, please. I already feel guilty enough about letting you change your Saturday plans. Please, let me do this."

"Okay, okay, but only the dress. I'll get the shoes and purse myself."

"There's no winning with you. Well, you'll have the credit card anyway. Get whatever you want. You're good for it. Besides, I know where to find you," Neal chuckled.

There was a beep on the phone line.

"That's my line Neal. Hold on." Rachel pressed the flash button on the phone.

"Hello."

"Hi," Ken greeted. "What are you up to?"

"I'm talking to Neal."

"Oh. Well, you want to call me back?"

"No, hold on." She knew Neal would understand if she had to go and talk to Ken. "We were just finishing up."

Rachel clicked back over to Neal. "Neal, it's Ken. So, I'll talk to you tomorrow."

"All right, and Rach,"

"Yes?"

"Thanks again. You came through in a big way this time. It means a lot to me."

"What are friends for? Lord knows you've come through for me enough times. I'm glad to be able to do something for you. Talk to you later."

"Bye."

She clicked back to the other line. "Ken, I'm glad you called. I was just talking about you."

"Oh yeah. About what?"

"Neal has an important function to attend this Saturday, and his girlfriend, Nicole, got sick and can't go. So," and she paused in anticipation of his response, " I volunteered to go."

"You did, huh."

She could hear the disappointment in his voice.

"I know we didn't have concrete plans," Rachel paused. "It really is important to him. I hope you don't mind." She was hoping he wouldn't start trippin' about her going out with her best friend. If he did, it would mess up everything.

"Tell you what. I did plan to see you Saturday. I suppose I took it for granted without actually asking you out," he confessed.

"It wasn't all you. I also made some assumptions. That's not a problem," Rachel chimed in. She was glad they had evolved to the point where they automatically planned to spend weekends together.

"Anyway, maybe you can do something important for me."

Wait a minute! She wondered if this was a red flag? After thinking on it for a moment, she realized it was reasonable for a man to feel uncomfortable knowing his girlfriend's best friend was a guy, single, and straight at that. Still, Rachel felt like she was about to be put into a compromising spot. In order to help her friend out, she was now going to have to appease Ken. She hoped his request wasn't a sign of jealousy or even worse, selfishness. She was half afraid to ask what was on his mind, but had no choice. "Yes, Ken, what is it?"

"My family is having a small get together Sunday at my Dad's house. Ever since my mother died, we try to meet at his place a couple of Sundays out of each month. I would like for you to go with me. I've told my family so much about you. They really want to meet you."

That's it! Meeting the family was the best news she could hear. It equated to seriousness. Without hesitation, she responded "I'd love to."

"I'd also like for you to go to church with me Sunday. It would mean a lot to me."

There it was. Pay back. Rachel didn't mind going to church. She went at least once a month or so on her own, but going as a date added an element of discomfort. But, she had to do it in order to redeem herself with him for ducking out on Saturday. She chalked it up as a small price to pay for Neal's friendship.

"Yes, I'll go."

"Good. I really appreciate it, Rachel."

Yeah, sure, she thought. He had put her in a catch-22, and there wasn't really any alternative. Since it was Ken, funny thing was, she didn't feel offended. Going anywhere with him seemed wonderful. Church was no exception.

11

Before it got too late in the evening, Roz was determined to give her sister a call. Roz's birthday was the Saturday before, and they had not, yet, spoken. Actually, they were cousins, but as far as the two of them were concerned, they were sisters. Rachel had grown up without any siblings. When she was a child growing up in Detroit with her grandmother, Roz would often come to visit during the college breaks and sometimes even weekends. Since she was at Wayne State for four years during undergrad, and then another two years for her M.B.A. at the University of Michigan, she got to spend a lot of time with Rachel. The fifteen year age gap didn't diminish Rachel's love for the time she spent with her big sister. They were as close as any two siblings could be.

The two had been playing phone tag for the past five days. It was often difficult to coordinate the two hour time-zone difference. Either it was too early to call Roz or it was too late for Rachel to stay up. The two didn't physically see each other often, but they remained exceptionally close. They had a ritual. Unless something earth shattering came up in between birthdays and holidays, they talked on the phone about once a month. They both looked forward to it. The conversations would last for hours. Strangely enough, they always seemed to be current with each other's lives, even though they didn't talk daily. Since their time was so limited, they tended to talk about the important matters and not just idle chit-chat. One of Roz's favorite lines was "get to the skinny," implying get to the meat of the matter and cut out the fat chit-chat. Roz dialed the phone, hoping Rachel was in this time.

By the third ring, Rachel had made it upstairs and grabbed the phone in her bedroom. "Hello."

"Oh my goodness, she's alive," said the bubbly voice on the other end of the line. "I guess Mr. Sanders let you off for the night."

"Please! Don't even try it. You sound like Neal. I do keep in touch, you know."

"Yeah, well, I don't know about Neal, but I have been trying to get a hold of you since I got the birthday message. By the way, thanks for the crystal elephant."

"Oh, you're welcome. I hope you like it."

"I do. It's different. All of these years in the sorority, you'd think by now, we'd both be tired of elephants."

"Huh. You know Deltas and their elephants."

"Yeah, I know. Hey, hang-up and let me call you right back. After all, this is your birthday call."

"Aah, don't worry about it."

"Nope. You know the rules. It's your birthday. I'll pay for the call. Hang-up, hang-up."

"All right. All right." Roz pushed and held the button down long enough for Rachel to call right back.

"I assumed from the note in your card, Ken has been the one occupying all of your time."

"I've just been real busy."

"I bet you have been," Roz responded in a mischievous tone.

"I don't mean like that."

"Now look, you know I understand. When a man comes on the scene, everyone else gets kicked to the curb. You know us girlfriends understand that." The two had established it as one of the unspoken, unwritten girlfriends' golden rule.

"Anyway, how are you doing?"

"Just fine. Tell me, girl, is Ken still Mr. Wonderful, or has he started to shed his skin?"

"He's still Mr. Wonderful, exceptionally wonderful."

"Good. How long has it been?"

"Almost three months."

"Oh, he's still new. Give him time to settle in and show his tail."

"Girl, you are something else. You are hard on brothers."

"Realistic, not hard. That's why I'm able to have fun, and accept them as they are, with no expectations. As long as I don't expect anything, they don't disappoint me."

"Speaking of brothers, are you still seeing that guy?" Rachel wondered.

"Who, Randy?"

"Yeah."

"I recently cut him loose," Roz admitted.

"Why? He seemed so nice Roz."

"He was nice in the beginning."

"What happened?"

"He was nice and all, but I wasn't trying to marry him or anything serious like that. He got too comfortable, too fast. All I wanted was some companionship and an escort. I must admit, he did clean up real well. Throw a tux on the boy, and he looked good. But holding a conversation was something entirely different."

"What do you mean?"

"I couldn't let him talk, especially around my clients. I was always afraid he was going to embarrass me, with all of his 'we-bees' and 'you-bees'. You would have thought he was the poster child for Ebonics. He spent so much time trying to be deep, and girl, he was plain ignorant. Instead of being profound, he sounded stupid most of the time."

"He wanted to impress you."

"I don't know why?"

"Because, you're down-to-earth. Everybody that knows you knows that. But, for others, they draw the conclusion, before getting to know you, that you're snobby and feel like you're better than them because you have a successful career."

"How do you know that?"

"I know, because that's how people treat me. Some feel like they have to impress us and others blindly label us as stuck-up."

"That's too bad, because I accepted the man for who he was. He was actually a nice, simple guy. Everything was fine until he started trying to show-off. As a matter of fact, instead of being impressive, all he did was look more and more like a fool with every word."

"Girl, you're crazy."

"It just dawned on me," Roz was laughing so hard, she could barely finish the statement, "maybe you can take him off my hands. You always talk about wanting someone who's down-to-earth and a little rough around the edges. Well, here you go."

"Girl. Uhn uhn. When I say down-to-earth, I mean fun to be around. Rough is not the word from what you described. No thanks, sis. Admittedly, I like them rough, but not ignorant." With that, Rachel joined in with the laughter.

"Speaking of ignorant, girl let me tell you this story. I actually let him stay over one night after we got back from a banquet. It was late, so I thought it would be better to let him stay rather than have him drive home. Girl, he was so happy. The next time he came over, he had an overnight bag. I couldn't figure out what it was for. I happened to go into the bathroom and saw that he'd put his toothbrush in my rack."

"No he didn't! You said the poor man still lives at home with his seventy-some-year-old mother. What do you expect? When he got his foot in your nice big house, he felt right at home. He probably felt like he'd won the lottery. I bet he told his dear old mom all about you. No doubt he was in 'luv'." Rachel could barely finish the statement before chuckling. Even Roz had to laugh.

"Can you believe that? I asked him why his toothbrush was in my bathroom!"

"I can imagine the tone you had when you asked him. What did he say?"

"Get this, girl. He said it was time to leave a few things at my place, since we'd gotten so close."

"Oh, no he didn't."

"Yes, he did. It reminded me of a cat spraying his territory. You remember being young and dumb, hooking-up with a man, getting close, and then trying to lay claim by leaving a few items at his place," Roz depicted.

"I've been there, done that, felt like a fool. That little tactic was suppose to let any other woman coming over know she was in claimed territory."

"Now we're older, and hopefully not as dumb. We know those tricks don't work," Roz confessed.

"I know that's the truth."

"See, now we know all the men did back then was scour the bathroom and bedroom after we left, with the intent of removing any and all evidence. Let alone toiletries and lingerie, I bet they even cleaned up the strands of hair on the floor."

"I guess guys pull the same tricks as girls, although they'd never admit it. Oh my goodness. I know you hurt his feelings."

"No, you would have been proud of me. I was nice and calm. I don't know what gave him the impression that we were serious. So, I told him I was accustomed to living alone and felt uneasy with someone else in my place, on a regular basis."

"No, you didn't tell him that!"

"I sure did."

"Now you know you would hook-up with Mr. Right if he came along."

"You know that, but he didn't need to know. He wasn't Mr. Right."

"So what did he say."

"Nothing. He just went and got his toothbrush and put it back in his little overnight bag. I couldn't tell if he was embarrassed, hurt, or angry. Either way, I definitely didn't want to mislead the poor guy and let him think something was really going on with us. Besides, I'm not trying to adopt a forty-some-year-old mama's boy. I'm way beyond the breast-feeding years."

"And I thought I was the only one who attracted weirdoes. By the way, Gary broke up with me."

"Gary! What do you mean broke up? You were never really together."

"In his mind we were an item. Oh girl, let me tell you. Last month, I made a nice, romantic dinner for Ken. Guess who showed up, unannounced?"

"No! Don't tell me that Gary came over while Ken was there?" Roz sighed in disbelief.

"Yes, he did and I was really upset with him. I tried to let him down easy, and just get him out before Ken saw him. It didn't work."

"I bet that was awkward."

"You know it was, but you, of all people, know I've been in worse jams. The funny thing is, the next morning, bright and early he called me up. I think he was checking to see if Ken was here."

"As though it was any of his business," Roz stated.

"Exactly. He was pitiful. But, he managed to get up enough courage to break up with me, never mind that I'd already called it off with him many times before. I let him have the last say, and, the good thing about it, it didn't cost me a dime. But, do remind me not to get into another one of those kinds of relationships again, no matter how lonely I might be for the moment. Whenever I feel like being reminded of how pathetic men can be, I pull out my copy of *Waiting to Exhale*."

"There you go again, throwing away a perfectly good man."

"Hey, I can't help it. I like my men fine and strong. You know, a little rough around the edges. Gary was too wimpy, to the point of being boring."

"What you mean is, you want a pretty-boy with a little 'thug' in him."

"Exactly. I want him to be comfortable in the board room, but also able to hang with the 'homeys' on the street corner."

"Good luck in finding that combination. When you get to be my age, Mr. Nice is Mr. Right. I don't want to have to do any polishing."

"I haven't given up on the perfect combination, yet. Thank you very much," Rachel admitted.

"So let's, get back to the romantic evening. Now, tell me. How was it?"

"It was beautiful. He definitely gets a check for being romantic, and believe it or not, there was no sex."

"No sex. That seems strange for a handsome, single, young man like Ken," Roz stated.

"I thought so too, but I'm glad he's upholding the gentleman image I've created for him."

"Why do you suppose he didn't make a move?"

"I figure it has something to do with his religion."

"Yeah, or maybe with his sexual preferences."

"What do you mean?"

"You know how it is today. Maybe he's gay."

"Nah," Rachel responded, partially in defense of Ken.

"You don't really know. At the very least, he could be bisexual."

Rachel hadn't even considered the option before now. He couldn't be. He was too wonderful to not be for real with her. She could detect a cheat, free-loader, womanizer, worshiper, and even a mama's boy a mile away, but a gay or bi wasn't one she had encountered before. At least not to her knowledge. Ken couldn't burst her bubble like that. "No, I don't think so."

"Why?"

"For one, he has a daughter, Ariel."

"And, what does that mean?"

"It means he's fathered a child. There's only one natural way to do that," Rachel stated.

"Any man with healthy sperm can father a child. Producing a child is no indication of the mother or father's sexual preference."

Rachel had to agree with Roz. She was making some good points. Rachel always valued Roslyn's advice. She was full of wisdom that came strictly from life's experiences. Roz was in her mid forties, and had never been married. She ran her own marketing company in San Francisco, and was extremely successful. Most men were intimidated by her wit and financial status. She spent much of her twenties in school, thirties developing the business, and forties enjoying the fruits of her labor. Her favorite line was, "If I'd known twenty years ago that I'd end up single, I wouldn't have wasted so much time looking for a husband."

Unfortunately, the cost of her success was seeming more and more like being, indefinitely, without a husband. Having kids naturally had become a non-issue, because she could always adopt if the motherly urge became too intense to suppress. She had given it serious consideration in recent months. Rachel felt women didn't seem to be able to have it both, success and a family. Roz had accepted her fate a long time ago and had adjusted nicely. The sad part was, Roz didn't know she was choosing one over the other, years ago when she was building the business. She was rich with friends, extended family, godchildren, and traveled extensively. Other than Neal, Roz was one of the few people who had both the time and money needed to go on spontaneous trips with Rachel.

All in all, Rachel didn't want to pay the same price that Roz had. As fairy tale as it seemed, Rachel wanted it all: children, a loving mate, and a fulfilling career. All she needed now was to find a man who wanted the same thing, and had also done at least as much preparation as she had.

Maybe he was gay, Rachel pondered. "Perhaps that's why he didn't make a move. That's interesting. Now that you mention it, he is dressed to the nines every time I see him, and you know homosexuals can dress."

"What about his friends? You can always tell a lot about a person by the company they keep."

"I've never really met any of his friends."

"None! Not even a sports buddy?"

"Nope. No one."

"Now that's strange. I hope he's not one of those glass-bubble kind of guys." Roz had a label for all guys, and at times like now, she would spring a new one on Rachel.

"What's that?"

"You know, the kind that tries to keep you under his thumb. Maybe he never hangs out with friends in an attempt to set the standard for you not to. Later on, you can expect his type to ask you to give up your friends and just be with him, all in 'luv'."

"You always tend to find some red flags no matter what. You know Roz, I was really feeling good about Ken. Now, you've managed to raise my eyebrows."

"Don't let it bother you. You have time to get to know him. Whatever he is, it will come out."

"You sound like Big Mama when she says, 'It all gone come out in the wash, chile'. Haven't I heard that enough times to be able to spell it in my sleep."

"Well, your Big Mama knows what she's talking about. If Ken is as nice as he has come across so far, then great. All I can say, is to be careful."

"I have to admit, guys have it tough," Rachel acknowledged.

"How so?"

"If they make a move and try to seduce us before saying 'I do', then they are considered disrespectful dogs, at the least. If they do the exact opposite and don't make a move, then you'd think it would be considered respectful and viewed favorably, but no. When they act like gentleman and don't claw and paw all over us, we call them gay. What a tough position."

"I guess you're right. Anyway, take it easy. There's no hurry to do anything, if you know what I mean."

"Yes, I do, and I definitely agree. I'm just going to enjoy the ride for as long as it lasts."

"Nothing wrong with that."

"We've been on this phone for over two hours," which wasn't unusual.

"We had a lot to catch up on."

"Well, I'm going to get ready for bed."

"So early?"

"Roz, it's not early here. It's almost midnight."

"Oops, I forgot. Go to bed."

"Yeah, I am. I'm really tired, and tomorrow's going to be a long day, between work and trying to get my shopping done for Neal's ball. Plus, I'm going to church with Ken this Sunday, and then to his dad's for dinner. I'm only getting one chance to make a first impression, so I don't want to get any baggy or blood-shot eyes between now and then."

"His dad's? Are his parents divorced or something?"

"No. Oh, I didn't tell you. Ken's mother died from cancer a few years ago."

"Oh, sorry to hear that." Roz paused. "Well, at least that means he's not a mama's boy. That's the last thing you need."

"You're right. Huh, your Randy was enough mama's boy for you and me both."

"Right. Oh yeah, let me say this, and then I'll get off. I was thinking about going to Michigan for Thanksgiving. I assume you are going home to see Big Mama that weekend. We can plan to hook-up."

"I haven't thought about Thanksgiving, but now that I know you'll be there, let me seriously look into it. I'll let you know soon." Since Roz always encouraged her to be patient, it was one of the few times Rachel chose not to make a quick decision. It really wasn't much for her to think about. In all of her adult life, she had never missed a Thanksgiving with Big Mama.

"All right, let me know. I love you."

"Love you too, sis. Bye."

12

It was the middle of October, and the Indian summer was still going strong.

"What am I going to wear?" Rachel asked out loud as she rummaged through the walk-in closet.

"I need something dressy for church." Dressing up was a requirement, if Ken's church was anything like the ones she'd gone to. "And what about the barbecue? Hmmm."

She pulled out a two-piece summer dress and short jacket set. Holding it up to her body, she said, "This should work." She twirled the dress around and viewed it from every angle in the full-length mirror. Pleased with her selection, she said, "Not bad, not bad. I can wear the jacket to church and take it off for the barbecue. Boy, I sure am glad I don't have to change clothes anywhere." Outside of traveling, she avoided the inconvenience of having to get dressed away from home. It meant not having access to her toiletries and accessories. Removing her robe, she headed for the shower.

Sunday morning clicked right along. Before Rachel could take a breather, she was entering the church with Ken.

In the sanctuary, Rachel immediately noticed the fairly large size of the congregation. She had guessed right about the attire. Looking around the sanctuary was like being at a fashion show. People were dressed to the hilt. Even the little old ladies had on big beautiful hats, color coordinated with their outfits. Based solely on appearance, everyone seemed to be prosperous. This was definitely not the church for the poor, unsaved street-bum wandering in off the street. Even the working-class-poor probably felt out of place.

She couldn't help but wonder how many people could really afford the images that they were trying to project. She hadn't been to this kind of church in a long time, and found herself being critical, as well as in awe.

The choir was about fifty strong, and they sounded heavenly. It was like a concert, with the instruments and the elegant looking choir robes. It was obvious that a great deal of practice and commitment went into the music. Positioned on the wall, next to the choir stand, was a building fund barometer. In big, bold, black print, the hand-drawn barometer read $4,450. The goal at the top was $100,000. Being the accountant that she was, Rachel found the low balance odd, in light of the wealthy-looking congregation.

During the altar call for prayer, a multitude of people filed towards the front of the church, filling the aisles from front to back. Many people were weeping and others were clearly experiencing some kind of emotional or physical pain as evidenced by the burdened looks on their faces. The prayer was long and sounded like a lot of rhetoric to Rachel. It was loud, but not very uplifting. Thank goodness she wasn't going through a hard time like some of those other folks appeared to be. The morbid prayer would have made her feel worse. It was hard to tell what was really going on with the congregation, but one thing was clear to her, they all looked good.

Finally, after the devotion, two prayers, offering collection, a charity plate, long-winded announcements, two responsive reading, testimonies, special announcements, and what seemed like a mini-concert of about five songs, the pastor was finally in the pulpit. No wonder Ken got out so late on Sundays. This was nothing like the Catholic church she frequented once a month. Rachel didn't really consider herself to be a practicing Catholic, but she attended the church, anyway. In comparing it to this church setting, it was just as regimented to her, but at least she was in and out in one hour, start to finish. It would kill her grandmother to know she was claiming to be Catholic just to go to a shorter service.

Big Mama was what some called non-denominational, full-gospel, apostolic, or charismatic. However it was labeled, she was a serious woman of God, filled with the Holy Spirit and speaking in tongues. Rachel grew up knowing what was right in the eyes of God. Big Mama did have some rules which Rachel felt were based on tradition. Rachel didn't necessarily agree with some of them, but it was too hard to break away from the training she grew up on. Sunday was the Sabbath. No work was to be done that day, at least not in Big Mama's house or even in her presence. No washing, no cooking, no cleaning, no lawn mowing, not even ironing. Rachel had to press her clothes for church no later than Saturday night, and the cut off time was generally around 10:00 p.m. Big Mama didn't want midnight to sneak up and catch labor being done in her house on the Sabbath. Rachel had to wear a wrinkled dress a couple of times before she really got the message. It was bad enough to wear a wrinkled dress to church, but even worse to get the double whammy of also getting a whooping for having to wear it.

Growing up, she could not wear pants to church. When she got to college, the services on campus were a mixture of all races, religions, and cultures. There was no set dress code. She had heard one minister say years ago, "be clothed in the spirit and mind, don't concentrate on the flesh." Those words had stuck with her, probably out of convenience. From then on, Rachel believed that as long as she was decent, it didn't matter whether she wore pants or a dress. What mattered was that she be there to receive what God had to tell her.

Big Mama was from the old school and wasn't budging off of what she believed, and why should she? God had clearly blessed her through the years. Out of pure love and respect, Rachel never wore pants to church with Big Mama. There were several things she would do behind Big Mama's back, but the conviction wouldn't allow Rachel to do it in her presence.

Big Mama's strong religious beliefs had gained her the respect of the entire neighborhood. People always came to her for prayer when going through problems. Rachel believed her grandmother had a special touch, because every time someone left, they would have a shiny forehead. She didn't realize until she got older that Big Mama used anointing oil when she prayed. Even so, Rachel still preferred to believe that Big Mama had the special touch. A touch many of the well dressed, church-goers right there in the service seemed to need.

After the pastor finished hitting on a couple of the 'Big Ten' sins, he started hoopin' and hollering about Jesus being born of Mary, rising from the dead in three days, and suffering like Job.

Deep down, Rachel hoped everyone in the congregation already knew those bible basics. It would be hard for a Christian to not know those things. It was like religion 1-0-1. Other than being long, the service was comfortable. The minister didn't hit on any real sin, none of the faith and God's will stuff Big Mama consistently taught. Unless the person was a murderer, drug addict, wine-head, or known crook, the service wasn't directed towards them. Looking around, most people didn't seem to be impacted by the message. That was the good news. The bad news was, most of the sad-faced people who went to the altar for prayer didn't get much help in the message. Rachel assumed that it was the price this good-looking congregation was willing to pay for comfort and complacency.

"Oh well," she mumbled softly to herself.

After the service, people stood in line to shake the pastor's hand. They praised him for a good service. She figured this service must be the norm. The women were friendly to her, too. She couldn't tell if it was their normal behavior, or if it was just a nosey attempt to see who this was attached to Ken's arm.

"So how did you like the service?" Ken eagerly asked.

She couldn't come right out and tell him the service was entertaining, but not spiritually uplifting. Since she only planned to visit from time to time, he didn't need to know her complete opinion on the matter. She decided to focus on the positives.

"The choir is something else. They were really good." At least the service was not intimidating. It didn't require one to really evaluate their shortcomings or make any real ethical or spiritual changes. It would be an okay place to go with Ken from time to time. "I'd like to come again."

"Good. I'm glad to hear that. Come on. I want to introduce you to Pastor Watts."

Pastor Watts was barely taller than Rachel, standing about five feet four inches. His robust body, coupled with his camera-ready smile reminded Rachel of a minister she'd seen on late night TV who spent two solid minutes begging people to send money. The word 'jack-leg' crossed her mind. It was Big Mama's phrase for a preacher with a lot of talk and show, but no Holy Ghost power. She couldn't be sure with only one meeting, but Pastor

Watts sure showed signs of a 'jack'. For Ken's sake, she hoped her assessment was wrong.

Both Pastor and Rachel extended their hands towards each other to acknowledge the introduction with a shake. "Pastor, this is my friend Rachel."

"Hi, Rachel. Is this your first time visiting?"

"Yes, sir. It is."

"Well, welcome, young lady. I hope you enjoyed our service. We're glad you chose to fellowship with us today." Turning his eyes to Ken, he said, "You have a nice young man here. We really appreciate him. We have got to get him into deacon training so he can be an example for some of the other young men."

Rachel smiled at Ken in acknowledgment of his compliment.

"Nice meeting you, Pastor."

"See you later, Pastor," Ken said with his hand extended.

"All right, Ken."

As Ken and Rachel walked towards his car, she could feel eyes on them. She chalked it up to be some of Ken's admirers. There was sure to be plenty of single women in the church with an eye on him. Religious pretty-boys were hard to come by. It was a single woman's dream.

Ken opened the car door, and she slid right in with all of the confidence and certainty that came with being his woman, at least for the day.

13

Ken's father lived in a ranch styled home in what appeared to be a nice middle class neighborhood. The homes were fairly new. It was easy to see the area was changing but still well kept. Ken's father was not college educated, but on the basis of the house, he appeared to have some money. In reality, they were just a normal working-class family.

Ken had told Rachel earlier about his parents purchasing their house about five years ago with some money they received from a law settlement, only two years before Mrs. Sanders died. Shortly thereafter, his dad retired from the post office with thirty-one years of service. Before doing so, he had made sure all four kids received some type of professional training. Dana was a paralegal, Sharon was an administrative assistant, Brendon was a salesman, and Ken was in computer systems.

Rachel was looking forward to meeting Ken's father. As they pulled up to the house, she felt butterflies in her stomach. She didn't know why she felt so nervous. Perhaps it was her desire to make a good impression.

Ken directed Rachel through the carport to the side door. The screen door was locked, but the one inside was open. Rachel saw a gray-haired man sitting with his back to the door. He was talking at the portable TV located directly in front of him.

"Dad, open up."

The man turned his head slightly sideways to see who was talking to him through the screen. Once he realized it was his son, the elderly man responded. "Oh, okay. I didn't hear you pull up."

As he stood and walked towards the door, Rachel saw the strong resemblance to Ken. His father was tall, light-skinned, and on the slim side. Ken was the spitting image of his father, just a darker version. Even though Mr. Sanders was elderly, she could tell he must have been handsome in his day. Ken had told her his dad was hurt on the job years ago, and, at times, walked with a cane. He unhooked the latch and pushed the screen door open.

"You must be Rachel."

"Yes, sir." As Rachel went to extend her hand, Mr. Sanders gave her a big hug.

"Sir! Nah, nah. None of that. Junior, didn't you tell her everybody calls me Red?"

"No, Junior didn't tell me that." Rachel gave a smile to Ken, and he knew exactly why. She hadn't heard him referred to as Junior before. Meeting the family was always a treat to her. In a normal, unrehearsed conversation, they always revealed more about a person in a few minutes than she could get in months, on her own. Even with the approval from Mr. Sanders to call him Red, Rachel found it awkward. She was raised not to call elders by their first names. It was viewed as disrespectful by Big Mama. She was a grown-adult, but Rachel still found it difficult to do. On her first job, it had taken a while for her to call the older managers by their first names. Co-workers were one thing, but Ken's dad was another.

"Red, it's nice to meet you."

"I'm glad to finally meet you, too. Junior and Sharon talk about you all the time." Mr. Sanders glanced over to Ken and spoke as though Rachel wasn't there. "She sure is pretty." As he turned his attention back to Rachel, he said, "I don't know why Ken hasn't brought you by before now. Guess he trying to keep you all to himself."

Rachel was cheesing from ear to ear. She could tell this old man was cool.

"That's right, Dad, I'm keeping her all to myself." Ken walked past Rachel, grabbed her hand briefly, and gave her a wink. "Do you want something to drink, Rachel?"

"Oh, no thanks."

"You sure?"

"Yes."

"How was service today?" Red asked. He was a CME member, which meant he frequented church on Christmas, Mother's Day, and Easter. Ken had told Rachel his dad didn't go to church often, because he'd run into too many hypocritical preachers. He didn't go, but always showed interest in his kids religious activities.

"It was good," Ken quickly affirmed.

"What was the message?"

Ken had to stop and think about the message. It obviously did not leave a lasting impression. It took him several minutes to recall the topic. Finally, he was able to recall a portion of the message. What a shame, Rachel thought. After all those hours in church, the main speech wasn't even memorable. "He was talking about Moses and the flood."

Rachel knew Ken didn't remember anymore than she did, but it was entertaining.

"Dad, who you watching?"

"Chicago and Minnesota."

"What's the score?"

"Bears up by three with about three minutes left before the half."

"My father's a big sports fanatic."

"Yes indeed. Got to have my games on Sunday afternoon," Red chimed in.

"Rachel is into sports, too," Ken commented with a smirk.

"Good for you. What's your sport?" Red turned to Rachel with his hands clasped.

Before she could respond, Ken jumped in with "golf".

"Golf! My goodness, I didn't know they let women play. Are you any good?"

"Pretty good," she modestly affirmed.

"I've been watching Tiga' Woods. The boy is bad."

"You mean Tiger Woods, Dad."

"That's what I said boy, Tiga' Woods."

"Right, Dad," Ken declined. He knew better than to try and correct Red.

"Anyhow, I knew as soon as they let a brother in the game he was going to take it over. See, Michael was going to be the next golf champion, but Tiga' beat him to it. Michael is really too busy with basketball right now to get his golf game off, but you just wait. He's gonna make something happen."

"My dad thinks Michael Jordan walks on water. Let him tell it, Michael can do everything."

"He can. He's the best to ever, and I do mean ever, play basketball. There are many greats, no doubt, but Michael is in a class all by himself. I was sure glad when he stopped screwing around with that baseball and got back on the court. That's where the boy belongs, on the court. By the way, son, why don't you get us some tickets to the game this year. I want to see one of Chicago's playoff games this time."

"Playoffs! Dad, they haven't even started the real season."

"So, what that mean to me? Michael's taking this team to another championship. I already feel it."

"Okay, Dad, whatever you say."

"I agree, Red. Michael is the best," Rachel affirmed.

"You better believe he is," Red confidently responded.

"Rachel, don't get my father started on sports, otherwise you'll end up getting the history lesson that we've all heard a thousand times."

"What history lesson?"

"Oh boy, hear it comes." Ken slapped his own forehead with the butt of his hand.

"See Rachel, this young generation don't know nothing. All this hoopla about fame and money. They didn't have that back in my day. Athletes played for the love of the game. They didn't make all this big money. It was more of a team thang. No, not today."

"Rachel, you might as well sit down." Ken pulled out the chair to the kitchen table. Rachel sat down and scooted closer to Red.

"Hello, hello, hello," came bellowing through the screen door.

"Hey, Dad."

Sharon and Nick were coming in with a roaster of food. Sharon gave her father a hug around the neck, and then clucked Ken upside the head.

"Hey, boy." Turning her attention to Rachel, "Hi, Rachel. Good to see you. This boy finally got you over here. It's about time. Besides, that's the least he could do since he stole you away. I hardly ever see you in the cafeteria anymore."

Rachel smiled in response.

"Rachel, this is my husband, Nick."

"Hi Rachel." Nick extended his hand. "I missed you at the cookout."

"That's right! Well, it's nice to finally meet you. I've heard so much about you." Sharon consistently spoke highly of her husband. Although Rachel had never met him, it was like she knew him.

"Uh-oo. That's scary."

It was hard for Rachel to believe Nick used to be a heroin addict, but had been clean for the past six years. He and Sharon were happily married for five of those years. Rachel, admittedly, wouldn't have looked twice at someone like Nick, because of his former drug problem. In her search for Mr. Right, Nick would have appeared too imperfect. Yet, he was one of the few young men she knew who was actually making a good husband. She had to admire Sharon for giving the brother a chance, and as a result, finding a rare gem in what appeared to be a burned-out lump of coal.

"Your wife said all good things about you."

"Cool." After meeting Rachel, Nick turned his attention to Ken. "Hey man, what's up?"

"What's up?" Ken acknowledged with an upper tilt in his head.

"Yo, Red, what's on?" Nick asked.

"Bears and the Vikings. It's half-time."

"Where's the food? Is the barbecue done?" Sharon asked.

"The barbecue is done. I did it early this morning." Red responded.

"Where is Dana, Terry, and Brendon?" Sharon asked.

"I guess they on the way. I haven't talked to Dana since yesterday. And Brendon, huh, you know how that brother of yours is about showing up when he wants," Red answered.

"They'll probably be here soon. We'll wait a little longer for them," Sharon decided.

Ken had strong-armed her into coming, but Rachel was glad to be there. She liked the way Ken interacted with his family. His down-to-earth personality raised his score to seven on the checklist.

It was too bad having-a-wonderful-family wasn't on the checklist. Ken would easily have earned the point. Rachel felt comfortable in the warm family environment. She knew potential in-laws like these would be hard to come by. She decided to give him an honorary point, even though he had already gotten the one for being family-oriented. Perhaps he could use the extra credit point in place of some other shortcoming, like already having a child.

"What were you guys up to?" Sharon inquired.

"Guess," Ken responded.

"What?" Sharon had a mischievous smile on her face.

"Dad was giving Rachel the history lesson when you came in."

"Oh no. I bet he told you about the first eleven out of twenty Kentucky Derbys being ...," Sharon began saying.

Ken chimed in unison with Sharon, "... won by Black jockeys before they were banned from the club." They both bent over in laughter.

"That's right. You all need to know about Isaac Murphy."

"We know, Dad. He holds the best record in the history of the derby with forty-four percent wins. We all know it. You've told us a thousand times."

"I never knew that, Red," Rachel interestedly stated.

"I know. That's why I try to tell you all things, so you don't walk around here sounding ignorant. Isaac made ten grand a year, even in the 1800's."

Rachel liked Red, so she found it easy to sit and listen to him. He told the story with such enthusiasm, it was difficult for a first-time-listener not to be interested. "Ten thousand in the 1800's! That's a lot of money for that time."

"You know it was. He was making ten times more than most white folks, and more than all blacks. They cut him out from jockeying soon as they realized how much money he was making. See, ain't nobody gonna tell you stuff like that, except me."

"Wait, wait. My turn," Ken mockingly jumped in. "I know he's going to tell you about the world champion cyclist, Major Taylor, who was outlawed from the sport for winning so much."

"Actually I find this all to be interesting." As educated as Rachel was, she had never heard any of this history before.

Ken and Sharon simultaneously looked at each other and started laughing.

"That's all right. Go ahead and laugh. See, cause I know what I'm talking about."

Sharon affectionately gave her father another hug around the neck.

"I know Dad, you know what's going on. You're cool like that."

"Junior, you're over there laughing. I'll give you something to laugh about. Rachel you want to hear some stories about Junior when he was growing up?"

"Sure." Rachel sat on the edge of her chair in anticipation. With Red being the great storyteller he was, she knew some good stuff was about to be told.

"Unh, unh, Dad. I know you are not going to go there?"

"Oh, I see I got your attention now. No more laughing, huh?"

Everyone inside heard car doors slamming. Sharon glanced through the screen door. She saw Dana and Terry coming up the walk with pots. As always, Brendon was empty-handed. As the rest of the gang approached the house, Sharon said, "Everybody's here, finally. Dad, I'm hungry. You have to save Kenny's little knuckle-headed stories for later."

Ken was relieved. He knew Red's story would be funny, but embarrassing.

"All right, we'll eat. But, don't worry Rachel. I'll get a chance to tell you. I know you'll be back, won't you?"

"I sure hope so." The warm family reception felt good to Rachel.

After all of the eating, talking, and laughing well into the evening, everybody went home, except for Sharon and Nick. She insisted on staying to clean-up the kitchen for her dad. Sharon was standing at the sink, washing the dishes. Nick was standing next to her, drying them. Red's head was plastered in front of his portable kitchen TV.

"I like that Rachel."

"She is nice, Red. You think Kenny will keep her?" Nick asked.

"Shucks, I don't know about that boy. Neither of my boys. They ain't like you. You got a good woman, and you stick by her."

Sharon looked up at Nick and smiled. He winked back in agreement.

"Dad, this might be the one for Kenny. I know he really likes her."

"He really liked the other one."

"Who?"

"Sandra. It don't make no sense the way they act around that baby."

"Maybe that's all behind him now since he's met Rachel."

"Hmmm," was all Red said in response.

Sharon folded the dish towel and laid it on the counter. "All finished Dad. We're getting ready to go home. We both have to work tomorrow. She walked over and gave him a kiss on the cheek.

"Thanks, honey, for cleaning up everything."

"Anytime, Dad."

"See ya, Red."

"All right now Nick, you take it easy, son."

"And, Dad, I'll tell Rachel you like her," Sharon said.

"You do that," Red said without turning towards her.

14

Ken walked around the car to open Rachel's door. She had grown accustom to his attentiveness over the past three months. It had become standard for him to reach for her hand as she stepped out of the car. Ken went a step further and put his arm around her waist as they walked towards her front door.

Before putting the key in the lock, she stopped and asked Ken, "Do you want to come in?"

"No, I'm going on home and get ready for the week."

Normally, that was Ken's lead into leaving. But tonight was different. The afternoon had, somehow, taken them to another level. She felt content with him. He leaned forward, pulled Rachel close, and initiated a passionate kiss. The move completely caught her off guard. She tried to resist, but allowed herself to be consumed by his affection. They had managed to keep the sexual fire turned down, until now. For Rachel, the kiss was like a match starting a forest fire in her emotions. It started off small and after catching on, it roared, uncontrollably.

"Rachel, I want to ..."

"Ken, stop. Don't say it."

"You know what I'm going to say?"

"I think so. Look, I take some responsibility for creating this mood. I guess you could say we got the train moving, and now I'm trying to stop it," she confessed.

"What's wrong? Do you think I don't feel anything special for you," Ken asked.

"No, that's not it."

"What is it then? I want to be with you. We've been together for almost three months, and we haven't had any sex. What's up with that? You know I really like you."

"I know. I really like you, too. But, I want to wait."

"Wait for what?" The tone in Ken's voice indicated his anxiousness. "You're not a virgin, are you?"

Rachel timidly responded, "No, I'm not."

"Then, why do you want to wait?" Ken softened to almost a whisper, and he seductively pulled her close to him, leaned over and gave a peck on the neck.

"I want to wait until I'm married."

"Married? Why? You're not a virgin."

"Because, I want to do this right. You are special to me. I don't want to mess this up by getting sexually involved with you too soon," she said and pushed back from his embrace. "Do you understand?"

Ken frustratingly said, "What choice do I have?"

"Can we agree to not have any sex without a serious commitment?"

"That's asking a lot," Ken paused.

Rachel remained silent.

"But, for you, I will agree to no sex, at least for now." Pulling Rachel back into his arms, he backed off the stoop and stepped down to the ground level. He pulled her close to him, and gave her a light kiss on the cheek. "But, if you keep looking as fine as you do, I don't know," he said with a grin.

His mahogany skin contrasted with his pearly white teeth drove Rachel crazy. Recognizing how attractive he was, it had been awkward for her to get the request out, but she was glad Ken was understanding. He was looking better and better all the time, in more ways than she cared to admit.

15

After over indulging at Red's weekend barbecue, Rachel opted to eat light. She grabbed a quick salad in the cafeteria. Standing in line, she heard someone talking behind her.

"Hey, Missy."

Rachel turned around and found Sharon standing there.

"Hi, lady."

"What brings you to the caf?"

"Food?" Rachel jokingly responded.

"I didn't think you ate anymore. I thought you were just living on love."

Rachel affectionately tapped Sharon's shoulder with the butt of her hand. "Stop."

"It must be true. We use to run into each other a couple of times a week. Now, I barely catch a glimpse of you leaving the building, let alone coming down here for lunch."

"Been busy. You know how it is."

"Sure do." Sharon raised her left hand, and wiggled her wedding ring finger in front of Rachel. "That's exactly how it was when Nick and I first got serious."

"Whoa! Wait a minute. Nobody said anything about getting serious."

"I know my brother." Sharon spoke with confidence in her revelation to Rachel regarding Ken's intentions. "This is serious."

Rachel put the salad dressing down, and turned to Sharon with undivided attention. "How do you know that?"

"For one, he brought you to the family get-together. That's serious stuff. He doesn't bring just anybody home to meet the family. Trust me."

"That's what he said, but you know how guys are in the beginning, when they're trying to impress you. I thought he might be telling me something he thought I wanted to hear," Rachel said.

"Well, you can believe him. It's the truth."

Rachel was glad to get the reassurance of Ken's interest in her. However, she was careful not to become too buddy-buddy with Sharon about the details of her relationship with Ken. Rachel tactfully changed the subject to something more appropriate. "Your dad was nice."

"He really likes you. Thinks you're good for Kenny. So do I."

During the conversation, Rachel and Sharon were progressing through the food line. As Rachel got her change back from the cashier, she briefly contemplated eating with Sharon. She ended up deciding against it. She felt it was better to save conversations like this one for important fact-finding sessions.

"You eating down here?"

"No. I have to get back upstairs and get some work done. Lately, I've been working through lunch so I can get off at a decent hour." Rachel couldn't hold back the grin, because she remembered what Sharon had said earlier about how people act when things get serious.

"All right, next time then."

"Next time for sure. See you, and tell Nick and Red hello for me."

"Will do, and tell Kenny hello for me."

When Rachel got back to her office, she noticed the sticky note on her computer screen placed there as a reminder to call Neal. They hadn't spoken since the Black-tie event, and it was only natural for Rachel to give him an update on how the family gathering went at the Sanders'. She picked up the phone to call him.

"Good afternoon. Mr. Pierce's office. May I help you."

"Hi, Gertrude."

"Hello, Rachel." Knowing how close Rachel and Neal were, his secretary had dismissed the formalities long ago.

"Is your boss around?"

"I don't know where he ran off to. His calendar is clear for the next hour. I do know that he wants to speak with you, though."

"Well, just tell him I called, and have him give me a call when he can."

"Okay, Rachel. I sure will tell him as soon as he returns."

"Thank you."

Rachel pushed in the receiver button and dialed into voice mail to get her messages. After retrieving the messages, she placed the receiver on the cradle and got up to make a trip to the copier. As she was stepping out of the door, the phone rang. She dashed back to the phone. Even at work, she got excited when the phone rang and it turned out to be Ken on the other end.

"Hello," Rachel anxiously greeted.

"Hey. It's only me. Not Ken."

"Hey, only me. I know that every time the phone rings it's not Ken. But, that would be nice."

"You really have the bug bad," Neal teased.

"What bug?"

"The love bug."

"Oh, get out of here. You know I'm always glad to get a call from you."

"Yeah, but us lowly friends of yours are no competition for Mr. Sanders. He's head and shoulders above us when it comes to your time. Poor Boots must be climbing the walls from loneliness."

"Not true. Mr. Pierce, I will always have time for my best friend and for my cat. Remember, I told you Ken doesn't like cats. It's been real interesting watching him at my place when Boots is out."

"Poor Boots. Do you stuff him in the room every time King Ken comes over?"

"No. I can't torture my cat like that. I put him away, sometimes, but not every time. I'm sorry, but Boots has stuck with me a lot longer than any other man so far, except for you."

"You might as well go and get another cat now so Boots can start adjusting to a new friend."

"I'm not neglecting my cat just because Ken and I are having a great time, right now. This love thing is too up and down. Ken might get on my nerves at any time, but Boots is loyal. My cat is not going anywhere. So long as Boots gets food, water, and fresh kitty litter, I see no signs of discontent. And I'll have you know Ken doesn't get all of my time and attention. I still save some for the faithful few in my life."

"I'm glad to hear it, because I'm calling about exactly that, your time and attention to us faithful few."

"My time?"

"Yes. You probably forgot all about the annual golf scramble."

"Gee. You're right. I can't believe it's that time again. This year went by so fast."

"You know what they say. Time flies when you're having fun, and you, my dear, seem to be having a lot of fun."

"I don't see you and Nicole sitting around, letting any grass grow under your feet."

"See, Nicole and I have a two-year-old love, whereas you and Ken are still fresh with the new stuff. You're still feeling each other out and trying to put on the good face. I've long been past that stage with Nicole."

"By the way, how is Nicole feeling?"

"Doing much better, but she still hasn't completely recovered from the pox."

"Tell her I said 'hi', and I hope that she gets better real soon."

"She'll be glad you asked. I'll definitely tell her."

Rachel and Nicole had come a long ways for the sake of Neal. When Neal and Nicole started dating two years ago, she and Rachel didn't seem to hit it off. It was difficult for Nicole to believe Rachel and Neal were only friends. The closeness seemed to threaten Nicole's ability to establish a meaningful relationship with Neal. Rachel didn't want to hinder them, so she backed off. For several months she reduced the frequency of her calls and visits. After about three months, both Neal and Rachel felt odd. The change in their friendship was actually distracting to other relationships. Neither could deal with the change. Even Nicole could see the loss in him, and attributed it to the alteration in his relationship with his best friend. The three months gave Nicole an opportunity to spend quality, and in her mind, non-threatened time with Neal. In getting to know him, she grew to appreciate his honesty and dedication. Oddly, it was her suggestion that he restore his relationship with Rachel. Ever since, Rachel and Neal remained devoted friends.

"So, are you on the team, or do you need to check with King Ken?"

"Stop calling him that," Rachel said light-heartedly. "Of course, I am on the team. I don't need to get permission. Besides, I'm not going to get too many more opportunities to play this year with winter right around the corner."

"That's right. You didn't play much this summer. Love is messing up your game."

"Ha ha. I still got a better game than you, whether I practice or not."

"Yeah, all right. Don't forget, I taught you how to play, and can still put a whooping on you any time, on any course," Neal boasted. The playful banter felt comfortable to them both.

"I just realized. This was the first year in a long time that we didn't go to Myrtle Beach or Ft. Lauderdale for our annual improvement party."

"Next year we'll have to get Nicole and Ken into the game so we can all meet up at one of those fancy resorts for some golf and sun," Neal suggested.

"Sounds good. Oh yeah. I keep forgetting to ask you whether or not you're going home for Thanksgiving?" Rachel was still unconfirmed, although the probability of her going home was about ninety-five percent.

"Definitely, I am. You know I can't miss out on all of that good cooking." Neal eased back in his oversized leather chair, tilted his head back, and closed his eyes. "I can't break every tradition we've established. What about you? Are you going?"

"Most likely. Roz is going this year, and I really want to see her."

"Is Ken going to meet Big Mama?"

"I don't know if he's going or not. I know his family gets together for the holidays, especially since his mother died only a few years ago. He might even get with his daughter. I'll ask him, but I don't know if he'll come."

"Same with Nicole. Her family is in Dallas. Normally, I wouldn't mind going home with her, but you know how hectic this year has been for me, with all of the travel. I feel guilty enough not going home more this year, especially with Pop gone. I need to go and check on mom. I am so grateful Nicole understands. Hey listen, Rach, Gertrude just slipped a note to me. One of my clients is on the line. I'd better go. Quick, everything okay with you?"

"Yes, 'daddy'." Neal was always protective of Rachel, overly at times. She knew, without question, she could depend on him for anything and everything.

"Good. That's what I want to hear, my girl is okay. I'll pick you up Sunday afternoon for the scramble."

As she hung up the phone, she thought about Thanksgiving for a few minutes. No matter what was going on, Rachel always tried to go home for the major holidays. This year was no different, not even with Ken in the picture. She was particularly looking forward to going home this year, since Roz was planning to be there. She was hoping that Ken could go and meet her family, especially since she'd met his. Really only Big Mama, Roz, Neal, and his mom made up her inner circle. Now, Ken was also a part of the circle. All of them being in the same place, at the same time, was an event she didn't want him to miss.

"Hopefully, he'll want to go to Detroit with me for Thanksgiving." Rachel picked up the phone and dialed Ken's number.

16

Friday was Rachel's designated wind-down day. Over the past four months, Ken and Rachel had established a routine of getting together after work on Fridays, and spending most of the evening together. The only problem they had with spending the night together was maintaining the no-sex-before-marriage-agreement. It had become increasingly more difficult to refrain. The touching and kissing had escalated to heavy petting. As long as they didn't go all the way, she felt the agreement was still intact. Saving themselves for something serious was a goal she truly wanted to achieve. She acknowledged it hadn't been easy, especially with the amount of private time they spent together. Roz's opinion on the matter was different. According to her, the intense petting constituted sex. Yet, Rachel still felt a sense of sexual purity in the relationship. Whether it was reality or not didn't seem to matter.

Since her place was more spacious, they typically met at Rachel's around 7:00. Dinner and a movie was commonplace. This Friday, they broke the routine by meeting at Ken's apartment. The plan was to get some Chinese carry-out and watch a stack of rented videos. He had run out to pick up the food and to get a few other snacks from the local convenience store.

Rachel was just getting comfortable on the sofa when the phone rang. She wasn't in the habit of answering his phone, although he encouraged her to. For some reason, she just didn't feel right about it. She, only recently, felt comfortable about him answering her phone. Since it could be Ken calling, Rachel decided to go ahead and answer the phone.

"Hello."

"I must have the wrong number," said the party on the other end before hanging up.

Rachel didn't think much of it. She assumed it really was a wrong number or more likely, it was some woman from Ken's past, still trying to make contact. It was probably no different than Gary, Rick, or even Luc calling her. She felt confident. Ken had given her permission to answer, and it meant everything. It meant she was his lady and all others had the back seat. Rachel felt good being in the front seat for a change. A few minutes later, the phone rang again. She didn't hesitate this time in picking it up.

"Hello."

"Is Kenny there?"

"No. Can I take a message?"

"Who is this?"

"Rachel."

"This is Sandra," the caller responded in a bold tone.

Rachel felt awkward, knowing who Sandra was. "Hi, Sandra. I met you in the summer, at Sharon's place." Rachel was expecting a response, but didn't get one. She tried to keep the dialogue going. "How's it going?"

"Fine. How are things for you?"

"Great. By the way, did you call a few minutes ago?"

"Uh, yes, I did," Sandra hesitated. Since she didn't know if Ken had caller ID, Sandra decided to go ahead and tell the truth. "I'm sorry for hanging up. I was surprised to hear a woman answer Kenny's phone."

"Yeah, I don't normally answer it. Since we've been going together for a while, I guess I feel okay with it."

"Going together!" Sandra's voice elevated. "Kenny never mentioned anything about you." Rachel had given the tidbit of information in complete innocence, although Sandra probably didn't think so.

There was a brief moment of silence on the line.

"Well, good for you," Sandra pretended.

"Why thanks, I guess."

"Why did you say, 'I guess'?" Sandra asked curiously.

"I guess, because we're only dating, not getting married."

"Please, Rachel, you don't have to tell me. I know he's not trying to get married."

"Why you say that?" Rachel responded defensively.

"I just know him very well. We go way back. I've seen many of his girlfriends come and go. He's not the serious type."

Whether Sandra was right or not, Rachel was only going to take her opinion with a grain of salt. She knew ex's always had a hidden agenda when they volunteered information. She decided to change the subject.

"How's Ariel?"

"She's fine."

"When is she coming to visit?"

"I don't know, maybe Christmas. I need to get her there to see Red. She loves her grandfather."

"Oh yeah, I know Red adores her."

"You met Red?"

"Uhm Hmmm. Every other Sunday, we meet at his place for the family gathering." Rachel stated boldly.

"You go to those, huh?" Sandra wanted to minimize any significance Rachel might be feeling. She knew that taking Rachel to the family gathering was a strong indicator of Ken's seriousness.

"Red is funny. I really like him."

"Yeah."

Rachel could tell from the tone Sandra was deep in thought about something. "So, Ariel might be here for Christmas? That's good."

"Why is Christmas good?"

"Oh, we're planning to visit my family on Thanksgiving. If she had come then, I would have missed her."

"Well, like I said, I'm not sure about the exact date. I have some things going on here, and it might be sooner than I had planned. Her father and I will have to get together and work it out. We'll let you know what we decide," Sandra simply stated.

Rachel suspected there was an underlying message. Perhaps Sandra was trying to make her feel like she was not a factor in the decision. However, she ignored it.

"Good, I look forward to seeing her, whenever she comes."

"Well, I'm going to get off this phone and take care of a few errands. It was good talking to you again, Rachel. Tell Kenny to give me a call when he gets a chance. It's important."

"All right, Sandra. Bye."

After hanging up, Rachel felt slightly edgy. She remembered the uneasy vibes surrounding her meeting with Sandra back in the very beginning. She discounted them over recent months, but hadn't totally blocked them out. Sandra had been a wild card from the word 'go'. She couldn't help but wonder what Sandra thought about the relationship. Rachel hoped it wouldn't trigger any episodes of interference. Only time would tell.

No sooner had Rachel placed the receiver on the hook when she heard Ken's keys jingle in the lock.

"Hi, babe."

"Hi, Ken," Rachel responded. She jumped up to help him with the three brown bags of Chinese food and the plastic bags of beverages and snacks.

"Let me help you with that," Rachel offered as she grabbed the snack bag dangling from his index finger.

"Woo," Ken blurted as he wiped his shoes on the door mat and tried to shake some of the snow off of his coat without dropping the food. "Boy, it's cold out there."

The Chicago weather had gone straight from an extended Indian summer to the dead of winter, with no fall interlude.

She leaned towards him, careful not to step her bare feet in the melted spot of snow on the floor. She gave him a kiss and said, "Yeah, but it's warm in here."

"Ah," was all the response he could give.

"So, let's see what we have here." She took the Chinese boxes out of the bag and peaked into each to see what delicacies he had brought. Some of the sweet and sour sauce from the shrimp spilled onto her hand. She licked it off immediately, to avoid getting her sticky fingerprints all over everything. She was serving the food onto the two plates when it dawned on her, Sandra had called. It didn't seem to be urgent to her, but she still wanted to give Ken the message before it slipped her mind. She didn't want it to ever be said that his calls were being blocked by some insecure, possessive girlfriend.

"Oh, honey, Sandra called while you were out."

Ken didn't immediately respond to her comment. She figured he must not have heard her, so she said it again. "Sandra called."

"Uh huh."

"She said it was important, and to call her back when you get a chance."

"I'm sure it's not urgent."

"How do you know?"

"It never is."

"She seemed surprised about our dating."

"Oh, you told her." Ken sounded surprised but not upset.

"Yeah, that's okay isn't it?" Rachel inquired.

"Sure. Doesn't bother me if she knows. I told you, my only connection with Sandra is Ariel, plain and simple."

His explanation was good enough for Rachel. The discussion about Sandra was over and Rachel was ready to get back to the business of their warm evening together.

She picked up a couple of the rented videos. "Which video are we going to watch first?"

"Whichever you choose." She had selected the movies on the way over from their local video store. The weekend special was rent four and get two free. They never made it through all six videos in one evening. Just in case, she preferred to have a broad selection including comedy, drama, romance, and action. Horror flicks were not part of the line-up. Rachel reached for *Wuthering Heights*, and placed it into the VCR just to kick things off.

The ringing phone startled them both. They must have dosed off during the third movie. Ken glanced at the clock which displayed 1:43. He wondered who could be calling so late.

"Hello," Ken greeted with a groggy voice.

"Uhm humn" grunted Ken. "Uhm humn" he grunted again, in a tone that seemed increasingly irritated. The conversation was definitely one-sided. Whoever was on the other end of the line must have been doing all of the talking, because Ken wasn't saying much at all. He seemed so disinterested.

"Yep." Then he hung up without so much as a goodbye.

Rachel thought the conversation seemed odd. Based on past experience, normally a one-way call meant there was another woman on the line, and the guy wasn't free to talk. Perhaps it was one of his female stragglers who hadn't been completely cut loose. It was good Rachel had been with Ken long enough to not feel threatened.

The call was odd with only a couple of groanings and an abrupt hang-up without him saying bye. She didn't want to ask, but was hoping he would just offer some insight into the conversation. Instead of volunteering any information, he dozed back off. As much as she wanted to just let it go, her curiosity was in overdrive. She tried to hold back, but Ken wasn't offering any information. She asked in as diplomatic a way as she could, "So, who's up this late, besides us?"

Ken's head was leaning back on the sofa. He opened his eyes slightly, leaned forward, and put his head on her shoulder while easing both arms around her waist. He then responded casually, "Sandra."

Rachel wasn't surprised. She responded to his cuddling gesture by lifting her feet onto the sofa and resting her back comfortably against his chest. With her back to Ken, she felt free to speak openly. She wanted a little more information without coming across as pushy.

"For Sandra to call so late, it must be important."

"No. That's just Sandra. She wanted to know if you were here. She also asked if I would call her back tomorrow."

"Is everything all right, I mean with Ariel?"

"Yep, she said something about Ariel coming to visit for Thanksgiving."

"Thanksgiving! She told me Ariel was coming for Christmas! Don't forget, we've already planned to drive up to Detroit on Wednesday. My family is looking forward to meeting you. I hope Sandra doesn't try to mess up our plans."

Ken gave Rachel a kiss on the neck. "Sweetheart, don't even give Sandra a second thought. Trust me, she is no one for you to be concerned about."

"You're probably right. After all, she sounded all right on the phone."

"Well, don't underestimate her. Don't get too friendly with her. She's good for trying to get close to my friends. It's the tactic she uses to get into my business. Whatever you do, don't fall into her trap."

She relaxed into his arms and accepted his reassurance.

"Do you want to rewind this movie since we slept through most of it, or just let it play out and catch the next one?" Rachel proposed.

Ken chose to let it play out, and spend the time cuddling Rachel. They watched part of a movie. Before they knew it, both were fast asleep, again.

17

Rachel dropped the garment bag onto her bedroom floor, and Boots pounced on top of it. With Ken in the picture, the amount of attention the cat got was limited. Rachel kicked off her shoes and stretched out across the bed.

Exhaustion from her flight back to Chicago O'Hare was setting in. This trip, she was glad to have gotten the last seat on the same flight with Neal, and not have bothered with driving. A week or so ago, she definitely wasn't singing that tune when Miss Sandra so graciously disrupted the original Thanksgiving plans she had made with Ken. Rachel didn't know how Ken felt about it, but she suspected it to be intentional. She knew men didn't always see through schemes like women did.

Sandra had called at the last minute, claiming to need some kind of critical outpatient surgery. Rachel knew the emergency didn't come up until Sandra found out Ken was into a seemingly-serious relationship. She asked Ken if he could take care of Ariel for two weeks, including the Thanksgiving weekend. Apparently she felt more comfortable leaving Ariel with her dad rather than a random family member. If it hadn't been so manipulated, Rachel would actually have agreed. In theory it was an opportunity for the child to spend time with her father. In reality, Rachel wondered if it was an opportunity for Sandra to break up some of the attention Ken was giving his new woman.

Overlooking Sandra's motive, Rachel accepted that if Ken was going to be anything more than an absentee father, he would have to make sacrifices and be supportive to his child when necessary. This seemed liked one of those times. Rachel didn't discourage his commitment, because she would want no less from him, if it was her own child. Ken had decided to keep Ariel, and he was glad Rachel understood. It really wasn't the most comfortable position for her, but she didn't want to make a big deal out of it at this point in the relationship. Things were still too new to make a stand on such a no-win issue. That was his daughter and his responsibility, in spite of Sandra's motives. Wanting to be supportive, Rachel suggested that Ken bring Ariel with them to Detroit. Much to her surprise, he declined. He preferred spending the shortened trip alone, with Rachel.

Up to now, Sandra had not really been a problem in the relationship. With her living in Cincinnati, the distance was definitely a positive factor. Every now and then, Rachel would overhear them in a heated argument on the phone. As tempting as it was, she would go out of her way to not listen in. She never asked for any details, and Ken didn't volunteer. She didn't normally date men with children, but with Ariel being so far away, it didn't seem to be an issue. It wasn't the kids that bothered Rachel in such cases; it was the clinging mothers, who too often used the kids as a way to stay in the picture. It was hard enough maintaining a relationship between two adults, three was simply out of the question.

With the last minute change, Ken felt badly. He decided to go to Detroit for the Friday after Thanksgiving and to drive back early Saturday morning. Sharon agreed to keep Ariel while he was gone. The little girl was adorable. It was easy to find someone to keep her for the one day he was gone. Rachel had tried to talk him into flying in order to increase the amount of time they would have together in Detroit. He declined. The rationale was that he wanted to have his own car while out of town. Rachel had no allegiance to a car. A short plane ride and a rental car was right up her alley. Given the choice, she'd jet every time. Fortunately, their traveling preferences had not been a problem. Then again, they hadn't really been anywhere together.

"I am glad to be home." Rachel scratched Boots' head. "Aren't you glad Boots?" she asked in an animated voice.

Boots' purring was a 'yes'.

Rachel rolled over and pushed the play button on the answering machine. She listened to the messages half-heartedly. Everyone close to her knew she was out of town. When the third message started to play, she took notice and turned the sound up.

"Hi, baby. It's mom. Give me a call as soon as you can." Mrs. Pierce, Neal's mother, called all of her children 'baby', and made no exception with Rachel. Ever since Rachel's parents died, Big Mama's neighbors, especially Neal's parents, had always extended their families to her. She was surprised to hear from Mom so soon after Thanksgiving.

"Hi, Mom."

"Hi, baby. What you been doing?"

"You know me, keeping busy."

"Well, I won't hold you long. Just wanted to let you know that we had to change the place for the Christmas party. I don't know all the details, but I guess the hall burned down over the weekend and won't be ready for Christmas. So, your Aunties Fannie, Lottie, Ada, and Tee-Tee are working on pulling something together.

"Okay, just let me know where and when. I'll be there."

"All right, baby."

"By the way, I forgot to ask how you're doing?"

"I'm fine. Truly blessed, baby. Can't complain at all."

"Need anything?"

"No doll, but thanks for asking. You're such a sweet girl, always have been. By the way, can you tell Neal? I tried calling him, but the voice on the phone said his message box was full."

"I'll tell him you called, Mom."

Rachel knew Neal was going to see Nicole tonight, before leaving for his three week trip to Thailand in the morning. He avoided telling his mother when he was going on international trips, because she tended to worry. He told her only when absolutely necessary.

"That's right, he was going out of town on one of those business trips. I didn't ask him where he was going. Do you know?"

"Who knows where he is right now. I know he will call me sometime between now and the weekend."

With the time difference on his international trips, it was hard to catch up with each other. When he was out of the country, Rachel let him do the calling on the company's nickel. "I'll let him know what you said about Christmas as soon as he calls."

"Good. I'll see you later."

"Oh, Mom?" Rachel chimed in, trying to catch her before she hung up.

"Yes?"

"If you need anything while Neal is gone, let me know."

"Okay, baby. I will, and I love you."

"I love you, too. Bye, Mom."

She said okay, but Rachel knew Ms. Pierce wouldn't ask for anything. She was too proud. Mom had been living on her own ever since Neal's father died three years ago. It was his stepfather, but he never referred to Pop as such. He loved him as his natural father. Why not, Pop was the one who raised him.

Since Clarence, his biological father, hadn't raised him, they didn't have a loving bond. The most Neal could offer him was respect. To Neal, the natural-parent-thing wasn't all it was cracked up to be. Natural didn't mean automatic love and closeness; it just gave a head start. When Clarence didn't try to nurture the bond with Neal, it died. For Rachel, that explained why selfish, absentee-parents, coming on the scene in a child's teens, tended to disrupt their lives.

At least Clarence was decent enough not to step in and try to claim Neal when it became evident his son was going to be successful. Rachel knew enough colleagues whose dead-beat-dads crawled out of the woodwork and tried to take undeserved credit when they saw their offspring doing well. Clarence found out when Neal was fourteen that he didn't need, or more importantly didn't want another father. Coming late in the game, Clarence was smart enough to know that, at best, he could be a friend. Blood was normally thicker than water, but not in this case. There was no way he was going to be able to upstage Robert in Neal's life, blood or not. Thank goodness Clarence spared a lot of people some unnecessary heartache and confusion.

Relaxed, Rachel expected to doze off at any minute. Before falling asleep, she wanted to call Big Mama and let her know she had made it back safely. She did the majority of the calling when it came to keeping in touch with Big Mama. At her old age, it was a struggle to see well enough to dial the phone. Plus, Rachel felt better having the long distance charge on her phone bill. Even on Rachel's own birthday, she took the initiative to call Big Mama early in the morning. It was already past 9:00, and although Big Mama normally went to bed by sun down, Rachel knew she was waiting for her call.

She pressed the speed dial button labeled #2. While the phone was ringing, she sat up so her voice would come across clearer.

"Hello," sounded the older voice on the other end of the line.

"Hi, Big Mama. You sleep?"

"No, I'ze just laying down here resting my eyes. I guess ya done made it home."

"Yes, ma'am, I'm home. Neal gave me a ride."

"Was yo'r flight all right?"

"Yes, ma'am."

"All right then. Do ya have to go to work to-morrow?"

"Yes, ma'am."

"Then I reckon you be going to bed directly."

Rachel loved her grandmother dearly, and respected her opinion. Big Mama didn't always tell Rachel what she wanted to hear, yet, her opinion was highly respected. Although Ken had only been in Detroit one day, Rachel knew Big Mama had made an assessment. She wanted to know what it was.

"Big Mama."

"Yes'm, chile."

"What did you think about Ken?"

"Oh, chile. Ya ain't usually too particular about what I gots to say about yo'r men folk. Rachel, ya know we don't see eye to eye when it comes to them there men of yo'rn."

"I know, but I want to know what you think about this one."

"Ya sure?"

"Yes, I'm sure," Rachel reluctantly responded.

"Well, ya know I go by the leading of the Holy Spirit. I don't know whicha way the Spirit is leading me, but for sure I know something ain't quite right with that man.

Big Mama's comment caught her by surprise. Rachel thought she had hit the jackpot with Ken. She was expecting Big Mama to be pleased with his religious side. In defense of his position, Rachel added, "He goes to church faithfully."

"So, what that mean? The Devil, he goes to church every time the door open up, too."

She knew better than to go tit-for-tat with Big Mama, especially on religion. Rachel, with all of her education, didn't have a leg to stand on when debating with this seventy-some-year-old, God-fearing woman. The kind of wisdom she had didn't come from books. It could only come from God, himself.

"He might go to church, but are you sure the church is in him? He was nice and all. He was surely mannerble, but I didn't see any Lord around him. Ya can't sit in my house here, know the Lord and me not see it. If'n ya serving the same God that I'ze is, it can't help but to show. I ain't seen it with him. True enough, I don't know the man's heart, but whats ever ya love is going to show up sooner or later. I know ya like him pretty good. Don't worry none. I'ze going to pray on it and see what God lay on my heart."

Rachel was disappointed that she hadn't gotten Big Mama's endorsement. She still liked Ken. Whatever it was that made Big Mama uneasy, would either surface and be dealt with or, even better, disappear over time. She hoped once Big Mama got to know him, she would feel differently. All she could do now was to trust that Ken was for real, because if he wasn't, Big Mama's prayers were sure to sniff him out. Since the assessment wasn't too promising, she decided to pursue another avenue of affirmation, Roz. It was late, but she was anxious to get some feedback. She went ahead and dialed the number.

"Hi, Roz."

"Hey, Rachel. You at home?"

"Yeah. I'm back in Chicago."

"When did you get back?"

"Just a little while ago." Although Rachel normally loved chit-chat with Roz, this call had a specific purpose. She couldn't wait to get Roz's rating. With no more hesitation, excitedly Rachel asked, "So, what did you think?"

"About what?"

"Ken! What else?"

"Well, he's definitely handsome. He's bound to make some pretty kids, and that's right up your alley."

"Girl, now you know I checked that out way back in the beginning."

"You always were attracted to pretty-boys," Roz commented. "He does seem to be nice enough."

Looks were the basics. Rachel wanted something deeper. She valued Roz's opinion and wanted more of an affirmation that she was making the right choice with Ken. Prodding for more input from Roz, Rachel asked, "What else?"

"What do you mean, what else?"

"I want to know if you like him!"

"He seemed nice enough. Rachel, I only saw him briefly. He was so quiet. It was hard for me to get a good read on him. You must really like this guy."

"Why do you say that?"

"Because, it seems like you want my endorsement."

In essence, an approval was exactly what she wanted. The way Roz stated it, made her suddenly feel embarrassed to admit it.

"Not so much approval, as much as your insight. You know I've seen you size up the best of them. No matter how good the knights look or present themselves, if there is a crack in the armor, you always seem to find it. I wish I had the same uncanny ability to assess people as quickly as you do. It has saved you from a lot of heartaches."

"Huh. It has also limited my dating opportunities."

"So what. Why bother to date a guy if it's not going to end up anywhere."

"See, that's your youth talking Rachel."

"What do you mean?

"You go out with the hope of making a long term relationship. I gave up on that over ten years ago. That's why I can go out with a guy and enjoy the evening, without being bent out of shape about his flaws. Flaws were an issue when I was looking for a mate. They are irrelevant when it comes to finding an escort. I'm in the escort phase. You, my dear, are still in the let-me-find-a-man phase."

"See Roz. That's what I mean. You always know how to cut to the 'skinny' and lay things out on the line, calling it just like you see it."

"At my age, dear, all I can do is be honest. My memory is not good enough, any longer, to remember a lie." They both found themselves laughing. "So where does he rate on that checklist of yours?"

"So far he has checks for being handsome, tall, church-going, and family-oriented." Rachel paused. She was trying to envision the twelve-point checklist in her mind and check off those that applied to him. She knew he had more than four on his scorecard, but couldn't think of them all at the moment. "Off hand, I don't know what the other ones are."

"Girl, you and that list. What did Big Mama say?" Roz asked.

"Ah, you know how she is."

Roz was familiar with Big Mama's disapproval of the men Rachel dated. That's why Rachel wasn't in the habit of telling Big Mama about the men in her life, and definitely didn't give up any details about her sexual indiscretions. She preferred for Big Mama to think there was some purity still left in her little girl. Regardless of what Rachel did and didn't say, Big Mama was no dummy. She was quick to get a revelation and tell a person all about themselves, without any input from the perpetrator.

"I know what that means. She didn't like him."

"I wouldn't go that far."

"Exactly how far would you go? Talk about me! Huh. I know Big Mama didn't hold anything back."

"You're right about that," Rachel affirmed.

"So, tell me her take on Mr. Perfect," Roz humorously stated.

"She said he was a mannerable young man, but there was something about him she just couldn't put her finger on."

"Oh boy, that means leave him alone." Ninety-nine percent of the time, Big Mama's assessment was right on the money. At times, both Roz and Rachel were convinced Big Mama had a direct line to God, because he always gave her the correct scoop. "She wasn't praying in tongues over him, was she?"

"No. You know she wouldn't do anything like that, at least not in his face. Nah, she just wasn't 'too particular' about him she told me, but you're more open-minded."

"What you mean is, I'm more worldly. Well, don't worry about it. Like I told you before, just enjoy the companionship. You're not trying to marry him, at least not this week. So let it play out. As you get to know him, you'll make the right decision. Whatever he's doing in the dark, it'll come out in the light."

Rachel and Roz both started laughing at what, in essence, was an inside joke. It was Big Mama's favorite line and Rachel believed she had heard it no less than a million times growing up. The phrase alone kept Rachel from doing many things that she shouldn't. Even in her lukewarm religious state, she was willing to go only so far to get and to keep a man.

Roz's advice was wise, nevertheless difficult. Rachel wanted a husband, and a good one at that. The eight month evaluation process was always a hassle, although Ken was almost five months into it and still rating pretty high on the list. At the least, she hadn't grown tired or embarrassed of him. So far, so good. She was hoping beyond hope that he could make the eighth-month mark. Rachel, like many women her age, had waited so long for a husband, they went ahead and planned out the wedding, selected the rings, fantasized about the honeymoon, did a drive-by on the new neighborhood, and named the expected kids, all without a specific groom in mind. In the marital process, the man was the final, small detail needed to start the happily ever after saga. All Mr. Right had to do was show up at the church on time for the ceremony. Everything else could and had already been done, without him.

18

Saturday after Thanksgiving, Rachel could count on one thing, a Christmas card from Laurie. If no other cards came during the year, she knew there would be at least one. Without reading the name, the Atlanta postmark was a confirmation. Sure enough when she opened it, there was a family portrait of Laurie, her husband Greg, and the four kids, including the six week old newborn. Rachel had received a birth announcement last month, so she wasn't surprised by the family addition.

Rachel and Laurie had known each other for about seven years. They initially met when she hired Laurie as an accounting clerk at the firm in Atlanta. Although fairly uneducated, Laurie caught onto the job quickly, and, in Rachel's estimation did exceptional work. Rachel, being the nurturing type, immediately took to her and became an unofficial mentor.

Over time, Rachel became aware of Laurie's home life, and what an unpleasant sight it was. Her husband was slightly older than Rachel, while Laurie was about six years younger, somewhere around nineteen at the time. It was hard to believe they had been married eight years. Laurie had churned out babies ever since, at Greg's request, or more appropriately, at his demand.

As promising an employee as Laurie was, she only worked with Rachel for about six months. Greg decided Laurie needed to spend more time at home. Instead of losing her faithful clerk, altogether, Rachel created a part-time position for Laurie. Greg let her work the reduced hours for about four weeks, then pulled the plug on the whole deal. Laurie was disappointed about giving up her little independence, but had no say in the decision. 'Daddy' had spoken.

The sad part was, Greg needed the little money Laurie was making to help make ends meet, but was too proud to let his wife work outside of the home. Oddly enough, he wasn't too proud to be broke.

Rachel viewed Greg as the new generation of men. The ones who wanted the big lifestyles with the little wallets. The ones who refused to work multiple jobs, even if the one they had was inadequate. She didn't think the modern day men were cut from the same cloth as her grandfather and Pop, true providers. Rachel knew the generations before her were willing to work as many part and full-time jobs as needed to pay the bills. Pop cleaned toilets, dug ditches, and slung hash. Many mornings, she remember her grandfather, Pa-Pa, getting up at the crack of dawn and working past sunset. He left the best running car at home for Big Mama, and often times caught a ride to work. They did whatever they had to do to make ends meet. Rachel didn't think the men her age wanted to get dirty on the job. They also wanted the best cars for themselves, usually to showboat in. She believed a part-time job would eliminate the time available for showboating.

Even before finally quitting, Laurie had started to miss days frequently. Rachel later found out it was to conceal the physical abuse she was encountering. Greg was such a pathetic man in Rachel's eyes. Somehow he felt like a big man dominating a little woman. It was too bad he hadn't realized that he could be a strong man without making Laurie a weak woman. He didn't comprehend that there was actually room for both of them in the adult world. He preferred to keep the dominant mind frame of a child. Rachel sincerely hoped one day he would appreciate Laurie, preferably before he caused some real physical damage. For right now, all Laurie was good for was beating and breeding.

Greg, no doubt, saw her as weak, but Rachel saw her as strong. Ironically enough, the strength required to stay in such turmoil far outweighed that needed to leave. It was hard for Rachel to imagine love keeping Laurie there, but then again, many less desirable marriages endured without love. Perhaps it was the kids, fear, sex, commitment, shame, companionship, need, religious conviction, or simply complacency that kept Laurie there. Maybe she didn't want the hassle of starting all over again with someone new. She had no guarantee a new relationship would turn out to be any better than the one she was already settled into. Whatever the reason, one thing was sure, it wasn't because of blissful happiness. Laurie stayed in spite of it all. Besides, where was she going to go! She had four kids, no real friends in the area, no job, no money, no support structure, and worst of all, no self-esteem. Greg had made sure of that.

No matter how bad the marriage got, Rachel knew Laurie was not going to leave Greg. A dependent woman and a dictating man seemed to fit hand-and-glove. All Rachel could do was provide a shoulder to cry on, without judgment. Perhaps that was all Laurie wanted or could handle anyway.

Rachel couldn't help but to feel sorry for Laurie. The situation reinforced Rachel's determination to never be needy of a man. If that meant working two or three jobs, her freedom and peace of mind were worth it. The more Rachel thought about Laurie, the more appreciative she was of her happy, fulfilling relationship with Ken. It had been a long time coming, but so far, it had been worth the wait.

19

Ken pulled on the screen door, but it was locked. Red wasn't in the habit of leaving it open in the winter. Ken rang the doorbell three times before Red heard him.

"Dad, open up," Ken yelled as he banged on the door. Through the sheer curtains, he could see his tall, slim father slowly walking towards the door.

"All right, all right. What's your hurry?" Red opened the door as slowly as he walked. Ken grabbed the door and went in.

"You knew I was coming. You got the TV blasting. No wonder you can't hear anything."

Red sat in his favorite, worn-down easy-chair, and laid the cane down beside it. For the last four Christmas', Sharon threatened to throw the chair out and get him a nice new one. Each time, he protested, saying, "This chair suits me just fine. It took years to get it just right for my behind. I ain't about to throw it away now, not after it's finally broken in." He always finished the line with, "Don't mess with my chair."

"If you had Rachel with you, I might have opened the door faster."

"Ain't that about nuthin'. I come over here every week to watch a basketball game with you, and now you're trying to put me down for Rachel."

"That's right," Red said as he fumbled with the sound button on the remote. "She's a nice girl."

"I think so," Ken agreed.

"You ought to try and keep this one. You can go a long ways with a smart, respectable, hard-working woman like her. You not going to find somebody like her every day. It's time for you to be settling down."

"Dad, please. Can't we watch the game without a speech?"

Red continued with his train of thought, as if Ken hadn't said a word. "Now you already got one child, and you didn't marry that baby's mama. Look like right when you was about to marry her, all of a sudden you pulled out. You ain't a boy no more, Junior. You gotta get yourself settled."

"So, what do you want me to do Dad? I have a good job. I go to work everyday. I never get into any trouble, and I don't hang out with wild women. So what if I'm not married? And Sandra is out of the question."

"That's all good, but, don't you want a wife? I ain't telling you to marry Sandra. I know you two don't get along too good. But, Rachel seems like she'd be good for you. You act like you're afraid to commit to somebody."

"It ain't that, Dad."

"What is it then?"

"I don't know. I guess I just never met the right person, at least not until now."

"Son, ain't nobody going to be perfect. If you can find a good woman, you better hold on to her. When it comes to marriage, you boys sure ain't like my girls." Red had said his peace, and turned up the sound to hear the second quarter of the game.

Ken thought about the conversation on the way home. Red had been partially right about him not wanting to commit to Sandra. He pulled out when the pressure of marriage and a lifetime of responsibility came too close to reality. Leaving Sandra also had a lot to do with her domineering personality.

Ken was glad Rachel was nothing liked Sandra. She was kinder and gentler. Most of all, she didn't nag him about this and that. He also liked her being the independent, self-sufficient type. He had less fear of her getting pregnant and trying to railroad him into a commitment. After seven months of abstaining with Rachel, Ken found himself having more respect for her than anyone else he'd ever dated. The waiting had been unbearable, but it increased his desire for her. Red was right. It would be hard to find someone else as perfect as her. It was time to get serious.

Ken turned into the mall parking lot. He and Rachel were planning to spend the upcoming Valentine's Day weekend together, in Lake Geneva. He needed to finalize all of the arrangements at the travel agency. After letting Red's advice soak in, he decided to pick up something else from the mall. The first store he ran across had a big sign out front which caught his eye. *INSTANT CREDIT -- NO PAYMENT -- NO INTEREST FOR SIX MONTHS*

"Perfect," said Ken. As he stepped into the door, the eager salesman approached him.

As Rachel placed the silk nightie in her suitcase, she smiled. She was excited about the weekend. It was hard for her to believe it had been seven months since she first met Ken at his sister's cookout. What was even more difficult to believe was how great everything was still going. There were so many questions racing through her head. Had she finally hit the jackpot? Was this Mr. Right? She couldn't ever remember being this happy for this long in a relationship. This was definitely serious, and she was loving every minute.

One thing was certain, she was Ken's woman. Spending Valentine's Day with him was confirmation. Roz had taught her early in the dating process how to read the signs. She felt special days and weekends were big indicators of a man's level of involvement. The main lady always got holidays. She knew whenever a man couldn't be with her on the holiday, then he was most likely seeing someone else, whether he admitted it or not. The sign posts didn't lie.

Weekends were trickier for her to interpret. Spending Friday with a guy didn't really give her any indication of his level of commitment. With little to no effort, it was easy for a date to extend the work day, and go out for happy hour. Saturday, well that was different. She believed a man had to make a real effort to see a woman on Saturday. It wasn't so easy to tip out on the main Mrs. without a serious reason. Saturday and sacrifice were synonymous. They were not to be taken lightly in the dating arena, and both represented a sure sign of seriousness. Sunday, much like Friday, was not a clear indicator. It was a day of rest and guys could break away from home, under the guise of watching sports with some pals. Spending holidays and birthdays with a man, hands down, was the strongest indication a woman had that she was the main lady.

Not knowing exactly what to expect, Rachel was a bit nervous. She couldn't help but fantasize about the events of the weekend. With Ken's religious convictions, she was actually surprised he wanted to go on a romantic rendezvous. There had been many quiet romantic moments over the past seven months, but they hadn't given into the temptation of going any farther than hugging and passionately kissing. So far, so good. But, a weekend together in a remote, romantic setting might lead to something more serious. Lingering in the back of her mind was the conversation with Roz, months ago, about the possibility of Ken being gay. Given all of the possible outcomes, Rachel was determined to focus on the positive and finish her packing.

Whenever Rachel was packing, her cat was never too far away. Boots was batting a travel size bar of soap that had fallen onto the floor. He hesitated for a brief moment when the phone rang. Rachel hurriedly placed the sweater, she was holding, into the suitcase and dove across the bed for the phone. She wanted to get it before the answering machine picked up.

"Hello," she greeted in a slightly elevated voice.

"Hi, dear," Ken's captivating voice echoed. "You packing?"

"Yes, I am," she rolled onto her back, allowing his seductive voice to mesmerize her. "Are you?"

"I'm done."

"So soon!" Rachel surprisingly responded.

"You know I don't waste any time when I have something to do."

She turned onto her side and propped her head up with her hand. She closed her eyes in order to visualize him. "Ken, I'm excited about this trip."

"Me too."

"You know it's really the first trip we've taken together. I'm a bit nervous."

"Why?"

"Because I don't know what to expect. We've gotten close, but we haven't, well, you know." Rachel was obviously nervous, because she stumbled over her words. That was unusual.

"You mean, we haven't had sex."

"That's exactly what I mean."

"Rachel, I've never had a problem getting sex. That doesn't phase me. I'm looking for something much more significant. I want a serious relationship."

She kind of anticipated how he would feel, but was relieved to hear the confirmation. "I never asked, do we have separate rooms, or are we sharing one?"

"Based on the description I was given, the room sounds big enough to accommodate two people, comfortably. Why? Is that a problem?"

"No, no. I was just wondering."

"If it's a problem, let me know. I might still be able to change it."

"No, I'm sure whatever arrangements you made are going to be fine."

"So, I'll pick you up after work tomorrow, around 6:00. That way we can get up there before 8:00 and have a late candlelight dinner."

"Sounds good to me."

"Then, I'll see you tomorrow."

There was a hesitation, like Ken was waiting for something. Neither Rachel nor Ken had verbally used the 'L' word. It was signed generically as a salutation on a few greeting cards they exchanged, but never the real deal of 'I love you'. Perhaps that's why he was stretching the conversation. One thing Rachel had been taught long before was to never confess the 'L' word first. For some unexplained reason, it was one of the unwritten, yet, fully accepted laws of love. Rachel wasn't about to break the rule, although she recognized every time her relationship ended, it really didn't matter who confessed love first.

"Okay. I'll see you. Bye."

"Bye."

20

The two hour drive from Chicago to Wisconsin had been uneventful. Rachel was anxious to get settled in and relax. As Ken turned the key and pushed the door open, her nervousness resurfaced. The room was better than she'd expected. He had made all of the arrangements. Until now, she only speculated about the accommodations. She knew, all along, he had good taste, and this room removed any doubt. The ceiling was at least ten feet high and vaulted near the center of the room. The fireplace was stone and spanned the full-length of the wall. The carpet was plush. The king-sized bed was in a separate room with a Jacuzzi and a smaller two-way fireplace.

Rachel was impressed with the beauty of the suite, but also recognized that it posed a major threat to the no-sex agreement. It would be difficult to stay there for the weekend and not give in to intimate temptations. Certain situations were bound to generate certain results, and this was one of those scenes.

"So, my dear, is it to your liking?" Ken asked as he stood behind her and placed his hands on her shoulders. He pulled the winter jacket down off of her shoulders.

She nervously responded. "This is beautiful Ken. Quite impressive."

He hung her coat in the entry closet and slowly returned to the comfortable spot behind her back. He placed his arms around her waist and she responded by putting her hands on top of his. She went with the flow of the moment and tilted her head slightly to the left and he laid his head on her right shoulder. He whispered into her ear ever so gently, "I wanted everything to be special."

"Well, it's special all right, and we've only been here for fifteen minutes."

"This is only the beginning." He spun her around so she was facing him. Ken gave her a big hug. Since Ken was eight or nine inches taller than Rachel, hugs seemed to completely swallow her up. She loved the warm-hearted embrace and so allowed herself to simply melt away into the moment.

"Are you ready for dinner?"

"I almost forgot how hungry I was on the drive up here. Yes, I am hungry."

"Good."

"Good?" she curiously asked. "Why did you say 'good' like that?"

"Aaaah. That's for me to know and for you to find out," Ken playfully teased, while all along peaking her intrigue.

She was boiling over with excitement from his impressive romantic nature. He was physically strong, and, at the same time, emotionally gentle. No matter what else happened this weekend, he had already confirmed his check for being romantic. She kept thinking it couldn't be this good. She decided he had to be for real, because it would be too difficult to fake and front this well, for this long. Even the best con-men couldn't front for seven consecutive months.

While Rachel was daydreaming, she noticed he was making a call. Not really paying much attention, she heard him say, "Thirty minutes will be fine."

"Rachel dear, I'm going to grab a quick shower before the food gets here. Do you want to shower, too?"

"Together?" Rachel winced.

Ken smiled and approached Rachel. "You can relax, I'm not asking you to take a shower with me."

"You're not!"

"No. You probably didn't notice, but there are two bathrooms in the suite, a his and a hers. I specifically asked for a room with separate bathrooms. Both have a shower." He gave Rachel a wink in acknowledgment of her nervousness. "You can feel relieved."

She did feel relieved for a moment. Then her thoughts and perspective changed. Didn't Ken feel like she was desirable enough to shower with? She wasn't exactly his little sister. She was a fine and flattering woman who had turned the heads of many in her day.

Why wasn't this fish biting? She didn't know whether to feel insulted or respected. She wondered why was love always so complicated?

"This place is incredible," Rachel complimented.

"I'm glad you like it."

"I definitely do," she answered.

Both grabbed their night clothes, robes, slippers, and headed towards their designated bathrooms. As Rachel turned on the shower water, she allowed her mind to wander. She had always wanted this, a wonderful man and a romantic relationship. Like a dream, it was finally happening. She felt like pinching herself to make sure it was real. On second thought, the pinching wasn't such a good idea. If it was a dream, she preferred not to snap out of it. All of the nobody-specials she had dated up to now were just stepping stones leading to Ken. The mounds of disappointment, hurt, and betrayal of the other relationships enabled her to appreciate this nirvana, all the more earnestly.

She could hear him in the front room. It took her a little bit longer to get dressed. She wasn't overdoing it, but even natural beauty had to be worked and nurtured. An Afro was natural, but even it had to be shaped into perfection. Rachel heard a knock on the door. She figured it to be room service.

When she finally stepped out of the bathroom in her silk robe, Ken had the lights dimmed and some soft music was playing. The table looked like a mini-buffet with fresh fruit, cheese, crackers, shrimp, and what appeared to be four entrees under glass.

"Ken, why so much food?"

"Some for now and some for later. You know, in case we talk into the wee hours of the morning and get hungry."

Ken dipped a shrimp lightly into the cocktail sauce and placed it on her lips. As hungry as she was, the shrimp was a welcome appetizer. He pulled out the chair for her, and she sat down to partake of the lavish meal. They both enjoyed the leisurely, romantic dinner.

"You out did yourself, Mr. Sanders. Dinner was wonderful."

"I'm pleased that you were satisfied. How about we have dessert by the fireplace?"

During dinner, Ken chilled a bottle of wine to have afterwards. Dessert in front of the fireplace, on the big bear rug, was going to be relaxing. Rachel was afraid the big meal, heat, wine, and the warm shower she took earlier might put her to sleep, prematurely. This was one night she wanted to stay wide awake. He reached for Rachel's hand to help her up from the chair, and proceeded to escort her to a spot in front of the fireplace. They both sat down on the rug side by side and glanced into the fireplace. The silence seemed to last forever.

Ken broke the silence when he offered her another glass of wine. "Rachel, I really enjoy being with you. You are so beautiful to me. I'm glad we met, and to think, I wasn't even looking for anybody. What's really funny about it is that if I had been looking I probably would not have found you. I love you, Rachel."

She was shocked at his openness. He was putting his feelings on the line. He actually said the 'L' word, first. Although Rachel loved him, it would seem too coerced to say 'I love you, too'. Since she didn't know what to say, she chose not to say anything. She opted to respond with a kiss.

"I'm glad we decided to spend the weekend together." He was laying on his side with his hand supporting his head. His other hand was tucked warmly in the robe pocket. "Happy Valentine's Day, sweetheart." He kissed Rachel on the cheek and handed her a gift.

As Rachel opened the small velvety box, her heart was racing. She figured it was a piece of jewelry, but didn't know what kind? The box was too big to be a ring, or was it. Thoughts flooded her mind. What if it was a ring? Was it too soon? Would she really like it or merely have to pretend she did? So many thoughts of commitment, romance, and details consumed her. It wasn't the anticipation of the ring that confused her. It was the implications of such a serious commitment which seemed overwhelming.

When she finally put forth the last bit of effort into her finger and pushed the box open, she smiled with relief. It was a ring, and a nice one at that. The ring had a small marquis in the center with rectangular baguettes on both sides. The stone was not a rock, but it definitely wasn't a chip. It was more like a nice-sized pebble.

No matter how simple she could be with other materialistic items, an engagement ring was different. Rachel wanted the world to know she was engaged, and had the ring to prove it. Somehow, a chip just didn't give the same assurance as a rock, or in this case, as a nice pebble. Gazing at the ring, there was an inner happiness resulting from her ability to wear the ring comfortably, with no shame.

"Oh!" she sighed in exhilaration. "It's beautiful." She clumsily leaned over and hugged Ken. "AhAhAhAh ...," Rachel screamed excitedly.

The surprise of getting a ring was enough, but she was also taken by the size and style. The ring made her feel good. Her eyes started to swell. All she could think of was that Ken, actually, thought enough of her to get something decent. It was a far cry from what she'd experienced in the past.

"Oh, Ken!" She leaned over to hug him with the box still in her hand. It took everything in her to hold back the tears. Connected to Ken in a tight embrace, Rachel told herself, "If this is a dream, please don't let me wake up."

"Here, let me put this on," he said.

"Oh yeah, that's right. I forgot to put it on." He leaned his body up on one knee and placed her hand into his. He took the other hand, placed it under her chin and gently lifted her head so their eyes were locked on each other.

"Rachel, my dear Rachel. You're special to me. I love you, and I want us to be together. Will you, officially, be mine?"

"Are you asking me to marry you?" This was a serious matter, and she wanted to be absolutely clear of his intentions. This was no time to be making assumptions.

"Yes, I'd like for us to be together. I like what we have," he assured.

"I do want to be with you," she responded, bursting with joy.

"I guess that's a yes."

"I guess it is," she happily answered as he slid the ring onto her finger.

"So now what do we do?"

"We have plenty of options. We can talk, eat, or go to sleep, for starters."

This engagement seemed too easy. Rachel had so many unanswered questions in her head, like when and where. She decided to go ahead and seek some answers while the mood was right. "I have a question about this marriage thing."

"Shoot."

"When did you have in mind for the wedding?"

"I was thinking sometime in the summer, of next year," he replied.

"That long, huh."

"I was thinking, perhaps we could live together. They say you don't really get to know a person until you live with them. Living together will give us an opportunity to really decide if marriage is as right for us as we think. Neither of us has been married. We need the extra time to get adjusted to each other. I, also, want to get some things straightened out on the finance end, before we hook-up." His financial concern wasn't good news to her. It was sounding like he wasn't going to earn a check for financial stability.

Rachel was willing to overlook the issues about money for the moment. She was more concerned about his offer to live together. She couldn't allow herself to live with a man. Once again, reliance in his religious convictions had failed her. Besides Big Mama blowing a gasket, Rachel had no intentions of giving away the milk before Ken purchased the cow. Sure, he had put a ring on her finger, but that was the extent of it. She was smart enough not to get caught in the long-engagement, live-together trap. Too often she had seen individuals get stuck living together and never graduate to marriage. If he was getting everything he wanted in the relationship, including sex, without a marriage license, then there would be no incentive for him to ever get married. Letting him have his cake and eat it too just didn't seem to benefit her.

One thing Rachel was certain on, the way to marriage was definitely not through the path of living together. It was interesting to her how Ken focused in on neither of them having been married. Yet, he was willing to live with her now and had lived with Sandra before. Surely that counted as a strike-off somewhere. He hadn't actually been married or divorced, but he sure wasn't pure either with several shackings under his belt. Rachel knew pre-marital sex and shacking-up were both equally wrong in the eyes of God.

Strangely enough, one seemed worse than the other. She didn't know why she felt the way she did, but shacking-up seemed less socially acceptable than having pre-marital sex.

"Ken, I just can't live together. My grandmother would just die if she knew. To be honest, I don't feel too comfortable about living together before we get married, either."

"I wouldn't want you to be uncomfortable, but I know we would enjoy being together day and night. Living in the same house would be special." He gently kissed her neck, her cheek, and then her lips. "I would love to go to sleep with you in my arms, and wake up with you every morning." Ken was trying to persuade her without coming on too strong.

The offer sounded tempting, but she knew it wasn't negotiable. She didn't dare allow herself to contemplate the thought, otherwise it might lead to a compromising set of circumstances. It was clear the two were on different wavelengths about living together. She wanted to change the subject.

"So," Rachel said as she intertwined her fingers with his, "now what?"

"Finally, I can make love to you."

"What makes you say that?" she asked with apprehension.

"You've always wanted a commitment before we get it on." He held her ring finger up and said, "This settles it."

"No it doesn't. Ken, I still want to wait for the wedding before we sleep together."

"What do you mean!"

"We still aren't completely committed."

"We're engaged!" He pushed away from her and spoke in an irritated tone. "That's commitment, to me. Baby, come on. What's the difference between now and later, anyway? You know I have waited, patiently, and I've done exactly what you asked of me."

"Please, don't make me feel guilty. It's hard enough to resist you."

Realizing how demanding he was being, Ken tempered his attitude. He didn't want to spoil the mood. "Come here."

He pulled Rachel close to him and let her sink into his embrace. "I love you, Rachel. We'll deal with the rest later."

His understanding drove out the tension. Comfortable in his arms, she chose to forget about the sex issue and savor the flavor of being engaged to a wonderful man, who she adored. Other issues would have to be dealt with later. Nothing was going to destroy the mood of this weekend.

21

"There's no place like home," Rachel chanted as she rubbed Boots' head. She stretched out across the bed and noticed there were eight messages on the answering machine. Busy weekend. She was still high on the events of the engagement. Since she was with Ken, surely the messages couldn't be from him, which eliminated any rush to play them.

Instead, she started to read the mail that had accumulated over the weekend. In the stack was a note from the florist. It read, '*We were unable to deliver your package.Please call the number below and arrange for delivery. Thank you.*' The note generated a smile.

She assumed it was from Neal. He had faithfully sent her flowers on Valentine's Day for the past eight years. It all started when Mr. Ed totally blew off Valentine's Day the year he was with Rachel. She was really hurt when he completely overlooked the most romantic day of the year. She cried and cried on the phone with Neal, after realizing Ed hadn't, and wasn't going to do anything special for her. She remembered getting a knock on her door at 11:30 that night. She didn't know how he did it, but Neal had managed to wire flowers from London, in the middle of the night. He was determined not to let the day go by without Rachel getting something special for Valentine's Day. Neal declared from that day on, he would not leave gift giving up to the inadequate men in her life. Instead of seeing his best friend hurt and rejected, he preferred to be proactive and take care of her himself.

At times it seemed like she took the flowers for granted, when in fact, Rachel really did appreciate them. On more than one occasion they came in quite handy, particularly when she was either in-between relationships or worse, with another inconsiderate jerk who didn't appropriately acknowledge the day. She'd experienced both kinds of scenarios one too many times.

After flipping through the mail she leaned over and pressed the play button on the answering machine. The computerized voice on the answering machine said, "You have eight messages." After the tape stopped rewinding, the messages started to play back.

"Hey Rach. Don't forget that I'll be in Paris for the next three weeks. Have a nice Valentine's Day and I'll call you next week," Neal requested.

"Hello, uh Rachel, it's Brian. Uh, I just wanted to say, hi. We haven't talked in a long time and I was sitting here thinking about you and, uh, just wondering how things were going. If you can, please give me a call as soon as possible. If you don't have plans for Valentine's Day, I'd love to take you out. Okay, uh, bye."

"Yeah right," Rachel chuckled. The brief interlude with Brian had long been over. She met him at a low point in her life and had no intention of rekindling the relationship. Unfortunately for him, she got involved with him on the rebound. Those relationships never materialized into seriousness for her. During the lonely, heartbreak times, Rachel wanted somebody to be there. She tended to lower her dating standards and tolerate a normally less desirable man. Once she started recovering, she would quickly discount the man as not being her type and tolerance for him immediately began to diminish. She remembered how Brian started to get on her nerves, that is, after she started healing emotionally.

She was even ashamed to be seen with him in public, and when they were together, often went to dark theaters, or stayed in to watch videos and order take-out food.

Despite her lack of interest, he was still trying to get something going with Rachel. Brian used to do everything he could to entice her, including wearing her favorite men's cologne, Donna Karan. Nothing could woo her to his bed, not even wild horses.

"Hi, Precious. I know you're busy with your friend, but I couldn't let this day go by without calling you. Happy Valentine's Day. By the way, I love you as much today as I did when we first met four years ago, and I guess I always will. Even you can't change that. Call me if you get a chance."

Rachel could hear what sounded like traffic in the background. Luc was probably calling from some pay phone on his infamous trip to the store. Back in the day, Luc would leave his family on Valentine's Day and rush over to spend a couple of hours with Rachel. Although the time was short, she was happy to get whatever time he could give, and always made the most of it. This Valentine's Day, it was nice to have a man of her own, all to herself, for the whole day. What she thought would never happen had finally come to pass; she actually preferred to be with someone other than Luc.

"Hey, Rachel. Happy Valentine's Day, girl. I know you're out with Mr. Perfect. Just thinking about you. My MCI calls were free today, so I figured I'd reach out and touch you, or is that AT&T's slogan? Whoever! You know every time they send me a check, I switch. So, really I don't know which long distance carrier I have right now. Oh well, doesn't matter." Roz was laughing at her own humor in the message. "Anyway, catch you later."

"If you'd like to make a call, please hang-up and dial the number again."

Rachel hated hang-ups on the recorder but understood some people didn't always want to leave a message. There were plenty of times when she didn't want to leave one herself.

"Hey Rachel, Gary here. Listen, I just wanted to say Happy Valentine's Day. I know that I broke up with you pretty harshly. I feel badly about hurting your feelings the way I did. It's been over six months since we last talked. If you want, maybe we can talk about patching things up."

"Oh, please," Rachel spoke out loud as she looked at her ring.

"Hi, Precious, it's me again. Just checking to see if you were back? I'll talk to you soon. I hope you had a nice weekend."

Rachel figured Luc must have told his wife he was making another run to the store. No matter. One thing was for sure, she needed to call Luc tomorrow at work and let him know she was engaged. Knowing she shouldn't be, Rachel was feeling obligated to tell him. Maybe it was the only way to close the Luc chapter in her life, once and for all. Recovery from the break-up with him had been a long, painful road, but she was now seeing the light at the end of the tunnel.

She wanted to call him immediately, but his home number was off limits. She appreciated the man she had now, more than ever. She could call Ken whenever she felt so inclined, as opposed to sitting around waiting for him to give her a jingle. Many a time she wasted an entire day waiting for Luc to break free from the family and come by her place. Sometimes he would arrive as late as 8:30 and then only be able to stay twenty minutes. Looking back, she couldn't figure out why she settled for so little, so much less than what she wanted.

"Hi, Ms. Matthews. Long time no talk. In case you didn't recognize the voice, it's Rick."

"How could I not recognize his voice?" How dramatic, she thought, but typical of a professional charmer.

"Just wanted to say Happy Valentine's Day. Perhaps we'll get a chance to talk soon. I'd like that. Take care," Rick closed with his smooth, charming voice.

It had been some time since Rick last called, but Rachel wasn't surprised to hear from him. She classified him as typical. It seemed like no matter what the circumstances were surrounding the break-up of the relationships, the playboys always came back. Some took longer than others, but by and large, they all came back begging, in one way or another.

Boy, this weekend they were really crawling out of the woodwork. Rachel was accustomed to feast or famine. Either every guy she ever knew was calling, or she couldn't buy a date. Where were they eight or nine months ago when she was going out with Gary just for companionship, until she could do better. It seemed to her the women who were in-between relationships and looking for simple companionship, couldn't shake a man off the tree. But, let her mess around and get into a serious relationship, then the dogs start to sniff and hang around as soon as they sense turf invasion. Rachel was convinced, danger to a man came in two forms, commitment, and competition from another man. Both caused men to act stupid. Fortunately, Mr. Sanders didn't seem to be running from either. Things were definitely looking up for her in the area of romance. It was a long time coming, but some stable happiness seemed to be on the way.

She glanced at the clock displaying 10:00. She did the quick two hour time-zone calculation in her mind, and came up with 8:00. It was still early enough to call Roz. Regardless, the news about the engagement was too big to sleep on. She had to share it with someone. She pressed the #3 spot on the speed dial containing Roz's number. A couple of months into the relationship, she had put Ken into spot #4. Rachel deemed the ranking appropriate since the constant people in her life were rightfully in the top spots. Her best friend Neal was always there for her, unlike many of the other jerks in her life. Now Ken, he was still going strong. Maybe he was on the move up in Rachel's speed dial list, but for now everything was status quo.

On the fourth ring, Rachel was about to hang-up when Roz picked up.

"Hello."

"Hey," Rachel sparked.

"Hey, girl."

"Well, it happened," trying to sound calm and not give Roz any indication of the news.

"What happened?" Roz inquired. "What, you're pregnant?"

"No girl, but I am engaged," Rachel squealed.

"Engaged! No, he didn't!"

"Yes, he did."

"Well you go, girl. Congratulations."

"Thank you."

"How long has it been?"

"Seven months."

"Did you have any idea?"

"No, not really. We had talked about it before, but only in general."

"So, do you feel okay with it?" That was Roz's way of asking was it too soon to make such a serious decision in light of Rachel's track record with men.

"I told him yes. Roz, these have been seven wonderful months with him. To top it off, the weekend was beautiful. He definitely earned the check for being romantic. It was all that!"

"How many checks is that?"

"I don't know. I guess about seven?"

"Out of twelve! That's barely half!"

"I'm not saying he's perfect, but he is definitely wonderful with me and to me. I really love him. I feel like I've finally met a good man," Rachel defended.

"Well, you know I'm happy for you, and as always I support you in whatever it is you do." Roz was always supportive, even if she didn't agree with Rachel's decisions. Rachel loved how Roz never forced an opinion or undermined a decision. She always respected Rachel as an adult, and perhaps that was a significant factor in their unquestionably successful bond.

"Thank you, sis. I always know I can count on you, through thick and thin."

"Now, let's get to the good stuff. Did he give you a ring?"

"Yes he did."

"And?" Roz asked looking for a description.

"It's medium-sized with a marquis diamond and baguettes on the side."

"Ah, sounds nice. So, Mr. Sanders has some class."

"Yes, I really like it."

"You didn't have to pay for it this time, did you?"

"Ha ha. Very funny. No, I didn't. As a matter of fact, that's what makes it so nice. Ken got what he could afford."

"Unlike Mr. Ed."

"Ooo, why did you have to go there. Ed, oh my goodness. What a joke! I've tried to block him and that whole ring thing out."

Ed was someone Rachel got engaged to about six months after she'd arrived in Atlanta. Back when she was young and naive, she met him her first week in town. Rachel later realized that meeting him so soon after she got there wasn't surprising. Leeches, like Ed, had a way of sniffing out fresh meat.

Ed was trifling. He always had a reason why he couldn't keep steady work. Somebody was always firing him for no apparent reason and from no fault of his own. Later, she came to find out how shiftless and no count he was, but at the time of their mock courtship, he was 'all that' in her eyes. Fine and fun-loving. He was more than a pretty-boy, he was down-right gorgeous. That was all she required back then. The twelve-point checklist was much shorter then. A job and substance used to be minor attributes. Now, understandably, they were inching their way to the top.

The whole engagement thing with Ed was a farce. He had asked her to get married in an attempt to prevent her from dumping him. He spared no expense. The ring was stunning, a 1 carat, heart-shaped, solitaire with another carat of baguettes along the side. Undoubtedly, a serious rock.

The price tag of the ring was forever registered in her mind, $4,372.21. That was the amount she ended up paying. Apparently Mr. Ed had purchased the ring on the one joint credit card they had. The purchase had been completely without her knowledge. She got the card with a 4,700 dollar limit in an effort to help build his sorry credit. In the end, all it built was her level of debt.

Four months after the engagement, Rachel finally kicked Ed to the curb. He was gorgeous, but she couldn't afford to keep him. She finally got fed up with having to take care of him. The meal ticket was over and the free-loader had to go. He was too expensive of a show-piece for her to keep on her modest salary.

A couple of months after the break-up, she received a statement from the credit card company. She had totally forgotten about the joint card. Since the relationship was over, she decided to go ahead and cancel the account while it was fresh on her mind. She opened the envelope to get the customer service number. When she opened the statement, her eyes were immediately fixed on the balance column. The $4,761.21 read larger than life. She was floored. She called the card company to see if there was a mistake, only to find out it was for the purchase of a ring. Not only was there a balance on the card, the customer service rep pointed out the accrued interest and late charges had taken it over the limit. After getting all of the information she could stomach from the rep, Rachel just eased the phone down on the hook. She was disgusted at both Ed and herself, him for being a jerk, and herself for being stupid.

Despite her gallant efforts, the jewelry store wouldn't take the ring back, because six months had already passed. She ended up selling the ring to a co-worker for 2,500 dollars, at a loss of over 2,000 dollars. And to think, she almost gave Mr. Ed the ring back when they broke up, because he was so persistent. It's a good thing she didn't. At least she was able to recover some of the money.

So, Ken's pebble was beautiful, and a big part of the ring's luster was attributed to it truly being a gift she didn't have to pay for.

"Well, I'm glad Ken did right by you with the ring. When's the wedding?"

"We didn't actually set a date, but I suspect sometime next year."

"Oh, a long engagement?"

"Yeah, Ken has some financial matters he wants to work out first."

Although this long engagement and financial issue was starting to look like a red flag, Roz couldn't burst Rachel's high, not now. She'd find a tactful way to address it later. Right now, it was Rachel's time.

"Well, the long engagement gives you some extra time to plan the big shindig."

There was a brief moment of silence on the line while Roz decided what to talk about next. After getting her thoughts together, she broke the silence.

"Tell me about this romantic weekend. Did you do it?"

Rachel knew exactly what Roz meant and responded quickly and firmly. "No we didn't. I told you, this time I want to wait and go about it the right way."

"So, you're telling me you were in this romantic room, huddled up together all weekend, and didn't do anything."

"No." Rachel's firmness softened to the point of seeming questionable. "Not really."

"Not really? What does not really mean? It's either yes or no."

"Well, we didn't go all the way, but there was some touching."

"You mean like kissing."

"Yes, that too, but, no sex," Rachel reiterated.

"You mean to tell me this strong, romantic, hunk of a man didn't want to make love to you after he gave you an engagement ring?"

"I didn't say that."

"So, he did want to?"

"Yes, he did."

"Woo - good."

"What do you mean, 'good'?"

"I was starting to really wonder about him. All this private time the two of you have been spending together, and he hasn't tried anything. Something was starting to sound a bit strange to me --- church boy or not."

"He was definitely ready to get it on, but I was able to resist."

"That's funny. He's the one all up in the church, but it was your religion, or at least the part of Big Mama in you, that kept the heat on the sex turned down. As many hypocritical things as you've told me about Ken, it's no wonder Big Mama didn't take to him. He's no more holier than I am. He might as well sleep in on Sundays, like the rest of us. Don't tell him I said that."

"You know I'm not telling him that. But, the main thing is, we didn't do anything."

"Well my dear, I hate to break it to you, but heavy touching, or as you younger people call it, petting, is sex. It won't get you pregnant, but it will sure get you into spiritual trouble. How many times have you heard Big Mama say that?"

Rachel had to stop and think. Had she messed up without realizing it? Even though they didn't complete the act, the thought was definitely there. According to Big Mama, that was just as bad. The more she thought about it, the less rationalizing seemed to work. Big Mama's words seemed to be amplified in her mind, like "What you do in the dark will come out in the light." The biggie was her reference to the verse in Proverbs about the eye of God being everywhere. Growing up, Rachel avoided doing many things, because she could imagine the eye of God on her, even in a dark room with someone. She started to feel guilty and disappointed, because she had so wanted Ken to be special. She really wanted to save herself for him, and, without consciously thinking, it might already be too late.

While Rachel was pondering over the sex issue, Roz changed the subject. "Have you told Big Mama the good news?"

"Stop. Don't even go there."

There was a beeping noise on the line indicating that another call was coming through. However, Rachel ignored it for the moment.

"What?" Roz piped in, while trying unconvincingly to seem confused. She knew exactly what Rachel was alluding to. They both knew Ken wasn't Big Mama's choice for Rachel, no matter how nice he appeared to be. Big Mama just didn't have a confirmation about him. Rachel knew her grandmother's opinion was nothing to take lightly. That was one call she was going to postpone till later, much later.

The line beeped again, and this time she answered it.

"Roz, that's my line. Hold on." Rachel pushed the flash button to pick up the other call.

"Hello," she greeted.

"Hello," Neal countered.

"How's Paris?" Rachel excitedly responded.

"Nice. At least the weather is good this time."

"Hold on a minute. I have Roz on the other line."

"Oh, I'm sorry. You want me to call back later?"

"No, I want to talk to you. Roz and I were getting ready to get off, anyway."

"All right. Rach, tell Roz hello for me."

"I will. Hold on." She pushed the flash button to get Roz back.

"Hey, Roz."

"I know, I know. You have to go."

"Yes."

"Tell Mr. Wonderful, I said hello."

"For your information missy, it's not Ken. It's Neal, and he says to tell you hi."

"Neal. That is Mr. Wonderful. Tell him hello for me, too."

"Bye."

Rachel clicked back over to Neal's line. She was so glad he called. She wanted desperately to share her exciting news with him, just like always.

"Neal, are you there?"

"Yes."

"Well, I'm finally going to be taken off your hands."

"How so."

"I'm engaged," she anxiously blurted out.

"Engaged! I guess congratulations are in order. When did that happen? I'm assuming it's to Mr. Too-fly." Neal had assigned the nickname to Ken months ago. It didn't bother Rachel, because she was in tune with his humor. He got the name from the 1970s Superfly character, representing a handsome, well dressed, big spending, smooth talking, ladies' man.

"Yes, it's Ken," placing emphasis on his real name, "and it happened on Valentine's Day."

"Did he give you a ring?"

"Yes he did, a nice one. You're worse than Roz."

"Don't fault us for those no class dead-beats in your life."

"I'm improving my quality of men."

"Good for you. Anyway, congrats Rach. No one deserves a good relationship more than you. You've definitely paid your dues. There's nothing but up for you now."

"Thanks, Neal. Coming from you, it means a lot."

"When's the big day? I need to be sure and have my tux ready."

"Especially since you'll probably have to give me away. With Pa-Pa and Pop gone, you're it, big brother."

"It will be my pleasure. Anything to get you off of my hands."

"Thanks a lot, friend."

"Oh, Rach, you know I'm just teasing."

"You better be. Look, let's get back to the date. We don't have one set, but it will probably be sometime next summer."

"Ah. Smart brother. He's just taking you out of circulation with the engagement."

"What do you mean?"

"Can't tell you. It's a man's thing, Rach."

"That never stopped you from telling me before. You know you're my tap into the male mind. Without your insight into men, I would have made even worse decisions in the past."

"I don't know what I'm going to do with all this time!"

"What time?"

"The time I won't have to spend worrying about you and how those losers are treating you."

"Ha ha. Funny. Funny."

"Golf, here I come."

"We'll still be golfing together, you and I."

"I doubt that!" he uttered.

"Why not," she asked.

"Ken probably won't go for that. Most men wouldn't. It was one thing for us to hang out when the two of you were single. It's totally different when you're married."

"Hey, Ken knows how close you are to me. You're my brother, for goodness sakes."

"You may see me as a brother, but trust me, Ken is a man. He doesn't see me as your brother. Trust me on this one Rach. I know how men are. Remember, I'm one, too."

"Uhm" Although Rachel hadn't given it much thought, she knew Neal was probably right. As much as she loved Ken and wanted a life with him, the thought of losing her best friend was inconceivable. He had been one of the few constant factors in her life for the past twenty-five years or so.

"No matter. You're still my girl. Maybe I can get married now that I've raised you up and am about to give you away."

"Thanks, Pop," Rachel affectionately teased.

"Anyway, go to bed. It's late. I'll call you in a couple of days. Just in case, write down the number here."

She jotted down the number, concluded the conversation, and prepared to turn in for the night. In ten minutes flat, she expected to have her teeth brushed, face washed, hair tied back, prayers completed, and lights turned out. Before she met Ken, the process took about a half-hour, with prayer counting for at least half the time. Now that things were going well, she had resorted to a drive-by prayer. Her knees weren't comfortably on the floor before she was finished. She figured there was no sense in bothering God when every thing was upbeat. She would lengthen the prayer on an as-needed-basis. Spiritually, she knew her time in prayer was not suppose to be shorter during the good times, but reality said it was.

Big Mama always said, "Store it up, chile, for when you need it. Keep the line open so you don't have to shake the dust off when you need him."

As happy as she was, at the moment, Rachel found consistent prayer easier said than done.

22

It was a few minutes after midnight. Rachel was into her routine when the phone rang. Immediately, she thought Neal must have been calling back for something. She finished tying the scarf around her head before moving towards the night stand to get the phone.

She grabbed the phone just as the answering machine was picking up. "Hello."

"Hi. The good news is ..." She could hear the answering machine message playing into the phone. "Hold on." She deactivated the machine. "I'm sorry about that Neal."

In the mild chaos, there was no immediate response on the other end. The first thought that came to her mind was Gary. Surely this loser wasn't still calling, especially at midnight. Had he no dignity. Rachel tried to let him down easy, but it hadn't worked. If it was Gary, she decided to tell him off, and get this joke-of-a-situation over once and for all. Enough was enough. "Hello," she said again in a serious tone.

"Hi, Precious."

When Rachel heard that voice, her heart sank to the floor. She could feel her pulse racing. "Hi Luc. I'm surprised to hear from you." Rachel never knew when Luc would show up or call. Things had been officially over between them for two years, but he was still able to tug at her emotions. Until now, no man had touched her as deeply as Luc, or left such a deep scar. Undeniably, his love had been a bittersweet experience in her life. Deep down she was glad to hear his voice from time to time. A phone call was fine, but she could only handle small doses of Luc at a time.

"I was thinking about you. I know you prefer for me not to call, but I decided to take a chance and say, hi." Luc always knew how to reach her. Fortunately for her, he called at a good time, a time when she was focusing on making a life with Ken. She couldn't afford to mess up her engagement by getting caught up in the moment and making the same kind of mistakes she had in the past. Rachel's strength enabled her to hold her ground and not let Luc woo her with his natural charm.

"How are you, my dear?"

"I'm fine, and you?"

"Much better now that I know you're okay."

Rachel could never figure out how he did it? What did he have over her? Most brothers would use a lame line like his, and she would automatically know what a fake they were. Luc was genuine. His words were poetic.

"How are your wife and kids?" Whenever Rachel felt like she was losing her perspective, she thought about his family. After all, that was why they weren't together. They were important to him, and rightfully so. She constantly reminded him of his commitment to them. Maybe, she was really reminding herself.

"They are fine." She could hear his voice dampen. Good, Rachel thought. She had to nip this feeling in the bud before it caused any more damage in her life. Thank goodness for Ken. What she had going on with him gave her the confidence she needed to resist Luc.

It was no wonder Rachel had such a deep attraction to Luc. He possessed many of the characteristics she wanted in a man. He was intelligent, compassionate, family-oriented, financially stable, and romantic to name a few. It wasn't on the list, but he had gained her favor for being an absolutely incredible lover. When they were together, she fondly remembered how everything he did was to give her pleasure, unselfishly. She couldn't help but to love him.

Once she found out he was married, his wonderful attributes seemed insignificant. He was simply unavailable. One quality she took for granted when looking for a mate was availability, and didn't even bother to put it on the list. Luc proved she couldn't take anything for granted. As caught up as she was with him, his being married forced her to deal with the relationship realistically and move towards getting out.

Being the family man, she knew Luc was going to stay in his marriage, at least until the kids grew up. Ideally, he wanted her to wait for him, but she had no intentions of putting her life on hold until his kids turned eighteen. By then, she'd be too old to have kids of her own. His youngest one wasn't even in kindergarten. And so long as he was still living at home with his wife, another child could spring up at any time. Rachel accepted that he was anything but available.

From the list of twelve, the three characteristics Luc failed in were biggies. He didn't go to church, couldn't be trusted, and already had kids. Rachel had trusted Luc with all aspects of her personal life, except with the most important thing, her unwavering love. She was smart enough to know that if he could cheat on his wife, then someday he would cheat on her. Whenever she was able to see clearly, she recognized him as a 'cheat'. By being with a married man, she was considered no better than him. Her focus was on cleaning this relationship up, once and for all. She needed to get free from this stronghold in her life. Her relationship with Ken had brought about a change in her. She wanted a clean slate before getting married. All loose ends had to be tied up. Whatever sexual and/or romantic sins she committed in the past were exactly that, in the past. She had gone to great pains to hold back from having sex with Ken, so everything could be picture-perfect. She wasn't going to let Luc ruffle her feathers now.

The bottom line was, he was untrustworthy. There were times when Rachel wanted to believe his wife, Aysha, was some mean witch or simply inadequate. Luc always said he and Aysha grew apart over the years. They were young and dumb when they got married. They married for the wrong reasons. There was no love left between them. They stayed together for the kids. Rachel was his true love. Luc wished he'd met her long before hooking-up with Aysha, and so on, and so on. Even if all of it was true, he was still married to the woman. If it was that bad, he would have been out of there long ago. As much as Rachel loved him and wanted to believe his tales, deep down she knew he was lying. Whether Luc knew he was lying was a different story.

He never had to tell her, but she knew he and his wife were still having sex. Why not? They were married, and still sleeping in the same bed. It used to bother Rachel to know Luc and Aysha were sexually involved, particularly right after he'd been with her. When Rachel finally came to her senses, she realized how absurd her feelings were. As long as Aysha and Luc were married, he was going to have his cake and eat it, too. Through much anguish, Rachel had decided two years before that Aysha deserved a chance to hold her marriage together, without any distractions. It was no less than Rachel would want as a women with kids, clinging to a struggling marriage, and a roving husband.

Rachel knew all about his wife, but she was sure Aysha knew nothing of her. There were times when she wanted Aysha to know she existed. No matter how Rachel felt about Luc, she didn't want to be labeled the other woman, begging and clawing for a few moments here and there. Rachel wanted Aysha to know she was a major threat. She wanted to feel validated and significant in his life. What better way than to let the wife know. Somehow, she knew it would only end up hurting Luc, and any future relationship she could possibly have with him. So, she never followed through with the urge. Now, she was getting emotional freedom from him. Rachel was glad she hadn't done anything stupid. It would have been something else to feel guilty about and have to get over later.

How sad, she thought. Two women, a wife and a lover, both catering to the needs of a man in the middle. In the end, it wasn't Luc, only the women who ended up hurt. Regardless of how she felt at any given time, Rachel believed in giving the wife her respect. It was the least she would want if the tables were turned. Being the other woman never felt right. One day, she finally realized that being with Luc enabled him to stay with his wife. She filled the void he had in his life by satisfying some basic needs, like peace-and-quiet, compatibility, adventure, and romance, without any responsibility. Rachel was his good-time girl. Time with her was all free. His wife and kids satisfied other needs, like stability and comfort. Coupling the two life styles allowed Luc to be completely fulfilled. It was Rachel and Aysha who were settling for second best, getting half a man and accepting it.

A significant part of Rachel was excited to spring the news of the engagement on him. Deep down, she wanted him to feel a small portion of the disappointment she had felt with him over the years. "Luc, I'm getting married."

"Getting married! Why, congratulations. I'm happy for you, but my heart is breaking at the same time. I was hoping we could be together."

With the engagement ring on her finger, and Ken on her mind, Rachel felt confident that the fantasy with Luc was over, once and for all. The confidence came through in her words to him. "Luc, you have a family all to yourself. Please, let me go so I can have one. Let me have that."

Luc couldn't discount her request if he truly loved her as much as he said. Love meant being able to let go. As always, Luc presented himself as a suave gentleman.

He reluctantly responded, "Rachel, I wish you the best."

"Thank you, Luc. That means a lot to me."

"Rachel, remember, you're still my Precious, and always will be."

"Thanks."

"Bye."

It wasn't easy saying goodbye to Luc and ultimately closing the chapter in her life, but thank God she did. The baggage going into the marriage was starting to get lighter and lighter. She was glad Luc hadn't called last summer when she had desperately wanted companionship. Even married, he would have beat out Gary, hands down.

23

"I'd like to order the two-pizza special."

Rachel was trying to balance the phone between her ear and shoulder, while ripping the forty percent off coupon from the flyer.

"Yeah, one barbecue chicken with the caramelized onions. Make the other one a veggie with extra cheese."

Ken grabbed his keys from the counter, gave Rachel a kiss on the cheek, and headed for the door.

She was waving the coupon at him. "Excuse me," she said to the person taking the order over the phone. "Ken, honey, here."

He came back to get the jaggedly ripped piece of paper.

"Don't forget the cider and some cinnamon sticks."

"Yep, I got it," he confirmed, holding up the crumpled list of all the things Rachel wanted him to get on his standard Friday night food and fun run.

"Okay, I'm sorry," Rachel said as she turned her attention back to the phone. "The name is Sanders. Someone will be there to pick it up in about twenty minutes. Oh yeah, throw in some garlic breadsticks. Thanks."

Rachel hung-up the phone and went to put the rug back up to the door. On a cold Chicago day, it was all she could do to keep the draft out.

Ring. Ring.

She knew it was the pizza place calling back to verify the order.

"Hello."

There was silence.

"Hello," Rachel said, with her voice raised.

"Oh, Rachel?"

"Yes."

"Hi, It's …"

"Sandra," Rachel cut in.

"Yes, how did you know?"

"I'm good at recognizing voices.

"Good for you. How are you doing?"

"Great," Rachel enthusiastically answered. "How have you been since the surgery?"

"Surgery!" Sandra was surprised Rachel knew about the surgery, given she had only told Ken. "Oh, Kenny must have told you?"

"Yes, he did."

She felt good about letting Sandra know Ken shared his personal information with her. Rachel was polite, but sharp with Sandra. She hadn't forgotten about the Thanksgiving stunt Sandra pulled.

"I'm surprised. He usually keeps everything confidential."

"Perhaps, but we can't keep a marriage together with secrets."

"Marriage! Did you two get married?"

"Oh, no."

"Oh." Sandra breathed a sigh of relief. "I was going to say."

"Not until next summer."

"Next summer! You're getting married."

"Uhm, humn."

"To Kenny?"

"Yes, to Ken." Rachel wanted to say, "To who else," but decided to let it go.

"Uh, when did this happen?"

"Valentine's Day."

"Whoa. Recently! Kenny didn't say anything about it."

"I'm not surprised. We've only told close family and friends, so far. I'm sure he will get around to telling you, too."

Sandra was speechless. It was an indication to Rachel that she was ticked off.

"By the way, I'd love for Ariel to be the flower girl. But, we have plenty of time to talk about that."

"Yeah, well congratulations."

Rachel knew it wasn't sincere, but didn't care. "Thank you."

"Look, uhm, is Kenny there."

"Nope, but I will tell him you called."

"All right. Tell him it's important."

"I sure will, but you know how slow he is about getting back to you." Rachel felt smug about the indirect way of letting Sandra know she wasn't a priority with Ken. "Take care and tell Ariel I said hello."

"Yeah, okay."

"Bye, Sandra."

"Bye, Rachel."

When Rachel hung up the phone, she felt good about putting Sandra in her place. The evening was well on its way to being fulfilling.

Rachel's internal clock went off, and her eyes slowly opened to the faint sunlight coming through the thin curtains in Ken's apartment. The TV was off, which meant Ken must have awakened in the middle of the night and turned it off. Friday night and Saturday morning generally followed the same routine. The two would, unsuccessfully, try to watch a bunch of movies, but were usually too tired to make it through the stack. The movie marathon was a great way for them to innocently spend the night together without much effort.

Once she got her bearings, Rachel hopped up in a frenzy. Ken was still asleep on the sofa. There was an entire list of errands she needed to do for the day. She also needed to go and feed Boots. She got her purse, shoes, and tipped out without waking Ken. She figured it would probably take a few hours to run the errands, a couple more to do work around the house, and another two hours or so for her sorority meeting. If all went as planned, she expected to be back at his place by 4:00, in time to cook dinner. She was in too much of a rush to leave a note, so opted to call back later and communicate her itinerary for the day.

When she got home, she wasted no time getting the laundry together. She hurriedly split the clothes into three piles, and tossed one load into the machine. The hardest thing about dating was finding the time to consistently keep up with her chores and paper work. It seemed like every free moment was dedicated to Mr. Sanders. Everything else seemed to get, at best, second priority.

Boots wasn't getting much attention these days. Whenever Rachel was home the cat was spastic, running around, and jumping on everything. Today, Boots was on top of her pile of dirty clothes.

"Boots, I see you. You don't have to do all this for attention. I guess it's the male in you."

Rachel noticed the full bin of mail was in need of some serious attention. As she was getting comfortable in the sun room, the phone rang. She glanced at the clock. Since it was still early, she suspected it to be Ken. She couldn't think of anyone else who would be calling on a Saturday morning. Normally she would guess Neal, but he was still on business in Australia. So, Ken it was.

She grabbed the phone while trying to balance the stack of mail on her lap. "Good morning."

"Good morning," Neal greeted.

Pleasantly surprised, she responded, "Hey, Mr. Pierce. What a surprise. I looked at the clock when the phone rang and just assumed it was Ken."

"That's you, guessing wrong. Well, it's not Ken. It's the other man in your life. The consistent one." The off-handed statement generated a chuckle from Rachel.

"Yes, you are. How's it going, and when are you coming back?"

"It's going fine and I should be back around Wednesday, if all goes well."

"Good. We haven't gotten together for lunch in a long time. What about Thursday or Friday?" she asked.

"That should be fine. It all depends on what happens here over the next couple of days. I'll let you know, either way. Actually, I'm surprised to catch you at home on a Saturday morning."

"Why so?" Rachel surprisingly asked.

Neal laughed before responding. "You know, Fridays at Sanders'." Neal was hinting at the romantic interludes that occurred every Friday.

"Oh, please. All we do is watch a bunch of movies," trying to discourage Neal from believing what seemed to be obvious.

"Uhm, huh. Yep," sounding unconvinced by her voluntary explanation.

"Really." She, unsuccessfully, attempted to add credibility to her statement.

"Rach, you don't have to convince me." He enjoyed harassing Rachel about her men. There had been many opportunities over the years to needle her.

"But I don't want to give you the wrong impression." Neal was the one person she never had to impress.

"The impression doesn't come from what you tell me; it's all in what you show me. Hey, Rach, it's me, Neal. You know no matter what you do, whether I agree or not, I'm going to support you. Haven't I always?"

"Yes, you have," Rachel stated with confidence.

"And, as far as Mr. Sanders goes, all I can say is follow your heart."

"Thanks, Neal. I needed to hear that."

Even with their joking, Neal detected a somber tone in her voice. He knew her so well. She didn't have to tell him when something was bothering her. He knew it from her mannerisms, and in this case, her tone prompted him to find out what was going on.

"Rach, what's up?"

"Nothing," Rachel responded unconvincingly.

"Uhn uhn. Something is up. Girl, I know you."

"I'm okay."

"Listen to me Rach, I know something is bothering you. If you want to talk, I'm here. If you want to tell me later, that's okay too, but whatever you do, don't tell me everything's okay. I know better. It's in your voice."

"All right. I'm thinking about Ken." Rachel loved Neal's ability to interpret her emotions without her always having to spell them out. Many times in the past, he figured out what was going on with her when it had been too painful for her to explain. She couldn't ask for more in a friend.

"What about him?" Neal worried.

"It's not him so much as it is this thing with Sandra."

"That's the baby's mother, right?"

"Right."

"What about her?"

"She called Ken's a couple of times last night, and it left an uncomfortable feeling with me."

"Why? Did she say something to you?"

"Nothing out of line. I did tell her about the engagement."

"How did that come up?"

"We were just talking, and I mentioned it."

"How did she react?" Neal curiously asked.

"Cordial, but I could tell that girlfriend didn't like it."

"And ..."

"And what?" Rachel asked for clarification.

"If she's the same woman who pulled the Thanksgiving stunt, then I'm sure she has a hidden agenda that includes Ken, and not you."

"That's what I was thinking. You know, I'm just not up for any confrontations with this woman, but I do sense some trouble brewing."

"Did you tell Ken how you feel?"

"Yes, I did."

"And, what did he say?"

"He assured me that Sandra is not a threat. He was adamant about his only involvement with her being Ariel."

"Do you believe him?"

"I guess so!"

"Good."

"Why you say that?"

"Because, I wanted to hear you say that you trust the man. If you're going to marry him, you have to trust him. Not only in the little things, but the big ones, too. Just take him at his word, until he proves otherwise."

"I guess you're right."

She knew Neal was right. For some odd reason, she couldn't explain, Ken hadn't gotten the check for being trustworthy. It wasn't like he'd done anything in favor or against getting it. Until now, it hadn't been an issue. She decided he did deserve the benefit of the doubt, and elevated him to eight points.

"No sense trying to fix the relationship if it's not broken," Rachel jovially stated.

"Sounds like you're feeling better, my dear."

"Yes, I am," Rachel cheerfully sounded.

"Good. Now I can get back to work and earn some money to pay for this call. It's probably going to cost over twenty bucks for these few minutes. By the way, why is it every time you go through a bad relationship, it always ends up costing me?"

"Maybe it's the price of our friendship?"

"At this price, who needs friends," he chuckled. "Talk to you soon. Like I said, I'll be back Wednesday. In the meantime, get a hold of me if you need to talk."

"You know I will."

"Yes. I know. Take care Rach."

"See ya, Neal."

After talking to her buddy, Rachel was feeling much better. She agreed with Neal. It didn't make sense to make a problem when there wasn't one. For the moment, Sandra was Ken's problem and not hers to worry about. As far as she was concerned, that was fine.

Time was zipping by and she still had a lot to do before the sorority meeting. She quickly rushed through the mail and wrote out the checks for her bills. She slammed the last load of clothes in the washer and ran to get dressed.

Afterwards, she grabbed up the items that needed to go to the cleaners, the post office, and the grocery list. She put the sheets and towels in the dryer, turned it on high, grabbed the keys off the counter, and headed for the door. On second thought, she decided to give Ken a call and let him know she'd be over by 4:00. She dialed his number in haste, and oddly enough his line was busy. She didn't have time to call back, so she left without talking to him.

24

When she walked into the community center's meeting room, several of her sorority sisters had already arrived. One lady turned to Rachel and said, "Soror, where have you been? We missed you at both the Jabberwock and the Art Auction."

"I've been so busy. How did they go? Did we make any money?" Rachel asked.

"They turned out nice. All together, we made about 13,500 dollars for the scholarship fund."

"Great."

"Busy, huh? What's keeping you so busy?"

"It must be a man," one of the younger sorors suggested.

Rachel blushed, but didn't respond.

"Yep, it's a man," someone else chimed in.

"You know the sorority takes a back seat when a man's on the scene."

Another soror grabbed Rachel's left hand looking for a ring.

"Ooooh. What's this?"

"You're engaged!" one of the ladies huddled around Rachel shockingly blurted.

"Engaged!" another responded.

"No wonder you've been a no-show to a lot of the functions," the fourth soror reacted.

"Honey, come on over here, sit down, and tell us all about this man."

"You got a picture of him?"

"Yes," Rachel smiled. She eagerly pulled his picture from her wallet, and the women took a glance.

"Oh girl, he is fine."

"You go, soror," another said.

All kind of questions were flying at Rachel from the five or six women surrounding her.

"When did you meet?"

"When's the big day? You know we're singing the Sweetheart song."

"Wait, wait, wait. I can't answer all of these questions at one time. First, I met him last summer. We got engaged on Valentine's Day. He's never been married, and we'll probably get married next summer." She chose to leave out the fact that he had an illegitimate child, with a potentially clinging ex. She would mention it only on a need-to-know basis.

"Good for you," the older soror said.

"Congratulations, soror."

"Yeah, congratulations. We'll talk more about it as the time gets closer."

Rachel was the topic of several side conversations during the main meeting. She was glad today's meeting was on time, and more importantly, it was ending at 3:00, as scheduled. She had enough time to stop at the grocery store and still get to Ken's by 4:00.

She thought about calling him on the cellular phone to let him know the meeting was over, and she was on her way. She rarely used the phone. The only reason she got it in the first place was to appease Neal. He got tired of her old car breaking down here and there, all times of the day and night. After much coaxing from him, she got the phone. Even she agreed, her road service wouldn't help if there was no way to contact them. To be sure, she rumbled through the glove compartment, and then felt under the seat. To the best of her recollection, the phone was in the trunk. Rachel decided there was really no need to call ahead, since she'd be at Ken's shortly.

She was right on schedule. At about ten minutes to four, she pulled into Ken's parking lot. She grabbed the two bags of groceries and headed for his apartment. Instead of ringing the buzzer and bothering him, she used her access card to enter the building. Approaching the apartment door, she juggled the bags in an effort to find the right key. When she opened the door, she could hear him and someone else talking. It sounded like he was in the bedroom. The tiny apartment made it easy for her to hear a conversation going on in the bedroom very clearly from the living room. The bags were heavy. She sat them down on the kitchen counter before doing anything else. Rachel eased the door closed and took off her coat. Ken was engrossed into his conversation, and he didn't hear her come in.

"I didn't get the money this month. Did you mail it, or were you too busy running around with your little girlfriend?" bellowed the voice over the speakerphone.

"What are you talking about Sandra?" Ken snipped at her.

"I talked to Miss Rowina last night, and she gave me the scoop on your Valentine's Day getaway, and the so-called engagement."

"And …"

"And you can't keep up with your funky little child support payments, but you can sure come up with money to wine and dine Miss Rochelle."

"Please. I don't want to hear this mess."

"Don't you think I have a right to know?"

"No," he calmly but firmly stated.

"No!" Sandra angrily yelled. "No?" she repeated as if she'd misunderstood him.

"What part of 'no' don't you understand Sandra." Ken's voice was elevated.

"Look Romeo, you can't just bring some strange woman around my daughter, and I not know who she is! I told you that at Thanksgiving. Have you forgotten, already."

"Listen, for one it's not your business who I see. Two, I don't question who you see, although, I'm sure you want me to. And for the record, not that it matters, you had nothing to do with my decision to leave Ariel here, Thanksgiving, instead of taking her to Michigan with me and Rachel."

"Yeah, right."

"Anyway, here's the bottom line. Sandra, I am engaged to Rachel. We're getting married. If you have a problem with it, keep it to yourself, because frankly I don't really care what you think, or how you feel about my personal life. And, when you call my house, I expect, no, I demand that you treat Rachel with respect. Otherwise you're not going to be calling here at all. Got that? Oh yeah, one more thing." Ken stood up in anticipation of ending the call. Slowly and distinctively Ken said, "Get the name right! It's Rachel. Not Rowina, Phoegina, Rochelle, or whatever else you think you might want to call her. Sandra, I am not going for your crap."

The only reaction Ken got from his demands was "click" from Sandra slamming the receiver on the hook.

Rachel heard everything. The Thanksgiving comment didn't sit too well with her. She remembered him saying Ariel wasn't going, because he wanted to spend time, alone, with Rachel. If Sandra did influence the trip, then Ken had lied, and was in jeopardy of losing his newly earned point for being trustworthy. She was taken aback. She didn't know whether to let Ken know she was there or not. Really, she wanted to disappear into thin air. That way, she could spare them both the embarrassment which was bound to occur from her overhearing this little conversation. She briefly considered just sneaking out, but what if he heard her. Her heart was racing. She was standing in the kitchen trying to build up enough courage to confront this awkward mess.

She took a step towards the bedroom, and heard the phone ring. The voice was unmistakably Sandra, again. The woman was really trippin'. Sandra had just hung up on Ken and now, thirty seconds later, she was calling back.

"I decided not to let you off that easy, Don Juan." It was Sandra's pathetic attempt to get his attention. "What do you want, Sandra," Ken disgustingly asked. The sharp tone in his voice indicated Ken was annoyed with Sandra, but he let it slide, without going off on her.

"What do I want! Don't you know? You have a child. Be a man, show some responsibility. If you can't be a man and take care of your child, then I'll have the law make you do it."

"Oh, not this again. Surely you can be more original than this."

"It's a shame you have to let 'the system' tell you how and when to take care of your child. You sure didn't seem to need any help getting me pregnant."

"Whatever, Sandra. Money hasn't been an issue before. You know I always send you something and buy extra things for Ariel, whenever you ask. What's the big deal now, or don't I know."

"Tell you what, I don't want this piece-meal money anymore. You don't want me to call your place in fear of offending the princess."

Ken interrupted in a bitter tone. Rachel could tell he was growing tired of Sandra's snide remarks. "Rachel doesn't have anything to do with this, Sandra. Face the real issue."

Although he didn't come right out and say it, Rachel wondered if he was alluding to Sandra's jealousy.

"Fine. Let's just get everything straightened out here. Starting next month, I want the amount of money the court says you should pay. What is it, twenty percent plus child care? In case you can't count too well, that's 96 dollars a week, unless you've gotten a raise. I want it next month, and if you think I'm joking, try me."

"Listen woman, haven't you learned yet, your little games don't move me. That's not going to get me back," he smugly stated.

"You are so full of yourself. Why would I want you back?" she bitterly asked.

"You tell me. You're always sweatin' me, every opportunity you get."

"Man please. Don't flatter yourself. We have a daughter together, or have you forgotten."

"Right, right. How could I forget? That's all I hear from you. Get a life, Sandra. What is it? Can't you find a man out there?"

"Another sorry-tail man like you! I don't think so."

"Maybe that's what you need, a man."

"Maybe you need to handle your business," she threw back.

"Look, this is nice, but I have to go. Believe it or not Sandra, I have something else to do with my time, other than jack around with you."

"This is not over, Kenny, not by a long shot."

"Well one thing is over, that's this conversation. Later," and Ken hung up, without giving Sandra time to respond. Unlike other nights, this time he was quite vocal on the phone with Sandra. He walked into the living room, which was adjacent to the kitchen. Rachel was standing in his view. His eyes enlarged and mouth flew open. Ken was surprised to see her standing there. The sheepish look on her face confirmed she had heard the sordid details.

"So, you heard," he awkwardly asked.

"Yes, I did, and it didn't sound too good."

"Sandra's trippin'," was all he could offer as an explanation of the embarrassing conversation.

"Why?"

"Who knows, although I have my ideas. Regardless of what her reason is, I'm not letting her get away with it. I'm not going to pay her any more money. I'm tired of her threatening me with Ariel. This last episode settles it. I'm going to do something about it."

"Like what?"

"I've been thinking about us raising Ariel. After we get married, we'll be a better family for Ariel than Sandra is by herself. That way, I won't have to pay her the money."

Ken's use of 'us' was a surprise to Rachel. They never talked about joint custody before. She knew he was coming to the marriage with a daughter. It hadn't been a serious problem. Ariel and, more importantly, Sandra, lived almost 400 miles away. Normally Rachel didn't hook-up with men who had children. She avoided getting in the crossfire between ex-lovers. The distance had given Ken the benefit of the doubt. Now, he was talking about, or at least thinking about making a major change to their relationship, without her input. This was starting to sound a bit uncomfortable. She was hoping the dust would settle between Sandra and Ken, over the next couple of days, and things would get back to normal. The sooner the better for everyone.

Ken was eager to change the subject, or at least get the focus off of Sandra. The grocery bags sitting on the kitchen counter were a perfect out.

"So, what's for dinner?"

Trying to muster up some enthusiasm, Rachel responded with "lasagna and a salad."

She lost interest in cooking up the pan of lasagna. She somehow wanted to talk this thing out, but Ken was not on the same wavelength. There was no sense rocking the boat on the subject. For sure it would come up again. She knew his question about dinner was an attempt to move from the matter, and she decided to let him have that one.

"Sounds good." He knew everything wasn't okay right now, but he appreciated Rachel giving him some room and not pushing the issue any further. An argument with Sandra was enough. He definitely didn't want a repeat performance with Rachel. He pulled her close and gave her a kiss on the forehead to reassure her everything was going to be fine. He didn't want her to start worrying, unnecessarily.

It didn't take long to whip up dinner. Before long, the two had finished eating and were washing the last of the dishes.

"Rachel, the dinner was scrumptious," Ken complementcd.

"Scrumptious! That's a new one. You don't usually use that term."

"I know, but I've told you so many times how good your cooking is. I didn't want to bore you with the same old praises."

She smiled in acknowledgment. "Thank you, Mr. Sanders. I'm glad you like my cooking. I get it honest from my grand-mother."

"No doubt. Even her left-overs from Thanksgiving were good. I can only imagine how one of Big Mama's fresh meals must be."

"Yeah, just ask Neal. Between his mom and Big Mama, he traditionally puts on a few extra pounds around the holidays."

"Ah, Neal. How is old Neal?"

"Fine."

"Is he seeing anyone these days?"

"He's still seeing Nicole. Why?"

"I'm just surprised."

"Why are you surprised?"

"Just surprised, that's all." Ken offcred no further explanation for his vague comment.

What did he mean? She contemplated whether or not to inquire further and find out where Ken was going with the discussion, but decided to drop it. She didn't want to touch his last comment with a ten-foot pole. With Sandra, custody, and child support hanging over their head, there were bigger fish to fry. Whatever Ken was trying to say about Neal would have to be done at some other time.

"Want to watch the rest of the movies? We still didn't see two of the tapes." Ken was clearly making every effort to diffuse the tension generated by Sandra, and get Rachel back on even keel.

The evening hadn't started off right, and she didn't want to sit there with a semi-nasty attitude. That could only make things worse. She decided to tactfully excuse herself for the evening and start fresh tomorrow with some of the tension behind them.

She put her arms around Ken and gave him a hug, before leaving. So they could have eye to eye contact, he lifted her up and sat Rachel on the countertop.

"Honey, I'm really tired. I also need to finish my laundry. I better go on home and get some odds and ends done. Maybe I can start the week off organized, for a change."

"What about church tomorrow? You know it's family day at Dad's."

Rachel loved the gatherings at Red's. She was smart enough to recognize that, like it or not, marrying Ken included marrying the family. Thank goodness the family part was working out great, better than she could have hoped.

"Of course, I'll go. I wouldn't miss an opportunity for Red to give me another history lesson."

"Uh huh. You just don't want to miss an opportunity for Dad to tell you how pretty you are."

"Hey. That too," she smiled from the flattery.

"Well, if that's all it takes to get a smile from you, I can tell you how pretty you are right now. No sense getting beat out by an old man."

Playfully she said, "If it makes you feel good, go ahead. I won't stop you." She was thankful that the awkwardness had eased for them both. She was still going home with the intent of starting over tomorrow, with some rest under her belt, and hopefully a fresh attitude.

After Rachel left, Ken hung his pants in the closet and stretched out on the bed, with his back against the headboard. There was so much on his mind. Deep down, he wanted to be a good father. If things had worked out better with Sandra, he could have been. Ariel was still young. He still had a chance to make a stronger bond with her. Since the engagement, he had been feeling nostalgic. He was ready for a family, wife, and a couple of kids. The wife was already in place, with the wedding no more than a year away.

Everything was falling in place, that is, if he could get his finances straightened out, and get some money saved to cover the wedding. He might even be able to buy a little house. He knew his place was too small for two people, and, being full of pride, there was no way he could move into Rachel's house. He viewed himself as the 'man', and needed to provide the roof over their heads. His plans were in trouble if Sandra carried out her threat. She couldn't have started to cause trouble at a worse time.

Ken pondered and pondered about what he could do. After a couple of hours had elapsed, all of a sudden he sat straight up in the bed and smiled. He had come up with a solution. He leaned over, picked up the phone, and started to dial Sharon's number.

25

It was too cold to keep the front door open, so Rachel periodically peeped out of the picture window to see if he had arrived. Right on time, as usual. When he pulled up, she ran out to the car and hopped right in, before he had a chance to get out. Usually, he opened and closed the car door for her, but she felt it too cold, today, for him to be concerned with chivalry. She leaned over and gave him a kiss, and then strapped on her seat belt.

"Uhm, you smell good, " he complemented.

"Thank you." She fully embraced her femininity and enjoyed being complemented by a tasteful gentleman.

"Did you sleep well?"

"Sure did. I'm ready for this day." The awkwardness of last night seemed light years away to her.

"And you?"

"So, so," Ken responded.

"What does that mean?"

"Let's just say I gave a lot of thought to the business with Sandra. I thought about it most of the night. I came to the conclusion that I really do want to improve my relationship with Ariel. I've always wanted to have a family, a wife and kids, all living under the same roof. That's how I grew up, and I want the same thing for my kids."

"That's reasonable. Our getting married is the first step towards that goal," Rachel pointed out.

"That's another thing."

"What?" She really had no idea what he was getting ready to say.

"If Sandra is able to get the child support she wants from me, then it is going to put a dent in the amount of money I can save for our wedding. My goal was to get all my bills paid off, save enough for the wedding, and a few other things."

"You know I'm going to help." She had managed to bank a few bucks over the past five years, thanks to the returns on her investments. She never expected him to pay all of the upcoming marital expenses by himself. They hadn't specifically talked about his salary, but Rachel assumed she would need to chip in, based on her estimation of his financial status. Unless he'd gotten a big inheritance from his mother's death, she didn't expect him to have a great deal of money squirreled away. Her speculations about Ken's financial stability were based solely on his initial proposal to delay the wedding, until he got some money together.

"I've made some decisions, but we'll have to talk about it later."

Later, she thought! Why couldn't they talk now. She was upset with his insensitivity. She wanted, or needed to talk now. When he refused last night, she had let it slide. How long did he expect her to keep silent? Rachel was fuming, as she considered the possibility that he'd made a major decision without her, his soon-to-be wife. Lucky for Ken, they were only minutes from the church. There was not ample time to force the discussion. This was definitely going to be continued later.

As usual, church was long and entertaining. No concentration was required. Today, this kind of service was perfect for her, because she had other things on her mind. Really, only one thing was on her mind, Ken's business with Sandra and Ariel.

The ride to Red's was pleasant, but quiet. Rachel didn't have much to say, and neither did Ken.

As soon as they hit the door, Red had them into a conversation. He had a natural way of drawing anyone around him in and generating a lot of fun. A few minutes with Red and already she was feeling much better.

"Junior, where are the two tickets to the Bulls game? You told me I'd have them for the Houston game. Next Friday will be here fore you know it. We are still going aren't we?"

"Next Friday. Ah nah. Ah Dad, I can't make it," remembering his other commitment.

"You!" Red proceeded to put his arm around Rachel's neck and pulled her closer to him. "Ah man. Ain't nobody talking about you going. You just buying the tickets. It's for my birthday. That means I can take whoever I want to with that other ticket." He turned to Rachel and asked, "You don't have any plans next Friday, do ya?" They all started laughing.

"Dad, you crazy," Ken laughed. Rachel was cheesing from the flattery. After all these months, she was accustomed to Red's humor and took no offense.

"I really would be crazy if I chose to take you over Rachel." Red never meant any harm with his comments. He was a cool Dad who was comfortable with his kids and their friends. Rachel adored Red. He reminded her of Pa-Pa. Since all of the elder men in her life had passed, Red was as close as she was going to get to a father-figure. And, he was just fine by her.

She was the first one to notice Brendon coming in. "I don't believe it," she blurted out. "You actually got here while it's still light outside." She got along well with Ken's family. They embraced her like a sister, and she loved it. Being an only child, she generally took to larger families.

"Yeah, yeah, sis. What's up?" Brendon gave her a kiss on the cheek. "What up Bro? Hey Red."

"Hey yourself. You may have gotten here on time for a change, but you still came empty-handed. Boy, I tell ya. I ain't never seen somebody freeload so much and always got a smile."

"He's a happy free-loader Dad," Ken pointed out.

"Boy, you can sho' put a hurting on a barbecue."

No matter how he joked about not wanting his kids around, Rachel knew how much Red loved the presence of his family, particularly with his wife gone. "You love it when we come over. Don't you Red?" Rachel added.

Brendon leaned over Red's chair and gave him a hug around the neck. "I know you miss me. Dad."

"Yeah, about as much as I miss my hemorrhoids." Rachel and Ken burst into laughter. It was easy to laugh when Red was on someone else's case.

"Ah man, how you gonna treat a brother."

Red always had a quick comeback. "Huh, I wish you were only my brother. I coulda gotten rid of your butt a long time ago. It's different with your own kids. They never leave. I thought all I had to do was raise you up to eighteen, and that would be it. I believe I've seen you just as much since you turned eighteen as I did when you were a child." No matter what Red said to the boys in jest, the truth was, he loved them dearly. They all knew it.

Brendon turned his focus to Ken. "Hey man, I heard about your plans. That takes a lot of courage. More power to you brother. I don't think I could do it."

"What?" Ken wondered.

"The thing with Ariel. You know, the custody thing."

Custody thing, overheard Rachel. What was he talking about? She had only been partially listening to Brendon up to this point, but now she was all ears. He must be mistaken.

Ken had only hinted at the notion of custody last night, in a moment of extreme outrage with Sandra she declared. Rachel hadn't taken the thought of seeking custody seriously. She wondered if he could decide on something major like that overnight. She chose to believe Mr. Ken hadn't made any major decisions without her input, and most certainly had not gone further to convey it to the family. Sleeping dogs just didn't want to lie down. This custody issue kept rearing its ugly head. Red put her in a good mood, and now she was about to spiral back down into a funky attitude.

"How did you hear about it?" Ken curiously asked.

'Where did he hear about it' was all he could ask! She didn't care when or where he heard it. Rachel just wanted to know if it was true. She was wondering why Ken wasn't at this very moment clearing up this obvious bit of confusion with his brother. She was biting her tongue so as not to jump into the conversation, prematurely, and make a bad matter worse.

"I talked to Sharon this morning and she told me."

"Oh."

If Brendon talked to Sharon this morning, then Rachel knew that could only mean one thing. After she left Ken last night, he made a decision and shared it with his sister. Rachel couldn't decide which was worse, Ken excluding her from the decision, or telling his sister before telling her. Neither felt good. By now she was practically biting her tongue off. All she could hope for was that there was some type of miscommunication. Clearly, this was not the right time to ask for clarification. She'd wait till later, and resolve it in private. She was sure Ken could explain the matter and put all of this craziness behind them and get back to the business of being happily engaged. Rachel had waited too long to get a man like Ken. She wasn't about to let some outside force, like Sandra, destroy an eight-month relationship with a thirty minute temper tantrum. If this relationship was going to struggle, it would be at her own hand, and not at Miss Sandra's.

Red was ready to eat. "I know Dana and Terry are still at the marriage retreat in Rockford, but where are Sharon and Nick? I'm hungry."

"They will be by later. Nick had some kind of special AA meeting today, a reunion or something like that. I don't know," Brendon explained.

"AA meeting on Sunday?" Red asked with a puzzled look.

"They meet all the time," Ken said.

"Ya know, I forget that Nick used to be an addict. He's come so far," Red proudly stated.

"He definitely got himself together, and then some," Ken agreed.

"Nick's all right with me. Rachel, did you know that I can count on him more than my own boys?" Red was too much. He talked about Brendon and Ken as though they weren't even in the room. "If Junior doesn't get our tickets soon, I'll have to ask Nick."

"Go ahead, Red. You're really going to hurt me by getting someone else to spend a hundred bucks on you. I'm really heartbroken."

"See what I told you."

No matter how they tried, Ken and Brendon weren't as quick-witted as their father. Red had a rapid-fire comeback for every comment. Even with the disturbing conversation earlier, Rachel couldn't help but feel jovial around Red. He had that way with people.

"Nick's your favorite boy now, huh. It's a good thing Nick got cleaned up before he came into this family, because Dad would

have made it hard on him. Remember, Brendon, how Dad u.
treat those crack-heads when we lived on Woodley."

The vivid picture came rushing back to Brendon's memory
and he chuckled at the thought. "Man, that was twenty-five years
ago, and I still remember Dad acting a fool in front of the house,
with his baseball bat. It's a good thing Mama was around then,
otherwise our father might have become a jailbird."

"You better believe it. Them drug-heads were taking over.
Look, I ain't got no shame saying I don't allow no crack-head, pot-
head, wine-head, or no other kind-of-head up in my house. Nick
about the only crack-head I allow in my house, and that's cause he
over all of that foolishness."

"He's not a crack-head. He used to be addicted to heroin, not
cocaine."

"So what. To a VCR, a crack-head and a heroin addict are all
the same."

"You a mess, Dad."

"Shoot. I'm old and can't smell and can't see too good,
neither. I ain't hardly gone be following a wine-head around to see
if he's going to pee in a corner. I'm sure not going to tail a dope-
head around my house to make sure he doesn't steal anything.
Truth be told, I prefer the wine-head over the crack-head."

"Why is that Dad?" Ken was attempting to egg him on.

"Cause a wino will get a nip and go on to sleep. They don't
usually bother nobody once they get a taste. But a crack-head never
goes to sleep. They will sit you out. They wait until you start to
look sleepy and try to act like they going to the bathroom. If you
don't watch out, that's when they get you. I ain't replacing nothing
around here. What I got now is in retirement, just like me. Them
dope-heads can move out a whole house in two hours flat. They
can steal, sell, and be high, all in two hours, and you know I'm right
about it."

Laughter filled the kitchen, and Rachel forgot about her
concerns. They seemed secondary to the wonderful afternoon she
was having with her extended family. Time seemed to fly by and
before she realized, it was almost 7:00. Ken noticed the time and
jumped up to get the coats.

"Rachel, are you ready?"

"Nah, she ain't ready. You go on. I'll give her a ride home," ⊥ joked.

"With those eyes of yours? You couldn't get out of the driveway. You've already run over one neighbor's cat, and had another close call with Mr. Smith's dog," Ken reminded.

"I can't help it if those untrained animals don't know how to look out for moving vehicles."

"Moving at thirty miles an hour into a residential driveway?" Brendon interjected.

"It ain't my fault if those driveways are too narrow for my driving machine."

"Driving machine! That's a gas-guzzling Cadillac," Brendon ridiculed.

"Ah, but it's got some power under the hood."

"Yeah, sure, Dad. Good-bye." Ken turned and walked towards the car. It was time to go, and he wasn't about to let Red pull him into another discussion.

"You sure you don't want a ride, Rachel?"

"Nah, Red. I'll let Ken drive me home so you can get some rest."

"See how well my daughters take care of me. You boys could learn something."

"See you on your birthday," Rachel affectionately stated.

"You don't have to wait for Ken to bring you by. You know the way. You're welcome anytime." Red hugged both Ken and Rachel on their way out. "Thanks for stopping by."

"My pleasure."

"I'll let you know about the tickets, Dad."

"All you need to let me know is when to pick them up from you."

"I hear you, Dad. Later."

26

Ken opened her door and Rachel got in feeling like all was well with the world, at least her small piece of it. With the tension being lightened, she decided there was no need to engage in a heavy conversation. It would be better to do it later, or better yet, maybe not at all. For now, things were good.

Before they could get to the main street, Ken broke the silence. "Rachel, I know what's on your mind and I want to get this behind us. We agreed to talk about it later and come to terms."

Come to terms! Rachel hadn't said much last night or this morning. Ken had done all of the talking. She was careful not to let her displeasure with his idea of pursuing custody show. She decided to take the low-road in broaching the subject. "I agreed to later, but you seemed to have found adequate time to discuss it with your family. Do you think that's fair?" Before he could respond, she loud talked him and continued having her say. "I know you would rather leave the issue of Ariel and Sandra alone, but I have legitimate concerns. I'm not sure if you're being inconsiderate by not addressing my concerns, or if I'm being unreasonable by asking you to address them. Either way, it's not a good feeling."

"I don't know what else to tell you. I've said Sandra is not a concern. You seem bent on making this a big deal."

It was a big deal to Rachel. She was less concerned about Sandra, and more worried about him seeking custody. Maybe it was selfish of Rachel, but she wanted to spend her first year alone, with her new husband, before taking on the role of a parent. Ken had never mentioned nor alluded to the idea that Ariel might be living with them, at least not right away. At best she could tell, he was as close as you could get to being an absentee-father without professing to be one. He sent a piece-of-money regularly, but by no means was it enough to provide for Ariel's livelihood. For him to think he was doing something big with his little lightweight contribution was ridiculous. She didn't want to broach a potentially explosive subject, but recognized the only way to get past it was to get it out on the table.

"What about Ariel?"

Ken defensively retorted, "What about Ariel?"

"You mentioned last night that she might come to stay for a while, and Brendon touched on it again today."

"And what about it! You knew I had a daughter when we got together. That's not new news."

"Yeah. I knew you had a daughter, thank you very much," she bitterly fired back. "What I didn't know is she'd be coming to stay with us, without you and I ever discussing it."

"I don't need to discuss it. She's my daughter."

"Yes, you do need to discuss it. She's your daughter, and I'm your fiancée. Have you forgotten?"

"You sound like you have a problem with my daughter?"

Rachel didn't like his tone. She could barely control her emotions. The desire to take the low-road approach was rapidly diminishing. How dare he try to go there. Mr. Absentee-Dad was all of a sudden trying to be a hands-on-father. Ken saw his daughter a couple times a year at best. He carried Ariel's picture in his wallet. That didn't impress Rachel. The ex was a problem, true enough, but the simple fact was, Sandra had sacrificed and taken care of her daughter, virtually alone.

"Don't get me wrong. I don't have a problem with you having a daughter. I do have a problem with you making major decisions without including me, particularly those that impact me. Just for the record, my problem is not with your daughter, ex-girlfriend, ex-roommate, ex-whatever, obviously, my problem is with you, your attitude, that is."

"My attitude. Huh. I wasn't the one walking around with my butt on my shoulders all day."

Rachel looked at him and her facial expression conveyed, "No, he didn't say that." She was shocked to hear such a negative comment coming from him. Didn't look like he was going to get the point for being compassionate. Before she realized it, a retort was on her lips. "I'm also not the one with the absentee-father-guilt-complex going on."

"What did you say?"

"Nothing."

"Nah. What did you say?" he demanded.

"Nothing," Rachel repeated.

She was shocked to hear herself actually arguing with him. This discussion had gone way too far. Both were testy and little was going to be solved if they pursued the issue. She decided to be quiet and not say something that would be hard to take back.

From that moment, there was complete silence in the car. The remaining thirty minute drive to her townhouse seemed to take an eternity. Both were fuming at the attitude of the other. Neither wanted to leave the conversation on such a negative note, yet, neither wanted to back down from their position. By the time Ken pulled up to her place, she had already gathered her belongings. Before he had time to say anything, she had the car door open. With her back to him, she got out and said, "I'll talk to you later." Even in the midst of anger, he was courteous enough to wait until she got inside before pulling off.

She went directly upstairs to her room. While taking off her shoes, it hit her like a ton of bricks. They just had their first major argument. This wasn't a happy ending. Sure, there had been minor differences along the way, but Rachel hadn't expected anything major like this.

"What just happened? Oh my God, what just happened? What did we do?" She slumped down on the bed and started to cry. She stayed sprawled out across the bed for a couple of hours, pondering the events of the past two days. Finally, she got up and dressed for bed, although, the last thing Rachel felt like doing was going to sleep.

She decided not to go to bed without talking to Ken. The first time she called, the line was busy. Since he had call waiting, it seemed odd. She called again. The second time, he answered. From the onset of the conversation the mood was strained. It didn't stop her from proceeding. She was determined not to let this unfortunate turn of events linger overnight. She wanted to make peace and clear the air. From his tone, it seemed like he was still angry and not as willing to resolve the dispute.

"I'm calling to let you know I was thinking about you ..."

She paused to clear her throat. She refused to let her emotions dominate the conversation.

"... and I want to make peace. I think it's safe to say that neither of us were pleased with what happened." She waited for him to respond, but he didn't say anything. She struggled to keep the conversation flowing. "Right?"

"Right," he agreed.

"I'm sorry for some of the things that I said," she apologized.

"Well, I'm glad to hear you admit you were wrong about Ariel and my situation with Sandra."

His comment came across arrogantly. It agitated Rachel, but she kept her cool. "I didn't say that. I'm apologizing for being wrong in how I said it, not necessarily in what I believe."

"What? Are we going to get into this again?"

"That wasn't my intent for calling," she sincerely stated.

"I don't know what to say. I don't know how to help you get over the problem you have with my daughter. I'm a father, plain and simple." Ken's tone was firm, but for Rachel it was still bordering on arrogance.

"I told you before, and I'll tell you again, my problem is not with your daughter. It's with your attitude."

"Perhaps you feel this way because you don't have any kids of your own. You just don't understand what it means to be a parent."

Why did he want to go there? She could feel her anger rising up with his smug and insensitive comments. Maintaining control of her responses was becoming more difficult.

"You think you do!"

"Yes, I do. I've been one for five years."

"You'd never know it," she murmured. Even though she spoke softly, he still heard it. She went further to say, "You think this will remedy your guilt of not being there when she was a baby."

"What does that mean?" he sharply asked.

"What do you think it means? By your own admission, you haven't exactly been the hands-on-father who changed diapers in the middle of the night. You weren't the one who rubbed Calamine lotion on Ariel when she had the chicken pox last year. Like it or not, it was her mother."

Regardless of how Rachel felt on a personal level, the bottom line was, Sandra was a good mother to Ariel. She had virtually raised the child alone, but for a few dollars, and a couple of shopping sprees thrown in from Ken. On a day-to-day basis, Sandra was Ariel's connection to the world. In a way, Rachel felt sorry for Sandra. She was just another sister who had gotten knocked up and left holding the baby.

"So what, I wasn't there in the past. I did the best I could."

"Did you really?"

It was easier for Ken, as a man, to get on with his life than it was for Sandra, the one bearing the child. Sending a few dollars was hardly the best he could do. He could be footloose and fancy-free for the first five to twenty years of his daughter's life, enjoy his single-hood, shirk his parenting responsibilities, save his money, hook-up with a new companion, get settled, and plop back into Ariel's life whenever ready. Sandra didn't have the luxury of turning on and off her parenting duties. Somebody had to keep Ariel alive while Ken got his fatherly act together.

"The best under the circumstances."

Rachel was unimpressed with his sorry excuses, and deducted one of his eight points. A dead-beat-dad was hardly someone who represented dependability.

"I told you I want to be more of a father to her."

"That's all well and good, but what do you really know about parenting?"

"It's not like you're an expert. Remember, you haven't raised any kids," he pointed out.

"Neither have you, and that's my point exactly. It's a big undertaking."

"I give you that, but that's my main reason for wanting to do something about it. I still say I want to be more involved with Ariel's life."

"Why now?"

"Because I'll be more stable. I'll have a wife and a home for her. Before I really settled down, it didn't make sense to even entertain such a thought as getting custody."

"You can be a part of her life, without getting custody. What makes you think Sandra's going to just let you walk in some five years later, and try to get custody of her baby."

"It's my baby too, and it's not just about what Sandra wants."

"Yeah, but she's the one who has kept the child alive for the past five years. What, you think she did that just to give you time to get your life together, only to hop up and want custody all of a sudden? Sure, it's convenient for you to want custody now, but what about last year, or the year before, or the year before that, when you were footloose and fancy-free, and it wasn't so convenient."

"Huh!" Rachel was talking too fast for Ken to interject a word into the discussion. "What about then? Why didn't you go for custody then? You can't make-up for the last five years. At least you can establish a stable relationship with her going forward. Get over the past."

"I'm not living in the past. This is about now, right now. Whether you understand it or not, I have rights to Ariel, too."

"Don't tell me. I'm the wrong one to tell. You can tell it to Sandra."

"Don't worry. I will."

"I'm sure you will," Rachel sarcastically agreed.

"Look Rachel, I don't know what you mean by your little comment, but this is strictly about my daughter."

"Is it really about your daughter Ken, or is it about control between you and Sandra?"

"What do you mean control?"

"You know, some sick power struggle between the two of you, with an innocent little child in the middle."

"Look, I'm trying not to hear this."

"Perhaps you need to hear it." Even though Ken was irritated, Rachel wasn't going to back down off of her position.

"Oh, yeah. What exactly is it that I need to hear, Rachel."

"For one, this whole thing started with Sandra asking for child support."

passed without her, even so much as, thinking about Rick. Weeks passed and pretty soon months.

Rachel decided to call Ken again. She did make an effort to pull herself together first. She didn't want him to know that she'd been crying. She pushed the speed dial and on the fourth ring, the answering machine picked up.

Ken sat in his apartment with the lights off, talking to himself. "I really do care about her." He scratched his head. "This arguing has got to stop. I get enough of this with Sandra. I just can't deal with it. I don't know why she's making such a big deal about the custody. She knew I had a child from the jump."

Both he and Rachel wanted a family. All Ken could do was shake his head in disappointment.

"We both want a family. Now that I'm working towards getting one together, why is she resisting?"

He heard the phone ringing, and decided not to answer. In case it was Rachel, he wasn't ready to talk.

She hesitated before leaving a message. She knew he was there and probably screening his calls. She considered hanging up, but decided to leave a message. She wanted to put the ball back in his court. Hours went by and no call came through. She called again and left another message slightly after midnight. It wasn't her style to call a man so many times, but Ken wasn't just anyone. He was supposedly her future husband. Surely their relationship allowed for a few extra calls of desperation.

She began her nightly ritual of slumping down to her knees and clasping her hands together in preparation for prayer. For the first time, in many months, she started to fervently pray. It was a position she hadn't taken seriously in a long time. The quick-hit with God wasn't the approach for tonight. She needed the real deal.

27

The anxiety caught up with Rachel. It was 4:00 in the morning when she woke up and looked at the clock. The bedroom light was still on. Boots jumped up onto the bed. Apparently she had fallen asleep, waiting for Ken to call back.

"Oooh." Her head was throbbing from the stress and the excessive crying. She sat up in bed, put a finger on each temple, and applied pressure. The pain subsided until she removed her fingers. She got up to get something for the pain. She preferred a headache over a heartache, any day. At least there was a quick, over-the-counter remedy for the head.

Rachel picked up the receiver and listened for the dial tone. "Boots, did you break the phone." She checked the cord to make sure it hadn't been chewed through. The phone was working.

"Why hasn't he called?"

She was looking for some reason why Ken hadn't returned her call. She was upset with him, but had still mustered up enough concern to call. She was willing to let bygones be bygones, and wondered why he couldn't do the same?

At daylight, she contemplated not going in to work. Besides being upset, she was sleepy. Her head was still aching. Since the pain medicine hadn't eased the pain, she chalked it up to a heartache, after all. Mulling over it for a while, she decided, "I'm going in. Hmmm. I'll save the vacation days for later."

All day she found herself glancing at the phone. It was too bad she couldn't call Ken. His job didn't allow him to have incoming calls. He generally called her during his lunch break. Today, lunch had come and gone with no word from Mr. Sanders. She was still disheartened about their argument, although she was starting to get angry about him being so stubborn.

She wasn't really hungry. Instead of getting a meal from the cafeteria, she bought some pretzels and juice from the vending machine. Approaching her office, she heard the phone. She broke her neck trying to get it before the voice mail kicked in. She grabbed it on the last ring.

"Hello." She was practically out of breath. In the excitement and anticipation of Ken calling, she didn't notice the telephone display.

"Hi, Rachel."

"Oh, hi, Sharon." Her tone was one of disappointment.

"I guess it wasn't who you thought."

"Not that. I was just coming back from getting a snack." She tried to clean it up. "What's up?"

"Just calling. I was hoping to see you at lunch since Nick and I missed out on Dad's yesterday. How was it?"

"We had a good time. Red was crazy, as usual. We missed you guys."

"Good. How's my brother?"

"Fine." Rachel didn't know exactly how to answer. Maybe Ken had put Sharon up to calling. Worse yet, maybe she already knew the events of the evening and was feeling Rachel out for information. Either way, Rachel was not going to get into her personal business with Sharon, sister or not. Rachel and Sharon didn't have that kind of friendship. Sharon had introduced them, but there was where her role in their affairs ended. No information was offered by Rachel. If Ken wanted Sharon to know anything, then he'd have to be the one to tell.

"Good. Tell him I said, hey."

"Sure will."

"I better go. You know how they bird-dog you down here with the phone."

"Talk to you later."

"Perhaps we could meet in the cafeteria one day this week."

"Yeah, maybe. See ya." Rachel didn't sound too convincing.

As soon as she hung up with Sharon, she checked the message indicator to see if Ken had called while she was on the line. There was also the possibility that he called and hung up without leaving a message. For the rest of the afternoon, she kept her calls brief, in order to keep the line clear. Periodically, she checked the message service at home, in case he had called there. She also wanted to confirm the phone line at home was working. By the close of business, there was still no call. She was hurt, but also starting to feel equally irritated that he hadn't called to make amends. After all, they were engaged to be married. If for no other reason, Rachel felt that should warrant a call.

On the way home, she thought about just going over to his place, but remembered how poorly such a move had turned out Saturday. She wasn't ready for a repeat performance. It would be wiser to talk first, get the bad feelings aired, and then get back to normal.

She checked the messages as soon as she got in the house. The indicator showed three. She got her hopes up that one of the three would be him. She eagerly pushed the play button.

"Hi. This message is for Rachel Matthews. I'm calling from the Community Outreach. I want to let you know that the board meeting for March is canceled due to a conflict with the chairman's schedule. We will resume in April. If you have any questions, please give me a call. Thank you."

"Hi, baby. It's me, Mom. Neal told me not to forget your birthday. I was sitting here thinking about it, and thought I'd better call right now. I can't remember, honey, if your birthday is this week or next week. Well, happy birthday and I hope you see many many more."

Rachel's birthday wasn't until next month, but she appreciated Mom thinking about her. Most years Mom forgot the actual date and just called within the general vicinity. That was fine with Rachel. She was just appreciative of the call, whenever it came.

Only one message left. "It had better be Ken." She was definitely acquiring an attitude.

"Hi, Rachel. It's, uh, Gary. I was calling to see if you'd be interested ... "

Before his message could finish playing, she pushed the erase button.

"So, he's not going to call. Well, I've already called enough times," Rachel voiced out loud. She proceeded to change into some sweat pants and a T-shirt. All of a sudden, she wasn't feeling sad, mad was more like it. She went through the house talking to herself and the cat. Boots was bound to get an ear full tonight, compliments of Mr. Sanders. Rachel was actually making herself angrier and angrier the more she rehearsed the chain of events. Her anger was no longer about what happened. It was all about Ken being stubborn and not trying to make-up.

All wound up, she didn't feel hungry. She heated up a can of soup and subsidized it with some crackers. She had grown tired of flipping through the channels with the remote. With nothing else to do, she decided to watch a movie. Whenever Rachel found herself in this kind of a funky mood, there was only three empowerment movies appropriate for the moment: *Waiting to Exhale*, *Thelma and Louise*, and the *Joy Luck Club*. Since she'd practically worn out *Thelma and Louise*, and had already exhaled last month with the engagement to Ken, the only logical choice was the *Joy Luck Club*. She popped in the tape and while it was queuing got herself some ice cream from the freezer and a bag of Chicago-style-cheese and caramel popcorn. Fortunately, she'd picked up the popcorn mix during a recent business trip to the Loop. Her favorite mix had a soothing effect that made everything look a bit brighter, or so she hoped. It was a good thing she had the essential snacks on hand. It was just one of those nights.

Granted, with Ken in the picture since last July, she hadn't hosted a pity party in almost a year. It was actually a weird feeling to be having one, and not a very good one at that. Ken was really in trouble. Not only was she mad at him about the argument, and how he acted, but now his not-calling was added to the list. She definitely attributed her lightweight pity party to him, just to round off his list of woes. Mr. Wonderful was in serious trouble.

"Trustworthy." Rachel viewed the list in her mind, making a mental note of Ken's check points. "Trustworthy, huh. Doesn't look like I can trust him with my feelings. Cancel that one."

At the blink of an eye, his total had shrunk to six.

She looked over at Boots who was curled up in front of the TV. "Boots, you're one of the two stable males in my life. I'm sure glad I didn't get rid of you, just because Ken didn't like you.

When the dust settles, look who's here and look who's gone a.w.o.l."

Even though she was really mad at Ken, she loved him and wanted to talk. She started to call him again, but decided against it. She refused to come across as a pest. Besides, she wasn't the only one in the relationship. She was hurt by the lack of interest and commitment he was showing. Since he obviously wasn't going to call, she decided to get on with the party and block the anguish out of her mind.

In spite of her gallant effort, it didn't work. All the movie did was make her feel worse. Before turning in for the evening, she pulled out the scratch pad she kept in the night stand. It contained Neal's number in France. He was her best friend and always had the male view on things. She didn't know whether to call and seek a friendly voice or keep the hurt to herself and hope the matter would quickly blow over.

She hesitated calling Neal, because the seven hour time difference would make it about 4:00 in the morning. It was probably selfish, but Rachel decided to do it anyway. If anyone would understand her need to call, and overlook the inconvenience, it would surely be Neal.

The hotel operator answered. "Hello."

"Puis-je parler á monsieur Neal Pierce, s'il vous plaît."

"Oui, madame."

The phone rang about five times. Rachel was afraid it would revert back to the front desk. She'd already spoken all of the French she knew and was hoping to be spared a round two. With the phone ringing so long, she figured Neal must really be sound asleep. She decided not to wake him. Her dilemma could keep until later. She was about to hang-up when a groggy voice on the other end picked up. "Hello."

Although he spoke fluent French, Neal sounded completely out of it. She felt badly. He had clearly been asleep. Here it was 4:00 in the morning, his time, and she was waking him from a restful nights sleep. She was too embarrassed to say, hello.

"Rachel?"

"How'd you know it was me?"

"Because, only three people have my number here, you, Nicole, and Gertrude."

"How'd you know it wasn't one of them?"

"I didn't, not really. I just guessed it was you."

"Good guess. I'm embarrassed about waking you up, though."

"Don't worry about it. I'll be getting up soon, anyway. What's wrong?"

"Why do you ask if something is wrong? Can't I just be calling to say, hi?"

"You, at 4:10 in the morning. Nope. Something is definitely wrong. What is it?"

Her words started to flow like a river. "Ken and I had a big argument about him getting custody of his daughter. Since the second argument last night, we haven't talked at all. I've called him several times, but have not gotten an answer. I've gotten no messages and no word from him. I'm not sure what to do! I don't know if I'm more hurt or mad. On top of it all, I really miss him."

"I can't believe you. I go out of town for a few days. I leave you there happily engaged, skipping down the yellow brick road, and out of nowhere, you're in divorce court."

"Cute, Mr. Pierce."

"I thought I got rid of you last month with the engagement."

"Never. We're friends for life," she spoke with confidence.

"What happened?"

"I don't know exactly."

"You know something. What prompted the war?" Neal was insistent on getting to the bottom of her problem.

"Sandra called and apparently got into an argument with Ken. She wants to take him to court and get the child support formalized. He thinks she's jealous about our engagement and is just being spiteful. You know those ex's use every trick in the book to hang on. Well, that is Sandra in a nutshell." Although Rachel had only heard one side of the story, namely Ken's, it was understandable that she'd side with her man.

"So, how did his argument with Sandra involve you."

"I accidentally overheard it. He didn't hear me come in."

"Ooooh. This is getting good. It's no problem that you woke me up. This should be worth it."

"Thanks, friend."

"Just kidding. Go ahead. Go ahead. What else happened?"

"Ken decided that instead of giving Sandra twenty percent of his check, he'd rather get joint custody. Personally, I don't know why he doesn't just pay the 96 dollars a week, and get over it."

"Whoa! Wait a minute."

"See, you're surprised like I was. That's exactly how I felt when he started talking about joint custody."

"Joint custody! Nah, nah. I'm talking about the 96 dollars per week. I'm shocked. Do you know how much that is?"

"What? In all the commotion, I didn't really think about it."

"Rach, you're the accountant, but even I can tell, it's not much."

"You know, I didn't even think about it. That's about 25,000 dollars per year."

"I thought you said he was in the computer field."

"He is."

"What is he, a computer operator? My goodness girl, he isn't making any money. Not enough to take on a child. You make at least twice what he makes. I'm surprised it doesn't bother him, especially since you told me that he has to always feel like the 'man' in charge. You know most brothers can't handle their woman making more money than they do. Boy, this guy must be someone special not to be bothered by what you make compared to his."

"We never really talked about it. It was never an issue. I have my place, and he has his. Our plan was to take the next year and save for the wedding. I'm sure we'll work out all these issues between now and then. Besides, I just assumed we'd put all the money together and have more than enough."

"That's great, but be careful. How you start off might be what you have to keep up. How does he live on that little money? "

"I guess his expenses are low. That's something I like about him." Rachel was unconsciously defending him. "He's not heavy in debt. He must bring home about 1,700 dollars a month after taxes. He doesn't have a new car. I can't imagine him still making payments on it. On second thought, he did say something about a payment of 250 dollars. The insurance is probably 100 dollars a month for a sports car like his."

"What about the apartment?"

"It can't be much. It's like a shoe box, and it's in the city. I can't imagine him spending more than 550 dollars a month, including utilities. Now, he does have some nice furniture. I do remember the bill being around 100 dollars a month." Rachel was starting to recall more details from all the conversations she and Ken had over the past months. "Oh yeah, the stereo is on credit, and it's about 100 a month."

"Doesn't he work out?"

"Yes, but the gym is only about thirty dollars per month."

"It may only be thirty dollars to you, but that only leaves him somewhere between five and six hundred dollars. With him being as religious as he is, you have to add in money for tithes," Neal suggested.

"Uhn uhn. I know for sure he only gives twenty-five dollars per week to the church," she confirmed.

"Are you sure?"

"Yes, I'm sure. Sometimes he has me fill out the envelope."

" I thought tithes was ten percent!"

"He's not in that kind of church."

"I didn't know there were different kinds," he commented in amazement.

"Well, from what I can tell, most of the people in his church seem to spend their money on clothes and cars. Every time I go, the pastor is begging people to tithe."

"They're probably afraid the pastor's going to start living large on their money," Neal suggested.

"You're probably right," she agreed.

"They sure wouldn't be able to hang in the church back home," he stated.

"Please, I can hear Big Mama now."

Neal jumped in and started imitating Big Mama, "First fruit, chile, first fruit, not the last, the first."

Rachel started laughing and jumped in with her addition. "Ten cents on every dollar gots to go back to the Lord."

Neal was laughing, too, but he managed to keep the dialogue going. "Don't whittle it down, then try to give him what's left."

"Ya give ten percent if ya can't do any better. The more he bless ya, the better you ought to be able to do."

The two knew Big Mama's position on the topic of tithing better than anyone. She was the one who made them put a portion of their allowance in the collection basket at an early age. Neither went to church enough to pay tithes, but consistently gave a big offering whenever they did attend a worship service. Some teachings were hard to get away from.

"Really, I don't know why some people bother to get religion if it doesn't change their lives for the better. They might as well sleep in on Sunday," said Rachel, repeating what she heard Roz say.

"That 1,700 dollars has whittled down, and we haven't even begun to talk about child support, food, or pocket money, let alone dating. Plus, the few times I've seen the brother, he's been sharp. You might as well add in some money for clothes and a cleaning bill. That, on top of everything else, should not only chew up the last 600 dollars, but put him in the red. I truly don't know how he lives so well on the money he makes. Maybe that's why he wants custody."

"Why?"

"Giving 400 dollars a month to Sandra is going to put him on a tight budget. That's going to put a hurting on the brother's livelihood. The truth of it is, I doubt if he can afford to take care of his daughter and be a fly-guy at the same time. I don't even know how he can afford to date. Maybe that's why he asked you to marry him."

"Why is that, Mr. Pierce?"

"Don't you know? Wives are cheaper than dates. You have to take a date out to a nice restaurant for dinner. All you have to do with a wife is bring home a bag of groceries and a hearty-man-appetite." As always, Neal found a tactful way to ease humor into the conversation, thereby lightening the tension.

"Ha ha. Remember Mr. Smarty, you've taken me to the finest restaurants in the country."

"Like I said, dates and you, my friend, get the best treatment."

"Sure, sure. I'm getting sleepy now. I'm going to bed," she said.

"Ain't that about nothing. You call me in the middle of the night, wide awake, and I'm asleep. You get cheered up and then get sleepy. Now I'm wide awake and ready to talk, but you're sleepy. I tell you, Rach, you got it too good."

"I know. I do, don't I. Seriously, thanks Neal. You came through for me buddy." As an afterthought, Rachel thought about how freely she was sharing such intimate information with Neal. She saw him as her buddy, her brother first, as a man last, and an outsider never. "I probably shouldn't be telling you all this stuff. I'm telling you all the man's business, but I needed someone to talk to."

It wasn't the first time she'd shared personal information with Neal, and with the way this relationship was derailing, might not be the last. Rachel could only hope to have the same kind of friendship with Ken that she had with Neal. It never seemed to work out whereby she had both in a relationship, friendship and romance. Only one seemed to be manageable at a time. Fortunately for her, Ken was Mr. Suave, and Neal was Mr. Devoted. If Ken could just get his part down, things would be perfect. For a brief moment, she imagined having a man who was the combination of the two.

"Why didn't you call Big Mama if you needed someone to talk to?" Neal wasn't serious. He knew Big Mama didn't have the warm and fuzzy feeling about Rachel and Ken's relationship.

"Funny, Neal. Besides, she was sleep. Guess you win the lucky prize at 4:00 a.m."

"About Ken, I don't know what to tell you. He'll call sooner or later. Trust me, he's missing you just as much. He may never admit it, but he is. Just prepare yourself. I don't know, though, about the money thing. That concerns me. Perhaps the brother has enough self-esteem to be cool with the whole thing. As long as he sees your relationship in more than just dollars and cents, then you'll be fine. I'm not really worried about you. You always end up on your feet. Now as for ole' boy, that might be a different story."

"I feel much better since I've talked to you."

"Good, don't go and give the man too much grief."

"I won't. The way I see it, he's bringing Ariel, and I'm bringing Boots. I don't particularly care for his position, and he doesn't like my cat. Looks like we'll both have to give and take on this one. If you really look at it, he's getting the better deal. My cat is low-maintenance. Two square meals a day, and Boots is good to go," Rachel hesitated. "What do you think?"

"Sounds fair to me, but I don't really know. Of course I like cats, or at least Boots, but you can't consider me an expert on the subject. I don't have kids."

"Yeah. Why is that, I wonder?"

"You know why. The past ten years have been devoted to work and building a foundation for my family. I don't have the time right now to dedicate to a wife and kids. You know I'm out of town most of the time. Keeping a girlfriend has been challenging enough, let alone a wife. The travel is just too intense for me to be trying to father somebody right now. Plus, long distance relationships never appealed to me."

"It's too bad. I know you'd be a good father."

"One day, it'll happen. Right now, I'm focusing on getting myself together."

"Exactly how long does it take?" Rachel and Neal were always on different wavelengths when it came to patience. Unlike her, he had only been serious with a few women in his adult years, and they were all long-term relationships. Neal decided in the beginning, whenever he took the marital plunge, it would be forever. He was in no rush to make a bad decision that he would have to live with the rest of his life. Rachel, on the other hand, wanted Mr. Right, and in a hurry. The dating scene had worn out long ago.

"Why? Do you have someone in mind?"

"No." Neal wasn't surprised at her response. She never introduced him to anyone. Deep down it was for selfish reasons. Generally, she had a male companion in her life. Rarely did they treat her as well as Neal. She really wanted her best friend to be happy, but she was afraid it would dramatically impact their relationship if and when he finally got married. The reality of it was, she was having her cake and eating it, too. She had Neal to fill the void where her romantic suitors often came up short.

"I figure that I need about 250 thousand dollars saved."

"Why so much?"

"So much! That's hardly anything nowadays. I need to buy another house, and that's about 250 to 275 thousand dollars. With the equity in the condo, I still need about 150 thousand dollars, cash. Plus, you never know. I might have to buy my wife a car, or whatever, after we get married."

"As big as your place is, why do you need another one?"

His place had a bi-level master bedroom with a fireplace, two guest bedrooms, office, three full bathrooms, family room, work-out room with a sauna, library, formal living and dining rooms, laundry room, two other fireplaces, and a two-car attached garage. Since the place was in a complex that let Neal own the unit and not the land underneath it, technically his home was considered a condo. Despite the legal mumbo-jumbo, Rachel classified it as a house.

"You are so rare. I'm glad you're my friend."

"Oh yeah, that's right. Part of the 250 thousand dollars has to be kept in reserve to bail your butt out of this and that."

"Thanks for the vote of confidence in my decisions."

"I figure in another couple of years I'll be ready to do the family thing."

"What if you meet a woman who has her own money? Does that move up your time line?"

"If she works, that's fine, but I plan to do my part. It's not in me to be a kept man. If my wife works, it will be by her choice and definitely not out of necessity."

"She'll probably be sitting at home eating bon bons all day."

"Fine with me. So long as I'm taking care of home and all of her needs, I'm sure she will take care of me."

"You're too good. Pops taught you well. I hope you get a great lady. You truly deserve one."

"Ah, thanks. Anyway, take care Rach. I don't even have to say call if you need me. You know where to find me. Au revoir!"

"Bye, Neal."

Rachel had new issues to think about regarding her and Ken, but for now she felt peace. Ken didn't know how much Neal had saved his butt by giving her an outlet to vent and get recharged. As always, good old Neal had come through in the pinch. His compassion seemed to be boundless, at least when it came to Rachel.

28

The week progressed without any contact from Ken. Rachel had grown equally stubborn over the past few days, and elected not to call him. She recognized the cold shoulder would eventually pass, but, for now, that was the way it was. She tried to stay clear of Sharon. Rachel had never gotten any indication Sharon was two-faced. Still, Rachel felt it better not to involve outside entities in her personal matters, while she and Ken were going through their thing. He was different. Neal was the exception. She knew Neal very well, and literally trusted him with her life. No matter how friendly she was with Ken's family, blood was always thicker than water.

Rachel wanted to call Red and see how he was doing, but decided against it. She knew this was his night for the Bulls and Rockets game at the United Center. Any other time it would have been fine, but with the strain in her relationship, it would probably come across as her trying to get in touch with Ken, in a round-about way. Her pride wouldn't let her give such an impression.

A bright red balloon with white letters spelling, *HAPPY BIRTHDAY*, was flying above the kitchen table. Red was sitting in his chair watching the Bulls and Knicks game with Ken. Everyone else was making a big deal about Red's birthday. Dana was putting candles on the cake. Sharon was setting the table, and Nick was watching the meat on the indoor grill. Brendon hadn't arrived.

"Where's my Rachel?" Red asked.

"She couldn't make it." Ken wanted to be as honest with his father as possible, without getting into the details of his personal business. Ken considered calling her several times to see if she wanted to come over, but he wasn't ready to deal with the conflict.

Sandra was enough headache at the moment. He preferred to let the dust settle, and give Rachel time to miss him.

"Couldn't make it! She hasn't missed a Sunday since you brought her the first time. I can't believe she would miss my birthday." Red kidded around a lot, but he loved visits from all of his children, including Rachel.

Ken had already lied once to his dad, and didn't want to do it again. He pretended to be deeply engrossed in the game.

"Junior, you two ain't on the outs, are you?"

Ken chuckled. His efforts to steer clear of the subject wasn't working. Red was too perceptive.

"I hope to goodness you didn't mess up with her. Can't you keep nobody? Good grief, Junior."

Ken started laughing louder. Sharon heard the laughter and came in to see what was going on. She stood in the doorway with an apron on. "What's so funny?"

"I don't know. I think the boy done lost his mind."

"What's so funny, Kenny? I could hear you all the way in the kitchen."

"Dad was yelling at me, about Rachel."

"What about Rachel? Where is she, anyway?"

"Before Ken could respond, Red jumped in. "This boy done messed up with her. I knew it was going too good. He can't keep nobody, too selfish, too bull-headed."

"What happened?" Sharon asked. "You and Rachel broke-up!"

"I didn't say anything like that. That's all coming from Dad." Ken was trying to skirt the topic, without really giving an answer. "All I said was that she couldn't make it."

"Uh huh. I hear what you said, but you can believe it's more to it than that."

"When I saw her at work this week, she seemed fine. I'm sure everything is okay, Dad, right Kenny?"

"You know you can't change Dad's mind once it's set."

"Brendon's here," Dana yelled from the kitchen.

"About time," Ken said. He was so glad to find a way out of his hot seat. He jumped up and headed for the kitchen. "Let's eat.

Sharon walked over to her dad and gave him a hug around the neck. "I'll bring a plate in here for you, Dad. That way you can finish watching the game."

"Thanks, dear. And when you go in the kitchen, tell your brother I said not to be a fool. He better work out his difference with Rachel. She too good for him to let get away. I don't want him sitting over here, up under me all the time. You go talk some sense into that boy. I didn't raise no fools."

Rachel was out of sorts this evening. Fridays were normally spent with her and Ken being together. This was the first Friday in eight months she was spending without Ken. It was awkward. Restless, she grabbed the TV guide to see if something entertaining was coming on cable. After flipping through the guide for a couple of minutes, disappointedly, she put it down. She picked up the new issues of Essence, Charisma, and Female Executives. Since her attention span was short, she just flipped through the magazines, not really focusing on any particular article. She glanced at the clock and realized it was still early enough to catch a movie. Although she had no problem going to the theater alone, her first choice was to have some company. The only person she could think of, besides Ken, was Neal. When they'd gone to lunch yesterday, Neal mentioned that he would probably be around tonight. She tapped the speakerphone button and pushed the speed dial. He answered on the second ring.

"Hey, Neal."

"Hey, Rach."

"Hey, Neal."

"What's up? I can't believe you're in on a Friday! Oh yeah, that's right. Mr. Too-fly is on the lamb. So, your friends get some time, now that he's a.w.o.l."

"Don't even start, Mr. Pierce. I called to see if you have any plans tonight."

"Actually, I do. Nicole and I are going to see a movie."

"Oh."

"You're welcome to come along if you'd like."

"No. That's okay. You two enjoy the movie."

"You know you're welcome to come along."

"No way. I'm not desperate enough to intrude like a third wheel. No thanks. You two have a good time."

"You sure?"

"Positive."

"All righty then. I'll be leaving in about twenty minutes to pick up Nicole. Call back if you change your mind."

"Thanks, but no thanks."

Since all else had failed, Rachel decided to curl up with Boots and a good book. She had picked up a book from the bookstore last week. This was one of her rare opportunities to actually read a book cover to cover. Being so tight with Ken over the past months, lots of things she used to do had fallen by the wayside.

Rachel stayed up most of the night reading the book. Periodically her mind would drift to Ken. She couldn't help but wonder what he was doing at that precise moment. The book didn't do much to boost her confidence in men. For as much as she missed Ken, there was an equal amount of disappointment and anger with the way things were turning out.

By the time she finished reading the book, it was about 6:00 Saturday morning. Instead of getting up and going to bed, she pulled up a comforter, stretched out on the sun room sofa, and fell asleep. The ringing phone startled her. For a moment, she was disoriented.

She reached for the receiver and dropped it on the floor. Deep down she was hoping it was Ken. She scrambled to pick it up.

"Hello."

"Hello. Rachel? Is this Rachel?"

"Yes, it is."

"Hi. This is Chelle Rogers from the Community Outreach. Did I wake you?"

"That's okay. I need to be getting up, anyway. How are you doing?"

"Fine. I was calling to see if you were interested in coming to the singles' luncheon at the Christian Center."

"Singles' luncheon?"

"You might not remember, but last month I mentioned that my church was having their annual church revival week. Well, today is the singles' luncheon."

Rachel had forgotten, but was interested in going. Anything would beat sitting around, feeling lonely all day.

"What time does it start?"

"Twelve noon."

"Sure, I'll come."

"Great."

"Just give me the directions."

Rachel was glad to have something to do for the day. She was glad there wasn't a sorority meeting. Since all of the sorors knew she was engaged, it would be too stressful to put on the happy face for three straight hours. She hated faking in front of others, pretending all was well when it really wasn't.

It was already 10:00. She pushed herself to get dressed and make it to the luncheon on time. When she arrived, Chelle was there to greet her. There was just enough time to get seated before the food was served. Strangely enough, there were about as many single men as there were women. That seemed strange to her, specially in a church environment where the women outnumbered the men three to one.

Half way into the meal, the speaker took the podium. Sister Jones was an eloquent, practical speaker. Her message centered around issues pertaining to single women. She implored the singles, at the luncheon, to get focused.

"Seek a relationship with God first, instead of trying to find a mate. Get that relationship right first," she kept repeating.

She emphasized how important it was to be happy and at peace being single.

"You have to be happy with yourself before you can be happy with someone else. If you don't want to be alone with yourself, what makes you think someone else does. Stop being so needy. You say that you need a husband, you need a wife, you need a better job, you need more money, you need companionship, you need to get married, you need kids."

Rachel could identify with most of the list. She listened, intently hoping that Sister Jones would reveal some golden nugget of wisdom that would enable her to fulfill the list.

"Need, need, need. What you need is the Lord. Stop needing and start appreciating. Apostle Paul said he learned to be content.

He didn't say he wanted to be, or chose to be, or desired to be. He said, 'learned'. That means, make yourself happy. Accept yourself, just as you are. That's what God does. Trust me singles, marriage isn't wonderful all of the time. Married people want to be single. Single people want to be married. Wake up people. Stop being so eager to leave one situation for another. Enjoy where you are in life, and wait for God to do what he's going to do."

Rachel was moved by the speech. It was all about God, but the manner in which it was presented made it easier to understand.

"If God can predestine a whole plan for your life long before you were even born, then surely he's capable of finding you a mate. Focus on getting yourself together. Then you will be ready to receive when God sends that special one. All right. Amen."

Waiting, being patient, giving the-husband-search over to God, wasn't exactly the golden nugget Rachel was looking for. The solution presented wasn't easy to swallow.

Sister Jones looked at her watch. "We have time for a few questions."

All around the room, hands popped up like mushrooms.

"You, dear," Sister Jones pointed towards the back of the room. "What's your question?"

The young lady, who looked to be in her early twenties, stood up.

"I'm single, and I want to know if it's spiritually wrong for me to take birth control pills?"

Oooh and uhm sounds came from all corners of the room.

"Honey, you say you're single, right?" Sister Jones asked.

"Right."

"You know birth control pills are supposed to help keep you from getting pregnant, right?"

"Yeah." The reluctance in the young lady's voice indicated to Rachel that she wasn't sure where the answer was going.

"Okay, and you are a born-again-believer, right?"

"Right."

Rachel was on the edge of her seat. She didn't know where Sister Jones was going, either. Whatever the answer was, Rachel wanted it quick, because she had also been struggling with whether or not to stop taking the pill. Some good insight here could aid in her decision.

"So, you know sex before marriage is a no-no, right?"

"Yes."

"Let's think about this. You're an unmarried Christian. That means you aren't having any sex. So, why would you need the pill? You can't get pregnant if you're not having sex, right?"

"Right," the young lady acknowledged.

"Ooo," Rachel grunted. Sister Jones' made perfect sense to her. That was at least one sound reason for not taking the pill. Applying it was easier said than done.

"You, honey, what's your question?"

The lady sitting next to Rachel stood up.

"I'm thirty-eight. My biological clock is ticking. How long do I have to wait for a man?"

"Oh boy, honey," Sister Jones said with distress. "You missed my whole message. You need to put your focus on God, not on getting a man. Read Matthew, chapter 6, verse 33. Get your eyes on God, he'll hook-up the rest. You see, how long depends on you. I don't mean no harm, but your question leads me to believe you're not ready for a husband."

"Why?"

"For one, you don't just ask for a man. You need to ask for a husband. Then, wait on God to answer."

Oh boy, Rachel thought. There was that waiting thing again. It was easier for Rachel in her twenties than her thirties.

"Don't be, too anxious. A whole bunch of people who couldn't wait, wishes they had. Don't get ahead of God. He knows how your biological clock works. He was the one who made it. He can stop or push the hands back, anytime he wants, and give you more time."

"Ahh," Rachel said. Finally, a nugget she could swallow.

"Honey, you be sure to get a tape of this message."

The crowd laughed.

"Seriously, you get the tape. Play it over and over, driving in your car, sitting at home. You play it until it gets in your spirit. Be happy while you are single. It's not so bad. It's time you can spend with the Lord that married folks with kids don't have. Remember to be content. Okay, sweetie. God loves you."

The lady shook her head in acknowledgment.

"And don't feel embarrassed by your question. There are other people here going through the same thing. You all need to get the tape, too."

Rachel knew she was right. It described her dilemma to the tee.

"What about some of you men? You mean to tell me that none of you have any questions?"

Rachel looked around. The men squirmed around in their seats, but none responded. She figured they were too embarrassed to ask what was really on their minds. And why not, she was.

"Come on men. None of you have any questions." Sister Jones waited another few seconds. "Okay, I'm going to take that to mean you guys have it all together. Looks like I just need to work on the women." Laughter filled the room. "See sisters, the men have their acts together. So, we have to get ours together. Amen. Brothers, when you come up, afterwards, to ask me questions, and I know you will, be patient. The line will be long."

The women were less intimidated by displaying their personal thoughts and concerns in front of a group of peers. They wanted help, at any cost. As soon as Sister Jones asked for more questions, the hands of women around the room flew up in the air.

"One more question. Kelly, is that your name? Honey, I can't see your tag too well without my glasses."

A lady at one of the front tables stood up. "Yes, it's Kelly."

"Kelly, what's your question." Sister Jones took a sip of water from a glass located behind the podium.

"How do I know if I've met my husband-to-be and maybe, even passed him up?'

"That's a good question. Like I told the other sister, spend this time with the Lord. Learn to hear his voice. Don't be anxious. He'll make it plain to you when the time is right, and confirm it with witnesses. He knows you're out here in Wheaton. Don't panic. He can get the man to you. He doesn't need your help. Concentrate on getting yourself ready to receive a husband. Oh, and ladies and men, too, when God sends your mate, look beyond their physical qualities. See them as God does, through the heart.

Rachel felt less alone, once she realized church-going, bible-reading Christians were having problems getting the right perspective on relationships, too, and not just the lukewarm believers like herself. She felt some conviction about her twelve-point checklist, but not enough to discard it.

Sister Jones continued with her insight on how to identify Mr. Right. "Grow up people. Grow up in the spirit. Stop throwing away the folks God sends you, because they don't look like this or have that. People with all kinds of shortcomings, and who knows what else, shouldn't be trying to find somebody perfect to marry. You might as well know, now, Christ Jesus was the only perfect human being. Listen, stop wasting your time and everybody else's looking for perfection."

Rachel wondered how many would hear the message and leave there with their minds still set on getting a mate, as soon as possible.

"That husband or wife you're believing God for, flat out, won't be perfect, and you aren't, either. Okay. Are we all clear on that."

Through the crowd's laughter, Sister Jones concluded with, "Amen. Let's pray. Father ..."

Rachel wondered how many people had taken the message to heart. Whether she acted on the message or not, she was impressed with the delivery, and decided to get the tapes.

"If you need personal prayer or ministering, don't leave here without letting some of the prayer-warriors lay-hands on you."

Rachel didn't feel bad off enough to go and get personal prayer. She decided that this was a good time to exit. Before leaving, she wanted to pay her money for the lunch, buy the audiotape, and also thank Chelle for inviting her. As she squeezed through the groups of people standing around the room, she reflected on the message. What it meant to be single and happy had impacted her. Near the front, she saw small groups of people praying. For a brief moment, she had eye-to-eye contact with the speaker.

"Ms., come here please."

Not sure who Sister Jones was talking to, Rachel spread her hand across her chest and mouthed the words 'me' to the speaker.

"Yes, you. Please come here. I have a word for you."

Rachel became instantly nervous, but she made her way over to the speaker. Sister Jones grabbed both of her hands and looked her in the eyes, and began to speak confidently, yet gently.

"Sister, God knows your hurt and he hears your heart cry. Seek him and you will find peace. Only in him will you find the perfection you seek."

Rachel couldn't say a word. All of a sudden, with absolutely no warning, her eyes filled with tears. She didn't know exactly why she was crying, but it seemed to feel good. Sister Jones gave her a hug and had some of the other women standing nearby do the same. After a few minutes, Rachel prepared to leave. On her way out, Chelle caught her by the arm.

"I'm glad you came."

"I'm glad I came, too. When are your Sunday services?"

"8:00, 11:00, and 6:00. Why? Are you interested in coming back?"

"Perhaps."

"Good. We also have a broadcast service on Sunday morning."

"On the radio?"

"No, on TV. If you're not sure about coming to the church, check out the broadcast. Maybe it will help you decide if you want to fellowship with us. You're welcome to come visit anytime."

"Thank you for inviting me." On the way home, Rachel recounted the message. She remembered the speaker's comment made to the single women. "The only man you should be focusing on is Christ." She smiled. Big Mama would be proud to know she'd gone to hear a power-packed, anointed, Bible-based message.

Saturday evening was uneventful. She spent time organizing receipts and papers for the tax return process. It was mostly busy work, but was ideal for keeping her mind off of Mr. Sanders. She had to take one evening at a time.

Sunday was no more thrilling than the day before. She did get up in time to catch the Christian Center broadcast. In the middle of the show, Neal called to check on her.

"What are you doing?" he asked.

"I'm watching the Christian Center."

"On what?"

"On TV. Turn it on. It's real good. The minister is talking about dating and why you should refrain from having sex before getting married. He's explaining the difference between lust and love."

"When did you start watching church TV?"

"Today?"

"Oh my goodness. First, you start calling your friends. Then you resort to religion. What next? You're not planning to become a nun, are you?"

"Neal, turn to the Christian network channel and spare me the lecture," she said.

"Why did you pick this service?"

"Yesterday, I went to a singles' luncheon that was hosted by this church, and it was awesome. I was actually touched." She wanted to relay what Sister Jones had told her, but decided to keep it to herself, for now.

"You're touched all right," alluding to her humorous side. "You're just now learning that."

"Anyway, I actually thought about the message after I left the luncheon. You know I never remember anything Ken's pastor talks about. This was different. It actually struck something in me. Maybe it's because they were actually teaching me something instead of preaching at me. Anyway, let me watch the end of it, and I'll call you back when it goes off."

"Sure thing, Rev. Rach. Talk to you in a little while."

29

A month ago, the farthest thing from Rachel's mind was being on the outs with Ken. It had been two, going on three weeks. She really felt like they had something special, not like the take-it or leave-it relationships of the past. He was supposed to be Mr. Wonderful, Mr. Right. At this moment, he was all wrong. He hadn't called in almost three weeks. She was hurt to know he thought so little of their relationship.

What she needed most was an esteem-booster. She needed to feel like someone special. This was the perfect time to hear from an 'old-shoe'. That was the term she used when referring to a man who she knew always made himself available for her, even though she had no long term interest in him. He tended to be nothing fancy, but extremely dependable.

She hadn't heard from Brian over the past three weeks. It would be easy enough to get a hold of him. On second thought, she didn't even want to open that can of worms. It would be difficult to get rid of him after her business cleared up. Gary was out of the question. He was too arrogant to realize her interest was only temporary. No way would she even remotely fuel his fire. It would take an ocean to put his flame back out after only ten minutes of harmless chit-chat.

Despite all of the deception and agony she had gone through with Rick, even he would be a welcomed caller. She didn't want to sleep with him. She just wanted to flirt, over the phone, for some much needed attention. The relationship with Rick was what she envisioned childbirth to be like. When she was with him, it was unbearably painful, but somehow over the years, the pain subsided and all she could really remember were the good times.

It was like she had forgotten all of the horrible events leading to their break-up, five years ago. The good news was, she'd only met him a few times since then. With each meeting, it only took a short time for her to be reminded of why they weren't together. They attempted to reconcile several years ago, and it didn't work out. Her tolerance for his games was nil. It was amazing how the tide had turned. None of these guys really mattered to her. They were only pacifiers for the real thing. Luc was a different story. She definitely did not need to hear from him at this moment, not while her defenses were down. He was too much of a temptation.

After thinking it through, she decided it was too risky contacting any of the guys from the past. Twenty minutes of an ego-boosting phone conversation would generate too much harassment long after. Instead, she called Roz to chat. With her, there were no strings attached.

"How's Mr. Wonderful?"

"He isn't so wonderful right now."

"What happened? Don't tell me he's finally shown his tail!"

"Kind of. Remember Sandra, his ex?"

"Yeah."

"Well she's trippin', he's trippin', and I'm trippin'. We're all trippin'."

"What happened?"

Since it occurred almost three weeks ago, Rachel didn't feel like rehashing the experience detail for detail, so she gave the short and sweet version.

"Sandra got mad about our engagement, and asked Ken for more child support money. He decided to fight for custody instead of paying. We argued and argued and argued, and haven't talked in almost three weeks."

"Wow! I'm shocked. You two seemed to be doing so well."

"We were."

"I'm sorry to hear that. How are you doing with all of this?"

"What can I do, girlfriend? I'm dealing with it."

"How did you two end up not talking for three weeks?"

"He didn't call, and I didn't either. Actually, I did call the night of the argument and left several messages. He hasn't called me back, yet."

"Sounds like he has a stubborn streak, like you."

"He's even more stubborn than I am, if you can believe that."

"This might be a serious red flag. Remember to watch those flags. They have a way of accumulating. They start off as small cracks when you're dating and grow into craters when you get married. Where does stubborn fit on your Mr. Right checklist?"

"Let's just say this little episode should cause him to lose a check."

"So much for the checklist in helping you find Mr. Right."

"Hey. That's a good list of characteristics."

"Sure, it is. It's all of the ingredients for Mr. Perfect. Sad thing is, you're not going to find him. He doesn't exist, Rachel. Dear, by now, you must have found out that nobody is perfect."

"At this point, I'm not looking for perfection. Shoot, I'll settle for a stable companion. Ken didn't have all twelve, anyway. I knew he wasn't perfect from the beginning, and it didn't bother me. There are only two men I know who meet most of my requirements. One has ten-and-a-half and the other nine."

"Who? I can't wait to hear this."

"Luc has nine, but he's already married. So, he doesn't count. Really, he could have twelve, and still not count."

"I'm surprised to hear you talk like that about Luc. He had your nose wide open for so long. What made you finally cut the chord? Was it Ken?"

"No, it wasn't really Ken. I can't trust Luc. You know that's one of my big twelve. It becomes more and more important with each break-up."

"Since Luc is out, who's the other Mr. Perfect, or close to it?"

"Neal is the other with ten-and-a-half."

"Ten-and-a-half? As wonderful as he is, why doesn't he have twelve?"

"You know he doesn't go to church regularly."

"You don't go," Roz reminded.

"I don't, but I want my man to. He has to set the example."

"Ken might as well not go to church, for all of the heathen-like things he does. What's the other half of a check that Neal lost?"

"Ah, that's for looks."

"Looks! Looks! What about his looks? I know you're not trying to say that good-looking man is ugly! I know you're not saying that."

Neal wasn't bad-looking. He was just average, not like Rachel's super-fine, pretty-boys. Not wanting Roz to think she was being petty, Rachel avoided giving an answer. "I'm saying he has ten-and-a-half, which is more than anyone else I know."

"So why don't you marry him?"

"Yeah, right. Get serious. I've known him all of my life. He's my best friend. I know practically everything there is to know about him. He's like a brother to me. I can't see him like that."

"Like what? Like someone who's perfect for you?"

"Sure, we get along great, but not like that, not like lovers."

"Oh well, go ahead and sweat it out with Mr. Wonderful, or should I say Mr. He'll Do. In the meantime, what are you going to do about the child support?"

"What can I do?"

"How do you feel about it?"

"I have mixed feelings. A part of me feels guilty about not wanting to have a child living with us right off the bat. There's nothing wrong with her staying during the holidays, even the whole summer, but not moving in right away. A live-in child wasn't part of the package when we got engaged. I'd like for us to have a little time together before we take on a family. I'm not prepared to be a ready-made-mom. Be honest Roz, am I wrong for feeling this way?"

"Rachel, I think it's a legitimate concern. You have a right to feel this way. Unfortunately, the feeling doesn't get your problem solved. Since I don't have kids, I can only speculate. I imagine it's tough for a single woman to marry a man with kids. You have to deal with the finances, clinging ex, lack of private time together, and who knows what else. I'm sure you're not the only one who feels this way, because there are a lot of single men with kids."

"Even now, I feel guilty. But, I guess there are two sides to this. If he were just the average Joe Blow, and not the man I'm planning to marry, then I wouldn't think twice about it. I think he should pay whatever he owes. Never mind Sandra's schemes for trying to come between us. The fact is, she deserves consistent support from Ken. He owes Ariel that."

"I agree. You know men want to have their cake and eat it, too." Roz was referring to men wanting to be a daddy, but also wanting to sacrifice as little as possible towards the child's livelihood. "There are a lot of 'daddys' who want the benefits of being a father, without doing any of the work."

"He may have fathered a child, but he doesn't know didley about being a father. If you ask me, he's already failed at sacrificing," Rachel strongly voiced.

"Why do you say that?" Roz asked.

"Anytime someone is willing to uproot their child, for selfish reasons, something is wrong. He's willing to put his innocent little five year old in a custody battle that he has almost no chance of winning. The only reason he's doing it is to try and save a few bucks with the support payments."

"His expenses wouldn't be cheaper with custody."

"I told him."

"Is it really about the money?" Roz asked.

"Mostly. I reminded him that he's not alone. I'll be contributing to the household when we get married. If he doesn't want to use my money, then he can always get a better job, or at least, a part-time gig."

For purposes of the checklist, she used intelligence and self-motivation interchangeably. So long as Ken showed some get-up-and-go about himself and made ends meet, then he could still earn the check for being intelligent.

"Don't count on that. Men nowadays aren't like your Pa-Pa. One job is all these young guys will take, whether it covers the bills or not. A part time job is probably out of the question, unless he's different, which he hasn't demonstrated thus far. Whether he gets a part-time job or not, one thing is certain. The money he ends up spending on an attorney could go towards the wedding expenses. I assume you are still getting married?"

"I don't know what's going to happen. I do sense that only part of this is actually about money. I think the biggest thing is his guilt-complex about not being there for Ariel during her first five years. Now that we're getting married, he wants to make up for lost time."

"Dealing with the guilt-trip is hard," Roz conceded.

"Don't I know it. If it were another woman, I could compete, or at least have some options on what to do. This guilt thing is hard to compete with."

"Well. Like I said, men want to have their cake and eat it, too. Ken has been living it up with the single life. He's only had to be responsible for himself. All he had to do was have fun. Now that he's worn out, he's ready to spring up and be a daddy," Roz noted.

"That's exactly it."

"You have to look at this objectively. What does all this mean to any children you might have with Ken?"

"What do you mean?"

"This is a two-edged sword."

"How so?" Rachel questioned.

"Whatever he does or doesn't do for Ariel is exactly what you should expect him to do with your children. A leopard doesn't change his spots. If he abandoned Ariel for five years, how do you know he won't do the same to you? Check out his sense of responsibility. Now, I know that's on your list, and seems to me, he should not get a check in that area." Roz's opinion had concluded on a humorous tone. It was a good thing, because Rachel was deep into thought about Roz's take on the matter. As always, it was painstakingly accurate, with a touch of sensitivity. That's why she loved her so.

"Good points, sis."

"I know you're mad about the spot you're being put into, but imagine how Sandra must feel."

"It doesn't really matter, because he won't get custody. For one, he lives out of town. For two, she is hardly an unfit mother. From what I can tell, she is pretty good with Ariel," Rachel admitted.

"In that case, you should just back up off the issue. Let it die a natural death, without you getting in the middle."

"Are you saying stay out of it?"

"Basically, yes. That way, he can't blame you later, when it falls apart. Face it, he is selfish to try and get custody, this late in the game. I could see if the woman was a bad mother, but it doesn't sound like she is. You said yourself, the probability of it happening is slim to none. Let him fail on his own. If you take sides against him, he'll find a way to blame you if it doesn't work out, even though it was his idea from the beginning. Trust me. Stay clear."

"That sounds like good advice to me. I'll take it."

Roz was filled with wisdom. Rachel didn't know what she'd do without her. It was too bad Roz had never met her own Mr. Right. One time, years ago, she was engaged to what seemed to be a wonderful guy. He turned out to be a dog in a nice man's clothing. He mooched off her for months, and as soon as he hit the lottery for a hundred grand, he moved out. All he left was a note and a miniature box of Sampler's chocolate. It took her years to recover, but when she did, Roz came back strong as ever.

"Don't make nothing into something. Follow your heart," Roz suggested.

"That's exactly what Neal said."

"Neal always did know what to say to you. You better look over that checklist again or get another one, because it's not helping you much."

"Give it a rest," Rachel lightly pleaded.

"All right, but the truth is the truth.

30

Ken unlocked his apartment door and headed straight for the bedroom. He was going to check his phone messages to see if Rachel had called, although she hadn't in weeks. He had grown accustomed to her companionship. He wanted to hear from her. Disappointed that there were no messages, he started to peel off the damp, sweaty workout clothes. He walked into the kitchen and opened the refrigerator door. Standing there, it dawned on him that it was unusual for him to be eating at home, alone. He grabbed some lunch meat, and a bottle of water. He sat down in front of the TV to pass the time, as best he could without Rachel.

The happy-go-lucky-facade wasn't working. Ken finally got up to get the only phone he had in his tiny apartment. He went into the bedroom and came back out with the fifty-five-foot phone cord dragging behind him. Too stubborn to call Rachel, he started to dial his confidant, Sharon.

She happened to be home, and picked up the ringing phone. "Hello."

"Hi, sis."

"Hey, Kenny. How are you doing?"

"Okay?"

"You don't sound okay."

"I'm fine. Look, have you talked to Rachel, at work?"

"No, why? Haven't you talked to her?"

"Nah, nah. Been busy."

"Boy, please. Don't tell me you haven't called that girl by now."

"Sharon, we needed some space."

"Space! Three weeks? Oh, boy," Sharon sighed. "You need to stop being so stubborn. It's your fault, anyway."

"My fault! Rachel was the one trippin' about Ariel. I love Rachel and all, but you know how I feel about a lot of fussing and fighting. I've been there with Sandra. Rachel's got to chill out with the nagging."

"Kenny, I'm sure there's more to it than just what you've told me. So, let's just leave it at that."

"I figure she'll call once she gets over her little mood swing. I've been waiting for her to call me."

"I don't want to run your business, but do you think that's smart?"

"I can't be jumping through hoops every time she gets an attitude," Ken stated defensively. In a softer, more affectionate voice he said, "But, I do miss her."

"Don't tell me, tell her. Call her, please," Sharon pleaded.

"I'll think about it."

Even though Rachel was keeping herself busy with various activities, Neal knew she was unhappy about the separation and needed a break. The pressure with Ken, Ariel, and Sandra had gotten to her. He wanted to help in some way, without prodding deeper into her business. After much thought, he came up with an idea. He was excited about it and called her up, anxious to share his thoughts. Without imposing his opinion on her in a direct fashion, he felt it wiser to try the indirect approach.

"Hey Rach, I just realized, some of my frequent-flyer miles are about to expire. I was wondering if you want to use them?"

"No, I don't feel like going anywhere."

"I meant a trip for you and Too-fly. Consider it an early birthday present."

"You and Nicole can't use them?"

"I have a trip to Orlando and another to Australia scheduled over the next two weeks. No, I won't be using them."

"What about Nicole?"

"What about Rach?"

"I don't know? I don't want to use a lot of vacation this early in the year."

"You can use some of the comp-time you've built up. Take a Friday and Monday off. Make it a long weekend."

"Hmmm. That's an idea. I sure could use it."

Neal felt that she could and should take the vacation, so he attempted to casually encourage her.

"What about Atlanta? You can see Laurie, or go to Detroit."

"I don't think so."

"Okay. What about Roz? Jet out to San Fran for the weekend. Check it out with Ken, and let me know by the weekend. Remember, if you're going to use them, you have to fly by the end of the month."

"You know I haven't spoken to Ken in three weeks."

"So call him."

"I don't know."

"Just do it. Someone has to break the ice."

"I don't know?" Reluctance echoed in her voice.

Rachel believed a vacation would be perfect. It was just what she needed. They hadn't talked in three weeks. She had even missed the gathering at Red's last weekend. She could have gone without Ken, but decided against it. She didn't want Ken to see her as needy and trying to manipulate her way back into his life, although, he was her fiancé. Neal was right. Somebody had to take the first step. Neal's offer was hard to pass up. After much dilemma, she decided to break the ice and give Mr. Sanders a call. All along, her heart had wanted to, but her pride wasn't too big on the idea.

In one hour, Rachel picked up the phone no less than ten times. She wanted to call, but didn't know what to say. Her palms were sweaty and heart was racing. Finally, the anticipation got the best of her and she made the call. Why shouldn't she call? It had only been a few weeks ago when they were planning to spend the rest of their natural lives together. With each ring, she was tempted to hang-up. Part of her was hoping he wasn't there. That way she could leave a message and wait for him to call her back. Before she could hang-up, he answered.

"Hello."

She melted. His voice hadn't lost any of his debonair charm. Needing a moment to get composed, she hesitated before speaking.

"Hi."

"Hi," Ken greeted in a low, strong voice. He was thrilled, but didn't want Rachel to know how happy he was to hear from her. He felt it important to maintain control.

Not knowing exactly what to say, she just opened her mouth and let the words flow naturally. Her biggest fear was rejection. "I was thinking about you and decided to call."

"Well, I'm glad you did, because I was thinking about you."

If he was thinking about her, why hadn't he called? She didn't even bother to ask. She just didn't want to go there. Right now, it didn't matter. They were communicating, and at the moment, it was good enough.

"So, what are you doing?"

"Washing my clothes."

Since they hadn't talked in three weeks, she treaded softly in the conversation. "Oh, I'm sorry. I can call you back later."

"No. No. I want to talk to you. I miss you."

His comment melted whatever coldness was still lingering. Whether he knew it or not, she was putty in his hand.

"I miss you, too."

"So, what are we going to do about it," he seductively asked.

She knew that he was alluding to them getting together for the evening. She was definitely up for it. It was a work night, but that wasn't a deterrent.

"Why don't you come over?" she asked.

"I have to finish my laundry."

She thought he was using this as an out. "Maybe tomorrow then."

"What about tonight?"

"It sounds like you're busy."

"Not too busy to come by and see you. Give me a couple hours, and I'll be there around 8:30, if it's okay with you?"

"It's fine."

"Then I'll see you soon."

"Bye."

"Oh, Rachel," Ken paused, "I love you."

She wanted and needed to hear that. Amazingly, those few words wiped away all of the tension that existed over the past three weeks. She was glad they were getting together. The past weekends had been unbearable without him. With this call, weekend plans were starting to look up for her. She had just enough time to freshen-up and whip-up a light snack. Even with the short notice, everything had to be perfect. He had to be reminded of the companionship he had missed during the separation. That was one way she knew to keep it from happening again.

When he arrived, the vanilla flavored candles permeated the entire townhouse, and the lights were slightly dimmed. The fondue was in full swing with fresh fruit and chocolate. She got in the habit of keeping some of his favorite items around. It was going to come in real handy tonight.

He let himself in with his key. Not wanting to startle her, he called out, "Rachel, I'm here."

She heard him from the top of the stairs. She had finished showering and was changing into a body suit and stretch pants. The Trésor cologne she was wearing could be smelled all the way down the stairs.

"I'll be right down," she responded.

As she gracefully came down the stairs, Ken couldn't take his eyes off of her. He walked over to the foot of the stairs and waited for her to complete the semi-grand entrance. He extended his hand to escort her down the last four steps. Before she hit the last two steps, Ken had her in his arms. No words needed to be said. They were both so glad to see each other.

He looked into her eyes and gave Rachel the smile she adored.

"I love you, Rachel."

"I love you, Ken." She clung to him like he was her life line.

They embraced for a couple of minutes, and then he let go. She wanted to stay there, in his arms, indefinitely. He lead the way to the sun room, holding her hand behind him. The sun room had also become his favorite spot in the house. It was perfect for a romantic, making-up session. She closed her eyes and could vividly remember last summer, the first time they sat in the sun room together. Now it was nine months later, with a major fight under their belt, this was no less romantic.

They spent hours lying in each other's arms, forgetting about the issues which had kept them apart. There wasn't much talking.

They relaxed together and soaked up the affectionate ambiance in the room. She had missed his presence in her life. Being in his arms, at this moment, reminded her of why she never wanted to have another major disagreement. The mood was right. She decided to use this opportunity to ask about taking a mini-vacation.

"Ken, how would you like to take a vacation?"

"Vacation? When? Where?"

"Sometime soon, and wherever you want to go."

"I don't know. I don't really have the money to pay for a vacation for us, not right now."

"It's not going to cost us much at all."

"How so?"

"Neal offered to give us two round-trip tickets to go wherever we want."

"You mean he's paying?"

"Not really. They are from his frequent-flyer miles. He has to use them or lose them. We'd actually be doing him a favor if we use them. What do you think?"

"Do you want a vacation?" he asked her.

"Yes! I definitely do. We both need one, together." She pulled closer to him.

"I guess you're right. When do we go?"

"Next weekend," she excitedly answered.

"Where?"

"You choose. Where would you like to go?"

"I've always wanted to go to New York City," he revealed.

"Well, here's your chance. Let's go." Rachel was full of joy stemming from the reconciliation and pending vacation.

Ken took a moment to ponder the suggestion and then replied, "Why not? Let's do it. New York, here we come." To seal the moment, he leaned over and kissed her on the forehead.

"Thank you, dear. Thank you. Boy, I really need this trip."

"No, we really need this trip."

Ken pulled her closer to him and they kissed. "Rachel, let me make love to you." He looked directly into her eyes, and took his finger and brushed the hair back from her face. "Let me love you. It will make us so much closer." Caressing her body, he so wanted to make love to her.

Rachel was both embarrassed and vulnerable. The no-sex-before-marriage agreement was still in force, although, the tension had mounted over the months. Since the engagement, Ken was ready and willing. She was determined not to give in, no matter how weak she got. This was one of those times.

"Ken, I, I," she hesitated. He had no idea how weak she was to his touch. Her resistance was at its lowest point. If Ken decided to keep pushing forward, she wasn't going to be able to resist. Her new found religious convictions were still in their infancy stage. Her spirit was willing to resist the sexual temptations, but her flesh was weak. She wasn't going to say yes, but she wasn't going to stop him, either. Ken respected her, and managed to catch himself before he got completely caught-up in the heated moment. They both knew this time was too close for comfort. The three week separation had added additional fuel to the already burning-love-jones.

31

It was still light outside, but they were too tired to get out and see the city. The two-and-a-half-hour flight, plus the extended cab ride through Central Park had worn them out. Ken started to unpack. Rachel took in the view from the 40th floor of their hotel suite. "This is breathtaking. This is my first time at the Waldorf."

Ken laid the shirt, he was holding, down and walked over to the window to share in the moment with Rachel. He pulled a chair up to the window and sat down. He extended his hand as an invitation for her to sit down on his lap and put her arms around him. The view and the moment started to set the mood. The passion was growing, undeniably. The two found themselves kissing. Standard practice was for Ken to push away. Not today. He pulled her close and she willingly let him.

She wanted the mini-vacation to be perfect. Coming off of the frightening separation, she didn't want to give him any reason to walk away, not again. The time apart had been awkward, not to mention emotionally draining. Being in his arms, made all of the hurt and rejection she'd experienced over the past weeks, vanish. His embrace seemed to be endless. She was glad to have her relationship back on track.

Ken whispered in her ear, "Rachel, I love you. I am going to marry you. You know we have something special. Please, let this be a special time for us."

All along, he respected her no-sex-before-marriage request. It hadn't been easy, but he had done it. With the romantic setting, coupled with the separation, and the warmth of her body, he found himself in a weak position. Ken was a man, not a sexual robot. It was a significant bit of information Rachel constantly took for granted. She couldn't expect him to keep letting her have her cake and eating it, too. If she didn't say 'no', flat out, then he was going to carry out his expression of love. They couldn't keep creating intimate moments, and stop just short of intercourse. The intensity Rachel felt let her clearly know that she was in a compromising position. She feared they'd been playing around the fire too long. It looked like the no-sex-arrangement was in danger of getting burned.

32

Rachel was ecstatic to see the trip with Ken go so well. The romantic ambiance was still lingering, a month after the spontaneous getaway. It had been a good time for them to reflect on what they meant to each other.

The dust had settled, and they'd gotten back to their normal routines. Rachel found herself dwelling on the events of the trip. In spite of all the wonderful moments shared with Ken, there was one nagging aspect that bothered her deeply. She was feeling guilty about being weak and giving into Ken's sexual advances. She wanted to hold the relationship together, but at what cost? The eight months of refraining had gone out the window in one moment of vulnerability. The intensity generated from reconciling in a romantic setting, away from the day-to-day routine, had been too enticing.

She wasn't ready to openly admit it, but Rachel admitted that a part of her gave in to prevent losing him. The separation had scared her. She had learned, first hand, it was easy for him to walk away. She didn't want to give him another reason to do it again. At the time, the intimacy seemed wonderful, but now, she wasn't feeling so good about it. She had really wanted the two of them to wait for the wedding night. She couldn't help but feel, somehow, all of the trouble leading up to their separation, had lured them into violating the agreement.

Ken felt fine with the whole thing. It didn't matter to him if they waited or not. Once he gave Rachel the ring, it was all-systems-go. He often said, "It's going to happen sooner or later, so why not sooner." With his decision to get married, the coast was clear to pursue as much intimacy as they could handle. Long ago, she had abandoned refuge in his spiritual convictions. He considered himself the religious-type but still felt completely justified in having sex with her. She hadn't gotten any indication that he was suffering from any guilt, whatsoever. His religion didn't really rule out too many wrongs, except for the 'Big Ten'. His professing to be religious, and then committing at least as many, if not more, sins than people who didn't go to church was confusing to her. Fortunately, the Sunday Christian Center broadcasts were giving her some spiritual direction. She knew better, and maybe that's why Rachel felt so guilty about what happened in New York,.

Other than the guilt, she was glad they were back together. All seemed well with the world. She glanced at her day-planner to see what was on the day's agenda. Penciled in was her annual performance evaluation scheduled for 1:30 and a note to order Neal's birthday gift. The reminder had been specifically written. It was something she did not want to forget. With all of the support and friendship he had exhibited in recent months, under no circumstances could she forget his special day. Before anything else distracted her, she acted on the reminder. She picked up the phone to call his office.

"Hi, Gertrude."

"Hello, Rachel."

"Is Mr. Pierce in?"

"No. He's in a meeting. It should be rapping up soon. Would you like for me to have him call you back?"

"Actually, I was calling for you. Do you know what next Wednesday is?"

Gertrude paused for a moment. She thought about what significance next week had and came up empty.

"Give up?" Rachel eagerly asked.

"I guess so."

"It's Neal's big three-three."

"Oh yeah, his birthday. That was going to be my next guess," Gertrude jovially commented.

"I'm calling to see what's on his calendar for Wednesday."

Gertrude flipped to next week's pages in the schedule book.

"He has some meetings in the morning and late afternoon."

"So, he'll be there all day?" Rachel inquired for confirmation.

"By the looks of it, I'd say, yes."

"Good."

"Why? What do you have planned for him?"

"Oh, nothing," Rachel mysteriously responded.

"Come on, tell me, please." Gertrude was boiling over with excitement. She and Rachel had established a positive rapport over the years and Gertrude was comfortable talking to her like a friend.

"It's nothing big. I'm just having a balloon bouquet sent over. Let's say something like three for each year."

"Ninety-nine balloons! Oh my goodness. I'd be lucky if my friends sent me one balloon on my birthday, let alone ninety-nine!"

"Yep. He'll be thoroughly embarrassed."

"Good for you. You two are quite a pair. I heard about what he did for you on your twenty-fifth birthday."

"He told you about sending me twenty-five dozen flowers!"

"He sure did."

"That was years ago," Rachel commented.

"I was so impressed to know a man could have the forethought to do something so special, on his own, and most importantly, be able to plan it out ahead of time. For my birthday, you don't know how many times my husband has grabbed a dozen miniature roses from the local convenience store. He thinks I don't know they're from the mini-mart, but you can always tell the difference between the ready-mades and the fresh-cuts from the florist."

Actually Rachel knew, oh too well, compliments of the jerks in her past. When she was in Atlanta, womanizing Ed even had the nerve to get an attitude when she didn't get overly excited about his $2.99 dozen roses that looked like he paid $2.00 too much. For this conversation, Rachel didn't want to open up any war wounds of the past. She let Gertrude continue with the flow.

"You must be a very special person to get a whole dozen fresh, full-sized florist flowers delivered on your birthday, let alone twenty-five."

Rachel definitely knew how fortunate she was to have Neal as her best friend and was always willing to openly acknowledge it. Throughout her unsuccessful relationships over the years, his friendship had filled the gap, abundantly. "Well, Neal is all right with me."

"By the way, your thirty-first birthday was just a few weeks ago. How did you like the gift Mr. Pierce sent?"

"I absolutely loved it. Why, were you one of the masterminds behind the gift?"

"No, no. He came up with the idea all by himself. I just helped with the coordinating. So, have you used any of them?"

"Not yet. I think I'll take one day and do the whole shopping spree thing."

"I still can't get over it, thirty-one 25 dollar gift certificates to all those places. I was so fascinated by the gesture. I'm still telling my friends about it. I think it's one of the niftiest gifts I've ever seen. Please, refresh my memory of what all was included. Since I'll never get such a gift, I'll have to live vicariously through yours." Gertrude was genuinely intrigued by Neal's creativity and generosity.

"Let's see." Rachel sifted through her purse to find the envelope of certificates. She carried them around, in case the urge arose to stop at one of the stores on the way home. When she found the envelope, she opened it and took out a bunch of certificates.

"Okay, there's two for my hair salon, one for a manicure, one for Body Works, three for Victoria's Secret, ten for Macy's, six for Marshall Field's, four for accessories, two for lunch and dinner, one for the theater, and last but not least, one for my popcorn." She tucked the certificates neatly back into her purse for safe-keeping.

"What a day you're going to have."

"Yep. That's my Neal. He came up with a good one this time. I must admit, the certificate for the popcorn was a nice touch."

"Well, he knows how much you like it. That was the first certificate he put on the list."

Just as the conversation was winding down, Neal was headed Gertrude's way. Trying not to give the surprise away, Gertrude camouflaged the conversation so he wouldn't know she was talking to Rachel. "I'll take the information down for you and forward it to Mr. Pierce. Thank you."

Rachel caught the signal. "Thanks, Gertrude. I'll talk to you later."

The birthday balloons were a go. The day was going well. Ken was still her love, and Neal's birthday gift was set. The bubbly mood inspired her to go out for a long lunch and relax before the evaluation scheduled for 1:30.

The stir-fry restaurant was just what she needed. Rachel got back to her office around ten minutes after one. She spent fifteen minutes winding down before the meeting. She dreaded the annual performance evaluation process, although it typically went well for her. She had developed a positive reputation on the job and was highly regarded, as consistently reflected in her evaluations.

Once the evaluation was underway, Rachel reviewed the comments written by her boss. She flipped the page over to see the total rating, careful not to appear overly eager. The overall score was five out of a possible five. That was unheard of. She assumed it was an error, because one had to walk on water to get such a rating. Most employees got a total of three, which meant that they were meeting expectations; a four was regarded as excellent, but a five. She was stunned. After allowing ample time for her to review the document, her boss initiated the dialogue.

"Well, any reaction?"

"Yes. Is this correct?" She was sure it must be a mistake.

"Indeed, it is correct."

"I don't know what to say!" Rachel said in astonishment.

"I know it must come as somewhat of a shock. I know we don't generally give out such a high rating, but you definitely deserve it."

"Why, thank you. This has been a good year for our entire department." Rachel was always good about acknowledging the contributions of others, particularly those who tended to be overlooked.

"Thanks primarily to your efforts, Rachel."

She blushed from the praise, but didn't comment in fear of coming across as too modest or too arrogant.

"Rachel, we value your contributions, and instead of losing you, we've come up with some ideas that might interest you."

She was all ears.

"We know you want to pursue a Master's program in Health Administration from either Harvard, Stanford, or the University of Chicago."

Rachel nodded in affirmation, but did not interrupt.

"What if we agreed to pay the entire tuition and fifty percent of your salary for the duration of the program? Would you be interested?"

She was flabbergasted. What an offer. It was hard to believe that this was happening. Over the past two years, she'd talked about getting a Master's. She never dreamed it would be handed to her on a silver platter. It only took a heartbeat for her to respond to the extremely generous offer.

"This is all so overwhelming. I do need a few days to think about it, but I am definitely interested in your generous offer. Thank you for the confidence in my abilities. It's overwhelming."

"Of course this is assuming you will get admitted into one of the three prestigious programs, and we have every confidence that you will."

"What about my current position?"

"We'd have to work out the details, but there's plenty of time for that. By the way, we want your input on the upcoming decisions that we will need to make. This is an unprecedented offer. We'll have to work our way through the details together. Remember, no one in the history of the hospital has received such an opportunity. This is quite an honor, Rachel. Needless to say, we think very highly of you. Keep up the good work."

"Thank you, Mrs. Beasley. This is great news."

Mrs. Beasley stood up from her winged-back arm chair and extended her hand. Rachel jumped up to shake Mrs. Beasley's extended hand.

Bubbling over with excitement, Rachel rushed back to her office. She could hardly wait to share the information with someone who would be equally excited for her, as well as appreciate the magnitude of the offer. She wasted no time in dialing Neal's office number. "Thank goodness he's in town today," Rachel whispered.

For a brief moment, she felt badly about not calling Ken, first. It wasn't that he was against advanced education; he just didn't have much interest in it. After he completed his initial computer training, years ago, he had seen no need to pursue further education. He was content with his lifestyle. From his view, he had a good job. It paid the bills, and that was enough.

Rachel saw advanced training as an integral seed in her career development. Their views were worlds apart, but she didn't see much harm in having differing perspectives. She affirmed that he was no dummy, but Ken wasn't the most intelligent person she'd ever dated, either. Unfortunately, his inability to figure out a way to pay for Ariel's support proved he didn't deserve to have self-motivation substituted for his intellectual shortcomings. As long as Ken kept a job and didn't hinder her motivation, she knew that was going to have to be sufficient.

She knew Neal would be pleased since he had encouraged her to go back to school. He had consistently offered his emotional and financial support on many occasions. She was eager to tell him about the great news.

"Neal Pierce."

"Hey, it's me."

"Hey, Rach."

"Guess what?"

"What?"

"I got five on my evaluation, and they offered me a fellowship to get the Health Administration Master's." From the excitement, she, unknowingly, was talking a-mile-a-minute.

"Wow. Congratulations, girl. I knew you could do it. That is fantastic."

Just as she anticipated, Neal was happy for her.

"We have to celebrate. I owe you dinner, your choice."

"Good, I haven't been to Spiaggía in a while."

"Should have known you would pick one of the most expense restaurants in town."

"That's right. Remember a few months ago you told me friends and dates get the best, so I'm requesting the best. Thank you very much."

"Which are you, friend or date?"

"Whichever one gets the dinner."

"Then Spiaggía it is."

"Gotta go, but just wanted to call and let you know the good news."

"Again, congrats, Rach. You deserve it, and we'll talk about the details later. Catch you later."

"Bye." Rachel was hanging-up when another thought crossed her mind. "Oh, Neal, wait."

"Yeah. What about the salesperson of the year award you were up for? Weren't you supposed to find out today who they selected?"

"Yes, they did announce the selection, just before you called."

"And, don't keep me in suspense. Who got it?"

"I did," Neal calmly announced.

"AhAhAhAh ..." Rachel gave out a loud scream. "Why didn't you say something?"

"Because, I didn't want it to take away from your good news. My award would have kept until later. This is your day, Rach. As much as you've been through over the past couple of years, I'd rather let you have the spotlight."

His sensitivity brought tears to her eyes. "You're too much, Mr. Pierce. Congratulations on your award, anyway."

"Thanks."

"Remember, dinner is still on you." She was attempting to humor her way through the pending tears of joy.

"Of course. I wouldn't have it any other way."

Between his award and her performance evaluation, the week was starting out superbly.

33

Wednesday, Rachel woke up about 6:00 in the morning with a queasy feeling in the pit of her stomach. She laid there for a while, enduring the nausea. The slightest movement seemed to make her feel worse. She glanced over at the clock to see how much time was left before she had to start getting ready for work. The clock displayed 7:05. It didn't leave her much time to get dressed and to get out of there.

While she was picking out an outfit to wear, she remembered it was the second day of her monthly. She termed the first days of her period 'the dark days', because she intentionally wore all dark clothing. There was really no justifiable reason for wearing a dark suit. However, she had unintentionally made a habit of it, and the routine was hard to break. She had expected her visitor to show up a few days ago, but nothing happened. She dreaded the monthly process. The only good thing about it was the consistency. Like clockwork, it started between 10:00 and 11:00 a.m. every fourth Monday, and was over by the weekend. Oddly enough, this was only the third or fourth time in the last ten years when her period didn't start right on time. During moments of extreme stress, she had been late a few times. Overall, she was regular. It was already Wednesday and no sign of her guest.

She leaned over to pick up a pair of pumps, and nausea set in. She bolted to the bathroom, barely making it there in time. Rachel leaned against the sink with her head close to the toilet, feeling completely out of it. With so many people being sick in the office, it was no wonder she was ill. There was no way she was going into the office throwing up all over the place. She decided to bag work, undress, and just stay at home.

Sitting at home was not her thing. Her lifestyle was active, including involvement with many organizations and auxiliaries. She flipped through the channels looking for something to watch. The only programs on in the middle of the day were old reruns, talk shows, and soap operas. She hadn't watched any soaps since her last day off, back in January. They were definitely on her TV line-up for the day. Cosby was in syndication, and she decided to save a few more episodes via tape. The only other show of interest was Oprah. The advertising plug sounded pretty interesting. The show was featuring the cast from Spike Lee's 'Get on the Bus' film. There was also some black man who reenacted the struggle of the former slave, Henry Brown, who mailed himself from Richmond to Philadelphia. Rachel planned for the program line-up, coupled with a nap here and there, to take her right into the late afternoon. By then, Ken would be off work.

She was finishing a bowl of soup and crackers when the phone rang. She was reluctant to answer, thinking it might be someone from work. Could it be Ken, she wondered. With the possibility of it being him, she took a chance and answered the phone.

"Hey, Rachel, are you all right?"

"Hey, Roz. Yes, I'm doing all right. I was just a little queasy this morning. I must have caught a flu bug from the folks at work. How did you know I was here?"

"I called you at the office, and they said you were out sick. I wanted to see how you were doing."

"I was a little nauseous. I should be back on my feet in a day or two. When I do get sick, it's usually over quick."

"I hope this flu bug doesn't last nine months," Roz said.

"Nine months!" Rachel played the comment off. She knew exactly what Roz was referring to, because it had, briefly, crossed her mind. Since she was on the pill, Rachel didn't take the thought too seriously.

"You know that no-sex-before-marriage agreement you two have, or should I say had. Well, maybe that's where you got the flu bug. Where was it, New York?"

"Roz, I am not pregnant. Remember, I'm on the pill."

"You're still on the pill? I thought you'd quit, because you didn't want to get fibroids?"

Rachel had told Roz, over a year ago, she wanted to get off the pill in order to reduce her chance of getting fibroids. She knew quite a few women with tumors, and she was glad not to have them. Her doctor said the pill didn't contribute to the fibroid tumors, but she wasn't convinced. It was too coincidental that the women she knew with the fibroids had all been on the pill for years.

"I haven't quit, yet. It's a good thing I didn't, with this little accident in New York."

"You know you're still not off the hook. The pill isn't one hundred percent effective. I think the statistics I read said one out of a hundred women who are on the pill get pregnant. With all of the heat you and Mr. Sanders have been generating, that one out of a hundred might be you."

"Girl, the pill is a sure thing."

"Now Rachel, I know you know better. The only sure thing is abstinence. I know after your getaway to New York, refraining is not an issue."

"After all these months of refraining, we slip up one time."

"I'm not surprised, not at all. It's amazing it took this long."

"Roz! Thanks for your vote of confidence."

"What? Look, I still love you. But, you should know when you keep leading a thirsty dog to water, eventually he's going to drink. And, you can't just blame the dog. The two of you were together almost every day for more than seven months. Then you go and separate for three weeks. To top it all off, you reconcile in a plush New York suite. It doesn't get more intimate than that. You couldn't keep setting up the buffet in front of the man, and expect him to keep fasting. You should have known the intensity would be overwhelming, and all kinds of things were bound to happen, like the flu."

"We had sex one time in nine months, and bam, I'm pregnant? How could that happen?"

"Well my dear, it only takes one time."

"It seemed like a good thing to do at the time, but if I could replay the moment over, it would be different. This time, for once, I really wanted to wait for the wedding to make love with Ken."

Rachel knew the possibility of being pregnant couldn't be ruled out, regardless of the pill.

"Hind-sight is always twenty-twenty."

Roz had worn down Rachel's confidence in not being pregnant. In a curious tone, she asked, "Roz, can you imagine if I were to get pregnant now, before I get married. It would be like the wrath falling on me."

"Well, I know the wrath of Big Mama would soon be at hand, too."

"I know. If I were single and pregnant, it would break her heart, particularly since she wasn't in favor of Ken and I getting together in the first place. I would have to see her in person to share that kind of news."

"Rachel, don't be so hard on yourself. We all hit bumps in the road. No matter what, we get up, kick the dust off, and keep stepping. Chalk this up to one of life's little growing experiences that's going to make you better and stronger. Having a baby now, wouldn't be the end of the world for you."

"You're right. I can't live on shoulda-woulda-coulda. I'm going to pick my head up and move forward like I've done every other time something happened."

"Good for you. Don't forget about me and a whole bunch of other people will be here for you. That reminds me of the reason I called. I have to go to New York in two weeks to meet with an advertising company. I was able to finagle a four hour lay over in Chicago on the return leg. Are you going to be around then?"

"That's what, the middle of May?" Rachel asked as she rummaged through her briefcase looking for the day-planner.

"Actually, I'll be there on Wednesday, May 9th. If you're free, I'll treat you to dinner."

"I'm definitely not going to pass up a free dinner."

"Consider it a belated birthday treat."

"I'll take it, sis."

"Good, we're on then. By the way, I keep forgetting to ask what Ken got you for your first birthday together?"

"I didn't tell you."

"Nope."

"Oh, I thought I did. Anyway, he got me a nice silk blouse and a beautiful pair of matching stretch pants."

"Ah. That's nice." Roz was being diplomatic. Although his gift was nice, she knew, before even asking, that Mr. Pierce had upstaged it. "I have to ask, what did Neal give you."

"His gift was nice." Rachel intentionally down-played her emphasis on his gift. She didn't want it to overshadow Ken's.

Roz could tell Rachel was holding back. Roz knew that it was something special, always was. She remembered the full-length fur coat Neal had gotten Rachel after she passed the C.P.A. exam. Even though it was presented as a joint gift from both Roz and Neal, in reality, he was determined to contribute at least 3,500 dollars towards the 4,000 dollar price tag.

Sure, Neal had some money, but what always impressed Roz was the extra effort he put into making Rachel happy. Roz and Rachel agreed the men they, generally, met were too insensitive or too self-centered to pick-up on the gifts they wanted. Not Neal. He took pleasure in giving Rachel what she wanted, and not just what he wanted her to have. How little or how much it cost was not the most important factor to him.

Roz recalled the time when Rachel mentioned how much she liked an antique brass and sterling silver hand mirror that cost all of twenty dollars. Over a seven month period, Neal visited over sixty-two antique and thrift shops during his travels, looking for that mirror. On a business trip to Philadelphia, he found it, exactly as she described. When he gave it to her, Rachel was in awe. She'd only mentioned the mirror on one occasion, and, amazingly, he remembered. She never knew the amount of effort he put into finding her 20 dollar gift. It was one of the best gifts she'd ever received, because it was precisely what she wanted. There had never been a limit to what extent Neal would go to make her smile. Making her happy, made him happy.

Roz pushed for the scoop on Neal's gift. "What did he give you?"

"Thirty-one gift certificates to all of my favorite places."

"I knew it. Girl, you're crazy to pass him up. And, on top of everything else, he doesn't have all of that baggage you're always talking about."

"You mean like kids and a lot of exs?"

"That's right, the twelfth characteristic on the Mr. Perfect list."

"Yeah, well?"

"Nowadays, you know how hard it is to find a man over twenty-one with no kids. I tell you, if Neal was five years older, I'd have to look his way myself."

"Yeah, right."

"Oh that's right. I forgot. You don't want him to be with anyone else. You just want to keep him pining over you to eternity. You don't want him and don't want anybody else to have him," Roz teased.

"Oh, please. Here we go on the Neal and Rachel kick. How did we get there? Get over it, sis. Neal and I are buddies, buddies you understand. You forget the man has a woman, remember, Nicole?"

"Uhm huh. Sure, I remember Nicole."

"Well?"

"Well, whatever you say. I have to get going Rachel. Take care of yourself, and call me if you need someone to talk to. Do yourself a favor, take a pregnancy test. If it turns out that you are pregnant, don't worry about what Big Mama's going to say. You know how much she loves you, and how dear you are to her heart. Remember, you are her only child, or grandchild, I should say. Anyway, that has always counted for a whole lot."

Rachel was more than willing to receive the encouraging words without disagreement. "Thanks, Roz. I'll let you know if anything happens."

As soon as Rachel hung-up the phone, she got up from the bed, threw on a few clothes, and headed for the local pharmacy. Her mission was to take a home pregnancy test before the anxiety intensified. The suspense, alone, was making her sick.

Upon her return from the store, she eagerly administered the test. Ideally, she wanted to wait and do the test first thing in the morning, but she couldn't hold out until then. The anticipation would be too overwhelming to wait another eighteen or so hours. The kit came with two tests. The plan was to take the first test now, and use the second one as a confirmation in the morning. Her nervousness managed to make Rachel mess up the test.

"Oh man, it didn't work," she sighed, leaned her body against the sink, and folded her arms. "Ooh," she signed again out of frustration. She twisted her body around to pick up the pregnancy test box from the countertop.

"I won't waste this one. I guess I'll have to do it again in the morning."

In her mind, it was only a formality. Deep down, Rachel suspected she was pregnant. Being on the pill afforded her a period of temporary denial, in spite of Roz's one out of a hundred statistic.

34

The first test hadn't proven anything, but Rachel still intended to have a talk with Ken about the possibility of being pregnant. She thought it only fair to share as much information with him as soon she could.

She picked up the phone and pushed the #4. After four rings, the answering service kicked in. "Hello. This is Ken. I can't take your call right now, but leave a message and I will get back to you. Remember, God has given us the victory. So, rejoice and be of good courage."

In the beginning, Rachel loved hearing his commanding voice spurting out religious words of encouragement. After hearing the message ump-teen times over the past nine months, it had lost the luster. She patiently waited for the beep.

"Don't forget to have a nice day." Beep.

"Hey honey, it's me. Just calling to make sure you're coming over after work." She couldn't decide how much information to leave on the message. After a brief thought, she decided to leave no details. It was better to let him hear the announcement face-to-face. "See you this evening. Love you. Bye."

After Rachel finished taping the Oprah show, she drifted off to sleep. The sound of Ken coming in the front door startled her, and she jumped up deliriously.

"It's me, Rachel," Ken called from the foyer.

Disheveled, she took a stretch to shake off the sleepies. "I'm in here," she called from the sun room.

He was sharp, as usual, wearing a black and white striped suit with lines so thin, it almost looked gray. The pants had a finely tailored cuff in the hem, about an inch wide. The tailored-looking suit hung perfectly on his toned body. He accented the suit with a soft white, finely-woven, collarless silk shirt with covered buttons. The cut of the shirt didn't require a tie. The black leather belt and shoes completed the ensemble.

"Uhm," Rachel grunted in acknowledgment of how good Ken looked. After all these months, she was still struck by his handsome demeanor. If looks were all it took, he was definitely the man. Between the two of them, she knew they would make some pretty kids.

He walked towards her with his arms open wide for a hug. "What are you doing home so early?"

"I wasn't feeling well, so I took the day off."

"How are you feeling now?"

"So, so." In replying, she scrunched her face up and rocked her right hand back and forth.

"What is it, some kind of a bug?"

"You could say that." Rachel's response sounded mysterious, but how else was she to answer his question? With the wedding so far off, and the thing with Sandra brewing, she had no idea how he was going to respond to the news about the potential pregnancy. She knew the timing was bad, especially, since they had just gotten back on track from the mini-break-up. She didn't want to prolong the anxiety, and chose to blurt it out.

"I think the rabbit might have died."

It took him a moment to understand what she was saying. Once he got it, Ken immediately plopped down onto the sofa. It was hard to tell from his facial expression exactly how he felt about the news.

"Are you sure?"

"Not one hundred percent, but a good ninety."

"So, you may not be?" he said, sounding a bit relieved.

"There's a small possibility that I'm not, but I do mean small." She was in tune with her body and was aware that something was going on.

"How did this happen?" he bitterly asked.

She couldn't believe he was asking such a question, with such a nasty tone. She immediately took offense. She wanted to say, "How do you think it happened, Romeo?" but held back.

After finally giving into the sexual tension, once, she was most likely pregnant. Neither were thrilled. Rachel had always dreamed that next to marriage, having a baby was going to be the happiest moment she would have. His distressful look made her feel miserable.

It wasn't supposed to happen like this. No matter how beautiful pregnancy was supposed to be, the timing had tainted it. She knew people who spent many years and lots of money trying to have a baby. She didn't like his tone, but could understand his lack of enthusiasm. It was also a bittersweet time for her. She couldn't figure out why their relationship seemed to go from one trying mess to another.

"Rachel, I'm not prepared for this, not at all. What are we going to do?"

"What is there to do, but have the baby?" While Rachel could understand his disappointment, she also wanted him to show some loving support.

"That's easy for you to say. You don't have any other kids. I do."

"And …"

"And that's enough for me right now."

"What are you saying, exactly?" Her tone was elevated.

"Nothing."

"No, you're definitely saying something. What is it? Are you saying you don't want a baby?" Her comments were sharp and to the point. He was sensing her anger rising up, so he opted to tone down his responses.

"I don't know what I'm saying. It's a shock."

It was funny to her how lovey-dovey everything was in New York. Ken couldn't wait to make love, and, as he said, "Get closer." Doesn't get much closer than this, Rachel thought. Even with his so-called-religious-self, she was the one who had pushed for refraining all those months. Never once, during the act in New York, did he seem confused or in doubt about any aspect of the relationship. There was nothing but love, love, love. Now it was the 'day after', and he was singing a different tune.

"Sex makes babies." Her head was bobbing from side to side. She was working her neck like it was attached to an ostrich. Her hand had become an extension of her hip. Her body language implied it was about to get real ugly in the conversation. She had been looking out for his feelings, and so was he. That didn't leave anyone to look out for her. She felt obligated to speak up for herself, since he wasn't giving her any consideration.

"Every time you sleep with somebody, you run the chance of them getting pregnant. If you didn't want another baby, then you shouldn't have been so eager to hop in bed. I didn't force you to do anything, you know."

Rachel didn't hold back in letting him know that she really didn't like his attitude. True enough, the pregnancy was unplanned, but she saw it as a moot point. It had happened. It had to be dealt with, and that was all there was to it. She was shocked and angry to see him act like they were strangers, particularly with a marriage pending. He made her feel like a one-night-stand.

"But we used protection!" He was referring to her being on the pill. He had opted not to use a condom, claiming he didn't like the feeling. In the heat of passion, nothing seemed significant except getting the groove on. Thinking back, Rachel realized it was naive to put herself in such a predicament. With all of the diseases out there, getting pregnant wasn't her only consideration. Nevertheless, she couldn't entertain any other life changing disasters, at the moment. One major crisis at a time was enough for her to handle.

"Protection is not everything, Ken. Read the labels." She sounded confident in her revelation to him. Ironically, it had only been a few hours before when she'd been in the same kind of denial he was experiencing. Yet, her tolerance for his denial was awfully low. She could only guess that it was due to his tone.

She had considered not taking the birth control pills six weeks ago, right after the New York trip. Until now, it had only been a thought. She hadn't actually stopped. Sister Jones' message at the singles' luncheon had vividly pointed out that a single woman seeking to live Godly and practicing abstinence would have no reason to be on birth control pills. The message had made sense, and she was inspired to move towards giving up the pill. At the time, getting off the pill had been merely a goal. She was smart enough to know the personal changes she wanted to make in her life

life wouldn't happen over night. The pill was a non-issue, now, since she was probably pregnant.

There was a strong possibility the pill hadn't worked for her in New York. Rachel was still glad she hadn't stopped taking them before the mini-getaway. The way Ken was trippin', she didn't want him to remotely think she tried to get pregnant on purpose. She wasn't the type to get pregnant in order to keep a man. It hadn't worked for anyone she knew, and worst of all, it hadn't worked for Sandra. Rachel, even at her lowest moment, wanted to believe she had more self-esteem than to resort to the acts of a really desperate woman, willing to comprise herself just to keep a man.

"I can't afford another baby, not right now. I'm already tied up with Sandra over some money."

"This isn't about money!" Rachel fired.

"Maybe not, but kids sure seem to end up that way."

"Don't forget, I work. I'll do what I have to do in order to take care of my baby," indirectly implying he should want to do the same thing.

"Don't get me wrong, Rachel. I mean, you know I want a wife, and some kids all living under the same roof, but this isn't the right time."

"Should have thought about that a month ago," was the snide remark she echoed. His negative reaction was really getting to her. She didn't feel good about being pregnant out of wedlock, but the damage had been done. She knew they had to deal with it. One thing was for sure, she had no intention of having an abortion, regardless of any inconvenience the pregnancy generated.

"There's no reason to get smart, Rachel. I'm doing the best I can with this news."

There he went again, supposedly doing the best he could. When it came to kids, Rachel found his 'best' effort was something to laugh at. This was starting to smell a lot like the deal with Sandra and Ariel. Rachel wondered exactly how close the two scenarios were. She was curious to know if Ken and Sandra had started off the same way as they had, all lovey-dovey and happy? It sure looked like they were going to end up the same way. Déjà vu. Handwriting had been on the wall, but she had chosen to ignore it.

Rachel thought that her having kids with him would, somehow, be different than his ordeal with Sandra.

Rachel should have sensed something was shaky with him from the beginning. Here he was, a handsome man, single, romantic, employed, unattached, and straight. She didn't know any perfectly good men between the ages of nineteen and sixty, sitting around, waiting to be found. She knew women were too desperate to let a good man be idle. She was starting to put some thought to why he was available. Perhaps, he wanted the American dream, house in the burbs, kids, cars, and vacations to Disney World, but didn't want to make any sacrifices for it.

In the midst of the heated dialogue, Rachel looked up at the wall clock. "Look, we've been talking for the past hour, and haven't resolved anything. I'm sleepy."

"I'm not."

"You're welcome to stay for as long as you like."

"I'll watch TV for a little while." He wasn't really ready to end the conversation, although he didn't have any thing else to say on the matter. He was disturbed, but wasn't ready to walk out. Things were too tense to leave with everything so messed up.

"Good night," she said without looking back.

Rachel was ticked off about his unyielding disappointment. She tossed and turned most of the night, feeling frustrated by his unsupportive reaction. Although it was doubtful, she was hoping her period would start at any minute and alleviate her from this trying dilemma. For the first time in over seven years, she was actually hoping for her dreaded period. It would be a welcomed visitor tonight.

"God, please let me not be pregnant. We wanted to get married first. Please let me get my period." Rachel prayed off and on throughout the night, something she hadn't done so diligently during the good times, particularly in New York. She was in real need, the prayers were flowing off of her lips like a hummingbird.

About 4:00, the anxiety became too great. She jumped up from the bed and headed straight to the bathroom for the retest. She had set everything up the night before, in anticipation of her desire to rush and potentially mess things up again. She had barely applied the test before it read positive. Her heart sank to her feet. She didn't know whether to cry or be tough and show no emotion.

She assumed Ken was still downstairs, sleeping on the sofa. He often slept there on his overnight stays. All along, he had wanted to sleep on the bed with her. She resisted as much as she could. She recognized that it might seem odd, to someone else, for her to still be against sleeping on the bed with Ken. The damage was already done. Still, she just didn't want to completely throw in the towel and start flat-out sleeping together. Perhaps it was a fairy tale, but for a brief while longer, she still wanted to maintain the facade. In a few months, it would be evident to the casual observer that abstinence was definitely not a reality in their relationship.

The strangest thought crossed her mind. As big as life, she could hear Sister Jones' and Pastor Ellington's plea to flee lust and pre-marital sex. Pastor Ellington summed it up very simply, "Five minutes of passion can lead to eighteen years of struggle, and some of you aren't even getting your whole five minutes." It was one thing to sin, and even worse to get caught. She wondered if the feeling would be different if she had slept with Ken, but not have gotten pregnant. She didn't know if the real source of her guilt was attributed to the sin or the consequences?

What had started off as such a vibrant and promising romance, was quickly turning into a bumpy, disaster-prone road. Worse yet, she was getting the impression Ken wanted to abandon her and the baby on that road. Well, she wouldn't really be alone. Sandra and Ariel were already there. His road of abandoned women and babies was starting to get pretty crowded.

Rachel laid across the bed and tried not to think about the test results. She dozed back off to sleep; it was Ken's coming up the stairs that woke her up. He went to the bathroom before coming into the bedroom in an attempt to avoid facing her. Finally, after about twenty minutes, he had to show his face and popped his head into the bedroom.

"Good morning."

"Good morning," Rachel returned.

"Are you going to work today?"

"Yes, I am," she flatly answered.

"Well, I better get out of here so I can get in on time."

"What time is it? she asked.

"It's almost 5:30," he kindly answered.

He was trying to avoid the pregnancy issue, but she couldn't refrain from sharing the news. It wasn't solely her dilemma.

"I took the test."

There was no response from him. He stood before her looking like a stranger.

"It was positive. I guess I'm definitely pregnant."

The only reaction he gave was, "Well, I have to go in order to get to work on time."

"Did you hear what I said?"

"Yeah."

"Are you going to say anything about it?"

"Like what?"

"Like you're happy, you're sad, you're mad." Her voice was elevated and sharp. Anger was at best only a couple of words away. "Even if you said dog, I don't want a baby. That would be better than standing there like you can't talk."

Indirectly, that's exactly what he had said. She refused to believe her fiancé, the man she was planning to marry, really felt so unattached. She wanted to give him the opportunity to redeem himself.

"What else is there to say? You know my situation."

"Your situation! This is only about you, huh!"

She was increasingly disappointed with his nonchalant stance. Too often the men in her past would clam up when a tough challenge arose. She figured Ken to be different, but, apparently, no such luck. He was whimpering in the face of adversity, like the rest. At that moment, she understood why women nagged. They were usually the one stuck with figuring out what to do, while the men sat back and watched life go by from the couch-potato-spot on the sofa, with a remote, CD, or a beer glued to their hand.

"Big Mama called it right, after all."

"Big Mama, Roz, Big Mama, Roz. That's all I hear. You do everything Big Mama tells you to do?"

"Obviously not."

Rachel so wanted to go further and tell Ken she wouldn't be with his sorry butt if she'd listened to Big Mama from the beginning, but didn't allow herself to go there. She now realized why he wasn't with Sandra. The answer to her initial question of why a perfectly good man in his mid-thirties was unattached, started to become clear. Unfortunately, the price she had to pay for her new found wisdom was an illegitimate child. What a price to pay, she thought. She mumbled under her breath, "I guess I just bought some sense."

"This is not a good time for me to be having another baby, Rachel."

"Like it's ideal for me!"

"I can't talk about this now. We'll just have to deal with it later. I have to go."

"Well, Ken why don't you get back to me when you can. I'll be pregnant for about nine months. So, there's no real rush, is there!" She jumped up from the bed, pushed past him, and stormed into the bathroom slamming the door behind her. She was fed up with his 'run and hide' attitude. Sticking his head in the sand wasn't going to solve anything. Where was the man when she needed him?

She yelled through the door, "You sure didn't mind giving me your undivided attention when we were laying up in New York. Now that the dust has settled, and I'm pregnant, all of a sudden you're confused and don't have any time. You are a pathetic excuse for a man, let alone a father."

He continued to stand there for a minute. He started to knock on the bathroom door, but realized there wasn't really anything left to say and decided to leave for work.

Rachel stood with her back to the door for a few minutes, and then sat down at the vanity table. She put her head down on the table and began to sob. As intelligent and successful as she was, it didn't prevent her from getting pregnant by an established 'dead-beat-dad'. The red flag had always been dangling in front of her eyes. She just chose to discount it, thinking this hang-up was exclusive to Sandra and not so much a quirk in his personality. She was well versed enough to know young, poor, and uneducated women weren't the only ones to 'get-knocked-up' and then left alone. Sad thing was, it was happening to her, cream of the crop. In the worst of moments, neither Rick with his playboy antics, nor Luc with his cheating self, nor Ed with his con acts had hurt her this badly.

After sobbing for what seemed like hours, she picked her head up and wiped the remaining tears from her cheeks. Glancing in the mirror, she looked like crap. She pushed the puffy pockets down underneath her eyelids.

"Oh my goodness. I can't go to work looking like this."

She had never abused the days off policy, so it would be no problem for her to take the day and potentially tomorrow off. The two days, coupled with the weekend, would give her time to regroup and figure out what to do about the baby and, more importantly, Ken.

Instead of lying around all day in a funk, she decided to pamper herself. The first step was to fill the Jacuzzi with warm steamy water scented with lilac body wash. She took the cotton nightie out of the box Big Mama had given for her birthday. She grabbed a new book and headed for the warm bath. The bubbles from the jet spray were soothing. After an hour of relaxation, she decided to get out before her skin dried up like a prune. She felt refreshed. The Jacuzzi had definitely made a difference. It didn't solve her problem, but she sure did feel better for a moment. All was well until a brief episode of nausea set in.

She layered her body with the lilac powder, lotion, and body splash; put her gown and robe on, and grabbed the door. Heading for the stairs, she picked up Boots and carted the cat down with her.

Downstairs, she put Boots down on top of the kitty playhouse and proceeded to wash her hands in the kitchen sink. She fixed a raisin bagel and juice to get her stomach settled. She took the continental breakfast to the sun room, grabbing the cordless phone on the way. She wanted to share the bittersweet news with her best friend, so she dialed his number.

"Is Neal in?" Rachel was brief, but courteous. She didn't feel like holding a long conversation with Gertrude today. All she wanted was to get Neal on the phone and share her ordeal with someone who truly cared.

Gertrude could tell it was no play-day and wasted no time joking around with her. "He sure is, Rachel. Hold on and I'll get him for you."

"Thanks, Gertrude."

It didn't take Neal anytime to get on the line. "Hey, Rach."

"Hi, Neal."

Neal could hear the television in the background. "Where are you?"

"At home."

"At home? Ah, vacationing at home, huh?"

"Nah. I wouldn't call it a vacation."

"Or is it that you needed a day to recover, because you and Mr. Sanders did too much celebrating for your fellowship award?"

"Nah," she answered strangely.

Neal knew her well enough to know something was not right. "Rach, are you okay?"

"Nah."

In anticipation of her sharing something personal, he picked up the handset to turn the speakerphone off. He didn't want her business spread over the speaker. "What's up Rach?" He could sense the seriousness in her voice, more so in what she wasn't saying, rather than what she was.

"Neal, I'm pregnant."

He heard her words, but just couldn't seem to get them to stick. He didn't know what to say. He was shocked, and wasn't sure why. Rachel and Ken had been in a serious relationship for almost a year. It shouldn't have come as a surprise to Neal that they were going to have sex sooner or later, but it did. He had always been supportive to her, but for the first time in their friendship, he couldn't get beyond his own emotion. He always knew she would eventually get married and have kids, but he never thought it would hit him so hard when the time came.

"Pregnant, huh."

"Yep."

"When did this happen!"

"During the trip to New York."

"The trip I treated you guys to?"

"That's right. I forgot. You did treat us. Thanks a lot." She struggled to find some humor in her situation.

"Look, don't blame me." He tried to joke with her, but his heart didn't find much funny. "Seriously, how do you feel about being pregnant?"

She took a big sigh and composed her thoughts in order to not speak out of pure emotion. "I am not happy about the timing, but I've always wanted children. I guess the good part is that I'm having a baby. The unfortunate part is that I'm not married."

"You're engaged. That's almost married. How does Ken feel about it?" This was one of the rare occasions when Neal referred to Ken by his real name, probably because the conversation was not of a joking matter. He knew this was serious business.

"He's still adjusting to the news. You know he's going through the child support battle with Sandra right now. The last thing he needed was for me to get pregnant."

"So what are you two going to do?"

"I don't know."

"Are you going to get married any earlier?"

"I don't know?"

"I guess this blows your fellowship out the window."

"Fellowship? I haven't even had a chance to think about it since Tuesday."

"How did Ken feel about the fellowship?"

"I never told him. I never got a chance to. We couldn't get past the pregnancy."

"Admittedly, I guess the timing is off."

"You know Neal, it's really crazy. I should be happy about having a baby with the man I love, but a part of me isn't. It's amazing how we took something so special, and ruined it. We let our hormones and emotions get the best of us."

"Ruined what," Neal asked.

"Ruined the sexual innocence we had before we went to New York. Don't get me wrong. I want to have children, but not under these circumstances."

"Neither one of you were virgins!"

"I know, but we were virgins to each other. It was like we were starting with clean slates. I really wanted to do the right thing. When we did, finally, get married, I wanted everything to be perfect."

"I didn't know there was such a thing as a perfect marriage. Do you mean happy or perfect? You know they are not the same."

"When I say 'perfect', I mean that I wanted our marriage to have every possible chance of being happy and beating the odds. I know I'm not the most religious person around, but I am working on it. I really wanted to avoid starting the marriage out with sin and baggage to deal with."

"Rach, I don't know what to say, except that I'm here for you. Whatever I can do, you know I will."

"Thanks, Neal."

"Oh, and Rach, I'm counting on Mr. Sanders to do right by you. This isn't just your baby. It's his, too." Neal sounded more serious than ever.

"I know, and I'm also counting on him."

"Catch ya later."

"All right."

35

Roz wasn't sure what to do about Rachel's current state of mind. The conversation from the day before left her worried. She couldn't call Big Mama and talk about it. The only person she remotely felt comfortable calling was Neal. Roz wasn't in the habit of discussing Rachel's business with others. This was different. She wanted to get some reinforcement on how to help Rachel through a potentially tough time.

Roz got up to get her electronic phone book. She typed in P-I-E-R-C-E-N, and his number popped up. She wasted no time dialing his number. It wasn't until the phone started ringing when Roz realized she didn't know what to say.

"Hello."

"Hello, Neal."

"Roz? Is that you?"

"Yes, it's me."

"Hey now. What's up, sis?"

"I didn't expect you to recognize my voice so quickly. How are you doing?"

"I'm fine," Neal enthusiastically answered. "How are you?"

"I'm good."

"I haven't talked to you since, when, Thanksgiving?"

"Yes."

"How's the marketing business going? I know you have it going on. Rach told me you are making all of the money out there. I hear you need Brinks to roll through for your bank deposits," he chuckled.

"Stop," Roz humorously said. Don't even try it. Matter of fact, I hear you're the one making all of the money, breaking all kind of sales records. You are the man. You go boy."

No matter how refined Roz and Neal were in the professional world, it was common for them to speak in a slang dialect among themselves.

"Yeah, the job is good. I can't complain."

"Even if you did, it wouldn't do any good," they both laughed.

"Right, right."

"Anyway, Neal, I know you're surprised to hear from me."

"A little."

"Well, I'm calling about our girl."

"Who, Rach?"

"Yes."

"Why, what's up?"

"I talked to her yesterday, and I'm worried about her."

"Worried! Why?" Neal instantly shifted to a serious mood.

"Mostly because of her relationship with this Ken. What's the story with him?"

"Ah, you know Rachel." Neal didn't reveal information about Rachel, not even to Roz. He never wanted to betray her trust.

"This guy is getting on my nerves. He gets mad and stops calling her. I hope he doesn't hurt her. She was so upset yesterday. It has really bothered me."

"Well, I know she's going through some things with him. But, I'm here. You know I'm going to look out for her. You know it goes without saying."

"I know."

"I don't get into her business, but I'll be here to help whatever way I can. I can guarantee you that."

"That's good enough for me. Rachel is so fortunate to have you. I hope one day she sees how much you love her."

"Hey, I'm her play-brother. You know me, good ole' Neal. Yeah, I love my sister."

"Uh huh. Rachel may not see it, and I don't know why, but it is obvious to me how much you love her. The real kicker is, you're that perfect man she's always talking about finding. She's pulling her hair out looking for Mr. Right, and she talks to him, practically, everyday. Talk about can't see the forest for the trees. You are a good man Neal, and I appreciate you taking care of my sister."

"Thanks Roz, but you don't have to thank me for caring about Rach. I don't know how not to."

"I believe it. Like I said, you're the best thing she has going. Anyway, I hope you don't mind me calling."

"Roz, come on. You're family. I'm always glad to hear from you."

"Okay. Well, take care Neal. I'll talk to you later."

"Bye, Roz. Oh, and don't worry about Rach. She'll be fine."

Rachel expected to hear from Ken during the day, but no call came through. She waited until 8:30 in the evening before calling him. The answering service picked up, "Hello. This is Ken. I can't take your call right now, but leave a message and I will get back to you. Remember, God ..."

"What a joke," Rachel bitterly yelled as she slammed the phone onto the base. "How can he talk about God, Mr.-Let's-Get-It-On-Because-We're-Engaged, Mr.-Let-Me-Get-To-Church-After-I-Try-To-Seduce-My-Girlfriend, Mr.-I'm-A-Happy-Daddy-In-Name-Only. Please! No wonder nobody else goes to church in his family. He's not exactly the best Christian role-model around."

She had already deducted the point he earned previously for being religious. She accepted that her definition and his way of life didn't equate to the same religious perspective. At one time, he had earned as many as eight out of the twelve possible points. With a few unexpected incidents, he was down to five and dropping fast. The one for family-oriented was questionable, although he did have a strong relationship with his father and siblings. The other four he had left were tall, handsome, romantic, and down-to-earth. Turned out those were the key ingredients that contributed to her getting pregnant. A good-looking man who likes romance and fun, without the worry of having kids.

Rachel was beside herself. Ken really had her stirred up. She was rattling off all kinds of comments, none of which would be said if he were there. But, it felt good getting the emotions off her chest, even if the only one getting an ear full was Boots.

Whenever she was feeling down in a relationship, it seemed like every show on TV had a couple holding hands and kissing. She didn't even bother to flip through the channels. She ordered in some Chinese food, and popped in a funny movie. The last thing she wanted to watch was a romance or tear-jerker. She planned to follow it up with another upbeat movie. This Thursday night was like a weekend, since there wasn't any work tomorrow. Rachel planned to stay up as long as she liked without feeling guilty or tired the next morning.

She tried Ken again around 10:30, only to get no answer. After the second movie and half a bag of cheese-flavored pretzels, she tried once again.

Ken heard the phone and chose to let it ring. "I know that's Rachel. I don't feel like dealing with her nagging right now."

This time she left a message. "Ken, it's me. Could you please call me as soon as you can. I'd like to talk. Thank you." The tone of her voice was curt. She was irritated with his irresponsible behavior.

"I don't know how this happened. How did I get myself into this mess?"

The last time they had gone days without talking turned out to be the motivation for reconciling on the New York trip. Ultimately, she ended up getting pregnant.

Rachel fell asleep on the sofa. She woke up when Boots jumped up onto her leg. At 3:45 the next morning, she turned the TV off and went up to bed. She was disappointed not to hear from Ken. She was annoyed at his childish act of avoiding the problem and cutting off communication. Based on his track record, she was wondering if this was how he always handled adversity, through avoidance? She started to call and wake him up in the middle of the night, but decided against it.

"No matter what, I am not going to beg him to do right by me. I have too many other options than to bow at King Ken's feet." She was determined to be strong for herself and the baby, regardless of the role he played.

Ken unlocked the door and went into his apartment. It had been a tough day at work. He had become increasingly bored by the repetitive nature of his job. Today, he had found a new focus. Rachel's pregnancy had caught him by surprise, and he couldn't seem to get it off of his mind.

He pulled a glass from the dish washing rack, grabbed some ice from the freezer, and opened a half-full bottle of liquor from the cabinet. He wasn't a big drinker, but drastic matters called for drastic actions. This was one of those times.

He took his glass into the living room. The first drink was tart, but effective. He plopped down onto the chair and tried to relax. This was one of the few Fridays he'd spent without Rachel. He turned the volume up on the stereo and the sound down on the TV. The combination allowed him to think. The TV was for motion, and the stereo was for sound.

Knock, Knock, was the sound coming from the doorway.

Ken wasn't sure if he heard someone at the door or not. He put the stereo on mute to see if he heard the knock, again.

Knock, knock.

"Who could that be. I'm not expecting anybody."

He put his drink on the floor, next to the chair and got up. The small size of his apartment enabled him to be at the front door within a few steps.

"Yes," Ken said, in lieu of a formal greeting.

"Mailman?"

"Oh, okay." Ken opened the door. "Hi, DeWayne. You're late today."

"Yeah, busy day today."

"I can understand that."

The mailman pulled the pen he had resting on his ear, and marked an X on the signature line. "Mr. Sanders, I need your 'John Hancock' right here." He handed the clipboard and the pen to Ken.

Pointing to the line with the big X, Ken asked, "Do I sign here?"

"Yep, that will be fine."

Ken scribbled his signature and handed the clipboard back.

The postman ripped off the signed portion of the label and handed Ken the letter with the rest of his mail.

"Have a good one."

"You too," Ken responded.

He closed the door, went back to his chair, and flipped through the mail. His eyes locked in on the certified letter. The return address was from the Department of Domestic Relations. He was more than curious to know what the letter was about. He ripped it open and pulled out the letter.

At the top of the page was the wording, State of Ohio. Department of Domestic Relations. Reading down the page, it stated Sandra L. Johnson, Plaintiff/Payee followed by Kenneth M. Sanders, Defendant/Payor.

He didn't need to read any further. His heart was pounding.

"I don't believe she actually did it." He leaned back in the chair and laid the papers on his chest. "Man, when it rains, it pours.

He gulped down the quarter-glass of liquor left and got up to get a refill.

Sunday morning, Rachel shuffled downstairs and grabbed a toasted bagel to help ease the nausea. She plopped down onto the sofa in the sun room and turned on the TV. It was just in time to catch the Christian Center broadcast. Neal called to check on her since he didn't like the way she sounded when they talked on Thursday.

"Did you watch the service?"

"Sure did," she emphatically answered.

"Good for you."

"Since when did you get all into the Christian Center?" she wondered.

"Ever since you told me about it a couple of months ago."

For the past month, he had faithfully watched the Sunday morning service she had turned him onto. He was really getting into the teachings and had even gone to the midweek service a couple times.

"The message was good. I didn't know nearly as much as I thought about being equally yoked." He was amazed to hear the depth of the spiritual meaning.

"What did you think it meant?" Rachel knew what it meant. She hadn't been able to apply it to her life, but had the theory down pat.

"You know, that religious-church-going folks should marry other people like themselves."

"So what part of the message surprised you?"

"Lots of it. The part where he talked about two people having the same direction, goals, philosophy on rearing children, spending money, working, praying, making friends, in-laws. He even talked about a couple being in sync on choosing a place to live. That's deep."

"But those all make sense."

"Yeah, but Pastor Ellington pointed out that most people decide those things after they get married. It's too late then to realize you don't see eye-to-eye on some serious stuff."

"Hmmm."

"I mean, think about it. Raising children and managing money are two of the biggest things married couples fight about. Most of them don't discuss those things before they get married."

"You're right. I knew that being equally yoked meant more than just being religious. It means to have the same view about God, the Father, and the Holy Spirit. Like Big Mama says, 'God, the father of Abraham, Isaac, and Jacob' to eliminate the slightest bit of confusion. Other than that, I hadn't thought about all of the other areas. It's hard enough finding someone you get along with, let alone having to be equally yoked in all of those other areas."

"I guess that's why we are suppose to let God bring us a mate, instead of trying to find one on our own. He's much better at match-making than we are," he attested.

"I guess that's the only way to get the perfect match-made-in-heaven, so to speak."

"You know me, I'm not looking for a person who's perfect in every aspect of their life. They just need to be perfect for me, flaws and all," he said.

"I know that's right. As hard as I've tried, looking on my own hasn't worked."

"Not even with that killer list of yours." he chuckled.

"Stop. Hey, that list has helped."

"Helped how? Helped you cut off the good brothers who fell short on a couple of points. But, the fine, smooth-talking brothers always seem to bypass the list. Rach, you better get a new list."

"Forget you. It has taken me over ten years and about as many heartaches to get my list tight. I'm not about to dump it, not now. When I find Mr. Right, then I'll put it away."

"You better find the Lord. Let the rest come when it comes."

"Hmm, listen to you. I didn't know you were into the ministry this much."

"I'm working on it. I'm glad you told me about it. Enough about me, how are you?"

"I'm getting by." She sounded melancholy. For a brief moment, his characteristics crossed her mind. Neal's religious pursuits raised his score to an impressive total of eleven-and-a-half. Rachel pondered why she couldn't find a good man, like Neal, who had as many characteristics as he did. She couldn't figure out why it was so hard to find Mr. Perfect. Neal was proof that such a man existed.

"Does that have some kind of a dual meaning?"

"No, not really."

"All right. How's Ken?"

"I don't know."

"What do you mean you don't know?"

"I haven't talked to him since he left here Thursday morning."

"You're kidding."

"No, I'm not kidding."

Neal gave an uncharacteristic sigh. "So he's trippin' again. Must be tough for a boy to try and play in a man's game."

"Neal!"

"What?"

"Why did you say that?"

"I'm sorry, but I don't like how he's treating you. All he can think about is himself. He should be giving you support, not a cold shoulder. For goodness sake, you two are engaged. Doesn't that mean something? It's not like you're his one-night-stand."

"He must have his reasons," she suggested.

"Sure he does, none of which I care to hear. Rach, you are so kind-hearted. Even in the midst of his childish behavior, you're defending him. The man is more fortunate than he'll ever know. I hope he doesn't screw it up."

"We'll see what happens. If he doesn't call soon, I'll have no choice but to rethink the relationship. Right now, I'm still holding out for the fairy tale."

"I hope the fairy tale doesn't turn into a horror flick, starring Too-fly."

"Funny, Mr. Pierce. Ha ha."

The comment Neal made was said in jest, but he was dead serious about it.

"Anyway, Neal, I'll be back to work tomorrow. Are you out of town this week?" Over the years, she had grown accustomed to knowing his where-abouts, just in case she needed to get a hold of him.

"No. I receive the award Thursday night. I postponed the Montreal trip until next week," he clarified.

"That's right. I totally forgot about the ceremony. You and Nicole have a great time, and I'll catch you later."

"See ya."

Neal wanted to make everything right for Rachel. He didn't always like her choices, but that never affected how he felt. She needed him now, and he knew it. Ken's cutting her off, at such a critical time, outraged him. He wanted to pick up the phone and give Too-fly a call, but resisted. It wasn't in his make-up to be confrontational.

Neal was mad about the whole situation. He was even mad at Rachel for getting herself into a spot he couldn't help her out of. He felt helpless. Neal pulled a snapshot from his wallet. It was a picture of him and Rachel, taken at Great America one summer. He sat down, next to the window, and stared at it.

"This girl is going to drive me crazy." He held the picture up in the sunlight. "When did I fall so deeply in love with this girl?" Even when Neal wanted to get mad at her, he couldn't. He smiled. "If she only knew, I'd be in real trouble. But, Ken is her choice, and that's that."

36

Neal was pleasantly surprised by the birthday bouquet. On Wednesday, he had a courier service take the gift home from the office. It was too big to fit into the Beemer.

Nicole happened to be at his place when the balloons arrived.

"Don't tell me, Rachel?"

"Yes." Neal didn't elaborate, sensing some dissatisfaction in her voice.

"Boy, what a surprise!" Nicole snidely commented.

"It is a lot of balloons." Neal tried to keep the tone up beat, even though he knew where Nicole was headed.

"Too many!"

"Come on Nicole. I thought we worked my friendship out with Rachel two years ago. I get the feeling you're upset about this gift."

"Upset? No, just out matched."

"What does that mean?"

"You honestly don't see anything wrong with the gift?"

"No, I think it's nice. Rachel always goes all out with her gifts. She didn't mean anything by it. That's the way she is with the people who are close to her."

"I don't expect you to see anything wrong with it. Why would you? They're from Rachel. I bet she could send you a box of mess and you'd be excited about it."

"Really, Nicole, do you think that's necessary?"

"No, I guess it wasn't. I'm sorry. But, it still doesn't change how you feel."

"Nicole, I'm not sure I know where you're going with this. I feel strongly about you."

"But not love me?"

"Love takes time." He didn't confirm or deny his love for Nicole.

"There will never be enough time to sway your feelings my way."

"I don't know why you're saying that. We're in a relationship right now. Excuse me if I'm wrong, but I thought we were getting closer every day."

"Don't you get it? I'm not the one, Neal. I never was, and probably never will be."

"Not the one what?" He wasn't following her train of thought. Her drastic mood swing was unexplainable.

"I'm not the one you want. I'm just the one you're with. Face it. I have. You love Rachel, not me."

"We have a good time together. You know I care about you."

"Yes, but I don't just care about you. I love you. This has been the best relationship I've ever had. You're rare Neal. You're honest. Your smart and romantic. I can honestly say that you are all I want in a man."

"I think you're nice, too."

"Yeah, well, too bad being nice isn't enough."

"You sound like there's a problem between us!" Neal was baffled how a bouquet of balloons could trigger such a deep reaction. He and Rachel had always exchanged gifts. It wasn't like he had short changed Nicole when it came to gifts. The gifts he gave her may not have been as sentimental as the one's given to Rachel, but were no less tasteful. Neal's defense for giving the high caliber of gifts to Rachel was their long standing twenty-plus years of friendship. Over time he grew to know what she liked. In time, he would learn all of Nicole's preferences.

"I would like nothing better than to spend the rest of my life with you, but I can't do that to you or to myself. As long as Rachel is in the picture, the most I can ever be to you is second best. That's simply not good enough for me. As wonderful as you are, I don't want to be with someone I know wants to be with someone else. We both deserve better."

"You act like I've short changed you in our relationship?"

"No. Not at all. Like I said, this has been wonderful."

"Whether you are right or wrong, how I feel about Rachel is not a negative reflection on you."

"Perhaps it was the timing?"

"How do you mean?" he asked.

"If things had been different with you and Rachel, then perhaps things would have been different with us."

"I don't know what to say."

"I guess a part of me wants you to say, no Nicole, you're all wrong. I do love you, and Rachel is really my friend, nothing more."

He couldn't deny her claim about his feelings for Rachel. It was true, but he was too much of a gentleman to knowingly hurt Nicole. It wasn't her fault Rachel had the key to his heart, and he adored her.

"See, I am right. You can't say it, can you."

Neal hesitated before responding, primarily because he didn't know what to say. He was too honest to flat out lie, and too chivalrous to crush her feelings.

"No, don't answer. I already know." Nicole knew breaking up with him, logically, was the right thing to do. Emotionally, it didn't feel too good.

"You know Rachel is engaged. Doesn't that change your mind about how you think I feel about her?" Neal asked.

He had to offer some sort of defense. He really did care about Nicole and wasn't expecting a sudden break-up. Sure, he loved Rachel, always had, but he resolved, years ago, to give up on that notion. He was faithful to Nicole and was anticipating a future together. This discussion was unexpected, and really caught him off guard.

"The real question is, does it change yours?" Nicole put the ball back in his court.

"She's getting married Nicole. Now, how could I possibly be pursing a romantic relationship with her?" The question was posed to Nicole, but Neal was really asking himself. He intentionally didn't mention the pregnancy, because Rachel had entrusted him with the information. Under no circumstances would he betray her confidence. He hadn't discussed any details with Roz and wasn't going to with Nicole.

"That's my point. Even though she's unavailable, you still love her. No one can compete with Rachel in your life. I know I can't."

"I don't deny our closeness, but it's not a romantic situation. It never has been." It wasn't clear whether he was trying to convince Nicole, or himself.

"I believe you're right when you say it's not romantic. That's even worse, at least for my chances. The two of you have a twenty or thirty year connection. You have loved her without even touching her in a sexual way. That's pretty deep. Surely you can't deny that as love."

"I don't deny our close friendship."

"Exactly. You're more than lovers, you're friends."

The phone rang in the middle of their discussion. Neal started not to answer it, but at Nicole's encouragement he picked up the phone.

"Hello."

"Neal."

"Yes, Mom."

"I got some bad news."

Neal didn't know what to expect, so he braced himself. "What is it, Mom?"

"Big Mama's sick. We just rushed her to the hospital."

"What happened? What's wrong with her? Is she going to be all right?" He had a flurry of questions to ask in his state of panic.

"We think it's either a stroke or heart attack. We're at the hospital right now. They're running some tests to find out what it is, so they can treat her."

"Oh my God. Rachel is going to be devastated."

"I know. That's why I called you first."

"I'm going over to her place. Give me the number where you are, so I can call you when I get to Rach's."

"It's a pay phone here in the emergency room, and I don't see a number. It will be easier for me to call you back."

"Can you wait about forty-five minutes, and then call over to her place."

"All right then. I'll call in forty-five minutes."

"Please, don't forget. Whatever you do, don't call any earlier. I want to be there for her when she finds out." All he could think about was Rachel's current state of semi-depression, attributed to the pregnancy and lame Ken. This was going to be hard on her.

"Talk to you soon, baby."

"Okay, Mom. Love you."

Neal had completely forgotten about his conversation with Nicole. She looked at him, and knew that both the conversation and the relationship were over.

"Nicole, I have to"

"Don't tell me," she interrupted. I heard enough to know that Rachel needs you and you're going to her. No matter where you are or what you're doing, she will always come first." She was right, and Neal didn't even try to deny it. There was no need.

"I want to continue this conversation, but I do have to get packed and over to Rachel's right away. I'm sorry. I really am sorry, Nicole." Neal was sincere in his apology. He never got involved with Nicole expecting the relationship would end like this.

Nicole grabbed her purse and keys before giving the parting speech. "There's no need to escort me to the door. I know you're in a hurry." She gave him a friendly peck on the cheek. "Take care, Neal, and oh I do hope everything works out for you and Rachel. As she opened the door to leave, for the last time, she turned to him and said, "If something changes, please, give me a call."

Nicole was barely out the door before he was filling his travel bag with only the bare essentials. He was completely packed in less than fifteen minutes. Anything else he needed would have to be purchased in Detroit.

Rachel was doing some work at the desk. With the three days off last week, there was a lot to catch up on. She was consumed with the financial statements. The phone rang about five times before she got it.

"Hello." She was distracted as reflected by the tone in her greeting. She'd answered the phone, but her mind wasn't on holding a conversation.

"Hi, baby."

"Hi, Mom." Rachel always recognized Ms. Pierce's voice.

"Did Neal get there? I called him before I called you."

"No, I didn't know he was coming over. I haven't talked to him today."

"He should be there by ..." Before she could finish, the doorbell rang.

"Someone's at the door. Hold on, Mom. Maybe that's him."

"Okay, baby." Mom wanted to make sure Rachel was in safe hands before she told her anything.

"Hang on." Rachel went to open the door. It was Neal.

"Hey, Rach."

"Hey. I didn't know you were coming over. Mom's on the phone."

"Did she tell you anything?"

"Tell me what? Is something wrong?" Rachel had a tone of fear in her words.

Without saying anything, he followed her to the kitchen, where she'd laid the phone on the counter. "Tell me what?" she asked anxiously while handing the phone to him.

"Hello."

"Hi, Neal. I see you made it."

"Yeah, Mom. I just got here."

"Did you tell her?"

"No, I prefer for you to tell her."

"Well, all right. I'll tell her what I know."

"Okay." Neal handed the phone to Rachel. "Here, Mom wants to talk to you."

The suspense made Rachel nervous, and she slowly reached for the phone, not knowing what to expect. "It's me, Mom."

"Baby, I called to tell you that we rushed Big Mama to the hospital."

"What do you mean you rushed her to the hospital? What's wrong with her?" Rachel was trembling.

"We don't know, yet, but it looks like a stroke or heart attack."

Her heart dropped. She broke out in a sweat and felt instantly faint. "What! Is she okay?" With all the problems going on with Ken, the last thing she needed was to lose Big Mama, who was a rock, no a pillar in her life.

As soon as she looked into Neal's eyes, she burst into tears and went limp. The phone fell to the floor. He grabbed her and took her back into the living room. After depositing her onto the couch, he went back to get the phone.

Bellowing out of the receiver was, "Hello. Is anybody there? Hello?"

"Mom, I'm here."

"Neal, I know she's going to be upset. Son, you take care of her and try to keep her from worrying. I'll let you know what's going on."

"I'll be here if you need to get a hold of me. I'll keep both the cellular phone and the pager on." After talking to his mom, he went back to the living room to give Rachel some comfort.

"Neal, what am I going to do? I need to go. I'm way out here. I don't know what's going on here. Nobody's telling me anything. I need to get to Detroit, fast." Rachel was in a frenzy. "I could probably get there faster by driving, instead of flying. But, I don't feel like driving all that way," said Rachel. She was clearly too shaken up to make any type of coherent decision.

"I know, Rach. Calm down, and try to pull yourself together." He took the box of tissue from the counter, walked over to Rachel, and wiped the tears from her cheeks. He pulled another Kleenex from the box and gave it to Rachel to blow her nose. "Go pack your bag and only get what you need. We're going to the airport."

"I have to stop and get some money," she said.

"I have some on me. On the way over, I stopped to get some money and called the airline from the car phone. Our flight leaves in about an hour and a half. So, you really need to hurry."

"You did! You said we." Her eyes lit up through the tears. "Are you going with me?"

"Of course, I'm going."

"But what about your award ceremony?"

"Now you know, a ceremony doesn't even come close to you and Big Mama."

She was overwhelmed by his support. "Oh, Neal," she cried. She hugged him tightly. "What would I do without you?"

"I have no idea what I'd do without you." he smiled.

She wiped her eyes and ran up the stairs to grab a few things for the trip. Between Big Mama's crisis and Neal's support, Ken briefly crossed her mind. She didn't bother to call him. He hadn't been in touch with her since he found out about the pregnancy, and there was no time or desire to hunt him down for sympathy. Besides, she didn't have time to baby him. Big Mama needed her and that was all there was to it. For once in a long time, Ken was not the center of Rachel's emotions.

She was edgy during the entire hour flight to Detroit. As soon as the plane landed, she was on the concourse and heading for the car rental. She had totally forgotten about the stress and the pregnancy. Neal had to literally run to keep up with her.

He hopped on I-94 and barreled east towards the Ford hospital. The giant-sized tire located outside of Detroit usually brought a smile to her face. That would start her countdown. Within twenty-five minutes from that point, she was in Big Mama's yard. Staring out the window in a daze, she looked right at the tire, but didn't see it. The landmark that ushered Rachel joyously into the safe, strong arms of her grandmother wasn't big enough to generate even a slight grin on this trip.

Neal zoomed into the hospital parking lot. It was not a minute too soon for Rachel. Her only desire was to lay eyes on Big Mama and know exactly how she was doing. Throughout her entire life, Big Mama had always been there for her. Rachel never discounted the tremendous sacrifices that were made to raise her. It hadn't been easy twenty-six years ago for Big Mama and Pa-Pa to take guardianship of a five year old. They did it without so much as a whimper. Big Mama was well into her retirement years when Rachel entered college. Despite her pleas against it, Big Mama did day-work. She was determined to help pay the college expenses for her only grandchild. Rachel grew up with an extraordinary amount of love, particularly considering that she had no parents or siblings.

They couldn't arrive at the hospital fast enough for her. When they hit the emergency room entrance, she bolted towards the receptionist station. She was out of breath and visibly drained. Neal stepped up and asked the receptionist for Emma Walker.

"Sir, are you a relative?"

"This is her only grandchild."

"She's in intensive care," the clerk directed.

Rachel went limp on her feet. Neal saw her dropping and caught her right before she hit the desk.

"Where is that?"

"Third floor - A Wing."

"How do we get there?"

"Go to the end of the hall, make a right and take the elevator up to three. You'll see the nurse's station when you get off the elevator. Tell them who you are when you get there. They'll direct you from there."

"Thank you ma'am."

When they got to Big Mama's room, Rachel braced herself. Neal's mother and two neighbors, Ms. Pauline and Ms. Lorena were already there. Big Mama had IV needles in her arm and a heart monitor attached to her chest. Tubes and needles were everywhere. It might not have been as bad as it looked, but nothing seemed to ease Rachel's concern. Neal escorted her to Big Mama's side and pulled up a chair. She sat down and placed Big Mama's hand tightly into hers. She leaned over and laid her head on top of her grandmother's hand. She wept silently. Neal's heart was heavy witnessing the pain Rachel was in. Plus, Big Mama had always been like a grandmother to him. He was also grieving.

He vividly recalled the many childhood days he spent at Big Mama's. She gave him the same love and discipline she gave her own flesh and blood, with no exception. He received the same kind of hugs and tail-whippings Rachel got. He could still remember the night, years ago, when he and Rachel were playing a game of war with the cards. Big Mama had warned them several times prior not to be gambling in her house. She considered any kind of card games to be gambling, even if no money was involved. In order to be semi-obedient, and still have some fun, they waited one evening until they thought Big Mama was nodding in her room. When the coast was clear, they took the cards back out. She must have anticipated their plan, because no soon had the cards hit the table when Big Mama came around the kitchen corner with discipline written all over her face. She snatched the playing cards and ripped them to shreds, right in front of them both. They dared not say anything.

He remembered a similar scenario which occurred with some dice. Rachel and Neal often played Monopoly. With him being two years older, he usually won. Rachel played anyway. The only problem with playing was using the dice to determine how many spaces a player could move. Big Mama forbid the use of dice. She considered them to be tools of gambling. Unsuccessfully, they tried to explain to their grandmother that the dice were harmless. They told her that everyone used dice when playing the game. Despite their attempt to convince her, it didn't work. Neal smiled to himself as he reflected on them resorting to writing numbers on pieces of paper and pulling them from a bowl in lieu of dice.

As a child it wasn't fun to get chastised by Big Mama. Now that he was an adult, Neal could look back and smile at the loving discipline she showed him. Looking at Big Mama laying there, helpless and weak, filled his heart with sadness. His image of her had always been one of a strong woman, able to endure most anything.

Rachel spoke softly. "Mama, I love you." A sigh followed every other sentence. It was her way of fighting back the tears. "You have been so wonderful to me. I would never have gotten this far without you. I need you. Please don't leave me right now. I need you so badly."

Big Mama's breathing got heavier. Rachel panicked and pushed the nurse's button. The nurse came rushing in.

"Did you push the button?"

"She's, she's breathing heavy."

The nurse came over, checked the monitor, and took her pulse. "All of her vital signs are fine."

"How is she, really?" Rachel asked as though something was being kept from her.

"She's still in critical condition."

"What does that mean?" Neal jumped in. He knew Rachel was operating on her last bit of strength, and he didn't want her to get stressed out anymore, if it could be prevented.

"That means we don't know what to expect until some other test results come in."

Neal and Rachel stayed in the hospital for hours. She refused to leave Big Mama's side. He had begged Mom and the two neighbors to go home, get some rest, and come back tomorrow. With his encouragement, they'd left a hour earlier.

"Rach, I'm going to get some coffee and a sandwich. Do you want to take a break?" Neal pleaded.

She shook her head, no.

"Then I'm going to bring you something to eat."

"I'm not hungry."

"Doesn't matter. You have to eat for the baby. I'm not about to let you get sick, too. Please, don't even bother to argue with me on this one."

It was rare for Neal to take a stern position with Rachel, but when he did she respected it and offered no opposition.

When he left the room, she pulled her chair closer to the bedside, and continuously rubbed Big Mama's hand.

"Big Mama, I'm here. I love you. Please, don't leave me." Big Mama had always prayed blessings for others. Rachel felt it was time she got some back. "God, please let my grandmother get well. Give her some more years, please God. I know I'm not right to come before you."

The conviction of sleeping with Ken and getting pregnant was hindering her ability to confidently pray for Big Mama. She wanted to be sure her prayers were getting through. Rachel felt she needed to come clean with God. If she hadn't learned anything else from Big Mama, she knew what it meant to repent. She wanted a clean slate, which meant asking God for forgiveness.

"God please forgive me for sleeping with Ken. Please don't let my sins hinder my prayer for my mama. I accept you as my Savior. I believe you died for me. Please forgive me for my sins." She was crying and praying simultaneously. "Let her get to know my baby. Let us have her for a while longer."

In the midst of her prayer, Big Mama's breathing slowed. Rachel's head was resting on her grandmother's stomach. She didn't notice Big Mama's eyes open, but she did feel her hand tighten.

"Chile, what ya crying for?"

Rachel heard Big Mama's voice, but she couldn't determine if it was real or merely a wishful dream. When Big Mama squeezed her hand again, Rachel knew it was real, but she wasn't able to respond. When she tried to answer, only a sigh came out. Neal walked back into the room.

"Don't ya cry for me. I'ze going to be fine. What ya doing here anyhow?"

"We came as fast as we could. I didn't want you to be alone."

"Ah, chile, don't ya know I ain't never alone. Jesus is always with me, no matter where I be."

"I know Big Mama, but I wanted to be here, too."

"Jesus is with ya, too, chile."

Rachel didn't feel this was the right time to burden Big Mama with the news of her pregnancy. It didn't matter. Big Mama had the spirit of discernment and knew what was on Rachel's heart. In addition to her anointed insight, she must have been coming into consciousness when Rachel was confessing to God about her involvement with Ken.

"Big Mama, at times, I feel like I've lost my way. I know you raised me right, and you taught me about God. Somehow, I just got away from all of that when I got out on my own. I'm ashamed to admit the only time I really think about God is when I need him to help me with my relationships."

"There ain't no relationship more important than the one you have with the Lord. Ya might have strayed some, but I'ze know ya going to find ya way back. The word says, train up a chile in the way ..."

Rachel knew that scripture. She chimed in with Big Mama to finish it out, "it should go, and it will not depart."

"That's right, honey. You know what it says. Now believe it."

"How can I Mama? I don't have as much faith as you. I've been disappointed and hurt so many times before. I just don't see a happy ending."

"Being happy ain't no more than getting what God gots for ya. Put God first, and all else will line up. Mark my words. You'll see. Everything is going to work out."

"How do you know this will all work out?"

"Cause the word says it, and that's good enough for me. The word is in ya, chile. It will be there when you need it the most."

"I need it now, but I feel like the wrath of God has fallen on me."

"Why come ya say that?"

"I sinned when I knew better, and now I'm being punished."

Big Mama lifted up Rachel's head with her free hand. "My sweet Rachel, ya always been a good chile. Jesus ain't punishing ya."

"You just don't understand Big Mama."

"I do. Life comes from God. That means, ain't nobody born that God doesn't want to be here. That baby ya having is a gift from God."

"How!" Rachel was shocked that Big Mama knew.

"Shhhhhhh. Let me say my peace. That baby is from God, and it ain't no sin. It's a good thing. Now how the baby got to be is something else. Yeah, ya gots to talk to the Lord about that and get it right with him. True enough, ya done sinned by knowing the man in a family-kind-of-way before marrying him. But, God is a forgiving God. He love ya more than Big Mama, and he can surely fix this up better than I can. All right, my sweet chile?"

"All right. I love you, Big Mama." Rachel laid her head back onto Big Mama's stomach.

"And chile, even if I'm wrapped up in the clay, I want ya to remember, two wrongs don't make it right."

"What do you mean, Mama?"

"True ya going to have a baby. Ain't nothing ya can do about that now, but that baby father ain't the man God got for ya. Ya ain't got to marry 'em just cause ya with chile. Ya done messed up once, now repent and move on. Ya ain't got to get in worse shape. Ya wait 'till God send ya a man. Hear me good. The mistake is done, but if ya mess around here and get into a bad marriage, then the Devil gone surely get a foot in on ya life. I sure don't wanna see that happen."

"Me either, Mama."

"Besides, the Lord has somebody for ya already, and I know you know who it is."

"Who? Tell me."

"Soon as ya get free from this here, ya will be able to see more clearly."

"That's exactly what Sister Jones said a couple months ago when she ministered to me at the Christian luncheon."

"Sure it was. The Bible says the Lord is going to establish his word among two or three witnesses. Ya got the word and the 'greement. Just let it come to pass."

Big Mama was not a sophisticated woman, but she knew how to make a person feel comfortable around her. Rachel was all prepared to deal with the consequences of her actions. She was expecting to hear the wrath of Big Mama expressed in at least one of her many sayings befitting the situation like, 'ya done made ya bed hard, now ya gotta lay in it', 'watcha do in the dark gone come to the light', or 'a hard head bring a soft backside'. Instead of getting the rod of correction from her grandmother and feeling condemned, Rachel received the arms of love. Deemed uneducated by most standards, Big Mama's direct line to the Lord explained her phenomenal wisdom. She always said there was a time and place for everything, and today must have been the time for support, instead of discipline. Neal, coupled with Big Mama's wisdom and love was all Rachel needed to stand strong through this pregnancy ordeal.

She felt spiritually clean. For the first time, she felt a desire to please God and not just Big Mama with her convictions. The repenting removed loads of the emotional heaviness she was carting. It felt good taking refuge in her spiritual beliefs. It gave Rachel tremendous peace about her relationship.

37

Rachel woke up in the middle of the night with an excruciating pain in her lower abdomen. The intensity prevented her from being able to move. She laid there sobbing, with a certain amount of the tears being attributed to fear. The thought of something being wrong with her baby was unbearable. She was hoping the pain would go away, and she could get back to sleep. Instead, it worsened. Finally, after two hours of suffering, she called 911.

At the hospital, she laid on the gurney worrying about the condition of her baby. It seemed so cold and lonely in the hospital. After what seemed like hours, the nurse came in to get some additional information.

"How's my baby?" she anxiously asked.

"Ms. Matthews, we're waiting on test results. Try to relax."

"I can't."

"You're not helping matters by getting all worked up."

"I know, but it's not easy."

"I know, but try and relax. It's better for the baby if you do. It's going to be at least another hour before we know anything. Do you want us to call your husband, so that he can come and sit with you?"

Rachel wrung her hands, glancing at her fingers. "I'm not married."

The nurse noticed the absence of a ring, and her red cheeks displayed embarrassment.

"Is there any one else you want me to call."

Rachel thought about who she should call. She had tried calling Ken right after 911, but as usual, there was no answer. The only other person she wanted to be with her was Neal.

"Yes, my best friend."

"Must be a very close friend if you can call them in the wee hours of the morning."

"He is."

"How nice." The nurse placed the stethoscope on Rachel's stomach to listen for the baby's heartbeat. "It's good to have someone to help you through the pregnancy."

Rachel didn't feel the least bit ashamed about being there without the baby's father. When she initially got pregnant, Rachel was concerned about her image of being unwed and pregnant. Thanks to Ken's childish behavior, she was learning to accept it. She wasn't proud of being an unwed mother, but like Big Mama had said, God had already forgiven her. There was no reason to continually beat up on herself over spilled milk.

"I'm happy to be having a baby that I can take care of," she affirmed to herself.

Rachel began giving the nurse Neal's name and then stopped. On second thought, she wasn't going to call him. He had a day trip scheduled to Milwaukee, and she decided not to bother him. She relied on him too much, and even he needed a rest.

"I got myself into this, and I'm ready to get through it , alone if I have to," Rachel said to herself.

Although it was lonely and cold in the emergency room, she managed to fall asleep near daybreak. When Dr. Anthony came in, he had to wake her up.

"Ms. Matthews. Ms Matthews."

Rachel rolled over onto her back and wiped her eyes. "Yes, Doctor?"

"You're feeling better, I see."

"A little."

Dr. Anthony sat down on the rolling chair which was located next to the gurney, pushed the glasses up on his nose, and opened the chart. "Okay, let's see here. Uhm huh, uhm huh." Rachel became more and more anxious with every 'uhm huh'. She didn't want to wait another second to find out what was going on.

"Okay," said Dr. Anthony. He took his glasses back off and let them dangle from the black cord around his neck. When he closed the chart, she could sense the seriousness in his voice. Instantly she grew nervous.

"Rachel, we've had a scare here."

She sat up and started to say, "My bab ..." The nurse stopped her halfway up and helped her to lay back down.

"It wasn't a miscarriage this time."

"Thank God." She was still worried, but at least the news gave her some relief.

"Everything appears to be all right with the babies."

"Babies?" She repeated it with emphasis on the plural.

"Yes. That's the good news. The ultrasound is showing two babies. Looks like you're having twins."

"Two! Well, are they going to be okay?"

"They appear fine for now, but we've got to get you to settle down for the next seven months. I have to let you know, this is a high-risk pregnancy."

"What does that mean?"

"It means you'll have to take it easy over the next months, no stress, no physical exertion, no worrying. Under normal conditions, multiple birth pregnancies don't usually go the full term. It is common for a mother to deliver twins anytime between the sixth and eighth month. With this episode tonight, I'm even more concerned about your welfare. I'm going to recommend that you be off work for the next two months, at least until the first trimester is over."

Knowing there was no one to take care of her during the proposed two months off, she immediately rejected his suggestion. "I can't do that. I can't be off work all of that time."

"How long can you be off?"

"A few weeks, maybe a month, tops."

"If you're concerned about the money, why don't you consider short-term disability? You probably have some benefits through your job."

"I hadn't thought about benefits. Perhaps that might be an option." Rachel sounded calmer with the doctor's suggestion.

"Do you have a good relationship with your employer?"

"Yes, I do," she confidently stated.

"Then, I suggest you go back and talk with them. Convey to them how important it is to the longevity of your pregnancy. You need to be off work for a few months. We'll see how the next two months go, and maybe you can do light duty after that. You might want to check on the short-term disability benefit. If you want, I will gladly talk to someone from your company, on your behalf."

"I will definitely ask about the benefit. If you could please call them, that would help."

"Good." Dr. Anthony stood up and patted Rachel on the knee. He could tell Rachel was feeling much more relieved than when she arrived several hours prior.

"Everything's going to be fine. Try to take it easy young lady. We want to give those twins every opportunity we can to go full term and arrive here healthy. All right."

"All right."

"Call my office and schedule a follow-up for sometime early next week. I want to keep an eye on you."

"See you doctor, and thanks for your help."

After the doctor left, the nurse helped Rachel sit up in the bed.

"Now, you can get dressed. When you're finished, come out to the receptionist desk, and I'll give you the prescription and a note to be off work for the rest of the week.

On her way out of the hospital, Rachel stopped in her tracks. It dawned on her, "I don't have a way home."

She had arrived at the hospital by ambulance, and was going to have to get back by cab. It was not a good feeling. This wasn't the fairy tale she had in mind. She dreamed of being whisked off in a horse drawn carriage with Mr. Right. Instead, she was rolling away in a big yellow cab that had an overwhelming cigarette stench. This scene was a far cry from her blissful fantasy.

38

All day Rachel tried to stay busy in order to keep her mind off of Ken. It was upsetting to think about him, and that wasn't good for her babies. She patted her stomach.

"I know it's not good for me to get upset. I have to take care of you guys."

She tried to stay distracted. Reading didn't work. It required more concentration than she could muster. She ended up dozing off a few times, playing with Boots for a while, and watching a few videos. The day seemed to drag on and on.

At least her boss had been supportive. It helped, but that wasn't enough to pull her out of the depressive mood. Once again, her job was fulfilling, while her personal life was creating chaos.

Rachel picked up the phone to call her grandmother. Big Mama had been out of the hospital a few days, and she was recovering at Mom Pierce's house. After second thought, she plopped the phone down. "I can't call her. She will know something is wrong, and I don't want to upset her.

It was finally 8:30 in the evening, and she still felt alone.

"Oh boy. What can I do? I can't take this." She didn't want to be alone anymore.

"Where is Ken? How could he do this to me," she screamed. "I can't believe this. He has really left me to go through this pregnancy by myself." She balled up her fist, crossed her arms, and pressed them into her chest. She bowed her head and placed it in between her fists to help calm down.

Surely, she didn't deserve this kind of treatment from him. Being at home all day had given her a lot of time to think, and to feel the affects of being on her own. Her concept of going through the pregnancy alone was noble, but stupid. At least she had Roz,

Neal, and Big Mama. Fortunately, Neal was less than fifteen minutes away. I have to get out of here. I can't take it." She decided not to sit there any longer and get herself all worked up. She needed to hold it together for her babies. That was paramount.

She pushed the mute button on the television in the bedroom, pushed Boots off of her legs onto the floor, and picked up the receiver located next to the bed. She pushed the speed dial slot #1 which contained Neal's number. After all of these months, she had never changed the speed dial directory and put Ken in the first slot. She was glad the change hadn't been made. As usual, Boots and Neal were left standing after the dust had cleared from, what appeared to be, another one of her perfect relationships turned sour.

"Hello," Neal greeted.

All of a sudden, her emotions took over. There was a big lump in her throat. She tried to talk, but the words wouldn't come out. Finally, after much strain, she was able to squeak out "Neal."

"Rachel, Rach, is that you?" Neal was starting to get anxious in fear that something was wrong with her. "Rach, please, say something."

All she could say was, "Neal."

"Rach, I'm coming over."

"No," she blurted through the tears.

"Then talk to me. You got me worried over here. I don't know what to think. I know something is wrong." He was anxious and concerned about her welfare.

"I'm okay."

"No you're not. Is it the baby?"

"No."

"Is it Big Mama? Did you get a call about Big Mama?"

"No."

"Rach, please, don't make me drag it out of you. Is it Ken?"

The sound of his name seemed to cut through her shield, and holding back went out the window. She wept openly.

"I'm on my way over."

"Neal, no, don't come over."

"I'm on my way over."

"Don't, I'll come over there."

"Rach, let me come over. You're not able to drive, not the way you sound."

"I can make it over. I need to get out of this house for awhile. I've been here all day, and I need to get out."

"Come on then."

He was on pins and needles the entire time it took her to arrive. He was afraid she'd get into an accident or something equally destructive in her emotional state of mind.

Rachel pulled into the garage and parked next to Neal's car. He had let the door up earlier for her. She sat in the car for a few minutes. Finally, she opened the door, got out, and walked towards the door leading into the house.

Neal had been looking out the window and saw her pull up. He opened the door, as she was about to reach for it. Neither said a word.

Rachel walked through the laundry room, past the powder room, and stepped down into the oversized family room. Next to his library, which contained over a thousand books, tapes, and artifacts, this was her favorite room in his house. She liked to lay her head back on the thick cushioned chaise-lounge-styled sofa and drift off.

She was still emotional. The more she tried to hold back the tears, the more freely they seemed to flow.

Neal was eager to find out what was going on, but was patient enough to let Rachel reveal it at her pace.

"Why can't I ever find a good man who loves me at least as much as I love him? Someone who actually cares about me?" she blurted out while trying to talk through the lump in her throat.

"You mean someone like me?"

She tried unsuccessfully to smile and acknowledge his attempt to cheer her up with his lighthearted comment. He always had a way of making her feel better, even at times when she seemed to be at her lowest point. "I know you love me, but I mean, you know, a regular guy."

"Oh, you mean somebody like Luc, the adulterer," Neal said in a snide tone. Out of all of her relationships, he knew Luc had dealt Rachel one of her most painful experiences, at least that was the case before Ken's a.w.o.l episode. Before she could respond to his comment about Luc, he followed up with "or do you mean someone more like the cheat Paul, and let's not forget about pesty Gary."

"Wooo," she chimed in. "Why did you bring up those guys?" She was puzzled by his openness and down right stunned at his attitude. For twenty-plus years, he had always been the one person she could consistently count on for support, without judgment. During those years, she couldn't recall a serious argument between them. They were typically on the same wave length. Nine times out of ten, they saw eye-to-eye. Not only was she confused by his tone, she was also hurt. She was wondering how he could be so insensitive at, what was clearly, another one of her darkest hours. Why did he pick now, of all times, to chastise her?

"I need your support, not your judgment."

"Rach, I don't want to seem hard, but you've been at this place so many times in the past. You're my friend, and you know I care about you, so I can say this. You might get mad at me, but I know you'll get over it."

"Say what?" Rachel inquired with some reluctance.

"I don't think you know a good man when you see him!"

"Yeah, right. You make it seem like there are tons of them beating down my door daily, and I guess you think I'm just turning them away?" She sounded irritated.

"Well, Rach, take me for example! I have loved you unconditionally for years. I've been there in the middle of the night when you called upset, because you didn't know where playboy Rick was."

"But," she blurted.

"No but. I'm going to do the talking now. You need to sit back and listen."

Realizing how serious he was, she thought it best to do exactly as he asked.

"Now, like I was saying, what about when Chris was trying to bang you off the wall? How do you think I felt? There were so many times when I seriously thought about going down to Atlanta and getting into that brother's face, but out of my love and respect for you, I didn't."

Chris! She wondered where that came from. He was someone from her past she'd forgotten about. It was more like she had blocked him out of her mind. She had no idea why Neal was drudging up the Atlanta incident.

Chris had been her first and only encounter with a violent man. True, the other guys she dated had been pathetic. Even they never stooped as low as Chris did and displayed abusive tendencies. She met him during her two-and-a-half year stay in Atlanta. He was a marketing manager with one of the local Fortune 500 companies. She initially figured them to be quite compatible, with a lot of the same interests and motivations.

He had also started off as Mr. Wonderful, but quickly became excessively possessive and controlling. He suggested living together after only a few months of dating. He seemed to always keep tabs on her where-abouts. She suspected that he secretively followed her around. With her active schedule, monitoring her comings and goings must have been too much for him, and one day he snapped.

He demanded that she cut off involvement with all of her extra-curricular activities and eliminate her calls to Roz, Neal, and Big Mama. Rachel wasn't having it. When she refused, he snatched the phone out of the wall in her apartment. She was shocked at the nerve of him. When she went to grab the phone back and have him leave, he took the backside of his hand and slapped it across her face. Looking back, she realized it was by the grace of God he hadn't hit her with the phone and done some real damage. He had her cowered down in the corner, hitting her while bellowing out his irrational orders. She couldn't believe it was happening.

All Rachel remembered was the terror she felt for what seemed like an eternity. Rachel later realized it had only been about five minutes, which was long enough for her to know how much danger she was in. She remembered the helpless feeling in the pit of her stomach, being all alone, ashamed, and confused.

The next morning, she waited for him to leave for work. She was praying he wouldn't find some reason to stay. All she wanted him to do was leave so she could get free. When he finally left, she immediately called Neal. He was the only one Rachel ever told about the encounter. She was too ashamed to tell anyone else. She did recall Neal being infuriated, and he forced her to call the police.

If she hadn't, Neal promised that he would. She did end up pressing assault charges against Chris, but it hadn't been easy. She was actually afraid of the man, and decided to leave Atlanta not long after that whole fiasco was resolved.

"How do you think I felt watching you nearly have a nervous breakdown when Rick had the baby by that girl? What about when Mr. Ed jetted off with your money and your dignity. Through it all, the real topper was watching you hook-up with Too-fly. Boy, what a 'perfect man' he has turned out to be. I mean, I have to give it to him. On the surface, the brother has it going on, but when you started scratching below the surface, beneath the good looks and charm, you found there wasn't much to him."

"Neal, I never knew you felt this way."

"Rach, how could you not? The way I see it, the only thing you don't know is how to recognize a good man. I have always loved you. I guess there is some truth to the saying, 'good guys either finish last or broke'! I've always stood by you, even when you made bad choices in your men. I have always been there to pick you up relationship after relationship, dust you off, build up your confidence, and unintentionally, send you on to the next loser."

"Why didn't you ever tell me? I mean, how was I suppose to know how you felt about me."

"How could you not know? You must be the only one who didn't know."

"Why are you speaking up now?"

"Because, Rach, timing is everything. I've always known you were a free-spirit. I knew you needed time to find out who you were and what you needed out of a man. I knew, from the beginning, you were the woman for me. You just didn't know I was the man for you. In my heart, I always knew, one day, you would come to your senses and recognize the relationship we have. You have always taken our relationship for granted, the mutual respect, the compassion, the genuine care, and most of all, you have underestimated our bond of friendship. You're so busy chasing some romantic pipe dream. You've never stopped and looked at what you have in me. Rach, my dear, you were always searching for the dream. What's so funny about it, you've had it all along.

Most married folks only fantasize about having the kind of closeness we have. Whatever happens to us now, know that the basis of our relationship is, and will always be, friendship."

"Neal, I don't know what to say."

"You don't have to say anything. Remember, this is my show," and he smiled at her.

There he was as usual, Rachel thought, making her feel comfortable in what should be an awkward conversation. She couldn't help but smile and feel relieved.

"Okay, okay, it's your show. Go ahead, talk, but let me ask one thing. Have you been waiting around for me to see you in that way all this time?" By that way, she meant romantically. As close as they were, she still found it surprisingly difficult to say it outright.

"In 'that light', huh. Rach, the bottom line is, we both needed time to mature. When we went away to college fourteen years ago, we were kids. Neither of us was able to appreciate a good relationship back then. You needed your time, and I needed mine. Apparently, I got through my growing period a lot sooner than you." The comment sounded harsh, but his smile that followed made it palatable.

They were sitting face-to-face on the sofa, both feeling relaxed as they always were when together. She had both feet on the sofa, with her knees bent and hands clasped together. The tears had stopped flowing long ago.

"There were times when I wanted to shake you and say, 'aren't you ready yet', but I never wanted to pressure you."

"You make me feel bad about sharing the details of all those bad relationships with you."

"No no, don't feel like that. Please, don't feel like that. The one thing I don't want you to do is to second guess our friendship, or try to associate any ulterior motives into our relationship. Besides, who else is going to understand your silly butt except me."

She slightly slapped her hand across his leg and unsuccessfully tried to suppress a smile.

"Seriously, Rach, how do you feel about me?"

"In all honesty Neal, I do have feelings for you, but I've always downplayed them. You're my play-brother. It was always hard or at least awkward for me to think of you in a romantic kind of a way." She paused. "I have to ask. How did you feel when I talked about certain personal issues?"

"If you weren't embarrassed, then I wasn't. My love for you is unconditional, Rach. Don't you get it? Your choices in men didn't stop me from loving you," he said with a grin. She couldn't help but to give him a grin back, coupled with another affectionate slap across the knee.

"Honestly, my hopes for us never clouded our friendship. I have often been put into precarious situations with you and have given objective advice, with no ulterior motive other than wanting what was best for you. Once I made the decision to wait for you, everything else was easy. Rach, I decided a long time ago that I would rather be second fiddle in your life than to not be there at all. It has only been within the last few years that I started to give up on our being together. That's why I went ahead and allowed myself to get involved with Nicole."

"Neal, you know you're special to me, but I didn't know you felt this way about me all this time. You have never tried to make a move on me. So, I never took any feelings seriously."

"It sounds like you're saying that since I didn't claw all over you, my feelings got ignored. I get penalized for showing you some respect. Girl, you should hear yourself."

"I didn't know." She covered her face with both hands. "I feel so naive."

"Come on. We've been in each other's lives for a long time. If you are really stunned about my feelings, then I am the one who should be shocked and embarrassed. I believe you knew, at least at some level. You tell me, all the time, that women can tell when a man is attracted to her. She may not react, but she can tell. Right?" Neal was awaiting her response, although he already knew the answer.

"Yeah, you're right. We have such a wonderful friendship. I was afraid to ruin the one good male relationship I have in my life. I never wanted to jeopardize our special friendship by crossing into the romance department. Once you cross, there's no way to come back."

"Why does it have to be either or?"

"What do you mean?" she asked.

"Why does it have to be either romance or friendship? Why can't it be both, with friendship being the foundation. You've said yourself, many times, you only know a handful of truly happy couples. I'm not talking about those who are just tolerating each other for the sake of the kids. Of the few truly happy ones, I bet they have the key ingredient."

"What's that," she paused, "friendship?"

"You know it. Rach, I know you don't think I'm your type."

"Why you say that?"

For one, I'm too skinny."

"Yeah, you are a little skinny," she said with a smile, "but you're okay."

She did feel his body was too thin for her. She had never even considered the thought of being in a relationship whereby she appeared bigger than the man. Maybe it was a possibility before, but not since the pregnancy. She expected to pick up at least twenty-five pounds.

"What I lack in weight, my dear, I more than make up for in devotion to you. That's something, sweetheart, you can't buy."

All Rachel could say in response to Neal's confidently spoken statement was, "Umm."

"Being skinny isn't all of the problem. I know what the other problem is."

"What other problem? There isn't anything else."

"Yes there is. I know you so well, Rach. The way you like pretty-boys, I don't look the way you want."

"Oh, Neal." It was true, but she didn't want to hurt his feelings. At one time, size was an important factor to Rachel. That was changing, because a significant amount of the men in her past only had the looks, size, and not much more. Good looks in a man wasn't enough to help Rachel take care of the children and herself.

"Rach, don't worry. I'm okay with the way I look. Like I said, I might not be as fine as some of your has-beens, but one thing is for sure. I can make you happier than all of them, put together. All you have to do is get past the physical features."

"You make me sound superficial."

"To an extent you are, but my unconditional love for you accepts the whole package, idiosyncrasies and all. As much as I love you, I know you're not perfect. No one is, not you, and certainly not me. We're not perfect, but we're perfect for each other." He raised his hand slowly and with his index finger brushed across her cheek with a feather-like stroke.

"I've been all around the world, and trust me when I say, we have something special," Neal said.

"Neal, you have been such a positive factor in my life. I do feel that you give a lot more of yourself to me than I do to you."

"You may not realize it, but you've been a real influence on me."

In an inquisitive tone she asked, "In what way."

"Well, did you know I started going to church and seeking the Lord because of you?"

"Because of me?" Rachel stated with her face scrunched up in reflection of her confusion.

"Yes, you. I knew if it was something important to you, then I wanted it to be important to me. I never wanted you to be anywhere I wasn't going to be."

"Yeah, but, spiritually, you've passed me up. You've clearly grown more, spiritually, than I have. You have really embraced religion."

"Rach, we all grow at our own pace. In the beginning I did it for you, but once I got into the teachings at the Christian Center, it just naturally seemed to flow for me. You know, spiritually, I wanted to be at least as strong as my mate. With all of the stuff you put me through, I needed comfort and support from somewhere." He slid his hand under hers and clasped their fingers together. "Now that I'm into the word, I am even more convinced you are the wife that God has for me."

"I'm not confident about what I hear and don't hear from God. Neal, I can't even really think about an 'us' right now. The timing is bad. I mean, you know the stuff I'm going through with Ken. I have to figure out what to do about that first."

"Rachel, you're not with him. I don't know why you tolerate him when you don't have to?" You're not married to him, and you don't ever have to be," he said in a raised voice.

"You make it sound easy to leave the relationship. I have to think about my babies. It is their father, you know."

"What do you mean, think? He's already gone. He's such a good example of a 'real man'," Neal sarcastically said. "You're the one left holding the baby, not to mention the bills. I know you have to be concerned about the welfare of the baby, but answer this. How stable of a life will the baby have with you and Ken arguing and separating all of the time? The child deserves a happy home, and the natural father is not the only one who can provide that. So far, he hasn't."

"You must not have heard me?"

"What?" he pondered. It was rare for him to miss anything. He always listened intensely to her.

"I said babies-ies."

"What do you mean babies?"

"It's twins," she excitedly responded.

"Twins!"

"Yep."

"Oooo, twins." Neal leaned over and gave her a hug. "That's nice, Rach. On second thought, it's even worse for you to be in such a bad relationship with two babies on the way."

"Well, this leads to a question I have. You always shy away from women with children. At my age, I'm already bringing a lot of baggage into the relationship. On top of it, I would be bringing two children. How do you feel about that?"

"Rach, what part of unconditional love don't you understand. Girl, sometimes I think you've been mistreated so long, you don't know how to act when you're treated right. Do you understand that I love you, period? Do you honestly think I could love you as much as I do, and not love your children? Besides, if I keep waiting for you, I'll be too old to have kids of my own. The closest thing I might get to offspring could be your twins. It's no secret you've gotten more time, attention, and support from me than that immature, figure-head father."

"What about Nicole? How does she figure into this revelation of yours?"

"Rach, my relationship with Nicole is over."

"Over! Why? When? How?"

In all of the confusion and concern about the pregnancy, Big Mama's health, and who knows what else, he had elected not to tell her about his ordeal with Nicole. Sensitive to her current situation, he intentionally kept it from her. He didn't want her to feel responsible for triggering the break-up by giving him the balloons. Eventually, the break-up was destined to happen, one way or another. He figured there was no sense in Rachel taking on the extra guilt.

"She didn't want to be second best to you. Unlike you, she knew that I loved you."

"What made her think that you loved me? Did you tell her?"

"No! I didn't tell her. Rach, I'm not that insensitive. Apparently I didn't have to. Besides, I told myself many times over the past two years that our being together was a dream. When I started dating Nicole, I tried to believe you were no longer an option. I tried to convince myself I only loved you like a sister. I guess I wasn't too convincing. It must have been my mind and not my heart talking. To be honest, my heart never gave up on you. Nicole was able to see it. She was a nice person, and I am really sorry that I hurt her. It wasn't too cool."

"Neal, I'm really sorry. It seems like I'm always causing some type of hassle in your life."

"Not at all. Loving you has taught me patience, and God knows, humility. I have to admit, it's been good loving you, mistakes, heartaches and all."

"Still, I don't know why you're laying all of this on me now?"

"I don't want you to give me an answer or anything, not right away. I know you're confused. As much as I want us to be together, I don't want you on the rebound. I'll admit there was a time when I would have taken you on any terms, Rach. Now I realize, to do that would make me no better than the other men who have taken advantage of you. No, I want you healthy, emotionally healthy that is."

He gazed into her eyes to affirm the sincerity in his statement. "Sweetheart, I'd take you physically sick without a moments hesitation, but not emotionally wounded. You need time to heal from your relationship with Ken, and I guess time to make some big decisions. Whatever you decide, I'm still going to be there for you." Neal grinned, which helped to ease the intensity that had transpired as a result of their conversation.

"Rach", said Neal as he placed her hand carefully into his palm and looked directly into her eyes. "If we get together, it will be because you chose me, and not because you just ended up with me. I don't ask much of you, but the one thing I will require is a commitment to me from your heart. Anything less, I can't accept, not even from you. I've waited a long time for this. I'm definitely not going to settle for anything less than everything from you."

What she loved most about Neal was his dependability. He was always there for her. What a great friend she declared. Although she had such admiration for him, Rachel never seriously considered a romantic relationship with him throughout her single life. She never saw him as a mate. He was her brother, for goodness sake. How could they be romantically involved?

No matter. He wasn't her type. She played the thought over and over in her mind. Then again, she had to think about what exactly was her type: the shiftless, controlling, unmotivated, selfish, immature, unfaithful, unavailable, broke pretty-boys. Her type hadn't worked out too well over the years.

Except for looks and body, Neal had all of the qualities she wanted in a man, plus some unwritten ones like being self-motivated, secure, available, and without excess emotional baggage. She acknowledged that he was intelligent, compassionate, romantic, down-to-earth, financially stable, family-oriented, tall, dependable, trustworthy, without kids, and religious. He was really into the Lord and not just playing church, like Ken.

Even with some discoloration in his skin, he still wasn't bad-looking. He was plain. Good thing was, any shortcomings in his looks were definitely overcome by his excellent taste, class, and attire.

The more she thought about it, the less significant his physique became. For the first time, she saw his beauty from the inside out. He had the perfect balance she was looking for. He was a man who was comfortable in the business world while also being able to roll up his sleeves and dig into a game of bid-whist, at the drop of a hat.

All along she'd been looking for Mr. Perfect, someone who shined like 18 carat gold, the real thing. Through her dating, all she had landed was gold-plated perpetrators, something far less than perfect. The characteristics of pure gold, the real thing, were becoming clearer to her. It was strong but soft, reliable, classy, rare, and slightly dull. That was Neal in a nutshell.

Rachel found herself caught up in the moment. Her mind was flooded with thoughts. Whenever one relationship ended, she would quickly embark on another to help her, superficially, get over the agony. In the process, she managed to create an internal mountain of emotional pain. She was finally in a position to hook-up with a wonderful man and couldn't. For once, she wanted to resolve the issue with Ken, instead of running to the next set of open arms, even if they belonged to Neal.

She did determine one thing. She was not going to be stuck in neutral any longer. It was like being dead, with no movement forward or backwards. Ken was going to have to 'piss or get off the pot', as Big Mama would say. She wasn't waiting around any longer for a repeat performance of shoulda-woulda-couldas. Hind sight had definitely been 20/20.

"By the way, did you do something for Big Mama's birthday?" Neal asked.

"Oh my goodness! I totally forgot about her birthday, to tell the truth. How can I be so distracted that I forgot Mama's birthday?"

"I figured as much, with everything going on with you right now, it's no wonder you forgot. When I was out earlier today I picked up a card and got a hundred dollar money order. I went ahead and signed your name. I sent it two-day priority mail. It should be there by Friday. I also ordered flowers to be delivered on Friday."

As she looked up at Neal, he could see the tears swelling up in her eyes. Rachel wanted to verbally thank him. She didn't, in fear of crying. Good thing was, their relationship didn't require her to explicitly say thank you for him to know how appreciative she was. He was too secure in their friendship to need the constant reassurance. She leaned over and gave him a big hug. She always knew how good he was to her. Rachel was starting to realize exactly how good he was for her. As Neal hugged her back, he seemed to squeeze the tears out of her, and at that moment, she let go and started to openly weep. She relaxed in his embrace and let the weight of the world fall from her shoulders.

She couldn't help but wonder whether Ken would have thought about sending her grandmother a birthday gift. Rachel resisted comparing the two men in her life. They were distinctively different people. However, she recognized that good treatment was nothing to sneeze at.

39

Rachel moseyed around the house Sunday morning, doing a little of this and a little of that. She was glad to be past the morning sickness stage of the pregnancy. The new attitude enabled her to focus on eating right and taking care of herself, for the welfare of the little ones. She fixed some instant cinnamon and spice oatmeal, toasted a piece of honey wheat bread, poured a glass of milk, and headed for the sun room.

She was in a hurry. The Christian Center broadcast was about to start. It had become a routine event in her Sunday morning schedule. When she turned the TV on, about ten minutes of the program had already elapsed.

Pastor Ellington was walking across the platform, boldly preaching, "Stop wallowing in your sins. Sure, you can expect to make some mistakes. But, you don't have to lay down in it. Learn to repent and shake the dust from your feet. Keep on keeping on. God is no respector of person. The same mercy and grace he extended to me, is available for you. Guilt and shame are not of God."

This was hitting home with Rachel. She was trying to keep her spirits up, but her emotions had been fluctuating up and down over the past months. She wanted to put the hurt of Ken behind her. His rejection was weighing heavily on her.

"That's the trick of the enemy, to keep your faults hanging over your head. God wants you to admit your mistakes by confessing them. Once you repent, walk in freedom. Turn to Romans, eight-one."

Rachel flipped to the Romans section of her New International Version of the Bible. It was easier to understand than her King James version. She didn't read the Bible often, but knew the order of the sixty-six books from memorizing it at age six in Sunday school.

"Therefore, there is now no condemnation for those who are in Christ Jesus," read Pastor Ellington. "That means God doesn't hold mistakes and sins over your head, like some other people. So, why do you keep beating up on yourself? Once you sincerely repent, that sin is dead in your life."

The past, including the mistakes, was an important part of the molding process. Roz had encouraged Rachel time and time again not to dwell on her mistakes and to try and live without regrets. She consistently reminded Rachel how people made the best decisions they could based on what they knew at the time. With growth came better decisions.

The Pastor stopped pacing. With his oversized bible dangling, he leaned his left elbow on the podium. He was ready to drive the message home.

"I beg you, get free people. Stop settling for less than your rightful place in the Lord. God loves you, whether you like it or not."

She was beginning to realize that bad decisions could be put behind her, but sometimes they left consequences. The good news was as long as she was still alive, there was another chance to pick up the pieces and try again, each time with a bit more wisdom. Her heart started to swell, and, with no warning, the tears began flowing. Before she could think about it, the confession was spurting out.

"God, don't let my sin affect my babies. Please, let them be healthy."

She didn't know how to talk to God. Her confession was spontaneous. She found herself talking to God the same way she would talk to Neal, openly, with love and respect. Like Big Mama had told her time and time again, God loved her, no matter what her mistakes were. He was a father who loved his children, when they're both good and bad.

"My heart hurts."

She was finally getting to know herself, strengths, weaknesses, vulnerabilities and all.

"Help me to be able to get over the pain of Ken. Please, God, don't leave me. I really need you."

Rachel didn't know where all of this was coming from. All she knew was that her conscience felt a thousand times better after it was over. The guilt, worry, and shame seemed to vanish into thin air. Her heart actually felt lighter. She felt a higher level of freedom than the dose initially experienced in Big Mama's hospital room. Rachel didn't feel lonely, even though she was alone. The encouragement was soaking in. She believed God did love her, just as she was. She felt free.

It wasn't going to be easy growing up into a truly self-sufficient individual, depending only on God and herself, instead of the companionship of a man. For certain, she was determined not to sit around and let her thirties drift by, waiting for the perfect relationship to fall into her lap. By the grace of God, she was going to continue moving forward, with or without Ken.

As usual, Neal called when he got home from church to check on her.

"Hey, Rach."

"Hey, Neal."

"How are you today?"

"Fine."

"Did you eat breakfast?"

"Yes, Neal."

"Did you have some milk?"

"Yes, Neal. Anything else, 'Daddy'?"

"I guess not right now. Oh, have you heard from Big Mama?"

"Yes, I called her yesterday."

"How's she doing?"

"Okay, I guess."

"You don't sound too sure."

"Well, you know she's probably not telling me everything. I wish I was closer to home. It would be easier for me to check on her more myself."

"I know it's hard, but don't worry. Mom's there."

"I know, but Big Mama is back at her own house. I don't like her being in the house by herself. I wish that I could do more for her."

"What can I do to help?"

"I don't know. Probably nothing. I don't even know how I can help. I'd like to work at least another three months before I take time off. If it wasn't for the pregnancy, I could take off and go stay with her. "

"Great idea. Going home would be good for both of you."

"I know, but I can't afford to take that much time off. The doctor doesn't want me working, but I have to go back. I need to work and save up as much as I can. I've taken my two weeks off, and that's it. I'm going back tomorrow."

"What about your health?" Neal asked out of deep concern.

"I will be fine. All I have to do at work is show up. Mrs. Beasley has divided my work up among the other accountants. So, don't worry. Besides, I would be bored to tears if I had to stay at home all day."

"I don't feel comfortable with you going back to work Rachel? What about the short-term disability that you told me about?"

"That only gives me sixty percent of my pay. I can get by on that, but it doesn't leave any for me to save. I want to have enough so I can be off at least nine months when the twins come."

"Is money the only reason why you can't take off?"

"Not really." After thinking about it, she recognized, "Well, yeah, I guess so."

"Then, consider it done."

"Oh no, Neal. I'm not going to let you do this. Uhn uhn."

"Look Rach, I was your friend before we had our little talk, and as far as I'm concerned, nothing has changed."

"No, I won't take that kind of money from you. No way."

"Okay, Ms. Stubborn. Then what about the slush fund? There's at least forty-five to fifty thousand dollars in there."

"What fund?" Before Neal could respond, it dawned on her what he was talking about.

"Oh yeah. I forgot all about that money."

It had been years since she had used the fund. They opened an account after college. When she was moving to Atlanta and Neal to Chicago, they pooled money together and started a fund. Early on, it was to be used for emergencies. After they both got established in their careers, it was used primarily for traveling. Neal still put money into the account, although less frequently than he did in the beginning. Whenever he got a large bonus or gift, he would sock some of it away in the slush fund. Rachel, on the other hand, had forgotten all about it. The money started off joint, but lately Neal had made all of the contributions. She didn't feel right using the money for her current challenge.

"I just can't use it for my predicament."

"That's why we started the account," he acknowledged.

"Yeah, ten years ago. Surely I haven't sunk financially to where I was ten years ago.

"Look, the money is there. Please, use it. It's your money."

"No, it's your money."

"Our money," he demanded.

"Your money."

"What's the difference. My money is yours. There is no way I could be your buddy and let you struggle financially, when I'm able to help.

"But I can't have you paying my way."

"Paying your way! I'm helping."

"Helping me to fix a problem that you didn't create."

"I don't care how you got into this bind. All I care about is how to help you get through it. Anything less would make me less than the friend I profess to be. Please Rach, take the money. Don't force me to watch you suffer. It would be cruel of you to do that to me. Besides, you're still my girl. If I don't spend the money on you, then who else do I have to spend it on?"

It was just like him to make her feel good, even when she needed help. She remembered how much he'd helped her, one time in particular. A couple of years before meeting Ken, she purchased a Camry at Neal's request. Her old car was on its last leg. Neal was out of town regularly, and didn't feel comfortable leaving her stranded. Even road service didn't solve the problem of keeping the car running late at night on some dark remote road. With her crazy hours, anything could easily have happened.

Rachel was never big on cars. So long as it ran, and she didn't have a car payment, her old clunker was fine. Neal was more extravagant. He drove a brand new spiffy black seven series BMW.

He, all but, paid cash for the car. Out of a 70,000 dollar price tag, he financed 10,000 dollars over two years, just to keep his credit rating current.

Neal finally talked her into getting a car, but, she was determined to get something simple. She was good with money management, but didn't have as much money as he did. Thanks to his financial advice, Rachel had started to build a nice little nest egg, of which she was in no hurry to spend. She decided to buy a four year old model. She figured with 2,000 dollars down, the remaining 8,000 dollars could be financed at payments of about 200 dollars per month over four years.

When she went to pick up the car, the salesman gave her the keys to a brand new Camry. She immediately explained to him that they'd given her the wrong car, in fear of being strapped with a ridiculously high car payment. She was determined to get the matter resolved as quickly as possible. She had the 2,000 dollar payment with her, and that was it. She expected to walk out with the car they agreed upon earlier in the week. After she haggled with the salesman for a while, the manager came out and explained what happened. He told her that Mr. Pierce had come by earlier in the week, just before going out of town. She remembered asking Neal to look over her selection and make sure it was okay. In doing so, he decided that the new car was much better for her than another used one. He put 10,000 dollars down to make up the difference between the new and the used car. That way, he wouldn't have to worry about her breaking down in the middle of the night and getting robbed, raped, or worse.

"I hope you don't keep track of everything I owe you, because I couldn't possibly pay you back, at least no time soon," was her way of saying thank you.

"You're right. You couldn't. Neither could I pay you back. The cost of true friendship is priceless. If it was affordable, everyone would have it. But, I do think your tab is a bit higher."

Neal, in his usual manner, added humor to keep the discussion light and stress-free for Rachel. He was forever going out of his way to help her. In spite of his willingness to help, she didn't want to take advantage of his generosity.

"Well, Mr. Pierce, I'll think about it. I must admit, I'd love to spend this time with Big Mama."

"Well Ms. Matthews, you just say the word, and it's done. Don't wait too long."

"Why?"

"Because I might want to take me a nice long Trans-Atlantic flight with the money."

"Yeah, right. As much as you travel, that's the last thing on your mind."

"Huhn. You're right. You know me too well. Anyway, I'll catch you later. I have some proposals to work on for tomorrow."

"All right then. Don't work too hard. Enjoy some of this nice weather."

"You too, and call me if you need something."

"Will do. See ya."

Rachel spent the rest of the day lounging around the house. It was a beautiful spring afternoon. She finished reading *Raptured* the night before, and had started reading *This Present Darkness*. She found both books to be mesmerizing, and she literally couldn't put them down. Prior to reading those particular books, she had been under the impression that all Christian-based fiction was filled with Bible verses and boring messages. She was actually surprised to read such intriguing Christian novels. It was just the level she needed to get a better understanding on how prayer and salvation impacted her personal life.

From time to time, she would think about Ken. It had been a month since they'd spoken. He didn't even know Big Mama had been sick, but she didn't expect that to matter to him. He wasn't concerned about his own babies, let alone someone like Big Mama, who wasn't too 'particular' about him. In her wildest dreams, she would never have expected to be going through a pregnancy without the babies' father.

Ken was the man she wanted to marry and had planned to settle down with. How could she have read his personality so incorrectly over the past year? She wondered how could Mr. Right have turned out so wrong? If Ken turned out to really be the jerk he was appearing to be, then she'd made the worst mistake of all in choosing this man. Pregnant or not, Rachel was too independent to have Ken hang around solely because of guilt and pressure. When the phone rang, her casual greeting was in anticipation of it being Neal.

"Yes."

There was silence on the other end.

"Hello, Precious," the seductive voice greeted.

"Luc!"

"Yes, it's me. How are you doing Rachel?"

"I'm fine." She was surprised to hear from him. The last time they talked was right after the engagement, about four months ago.

"I'm glad."

"I'm surprised to hear from you."

"You are! Why? I've always kept in touch with you, from the moment you stole my heart five years ago. Whether you know it or not, you still have my heart. I call to check on it from time to time."

Luc was too much. He knew Rachel was engaged, but his arrogance didn't allow him to seriously respect it. He had grown accustomed to getting the spotlight in her life, no matter who else she was seeing. He had seen men come and go in her life. His confidence in their relationship was not dampened by Ken's role.

Normally, she would buckle under his flattering innuendoes. Today was different. She was still feeling her Godly freedom. It gave her courage to say things to Luc she never could before, and mean it.

"Luc, I don't have your heart, Aysha does."

"No, she doesn't."

"You're the one I love."

"No Luc. We had an adulterous affair. There's nothing glamorous about it."

"Rachel, what's wrong? You sound different."

"I guess you could say that I am different."

"But, I know that you are still beautiful."

Nothing seemed to penetrate. She didn't need an esteem-booster. She was feeling good without his lustful comments. Funny how things change, she thought. There was a time, not so long ago, when she craved his pleasantries and devoured his every word. She had evolved to this point of being offended and despondent.

"Luc, I'm really glad you called to check on me."

"It's the least that I want to do."

"Well, I appreciate the call, but can you do me a favor?"

"Anything," Luc quickly responded, in hopes of getting back into her good graces and maybe her bed.

"Please, don't call me anymore."

"What!"

"Please, don't call anymore."

"You don't mean that, Precious."

"Yes, Luc, I do."

"No, Rachel. You couldn't mean that. Is it because of your boyfriend?"

"Not at all. As a matter of fact, we're not seeing each other."

"Are you seeing someone else?"

"No."

"If it's not because of your boyfriend, and it's not because of someone else, then what is it? Is it something that I did?"

"No. You didn't do anything. "It's me."

"You! Is there something wrong with you?"

"Not anymore."

"Rachel, you're not making any sense."

She didn't attempt to explain her spiritual enlightenment to Luc. He wouldn't want to understand. She knew the doors to her past needed to be closed in order to move on. She'd toyed with this relationship long enough. Rachel consciously decided not to reopen a sin area that her repenting had already closed.

"You're a married man. There is no future for us."

"You know I would marry you, if I could."

"But, I couldn't marry you."

"Since when!"

"Let's just say, you're not the man God has for me."

"How do you know that? You know how much I love you."

"For one, you're already married. God wouldn't send a married man to be my husband. Secondly, we are not equally yoked."

"Since when did you become so holy."

"Oh, I'm not holy, not yet, but I'm trying to get my act together. I'm cleaning out a lot of garbage in my life."

"Are you calling me garbage."

"No. You're not garbage. What you're doing is, and I don't want to be a part of it any longer."

"You sure this is what you want?"

"Positive."

"Okay, I'll have to respect your wish."

"Thanks, Luc."

"For what?"

"For understanding."

"What choice do I have?"

"You do have a choice, but thanks, anyway."

"Rachel, just remember, you are still Precious to me. I will always love you, regardless. You can't change that. If you ever change your mind, get a hold of me."

The comment rolled off her back and took no root in her spirit. "Bye, Luc."

"Bye."

40

This Sunday, the family get-together was no different than usual. Red and Ken were watching TV. Sharon and Nick were fixing the food. Dana and Terry were working. Brendon was late.

"See, I told you way back before the season started that Michael was going to be in the championship. He gone win it, too."

"Yep, Dad, you said it."

"See, you ought to learn to listen to me sometimes. It would make some things easier for you. Rachel didn't come, huh?" Red asked.

"Nah, she couldn't make it."

"Uh oh ... That don't sound good. Whenever Junior comes over here, by himself, it means that he's on the outs with Rachel." Red never took his eyes off of the TV. He had perfected a way of having hard conversations with his kids, while appearing not to be the least bit disturbed.

"Dad, you're too much."

"Uh huh, but I know I'm right."

Sharon and Nick stood in the doorway to catch a glimpse of the basketball championship.

"Had a love TKO, huh buddy?" Nick teased.

"It'll work out big brother," Sharon said as she walked over and gave him a hug. "You hang in there with Rachel. You will be married before you know it."

"Yeah, man. Before you know it, you will be another brother with a ball and chain around your ankle. Right, baby?" Nick gave Sharon a wink.

"Nick, will you go on out there, and get my barbecue ready."

"All right, Red. I'm on it." He turned to Sharon, "I will be in the breezeway, honey."

"Don't waste your time with Junior. He ain't going to marry nobody, less he learn how to stop being so selfish. Your mama sure did spoil you boys."

"Why are you riding me, Dad? Rachel doesn't show up for dinner, and you give me the third degree."

"Look boy, I ain't stupid. I know you can mind your own business. But, it's like I told you before, don't let that girl get away. Ain't nobody going to be perfect. You gotta make it work."

"Dad, why do I have to hear all this?"

"Cause, I'm tired of hearing you bellyache about wanting a wife when you don't know how to get along with anybody."

"Ah!" Ken sighed. "Red, I'm out of here." Ken was angry, but the most he could do in defiance was to call his father by his nickname. Red was old, but never tolerated any disrespect. Ken knew it.

"Run on out of here, but sooner or later you're going to have to face the music. See, I'm your father. I have to put up with your narrow butt, but other folks don't have to."

Ken stood up.

"Sharon," Red yelled, "call up Rachel for me. Tell her I said to please take Junior back. I don't want this grown man moping around here, looking pitiful."

Deep down, Ken knew Red was right, but he wasn't about to admit it. He walked into the kitchen with Sharon.

In a low tone, Sharon asked, "Are things okay with you and Rachel?"

Ken often confided in his sister and saw this as an opportunity to get some of the anxiety off of his chest.

"We found out that she's pregnant."

Sharon stopped shredding the lettuce and turned to face him. "Pregnant! How did she get pregnant?"

Ken gave Sharon a look that seemed to say, "How do you think?"

"I don't mean, literally, how. I know how. I mean, I thought you both wanted to wait and get married first."

"We did, or she did."

"So, what happened?"

"It just happened."

"Well, congratulations."

"Yeah."

"You don't seem too happy?"

"Why would I be?"

"Because Kenny, your fiancée is pregnant. Seems like reason enough for me."

"I already have to deal with Sandra and the child support for Ariel."

"So!"

"So, I can't afford all of this."

Sharon laughed, much to his surprise.

"Why are you laughing?"

"Because, it's kind of late to be thinking about money now. Dad is right. You're being selfish. This isn't just about you, big brother. What about Rachel? Is she happy about it?"

"I don't know?"

"What do you mean 'I don't know'. She didn't tell you?"

"Nah, I haven't talked to her since I found out."

Sharon stopped chopping the carrots and said loudly, "What?"

"We stopped talking for a while, until we could think things through."

"We or you? What's there to think about?"

Sharon paid no attention to what he was saying. She was so stunned at her brother.

"I'll admit, I, no we both needed time to think."

"I'm really disappointed in you Kenny. I can't believe you left her at such a critical time. If you're going to act like this, I'm sorry that I introduced you to her."

"What do you expect me to do?"

"Take care of your responsibilities. If it's about money, then get another job. Grow up, Kenny!"

"Look, both you and Dad are trippin'. I'm out of here. I'll see you later."

"Aren't you going to eat first?"

"Not hungry." Ken was angry, mostly at the situation and not his family. On the way to the car, he admitted, "I know they're right."

He didn't really know where he was going. He backed out of the driveway and cruised down the street, headed nowhere in particular. The drive was dazed, as his mind wandered.

"What am I going to do? I'll be forty soon. I don't want to start all over with someone else."

He pushed in some jazz music and let it relax him.

"I do love her. Dad's right. She's the best woman I've had. I want to have a family with her. Ah, man, I'm going to do it."

Beep, beep.

The noise startled him. Glancing into the rearview mirror, he saw the driver behind him pointing to the traffic light. It was green, and he hadn't noticed. He eased off from the light, feeling much better about his decision. He dropped the car into second gear and got on. Ken wanted to get to Rachel's place, quick. He had missed her long enough.

He pulled up to the townhouse. It was a spot he had sat in many times in the past.

"Maybe I should have called first. Maybe I should come back later?"

He sat in the car for about fifteen minutes, contemplating whether he should go up to the door or not. He wasn't normally the nervous type. Finally, he opened the door and got out.

"Let me do this."

He went up the walkway. At the door, he hesitated before ringing the bell. This was it.

Ding Dong.

Rachel had dosed off lying on the sofa. The second time the bell rang, she sat up.

"Oh no, I know Luc didn't bring his behind over here!"

She stood up and shook out her robe. The material was wrinkled around her body.

Approaching the door, she asked, "Who is it?"

There was no answer.

"Who is it?"

This time, a familiar voice responded. "It's me, Rachel."

"Ken," Rachel winced. It had been a while since they last spoke, but not so long that she didn't recognize his voice. Shocked, she stood there trying to compose herself. She had many mixed emotions, like why was he there?

After all of these weeks, critical ones at that, he was just now showing up. He hadn't called to see how she was doing or anything.

"How pathetic," she mumbled. She was carrying his children, and he couldn't even bother to get beyond himself to check on her from time to time. "I could have been dead for all he knows."

The more she rehearsed the thought of his total disregard for her feelings, the angrier she became. "How dare he show up." The spiritual freedom she had received earlier from the Christian Center broadcast was rapidly eroding. She could literally feel herself being drawn back into a funky mood.

She opened the door slowly. There he stood, GQ, and handsome as ever. She was glad to see him, but was also ticked off that it had taken him so long to get in touch. She had made every reasonable attempt to keep the lines of communication open. Over time, she got use to the thought of parenting on her own. Still, Rachel wanted to hear what Mr. Sanders had to say. A significant part of her heart was aching to talk with him, so she toned down the anger and went with the flow.

"Hi," Ken greeted.

"Hi," Rachel softly spoke.

"Hi," he responded again, for lack of something else to say.

She unlocked the screen door and pushed it open. He grabbed it and walked in. Neither knew how to proceed. Both were momentarily silent and then spoke simultaneously, in an effort to smooth the tension.

"So," they blurted.

"I'm sorry," both offered. They laughed.

"You go ahead, Rachel"

"No, I insist that you go, Mr. Sanders."

"Uh-o. Mr. Sanders! I know what that means."

"What?"

She turned and walked towards the sun room. He followed close behind.

"That you're ready to bite my head off."

"Not today. I think we've done enough biting and fighting over the past few months. Don't you?"

"Yes, I think we did do a pretty good job of messing up our relationship. I just hope it's not too late to fix it."

She didn't want to comment one way or another. She was glad to know he was interested, but she wasn't the same naive woman he cut off communication with a month or so ago. Much had happened to change her perspective. With Big Mama getting sick and the potential problems with the pregnancy, she had no choice but to change her outlook. She needed to be strong for her loved ones. It wasn't about what she wanted and needed anymore. Unlike Ken, she had others to consider.

"How have you been?"

"I'm making it."

"Rachel, I'm so sorry that I, well ..."

She figured it was his guilt that caused him to tiptoe through the conversation. Normally, she would have jumped in and spared him the agony of having to apologize, but not this time. She not only wanted him to apologize, she also wanted an explanation of why he'd let a whole month go by without any contact. It was inexcusable, and even her easy-going nature couldn't brush it off. Once he realized that she wasn't going to save him from completing the apology, he started fumbling for words.

"Uh, uh. Well, I'm sorry I haven't been here for you."

Rachel maintained her silence. The apology felt good to her, but it didn't seem to be enough. She needed more to justify his existence in her life. The days of charming her with his voice and smooth talking ways were eroding.

"How's the pregnancy going?"

"I'm making it. I did have a scare a couple of weeks ago."

"What kind of a scare? Is everything all right?"

"It is, so long as I don't get too stressed. After I almost miscarried, the doctor put me on light duty. I've been off for two weeks. I'll be going back tomorrow. All I plan to do is go to work, come back home, and keep my feet up." She suspected the news would make him feel guilty. She was right.

He was silent before responding. "I really feel badly about that Rachel."

His jerk-like actions over the past months hadn't minimized the soft spot she had for him. After all, his inadequate behavior didn't change the fact that she loved him. It was his actions that changed the relationship's tempo, not hers. She sensed the sincerity in his regrets.

"What could be so bad that it made you almost have a miscarriage?"

She wanted to answer with 'you', but she recognized he had not been the only factor in the miscarriage scare. Plus, she found no joy in intentionally adding to his current level of guilt.

"Apparently, it was a lot of things."

"Like what?"

"Between the pregnancy of twins and Big Mama's heart attack, I guess my body just couldn't handle all of the pressure."

"Big Mama and twins! Wow! What a shock."

He was sounding more relieved, because she hadn't included him in the list of possible factors that initiated the strain on her pregnancy. But, she wasn't finished. She was in no way going to let him completely off the hook. Clearly his behavior and abandonment was a major contributor to her misfortune, and she had every intention of letting him know it. After Big Mama's illness, she started being more open about her feelings. Life was too short to waste time and emotions on dead-end projects. It was time to come clean with him about how she felt.

"And I have to add that our break-up didn't help matters. That was probably the biggest factor."

"I know. I should have been here for you, with Big Mama and with the baby, or I should say, babies." He gave a sigh. He hesitated to ask about Big Mama. He didn't know if she was still alive. "How is Big Mama doing now?"

"She's doing well. You know how strong her faith is. She'll be fine."

"Are you going to be fine?"

"I'll be fine. It might take a while," Rachel said in a strong voice, "but I'm going to be all right."

"That's good."

"So, how are you?" she asked.

"Could be better."

"What's going on?"

"Last month, I received the papers from Sandra's attorney."

"Boy, she didn't waste any time. She really was serious."

"I have to go to Ohio next week for the hearing."

"Well, I guess it was bound to happen sooner or later."

"I wish it wasn't happening right now. It's not good timing for us, or for our babies," Ken professed.

His use of the phrase 'our babies' struck Rachel as odd. Somehow over the past month, she'd started to think of them as her babies. True, she hadn't been overly excited about getting pregnant out of wedlock, but had evolved to the point of being happy as ever to be having her babies. Since the trip to Detroit, she was determined to get herself together, especially spiritually. Seeking forgiveness from God had been her first step. The second had been to let go of the guilt, once and for all.

She accepted her babies as a gift from God and started holding her head up high. Rachel intended to do everything she could to keep her babies healthy until the due date. With twins, it was already a high-risk pregnancy. She promised herself that anything causing her stress was going to be eliminated. Ken was no exception. Perhaps it was her motherly instinct kicking in. Whatever it was, her first allegiance was to her babies, not Ken. She had always tried to please her men, particularly Luc and Ken. In the end, what did it get her? She felt it was time to start thinking about herself. A part of her wanted the relationship with Ken to work out, but it was not the top priority anymore. Keeping those babies alive for another six months was.

"Twins, huh. Red will be glad to hear that."

"I'm sure, but tell me Ken, what about you? How do you feel about it?"

"How do I feel about it? I'm happy. How often does a man find out he's having twins? It's really good news."

In spite of his words, she couldn't figure out whether he really meant it or not. At this moment, it really didn't matter one way or another. She was happy about her twins.

"Twins are going to be expensive," he added.

"All kids are expensive. I think it's a small price to pay for the joy of having a child."

She didn't want to get into the money thing with him. Plain and simple, she felt he should either step up to the plate and find a better job to take care of all his responsibilities, change his flashy lifestyle, or get a part time job to pick up the slack. His lack of motivation was a complete turn off, and as far as Rachel was concerned, inexcusable.

"Yeah, I guess you're right. I guess I'm still thrown off by this child support thing with Sandra."

"I guess you would be."

She didn't want to side with Ken or Sandra. Now that she was soon to be a mom, Rachel could understand both sides. Sandra's perspective was much clearer, at least the part pertaining to Ariel. She still believed Ken should pay whatever he owed, plus some, to take care of his daughter. She couldn't figure out why he was having problems seeing it.

"So, when are we getting married?"

"Married! I'm surprised you still want to."

"Yeah, I do."

"After I didn't hear from you in over a month, I put it out of my mind."

"Well, put it back." He moved over to the sofa and sat next to her. Placing her hands in his, he said, "Seriously, Rach, let's get married."

"When?"

"Before the babies come."

"Why the rush?"

"Because ..."

"Because what?"

"Because I want you, me, and the twins together. I want us to do this thing right." Glazing lovingly into her eyes, he said, "I miss you."

His charm had found a hole in the armor that she'd place around her feelings, and it was starting to show signs of penetration. Her tough demeanor was melting. She always wanted a home, and a loving husband to help raise the kids. Perhaps it was finally happening. Ken was getting his fatherly act together. She had lost some faith in him, but hadn't completely given up hope.

"I miss you," Rachel emotionally responded, without really giving thought to what she was saying.

Looking at him, she still saw the same captivating demeanor that had always been there. What she saw differently were his internal characteristics. He was a mere man, full of flaws, idiosyncrasies, and imperfections like everyone else. He was no different than she was. She recognized that there were areas where he needed to grow just like she did. He wasn't perfect, but then neither was she?

Even as wonderful as Neal was, she felt it unfair to put him on a pedestal. By elevating Neal in her life, there was nowhere for him to go but down. He, too, was a mere man. She never again wanted to create a scenario whereby the men in her life might be lead to fall.

Perhaps that is how Rachel knew she was growing. Her faith was no longer in a man. It was in God. He was the only one she could completely count on where her twins were concerned.

"I'm glad I came over." Ken hugged Rachel and gave her a kiss.

"Uhm."

She laid her head on his shoulder, and they both enjoyed the quiet. Her relationships were looking up. The good news was, Ken was showing interest in her and their babies. The bad news was, she had began giving Neal some consideration. The last thing she wanted to do was get confused about choosing between the two men. There were reasons for selecting both. While she trusted Neal with her life, Ken was the father of her expectant children.

Playing over and over in her mind was, "Get your relationship right with the Lord first, first, first." The internal struggle was escalating, between wanting someone now, and simultaneously trying to build a solid foundation in Christ. The whole thought of deciding was too much to deal with.

She decided to enjoy the moment with Ken and deal with the rest, later. All was right with her little corner of the world. She was finally finding some peace and happiness in the dating game. She snuggled her head deeper into his shoulder. Like old times, he put his arm around her. Time seemed to stand still for Rachel while in Ken's arms.

Reluctantly, Ken had gone home around 9:30. Rachel was meditating before going to bed. She read a few of the scriptures that Sister Jones had recommended. It helped her to keep hold of her new found focus. She slid to her knees for prayer.

"God, I don't have to decide on anything. It's just me, my babies, and you. Help me to take one step at a time. I don't want to be needy of a man. Please God, help me to be happy with myself. Help me to make the right decisions. Amen."

Rachel got up off of her knees and turned back the bedding. She snuggled in and turned out the light. "I guess it's me and you, Lord. Help me to be patient until you show me what to do."

41

Rachel grabbed the bundle of letters from the mailbox. Like clockwork, Laurie's Christmas card was in the stack. Noticeably, the Savannah return address was different than the Atlanta one that Laurie and Greg had maintained for the past seven years. When Rachel tore open the envelope, a picture fell out. To her surprise, the picture included Greg, Laurie, the four kids, and a newborn. She was shocked to see the fifth child since Laurie had the last baby barely a year ago. She glanced over the text in the card, and found the phone number. It had been a while since they last spoke.

"I wonder how Laurie's doing?" She wasted no time in picking up the phone to call.

"Hello."

"Hi, stranger."

"Rachel?" the excited voice said on the other end of the call.

"Yes, it's me. How are you doing Laurie?"

"Fine. I'm glad to hear from you," the excited voice echoed on the other end of the call. It's been a long time."

"Yes it has been, too long."

"By the way, I did get the invitation."

"Good, I know you might not be able to come, but I wanted to include you, anyway," Rachel said.

"Thank you for thinking about me. You know, when I saw Rachel Matthews on such a formal envelope, I couldn't figure out if it was a graduation announcement or an invitation to your wedding."

"I bet you were surprised when you opened it."

"Sure was. I have to say, it was a shock."

"Leave it to Neal. He always goes overboard."

"Is it his idea?"

"Well, kind of. Since he's going to be godfather to the boys, we both wanted to have a baby dedication service. But I was planning on a small church service. He's the one that arranged for the fancy invitations and the big reception at the country club."

"Well, it sounds great. It's hard for me to think of you with kids."

"Sometimes, it's hard for me to believe."

"You sound so happy," Laurie acknowledged.

"I really am. I couldn't have asked for two healthier sons and a more wonderful friend."

"You're so lucky."

"No, not lucky. I'm blessed, and now I know it. Anyway, tell me, why did you move?"

"It's a long story. Let's stay on a positive note. Tell me, are you and Ken still getting married?"

"No, we're not."

"You're not! I'm surprised. The card you sent me back in the winter said you were engaged. What happened?"

"We tried, but we weren't able to get it together. We decided to go our separate ways."

"I'm sorry to hear that."

"Is there any possibility of it working out? I remember when you were in Atlanta, you always talked about wanting to raise your children with their father."

"I know, but it didn't work out that way. When I do get married, it will be to Neal."

"Neal!"

"Yes, Neal."

"Your best friend! How neat."

"Yeah, I finally matured enough to appreciate God's gift."

"When is the wedding? I do want to come."

"We haven't set a date."

"It definitely won't be before next summer."
Why?"

"Because, he strongly suggested that I do self-enrichment counseling."

"What's that?"

"We nicknamed it baggage-debriefing. It's a cute way of describing all of the hurt and emotional damage I have accumulated over the years."

"Why? You've always had your act together. I can't see why you'd need something like that."

"Oh no, I definitely need it. I was lugging around so much baggage. Neal didn't want me lugging that into the marriage, and neither do I. I didn't even realize how much anger, hurt, distrust, low self-esteem, and stress I'd acquired as a result of all those bad relationships. Without realizing it, they had taken a toll on me."

"Well, it will be nice when you two are finally married."

"Yes, it will be. It has been a long time coming, but God worked it all out in his timing."

"I didn't know you were into the Lord."

"I am now. Had to. Things got too tough for me on my own. I didn't have the best track record with relationships when I was doing it on my own. God is much better at understanding this love thing than I ever could be."

"I can relate to that."

"You! Are you into the Lord?"

"Yes, I am."

"When did that happen?"

"When Greg and I were going through some things, my parents talked me into joining a woman's support group. I guess it's kind of like you described earlier, a baggage-debriefing session. I ended up meeting a lady there who invited me to her church. One day I went, and the rest is history. I've been working on my life ever since. It was exactly what I needed to get through the tough times. I'm not where I want to be spiritually, but I'm a thousand times better than I was this time last year."

"I know that feeling. We're all growing one day at a time."

"Is Neal into the Lord?"

"Sure is. He's even stronger than I am. I feel really secure having him as a future mate and as the leader of our family. When I think about all of the stupid things I did. How desperate I was to find a man. It brings tears to my eyes to see where God has brought me from. He gave me Neal, a wonderful man, a shot at happiness, in spite of my past."

"Wow, that's wonderful."

"Yes it is. Can you believe I finally hooked up with someone who feels comfortable with me just being a woman and a mother. He doesn't expect me to be superwoman, the bread winner, or a doormat. It's just another one of the many reasons why I love him so."

"Ah, so you do love him?"

"Yes, I do. We have friendship, respect, and love. It's the ideal combination. Sometimes when I think that I might have passed him up, it's scary. Thank goodness God woke me up before my blessing got away."

"How's Ken?"

"He's fine. It took some time for me to get over the feeling of rejection and anger that I got from that relationship. By God's grace I did."

"How is he with the kids?" Laurie wondered.

"I can honestly say that he's cool with the whole thing. He really is. He sees them once a week. His father and the rest of the family, have been wonderful with them."

"It's good that he wants to be involved."

"He would have the boys even more if I let him. They're still too young to stay all night with him. I'm not ready to let my babies go away with anyone. I suspect it will take me a while before I am ready for that. Speaking of which, I know how hard it is with two babies. It can't be easy for you with five children. Does Greg help out?"

"A little here and there, but nothing consistent. It's an area that he's working on."

"Some men know how to receive, but they need help with the giving part of the relationship."

"Sounds like Ken is helping out?"

"He is doing fine with the visitations, but not the money. It doesn't really matter, now. My job gave me a special deal while I'm off. It's not my full salary, but every little bit helps with the twins. Now that Neal is the godfather, he feels obligated to help take care of the boys while I'm on maternity leave. I begged him not to, but you know he didn't listen. I'm fortunate enough not to need Ken's money."

"You really are blessed."

"Since he's not pressured to pay, he seems more eager to maintain a relationship with the boys."

"Marriage, next year? I bet you're anxious to get the wedding over?"

"It's funny. I used to be eager to get married. Now that I've found peace, there's no hurry."

"So, when are you planning to get married?"

"Sometime after we complete the pre-marital counseling. Our pastor won't release us to get married before then. I imagine it will be sometime next summer or fall. I'm not anxious anymore. Whatever time God puts on our hearts will be it."

"That's good. It gives you plenty of time to plan the wedding."

"Oh, I don't need much time. Whenever it is, it will be a simple wedding."

"I remember Neal being very extravagant. I can't imagine him wanting a simple wedding."

"As usual, he's been unbelievably supportive. He's left the details up to me, all except paying for it." Rachel and Laurie both chuckled, not really out of humor, but more so as a cheerful affirmation of Neal's willingness to take on the responsibilities of a real man.

"I know he gave you a ring for the engagement?"

"He picked one out, but he hasn't given it to me."

"Why not?"

"He's waiting for the right time. There's no hurry. I'm comfortable with the whole thing. It feels good to not be anxious about hooking up with a man. Those days are long gone. I know that I'll get the ring when the time is right."

"I bet it's nice."

"You know Neal. He over did it."

"Tell me. How does it look?"

Before responding to Laurie's request, Rachel reflected back on the time when Roz asked for a description of Ken's engagement ring. So much had happened in the nine months since then. She smiled in recognition of her maturity. Rachel had actually grown to the point where she wasn't comparing Neal and Ken anymore. She was able to appreciate that Ken and Neal were unique, and each was created for different purposes. It so happened that Neal, not Ken, was the one for her.

"It's a two carat, heart-shaped, diamond solitaire, with a carat of baguettes around the side."

"Boy! I knew it. That man has such class. And you still expect to have a simple wedding, huh. With a three carat ring, nothing is simple."

"It will be."

"Sounds like you have it all together."

"Not at all. I'm tired of always planning out everything. For once, I'm letting God and Neal have a say in the plans."

"What about your big, story book, wedding. The one you always wanted?   What happened to that?"

"It went out the window with all the other nonsense. Once I knew Neal was the one for me, all the superficial, unimportant stuff went away. My focus is on getting myself together, first, and then the marriage. It's not about a wedding, like it use to be."

"Will you work after the marriage?

"No. Neal and I talked about it, and agreed that I need to be home with the kids. He'll work, and I'll manage the funds. Together we should make quite a team."

"So, how long do you plan to be off work?"

"I don't know. Probably six years."

"Six years?"

"Yes. I'll be off at least another five months for the maternity leave. Then, I will be starting at the University of Chicago, next September, for my Master's in Health Administration."

"A few years ago, you wanted to go to Harvard or Stanford."

"They are too far away. The degree isn't important enough for me to leave my family, not now. I would miss my babies too much. Even if I took the kids with me, I wouldn't want to be so far away from Neal."

"Sounds like you really love him."

"Yes I do." Rachel had to smile. God had made such a difference in her outlook on love. "It's funny. There was a time when I feared that my feelings for him were based on need, instead of genuine love. When we first contemplated getting together back in the summer, I was afraid to get involved with him."

"Why? You've known him for so long."

"That's why. I didn't want to mess up our friendship. The real reason is, I didn't think we would have any hot fire-burning passion in our relationship."

"You mean the kind where you look all dreamy-eyed at each other, and hold hands all of the time?"

"Exactly. That's what I wanted, and was afraid I wasn't going to get."

"How did you two finally get together?"

"I still don't know what happened. All I know is that one day I looked at him, and it was like a different person standing before me. I saw him as being perfect for me. Once we got into the church together, it's like God opened my heart, and the feelings poured out. I sincerely love him. And I do look at him all dreamy-eyed," Rachel giggled.

"Ahhh."

"And it's not in a lustful way. I have so much respect and admiration for him. The love seems to come oozing out. We have the kind of love where you don't have to say I love you back, every time one of us says it to the other. I am so grateful to God for putting us together."

"You're fortunate. You don't have to go through the learning period. You already know him so well."

"I know him. I should! It has taken, what, twenty-five years to really get to know him. I guess it's time to get married. And to think, I used to judge a good relationship on whether or not it could make the eight-month mark, that's nothing. You don't really know anybody well enough to get married in such a short time. Like I said, it took us twenty-five years, and only a few of those were extra."

Without knowing it, she had been laying the groundwork for a solid relationship, all those years, by developing a friendship that excluded sex. They took time to get to know each other, without their distracting hormones taking over and clouding the feelings. Perhaps that was the way it had to be. She was finally able to appreciate Neal.

"I guess you could say we were hooked up by the match-maker who has a hundred percent success rate with couples."

"You mean the Lord?"

"Exactly. I couldn't have made such a great choice on my own. It was all a matter of luck when I was trying to look for a husband on my own. I know now it was, at best, hit and miss."

"Not even with the list you use to keep of all the things you want in a guy?"

"Please! My list almost let the love of my dreams get away. I say that with all sincerity. I have honestly never loved any man as much as I do Neal, and I know it's only going to get better. It's probably because he's the only one I really respect."

Laurie was shocked at Rachel's comment about Neal being her great love. Even she knew Luc had been Rachel's heart throb for a long time. "Not even as much as Luc?"

"Especially not Luc. I use to love the ground man walked on. I used to think he was so perfect for me. I was so wrong. I didn't love him. I thought I did. I didn't. I felt something for him. It sure wasn't love. It was more like a sinful, sick lust. I can honestly say that, now, because I know how God works. There's no way God would send a married man to me, and expect him to be my husband. God wouldn't put me into an adulterous relationship like that. He wouldn't do that. That was all my doing, getting caught up with Luc. He was definitely not the man for me. Boy, when I look back at all of the mistakes I made in my relationships, I thank God all the more for forgiving me and then letting me have Neal. I love God more and more."

"With Neal traveling so much, how are you going to be able to go to school with the twins?"

"Ken's family will help, and Neal has already hired a live-in to help with the kids in April."

"Why doesn't his mom come down and help out?"

"It's better if she stays in Detroit to help Big Mama. You remember my grandmother?"

"Oh, yeah. How is she by the way?"

"She's coming along fine. I didn't get a chance to tell you about the heart attack she had last May."

"I'm sorry to hear that."

"Well, she's doing well. As a matter of fact, she's here with me now. She'll be here until March or so."

"That should be a big help."

"She is a big help. I'm really glad she's getting an opportunity to spend some quality time with her great-grandsons. About school, Neal will be officially self-employed as of next July. He is determined not to do any major business traveling once we get married. He doesn't want me and the kids to be left alone. It works out. I want him to be able to spend quality time with the boys. I want them to really get to know him."

"It sounds like you have it all planned."

"Not really. We are both excited about everything, but I'm letting things flow. I'm not rushing anything. Like my grandmother says, 'what's for ya, ya going to get. Ain't no need runnin' head. Slow ya road, chile.' "

"You go, girl."

"For the first time in my life, I actually feel free and happy. It sure does feel good."

"Oh yeah, thanks for the picture you sent of the twins. They are adorable. What are their names?"

"Lewis and Lane."

"How old are they now?"

"Six weeks old."

"Were you pregnant when you sent me the card around Valentine's Day and told me about the engagement?"

"No, I got pregnant about a month after that."

"They were premies?"

"Yes. They were two months premature."

"How are they?"

"Healthy and happy as can be. I told you, girl. I am so blessed. They are two very healthy boys. They stayed in the hospital two weeks after the delivery and have been home ever since."

"That's great."

"What about your last one?" Rachel asked.

"David? He's almost four months old."

"Four months! I didn't even know you were pregnant."

"I found out at my six week check-up, after having Breanna."

Rachel didn't know if having another baby was a sensitive spot or not for Laurie, so she attempted to add humor. "If I keep having twins, I could catch up with you in no time."

Laurie laughed.

Rachel could hear her twins crying. They were awake from their nap.

"I better get going. It's time to feed the twins."

"Okay. Well, it was good talking to you Rachel. Tell Neal I said, hi, and your grandmother, too."

"I sure will, Laurie. Take care of yourself and let's keep in touch, especially since we have two more things in common."

"What two things?"

"Our faith and our children."

Laurie smiled. "You're right. Take care and be blessed."

"You, too. See ya."

As she placed the receiver on the hook, Rachel smiled. She knew everything was going to be all right for both her and Laurie, so long as they kept the Lord in their lives.

WAIT - IT'S NOT OVER ! !

Now that you have read *Nobody's Perfect,* aren't you curious to know what happened at Big Mama's during Rachel and Ken's Thanksgiving trip to Detroit?

If so, visit the website **www.anointedvision.com** and click on *Nobody's Perfect* editing floor to read the extra chapter. Enjoy.